Murder at the Theatre

GREG MOSSE is a 'writer and encourager of writers' and husband of internationally bestselling author, Kate Mosse. He has lived and worked in Paris, New York, Los Angeles and Madrid as an interpreter and translator, but grew up in rural south-west Sussex. In 2014, he founded the Criterion New Writing playwriting programme in the heart of the West End and, since then, has produced more than 25 of his own plays and musicals. His creative writing workshops are highly sought after at festivals at home and abroad. His first novel, *The Coming Darkness*, was published by Moonflower in 2022. *Murder at the Theatre* is the third book in a new cosy crime series featuring amateur sleuth Maisie Cooper, following *Murder at Church Lodge* and *Murder at Bunting Manor*, which published in 2023.

Murder at
the Theatre

Greg Mosse

HODDER &
STOUGHTON

First published in Great Britain in 2024 by Hodder & Stoughton Limited
An Hachette UK company

2

Copyright © Mosse Futures Ltd 2024

The right of Greg Mosse to be identified as the Author of the Work has been
asserted by him in accordance with the Copyright, Designs and Patents Act 1988.

A CIP catalogue record for this title is available from the British Library

Paperback ISBN 978 1 399 71519 5
ebook ISBN 978 1 399 71521 8

Typeset in Monotype Plantin by Manipal Technologies Limited

Printed and bound in Great Britain by Clays Ltd, Elcograf S.p.A.

Hodder & Stoughton policy is to use papers that are natural, renewable
and recyclable products and made from wood grown in sustainable forests.
The logging and manufacturing processes are expected to conform to the
environmental regulations of the country of origin.

Hodder & Stoughton Limited
Carmelite House
50 Victoria Embankment
London EC4Y 0DZ

www.hodder.co.uk

For Benj

CAST OF CHARACTERS

Maisie Cooper
Mohammed As-Sabah, an old friend
Sergeant Jack Wingard of the Chichester police
Florence Wingard, Jack Wingard's grandmother
Phyl Pascal, owner of Bunting Manor
Zoe Pascal, Phyl Pascal's ward
Keith Sadler, waiter at the Dolphin & Anchor Hotel, night-watchman at the theatre
The manager of the Dolphin & Anchor Hotel
The chef of the Dolphin & Anchor Hotel
Harry Farr, an elderly farm labourer fallen on hard times
Inspector Fred Nairn of the Chichester police
Police Constable Barry Goodbody of the Chichester police
Detective-Sergeants Tindall and Wilson, forensics officers with the Chichester police
Dorothy Dean, theatre manager
Sam Smithers, theatre electrician
Mrs Harriet Belt, volunteer stage door attendant
Micky Petherick, stage manager
Nils van Erde, theatre director
Adélaïde Amour, playing Polly Peachum
Andrew P Bradshaw, playing Macheath, Polly Peachum's lover
Esther Canning, playing Mrs Peachum, Polly's mother
Clive Canning, playing Mr Peachum, Polly's father
John Hermanson, playing the Beggar
Winnie Brahms, playing Lucy Lockit, Polly Peachum's love rival
Kitty Farrell, understudy to Adélaïde Amour

Liam Jukes, understudy to Andrew P Bradshaw
Beryl Vere, wardrobe mistress
Two male stagehands, one old and grey, one young and blond
Mr Chitty of Chitty's Cycles
Maurice Ryan, solicitor
Charity Clement, Maurice's assistant and wife

PROLOGUE

In her dream, Maisie Cooper was back at school. It was a warm summer's day and the sixth-form boys and girls had been brought together to read a play, *The Beggar's Opera*. She could smell the fresh cut grass and hear the persistent hum of the groundsman's mower on the playing fields outside the open windows. She could hear the voice of Jack Wingard, the boy chosen to read the lead, sitting two rows ahead of her in the stuffy classroom.

Then the dream moved forward in a kind of woozy surge and she and Jack were suddenly facing one another on stage, with an intimidating audience of teachers, parents and grandparents, brothers and sisters, aunts and uncles and friends. Under the lights, in full eighteenth-century costume, Jack tentatively took her face in his hands and kissed her.

The dream flipped for a second time, to a damp gravel drive and Jack, now grown up, clasping her in his strong arms, angry that he had allowed her to put herself in danger.

The confused memory lasted for only a moment before she was back on stage at Westbrook College and Jack was being led up the steps to the scaffold. Another boy, with a canvas hood over his adolescent acne, placed a noose around Jack's neck...

Maisie spoke without waking: 'No!'

She turned over, her face to the wall. For a time, she slept soundly, though her subconscious still roamed the world of the play: the character she was portraying, Polly Peachum, in love with Jack Wingard's, the highwayman Macheath.

Then, cross-fading like a film, the dream found her at the end-of-term afternoon summer party on the cricket lawn, enfolded in a moment of unexpected intimacy in the shadows behind the pavilion, when Jack had kissed her in real life, not in the play. With no one watching, their teenage destinies became entwined – perhaps for all of time – only for circumstances, good and bad, to rip them apart once more.

Then, she was back in the play once more, competing with another girl, in old-fashioned dialogue, for Macheath's affections – for Jack's affections. Then, suddenly, they were allies, desperate to save him from hanging and—

Maisie woke in a tangle of bedclothes, her strong limbs constrained by the narrow single bed, her eyes reluctant to open. She could hear faint night-time sounds from the streets of the cathedral city outside the narrow window of her poky hotel room.

At last, she opened her eyes and sat up, wearily rearranging her lumpy pillows, the image of a lithe and youthful Jack Wingard still vivid in her mind. She heaved an unhappy sigh.

How long ago was all that? Sixteen years? And he says he still loves me, that he has never loved anyone else.

Did she love him back?

The truth was, she didn't know.

On the bedside table were her three birthday gifts, touchingly wrapped in identical patterned paper. In the gap between her flimsy curtains, she had a view of the backs of other buildings and a grey sky with no hint of dawn, despite the lengthening of the days as April finally drew to a close.

Maisie groped for the light switch and turned on the table lamp – a weak, forty-watt bulb beneath a fussy beaded shade.

Why do I feel so trapped in the past? Why don't I yet feel free? It isn't fair.

The trial arising from her brother's murder was over, taking much longer than she had anticipated, with the defence lawyer cruelly undermining Maisie's actions by contemptuously referring to her as an 'interfering amateur detective'. She had found it exhausting and upsetting, though guilty verdicts were finally pronounced by the jury and appropriate sentences handed down by the judge.

The trouble was, she had yet to face the repercussions of what the local paper, the *Chichester Observer*, called 'the murder at Bunting Manor'. While she wished – almost to the exclusion of everything else – to finally feel properly free to grieve her brother's death, her heart seemed numb and unable to do so.

She got out of bed and went to stand at the north-facing window. Was there a little lightness in the sky?

No. And there was no lightness in her heart, either.

Not only was she conflicted by her longing for Jack's embrace – while still worrying that what she felt for him was simply a reaction to the series of shocks she had endured in two successive and unexpected murder investigations – there was also her duty to the owner of Bunting Manor, Phyl Pascal, a hearty country woman, Maisie's mother's sister.

No, not just my mother's sister, nor my aunt. The woman with whom my father had an affair, who carried his child.

A child who turned out to be … me.

Maisie turned back to the room. For a moment, she was tempted to open her birthday gifts. She remembered Jack and Phyl singing 'Happy Birthday', desperately wanting her to join in. Phyl's sixteen-year-old ward Zoe had been there, too, her lovely clear voice raised above the others, looking up to Maisie with a kind of hero-worship.

They all want something from me that I'm not certain I can give.

She relived the scene in memory, stark and upsetting, telling them to stop, that she needed time alone. She remembered Phyl's pained response.

3

'Obviously, I think you'd be better off here with Zoe and me, but Jack's persuaded me that you need to ... to reassess. Have you thought about where you will go?'

'I'm not sure—'

'I thought you might say that, so I've booked a room at the Dolphin & Anchor in the centre of Chichester,' Phyl had said decisively.

'I'll need their cheapest room,' Maisie had harshly replied. 'I insist on paying my own way.'

'I'm your mother,' Phyl had protested, aghast. 'And I've brought you nothing but trouble. Please let me do this small thing.'

Maisie had felt herself weaken at the sight of Zoe on the edge of tears.

'No,' Jack had cut in. 'We should all trust Maisie to know her own mind.'

Soon after, Maisie's brief stay at Bunting Manor had ended, her small travel suitcase on the back seat of Jack's Ford Zephyr police car as he had driven her in unhappy silence to Chichester.

'Don't worry. I won't come bothering you,' he had told her, smiling his charming smile, but looking defeated.

'I'm sorry, Jack. I know this isn't fair on you—'

'Let's leave it at that,' he had told her quietly, refusing the offer of her outstretched hand, looking like he regretted his words but knowing that walking away was for his own good. 'Well, goodbye.'

Back in her dismal hotel room, Maisie was unable to bear the dreams and memories any longer. She slumped down on the end of her uncomfortable single bed.

I've rejected poor Phyl, I've abandoned Zoe and I've pushed Jack away – so far that I'm frightened he might change his mind and never come back to me.

★

4

When, finally, Maisie climbed back into bed, having washed her hands and face in the unfriendly shared bathroom on the corridor outside her room, the cathedral bells were chiming half-past-two. The immemorial peal drifted over the Roman walls to a park at the northern edge of the city, where the impressive Chichester Festival Theatre sat, incongruous, like a concrete-and-glass spaceship.

Keith Sadler, a porter at the Dolphin & Anchor Hotel, had a second job at the theatre as nightwatchman. He didn't hear the bells because – once again burning the candle at both ends – he was asleep. Neglecting his duties, his head instead lay upon his arms in the green room, the space where the cast and crew of *The Beggar's Opera* went to relax and eat and drink at the management's expense.

He ought to have been alone in the enormous 1200-seat building. The actors, creatives, technicians and management were all supposed to be in their respective accommodation; their homes, their hotel rooms or their bed-and-breakfast digs.

One of them, though, had contrived a makeshift bed out of a pile of dusty curtains in a neglected storage space, deep in the theatre basement, and lay awake, thinking bitter thoughts of avarice, unlikely prosperity and revenge.

I

THOUGHT

ONE

Four days later, on Friday evening, the Dolphin & Anchor Hotel was all in a ferment, due to the arrival, fresh from the London train, just in time for a latish supper, of several more members of the Chichester Festival Theatre company. The celebrated Dutch director, Nils van Erde, and two or three of his entourage were occupying rooms on the first floor.

Miserable from her spartan week of penny-pinching solitude, Maisie ran into the famous director at the base of the stairs, as she returned from another interminable trudge around the walls of the city. She tried to slip past unnoticed, but she caught his eye. He seemed in an expansive mood, perhaps fuelled by alcohol.

'Call me NVE. Everyone else does. "Nils-of-the-Earth" is too much of a mouthful.'

'I thought that was what Nils van Erde might mean,' Maisie replied, politely. 'Are you opening the season?'

'*The Beggar's Opera.* You might know it better from the Brecht and Weill version, *Die Dreigroschenoper.* That's—'

'Yes, *The Threepenny Opera,*' she interrupted. 'It's a big cast.'

She took off her mackintosh and his eye travelled the length of her, re-evaluating what he saw. His expression became more alert.

'You know it?'

'A little.'

'Are you, perhaps, in the business? Am I being indiscreet? Are you employed at the Festival Theatre, Miss, er…?'

'My name is Cooper and no, I am not associated with the theatre. I am glad to have met you, Mr van Erde. Good luck with your production.'

NVE seemed inclined to keep the conversation going.

'Four weeks rehearsal in London and I have high hopes. Do you know the Drill Hall?'

Maisie had heard of it.

'Isn't it somewhere off Tottenham Court Road?'

'Four weeks of long days and bitter struggle with nervous actors wrestling with John Gay's archaic – but magnificent – text.' He shook his head, showing her a rueful smile. 'Now, we are in Chichester for a final week of polishing and technical run-throughs, trying to transfer what we discovered in the dusty rehearsal room onto Chichester's enormous and intimidating thrust stage. You know it?'

'I am local so, yes, I know it. I hope it's a success.'

Nils van Erde still didn't take the hint.

'The process is simple and has existed for all of time. The incomparable Aristotle set it out in the fourth century BC, the six fundamental elements of a play.' He counted them out on long narrow fingers. 'Thought, Song, Plot, Character, Spectacle, Speech.'

'That's very interesting,' said Maisie. 'I didn't know that. Now, isn't it late…?'

NVE leaned in.

'In some plays, plot is the key ingredient. In others, spectacle. In still others, song. But all must be present.'

Her right hand was on the banister. Surprising her, he took it in both of his, enclosing her fist as though it was something precious.

'It's a challenge,' he said.

'Is it?' said Maisie, holding his gaze.

'From the rehearsal room to the stage, you must bring the play, you understand, Miss Cooper, palpitating and frightened, like a small songbird that wishes only to escape. And you must hope that, after the trauma, despite the dislocation, your songbird still takes flight.'

'It sounds like a very tricky time,' said Maisie, politely removing her hand. 'Good luck.' He was standing in her way at the foot of the stairs. 'Would you excuse me?'

He stepped aside with a flourish.

'Good night, Miss Cooper.'

Maisie went upstairs to her room at the end of a drab corridor. She undressed and got into bed but was disturbed, several times, by the sound of footsteps and doors opening and closing until well after midnight.

*

On the following morning, the Saturday, Maisie was confronted with further direct evidence of the general ferment at the Dolphin & Anchor – the presence of the famous female lead of *The Beggar's Opera*, a young French actress called, unfeasibly, Adélaïde Amour.

Maisie didn't like gossip, but she found it hard to quash the enthusing of the young man – Keith – who served her wet poached eggs and burned toast.

'She's a doll. She's gorgeous, but they say she can't act for toffee.'

'Who says that?'

'My film magazine. I buy it at the railway station.'

'I think I know who you mean. She's a film actress first?'

'She probably won't be able to make herself heard. Have you been to the Festival Theatre? I saw the Royal Marines at Christmas.' He pursed his lips judiciously, like a connoisseur. 'That was loud.'

'I expect it was.' Maisie gestured to her plate. 'These eggs aren't quite cooked, and the toast is overdone. I expect it's difficult to get the timings right when the kitchen is so busy. Could you ask the chef to repeat my order, please?'

'I'll do it myself,' said the boy, nodding enthusiastically.

'Thank you, Keith. That's very kind of you.'

'Aren't you the one who was in the paper with the murders?'

Maisie sighed and admitted that she was.

'But please don't pass it on to anyone else.'

'You were clever and brave. Will you tell me about it?'

'Perhaps, if there's a moment,' said Maisie, surprising herself. Normally, thoughts of her accidental investigations made her extremely reticent, but the young man seemed innocently fascinated. 'But not right now, Keith. I'm hungry.'

A young woman of great beauty, wearing a floaty, diaphanous creation of white silk, appeared in the doorway, glancing round the tables. Maisie was struck by the perfection of her complexion, the depth of her dark, wide-set eyes and her generous mouth.

'What did I tell you?' whispered Keith, a comical expression of longing on his boyish features. 'What a doll.'

Keith bustled off to remake Maisie's breakfast and Adélaïde Amour seemed to change her mind, turning away without ever fully entering the breakfast room. Maisie heard her nicely accented voice telling someone that she would like 'coffee, lots of coffee, upstairs'.

After Keith's second stab at breakfast, Maisie returned to her room and finally opened her birthday gifts. Knowing she was a big reader, Zoe had chosen a murder-mystery story by the New Zealand writer Ngaio Marsh and inscribed it: *Thank you for everything. Love, Zoe.* It made Maisie feel like crying. Jack's gift was equally touching – a copy of *The Beggar's Opera*, bound in leather, probably from the second-hand bookshop on South Street. His dedication simply said: *Yours, always. Jack.*

Can that possibly be true? she wondered. *And will I ever deserve it?*

On a whim, Maisie went out and wandered down to the kiosk at the railway station to look at a copy of the film magazine Keith had mentioned. It had a photograph of Adélaïde Amour on the cover. Inside, she learned that Adélaïde had been twice engaged but never married, that she was born and raised in a village in Brittany, close to the western peninsula of Finisterre, loosely translated as 'the end of the Earth'. She was a campaigner for animal rights and had once been arrested while protesting against an oil company responsible for a black tide of crude that had washed up on her native beaches.

Maisie thought she rather liked her.

'Are you going to buy that?' asked the vendor.

'I'm sorry, I've forgotten my purse,' she lied.

The interminable Saturday became a tiresome Sunday, and Maisie found herself reduced to watching an afternoon musical in the hotel television room. At its conclusion, as dusk became night, she went out for a long walk, the sound of her sensible shoes echoing on the damp pavements. Returning to the Dolphin & Anchor, her cheeks stinging from the chilly evening air, Maisie hesitated in the lobby. The bar was busy with competing voices raised in joyous conflab, and she found she would like the opportunity to sit among strangers for an hour, letting the noise of their enthusiastic gossip help the time to pass.

She found a low table in front of a wing-back armchair, not far from the fire. Keith was on duty at the bar – though he seemed under-age to do so – and automatically brought her a small bowl of oily salted peanuts.

'What else can I get you?' he asked, his hungry eye flicking involuntarily towards the other side of the room.

'Actually, just a glass of water, please.'

13

Keith didn't seem to hear. Maisie followed his gaze. Adélaïde, in a voluminous patterned kimono, was in a circle of chairs, dragged together to make an audience for Nils van Erde. NVE was holding court simultaneously in several languages – his native Dutch, his willing French and his very smooth English.

'Keith?' said Maisie. 'My glass of water?'

'Oh, er, sorry.'

He slipped away.

The local paper, the *Chichester Observer*, was on her low table. Maisie picked it up and leaned back, shielding herself from the theatrical group. The front page carried an announcement of the Festival Theatre season and, inside, there was an interview, given by NVE, extolling the virtues of his star and noting her 'remarkable performance' in an avant-garde production in a small Parisian theatre that Maisie had never heard of.

It was clear that Adélaïde was NVE's casting choice. Maisie hoped the director wasn't selling the young woman beyond her ability to fulfil his boasts. If, as Keith suggested, she wasn't physically ready or sufficiently well-trained to perform a stage role in a major theatre, it would be extremely damaging for NVE as well as for her.

But isn't that his job, Maisie thought, *to make sure she's ready*?

Keith brought her water. She sipped it and looked up at a large mirror in a gold-painted frame above the fireplace. In it, she could see NVE – she could still hear him as well – talking to Adélaïde, making a great effort to put her at her ease, to encourage her. Then the actress stood up and NVE switched back to English to confer with a rugged man he addressed as 'Micky'. Adélaïde drifted away to stand in front of the fire, quite close to Maisie's chair. The silken patterned kimono flowed with her, drawing the eye.

Maisie closed the newspaper and put it aside. Adélaïde saw her do this and gave her a glance of enquiry. Maisie felt it would be rude not to speak.

'*J'espère que tout se passera bien, que le public vous appréciera,*' Maisie said.

I hope the show goes well, that the audience enjoys your performance.

Adélaïde looked at her without replying, her dark, wide-set eyes expressing slight surprise and, Maisie thought, a worried intensity.

'*Merci,*' she said, finally.

Maisie found she no longer felt comfortable sitting among strangers. In any case, she feared NVE would try and draw her into his circle of acolytes if she stayed too long. She stood up.

'*Bonne nuit, Mademoiselle Amour.*'

Maisie left the bar, climbed the stairs to the second floor and returned along the drab corridor to her rear-facing room. She read for an hour from Zoe's gift. The murder-mystery was called *Opening Night* and it was set in a theatre – beautifully written but the set-up was quite long, with many pages devoted to the intriguing depiction of character and backstory, and no sign yet of a murder.

She put her book aside, got off her narrow bed and opened her window with a screech of unoiled hinges. She stood quietly, breathing in the night air. The weather had changed. A warm front had rolled in and mild drizzle was falling from a grey sky without moon or stars.

Suddenly, she heard a balcony door open and two voices, floating up from below. Maisie took a step back. She wanted to close her window and shut out the noise, but she couldn't do so without the hinges giving away her presence.

It was Nils and Adélaïde – he, insistent and determined, she, monosyllabic and bored. He spoke in English and she replied in French. They were either unaware that they might be overheard or didn't care. And it was, inevitably, a 'love scene' – though perhaps it would be better described as a 'failed seduction'. NVE was deploying all his charm, all his authority. Adélaïde was having none of it.

'But you cannot leave me like this?' he protested.

Would the conversation turn nasty, Maisie wondered? If Nils became too persistent, might she feel herself obliged to go downstairs on some pretext or other and intervene?

'You know I am devoted to you,' said Nils. 'Am I not better looking than my brother?'

'Mais, non,' Adélaïde replied.

No, you aren't.

'Haven't I protected you from him?'

'Même pas,' she told him.

Not even.

Then, abruptly, there was the sound of a scuffle and something heavy fell to the ground. What had happened? Had Nils tripped and fallen? Maisie went quickly to the door of her room but stopped when she heard Adélaïde's voice in English.

'That is enough. Get up and go away.'

Not another word was exchanged. Faintly, Maisie heard a door open and close, then Adélaïde swearing copiously as she slammed shut her balcony doors.

*

Maisie slept poorly, once again, haunted by feelings of loss and betrayal – and her own resistance to confronting the demons of the past. On Monday morning, therefore, she went downstairs early, just before seven, and hesitated on the threshold of the dining room, seeing that she was alone with only Adélaïde for company. The young woman hadn't seen her arrive and was singing a song Maisie recognised from *The Beggar's Opera*, as she buttered her toast.

'No power on Earth can e'er divide,
'The knot that sacred love hath tied.
'When parents draw against our mind,
'The true-love's knot, they faster bind.'

Adélaïde sang with such effortless charm that Maisie was unable to move until the last gentle notes had faded.

Then, as people often do, Adélaïde realised she was being observed and looked up.

Surprised into speech, Maisie told Adélaïde, in fluent French, that she was sorry to have eavesdropped but that to hear Adélaïde sing was an unexpected and incomparable pleasure.

Adélaïde promptly burst into tears and ran from the room.

Two

A little later, Maisie once more found herself waiting for time to pass, this time under the cobwebby roof of a bus shelter.

Should she have tried to slip away from the breakfast room, before Adélaïde had noticed her, then come back in again, moments later, making a noise so as not to take the young woman by surprise? She wished she had. Over the last few weeks, she had endured enough upset and drama to last her a lifetime.

There was almost no money left in her purse. Her travellers' cheques were cashed and spent. She had her depressing hotel room and half-board till the end of the week. That would be fine if she went without lunches. After that...

It was raining, again. February had been sleety and cold, March little better. April, when all of nature ought to be celebrating the burgeoning of spring, seemed determined only to prolong the depressing winter. Even the daffodils round the edges of the cathedral green looked bedraggled and depressed.

Maisie would still be welcome, she knew, in Bunting. Phyl had written to her, care of her solicitor, reiterating her offer. But it was too soon. The extraordinary revelation that Phyl was her birth mother, not her aunt, still made Maisie feel nervous and queasy – lied to.

She could ask for help from Jack, but would that be fair? She still felt the pull of her first love and believed she might be able to love him again, to want him, but not now, not yet.

Not with the shadow of death still lying so deep and dark across their lives.

And, of course, Jack was a police officer, a well-liked and respected sergeant working out of Chichester police station. That fact alone made it difficult to pursue their relationship, what with her involvement in the Bunting Manor murder yet to be resolved in court.

Returning to Chichester from Paris, she had taken the precaution of buying an open return ticket on the boat-train. If only she were allowed, she would stride off down South Street to the railway station this instant and set off – never mind the forecast of gales in the Channel and the likelihood of an extremely unpleasant crossing on the small passenger ferry, surrounded by the oppressive rumble and stench of the diesel engines and the inevitable consequences of the choppy seas on the more fragile passengers.

But she couldn't. It wasn't like in a detective story where the problem posed by the locked room mystery or the deadly country house weekend party is solved by an explanation on the final pages and everyone says 'oh, I see' and goes on with their lives. No, in the real world, the police were obliged to follow up on all the evidence, organise the sequence of events into a convincing timeline and demand everyone's presence in court so that the alleged facts might be presented by the prosecution and challenged by the defence.

And the truth finally and definitively established.

What a waste of time that all was. Maisie knew what had happened in Bunting – the motivations and objectives of all the damaged and unhappy protagonists. She had to accept, however, that knowing was not enough. The facts had to be proved in a court of law to the satisfaction of a jury of the peers of the accused.

From where she sat, with the rain dripping from the edge of the bus-shelter roof like a curtain of water-beads, she could see the clock face on the medieval Market Cross. It was nine-thirty. The town – she ought to remember to call it a city, because of the cathedral, but it really was no more than a town – was bustling into life. She saw four or five people enter and leave Morant's, the department store. What luxuries were they buying well before lunch on a Monday morning? Make-up? Fine china? Glassware? Bed linen? Next door, the Post Office was doing good business, too. Meanwhile, she could do nothing but wait for the wheels of justice to turn and grind – oh, so immeasurably slowly – and trust that, eventually, she would be released from her excruciating limbo.

Maisie sat up a little straighter, telling herself to buck up. Soon, she would be able to go to her appointment with her solicitor. Perhaps there would be news – confirmed dates in court. She would, inevitably, be offered tea and bourbon biscuits which she would refuse, having only recently finished her breakfast in the damp restaurant room at the Dolphin & Anchor Hotel.

The hotel wasn't far from where she sat. It was on the opposite side of the road, close to the Cross. She hoped, when she got back, that her room would have been made up, but she wasn't optimistic. She thought it was something to do with the fact that hers was the cheapest room in the building, right at the back, with a view of the loading bay at the rear of Woolworths. To the experienced house-keeping staff, she probably looked like exactly what she was – someone unlikely to come across with a good tip at the end of her stay.

All the same, however low the price, however distant the room, didn't she deserve the same consideration as other guests?

That will do, she decided. *Think of something else.*

High up above her head, ten o'clock chimed in the bell tower. Maisie stood up, straightened her clothes and walked the short distance to her solicitor's office – the solicitor she had inherited from her murdered brother. Charity Clement was unlocking the door when Maisie arrived, and the two women said hello and went inside. Charity took off her bright yellow plastic raincoat, revealing a fetching twinset – a short-sleeved sweater and matching cardigan – somewhere between pink and tangerine.

'You look half-asleep,' said Charity. 'Is everything all right?'

'Hm?'

'Maisie, réveille-toi.'

Wake up.

Charity – more properly Charité Clément – was originally from Guadeloupe, where the official language was French.

'I am awake.'

'You don't look it.'

Maisie sat down on one of the three hard dining chairs lined up against the wall of the office, opposite Charity's desk.

'You do love bright colours, don't you?'

'Guilty,' said Charity with a smile, opening the door to the rudimentary office kitchen to make the inevitable tea.

'Any news?' asked Maisie, raising her voice to be heard above the rumble of the electric kettle, 'How long until the—'

'The Bunting Manor hearings?' Charity called back. 'That depends on what happens next – on the disclosure of evidence by the prosecution and the length of time the defence can request in order to prepare their response.'

Leaving the tea to brew, Charity came back into the office. In a few words, Maisie told her the story of Nils van Erde and Adélaïde Amour, with the unexpected climax of sending the young woman running from the breakfast room in tears.

'You do see life, Maisie,' said Charity, looking pleased with the vernacular expression. 'Anyway, Mrs Pascal came to see me.'

'Oh.'

In theory, Maisie had been in gainful employment at Bunting Manor. Phyl Pascal had promised a wage equal to that of Maisie's former Paris salary but, in the end, the investigation and its awful conclusion had only taken a few days. Despite this, it appeared that Phyl had deposited a substantial sum with the solicitor, for Maisie to call upon whenever she needed it.

'Maisie, you are looking the gift horse in the mouth. Is that the correct expression?' Charity said when Maisie immediately shook her head at the offer.

'Yes, it is.'

'What does it mean, exactly?'

'It means, if someone's giving you a horse for free, don't go looking to see if it's too old from its teeth.'

'Good.' Charity smiled. 'That's exactly what I meant to say.'

They drank their tea and Charity opened the safe in the corner of the room. She pointed to a plain brown envelope on the top shelf.

'Here it is,' she said. 'One hundred pounds in cash – a payment, not a gift.'

'No, thank you.'

'*Ce que tu es têtue.*'

How stubborn you are.

Charity relocked the safe and set about opening her post. Just then, the phone rang. Charity picked up and, after a few seconds, mimed that the call would not be brief. Given there was no news of a trial date, Maisie smiled her good-byes and left, hurrying back to the Dolphin & Anchor in the rain.

She headed for the first-floor sitting room, intending to pass the time with the morning papers, perhaps doing a crossword. She opened the door onto a shabby space furnished with wooden armchairs with green velvet seats and backs, and several coffee tables, each supplied with magazines. The day's newspapers were hanging on hooks with long wooden poles down their spines. A small coal fire was burning in the hearth.

To her surprise, she didn't have the room to herself.

THREE

In the first-floor sitting room of the Dolphin & Anchor Hotel, Adélaïde Amour was draped across a window seat, looking immensely decorative in voluminous white cotton pyjamas. Standing in the middle of the room was a formidable-looking woman, short and stocky but upright, in a dark blue trouser suit that was a little too small for her, her grey hair set in tight curls. She was holding a briefcase. Maisie heard the cathedral bells ringing the half-hour and wondered if the star was complaining that they were too loud. It wouldn't be the first time.

'I'm sorry,' she told them both. 'You're busy. I'll leave you in peace.'

Adélaïde jumped up.

'*Mais non, restez*. Stay, please,' she translated in her charming Gallic accent, then turned to the other woman. 'This is what I need, or someone like her. This one, she is … *sympathique*.'

'I beg your pardon?' said Maisie.

'I'm Dorothy Dean,' said the other woman, holding out her hand. 'General manager of Chichester Festival Theatre. And you are?'

'My name is Maisie Cooper. I'm staying in the hotel, but—'

'You've met Mademoiselle Amour?'

Maisie glanced from one to the other. 'Briefly.'

'More than once, she tells me.'

Maisie thought back.

'Twice … no, three times, I think.'

24

Maisie began to wonder if she was about to be told off for importuning the star. Usually very sensitive to other people's emotions, this morning she had brought her own – comprised of boredom and frustration and worry – so she hadn't immediately noticed quite how tense was the atmosphere in the room. Instead of rebuking her, though, Dorothy Dean smiled a rather wolf-like smile.

'Mademoiselle Amour says you were very kind to her this morning.'

'Oh,' said Maisie. 'I just told her what a charming voice she has.'

'That was very nice of you, I'm sure.'

Dorothy Dean looked from Maisie to Adélaïde and back again.

'Is that all?' asked Maisie.

'*Il me faut quelqu'un,*' said Adélaïde.

Dorothy Dean made a frustrated grimace and spoke loudly in Adelaide's general direction.

'I – have – no – idea – what – you're – saying.'

Yes, of course, thought Maisie, the tension must have arisen in part out of mutual incomprehension. First, the language barrier, of course, but also because she didn't suppose there was much common ground between these two very different women.

'She says she needs someone,' Maisie explained.

'Miss Amour's assistant has had to return to France to look after a sick relative. And you,' replied Dorothy Dean, 'speak French like a native, so she tells me. Will you please help us?'

'Help you?'

'Translate for me in the first instance? It won't take a minute. I'll be glad to give you tickets to the preview as thanks.'

'Oh, is that all? I would be glad to help,' said Maisie. She had only been to the theatre once before, soon after it opened, to see the mesmerising Laurence Olivier in Chekhov's *Uncle*

Vanya. Then her parents had died in a road-traffic accident in a 'pea-souper' London fog and she had moved abroad to Paris, taking only her grief. 'I mean, I'll do my best.'

'Could you please explain to Mademoiselle Amour that she is under contract to perform as Polly Peachum and that the opening night is at the end of the week.'

Sensibly, Dorothy Dean stopped and let Maisie translate what she had said. Maisie left out the character name as that didn't seem essential to the meaning of the sentence.

'And,' continued Dorothy, 'she was contracted at the insistence of the director, on the strength of her own assertion that she is capable of performing, in the English language, in a major theatre, without amplification.'

Maisie took a little longer to translate this convoluted set of ideas. In reply, Adélaïde muttered: '*Je sais, je sais.*'

'She says she knows,' said Maisie.

'I'm glad she does,' said Dorothy. She fished out an official-looking paper from her briefcase. 'Here is her contract. Here is her signature.'

That's very high-handed, thought Maisie.

'Do you want me to translate that?' she asked.

'Yes. And tell her that it is extremely late to be getting cold feet.'

After Maisie had communicated these brutal thoughts, there was a pause as Adélaïde thought things through. Finally, she got up out of the window seat.

'Come, please.' She drew Maisie aside to the far corner of the room and spoke rapidly in French in a low voice. 'This woman, she is concerned only for money. She has economised on my costumes. She has provided this third-rate accommodation.' She waved a hand. 'What do you think of this hotel?'

'It is adequate,' said Maisie.

'For you, perhaps. But for me…? Anyway, now, when I say that this is all beneath me, she comes back with threats that

I am not good enough, that I cannot say the stupid old-fashioned lines that anyone can learn but it would take a goddess like Deneuve to breathe life into.'

'Do you want me to translate any of this for her?'

'I do not,' said Adélaïde. 'Furthermore, it seems I am to be pawed at and fawned over by an old man who believes himself to be a god, in his own way, a god of the theatre with a "unique vision" which, in the end, is just to put the beautiful woman opposite the handsome man and have them take their time over falling in love. And, like all such men, he believes his scrawny old carcass remains irresistibly attractive to all the pretty actresses in his company, even the star.' She made the sound usually written as 'pfff'. '*Non, merci!*'

'I don't understand how I can help—'

'Then the leading man, who resembles the director in a way, believes that he must take advantage of me if the director does not.'

'I see that this must all be very difficult and annoying—'

'I am a good actress,' said Adélaïde complacently, 'and perhaps I can be great. But it is a question of ... of strategy. It will not help me if people can say: "Oh, Adélaïde Amour? She is very difficult. You know, NVE gave her a chance and she was a nightmare to direct." You understand?'

'Yes, you are trapped between demanding respect and not wanting to be cast as a troublemaker, but—'

'You can be my assistant. That is what I am saying.'

'I can?'

'You are an attractive woman,' said Adélaïde, judiciously. 'You will help me with all that I need, but you will also deflect attention, perhaps, and assist me with the old-fashioned words. But, above all, you will be always by me so I cannot be importuned.'

There it is, thought Maisie, *the very word I was imagining. But, instead of being accused of it myself, I am to be cast as the shield, the distraction.*

'But why me?' she asked, a little helplessly.

Adélaïde shrugged.

'Who else will I find in this awful town?'

Maisie didn't reply straight away. The insult to Chichester was, she thought, unfair. From the far side of the room, Dorothy Dean interrupted, with an edge of anger: 'I am a very busy woman, Miss…'

'Cooper,' Maisie reminded her.

'Would you be so good as to communicate? Just the gist will do.'

'Let me make certain of something,' said Maisie, prevaricating. She quickly asked Adélaïde to confirm what she meant, concluding by enunciating very clearly in English: 'You want me to replace your assistant who had to return home to France, even though I have no experience. And you are certain that this will help you?'

'I am,' confirmed Adélaïde.

Maisie looked from one to the other: the delightful but wary features of the beautiful star; the severe but practical expression on the face of the business manager. She took what felt like a bold decision.

'For a modest consideration of fifty pounds for the week, I am prepared to act as assistant to Mademoiselle Amour, to help her with her lines and to accompany her at all times in rehearsals and wherever else she might need me.'

'Sixty,' said Dorothy Dean.

'I beg your pardon?'

'Sixty pounds – and, if you get her to opening night without another tantrum from her or from NVE, I'll make it a round hundred.'

'I see. That sounds more than reasonable.'

28

Maisie turned to Adélaïde.

'Yes, I understood, it is not much money, but…' said Adélaïde in French.

'*Vous êtes certaine*?' Maisie insisted.

You are certain?

'*Absolument.*'

Maisie turned back to Dorothy.

'It's a deal.'

For the second time that morning, Maisie Cooper and Dorothy Dean shook hands.

FOUR

A theatre is a complicated thing, a kind of organism, or a complex machine, full of moving parts. Because of this, there are many places where someone can hide, where something can be hidden. Even in a modern theatre – and Chichester Festival Theatre was a modernist building *par excellence* – there were cubby holes, dark corners, forgotten spaces.

For several months, the theatre had been idle and unobserved, apart from a few routine maintenance jobs and infrequent visits from police and fire brigade. Now and then, Dorothy Dean had popped in to use the office known as 'Fort Knox' to write cheques and draw up contracts, to file things away until the theatre machine should be roused once more for its summer season.

The previous week, Dorothy had made a tour of inspection, in company with young Keith Sadler, whom she had reluctantly taken on as nightwatchman, in the absence of any other convincing candidates.

'I would have preferred a mature gentleman,' she had frankly informed the hopeful young applicant. 'I hope you won't let me down.'

'I promise I'll do my best,' Keith had replied, uncertain how long he would be able to combine his work at the Dolphin & Anchor with this additional new job.

On that day, neither Dorothy nor Keith had known that they were not alone in the building. There were, after all, so many places to hide.

To start with, there was the grid, the network of metal high up in the hexagonal roof: bars for hanging the theatre lights; dusty walkways in perforated steel; places for the follow-spot operators to sit or crouch; electrical cables and sockets; devices for raising and lowering pieces of the set, pulleys, winches and counterweights.

Because of the shape of the stage, thrust out into the midst of the auditorium and surrounded on three sides by well over a thousand seats, most of the time it was possible to see what has happening up aloft – but not when the theatre was dark, or when the only light came from the blue lamp in the prompt corner or the tips of a few cigarettes as the crew went about their business in the gloom.

Next, there were the disregarded corners backstage, places people seldom chose to go unless they had business there: storerooms full of costumes from previous shows; awkward corners stacked with bits of old sets; here and there a baited box containing poison, destined for rats or mice.

Where might the vermin go to curl up and die? Other quiet corners?

Some wardrobes and cupboard spaces smelled strongly of naphthalene, the principal ingredient of mothballs, used to protect the natural fibres of the clothes and curtains and rugs. In sufficient quantities over sufficient time – trapped, for example, in one of those cupboards – naphthalene might be poisonous even to humans. The result would be haemolytic anaemia, a breaking down of the red blood cells.

Then, there were the two locked rooms. The first, known to members of staff by its nickname of 'Fort Knox', contained sensitive financial information related to five separate bank accounts in lever-arch files, minutes of meetings of the theatre's executive board, as well as copies of contracts with rights holders, creatives, performers and suppliers. There was also a safe with a combination dial and a large keyhole, containing – among other things – a metal cashbox with a float of notes and coins left over from the previous season.

The second locked room – known as the 'armoury' – was crammed with swords and pikes, old-fashioned shields and helmets. There were three crystal-encrusted daggers and two scimitars from a play set in Ottoman Istanbul that, in the end, hadn't ever been produced. Leaning in a corner were half a dozen wooden rifles for an upcoming Shakespeare set in World War One. Next to them was a tall metal cabinet that was always supposed to be locked. The cabinet concealed some imitation grenades, landmines and shells, all carved from lightweight timber and painted to look like the real thing. More importantly, on an upper shelf, there were three service revolvers left over from World War Two – one German and two American. Because the outer door to the armoury was usually secure, the cabinet seldom was.

At the rear of the theatre was the scene dock with its access to the outside world – huge doors that could let in air and light but also served for the passage of bigger elements of décor: complete staircases or balconies; façades of buildings strong enough to be climbed by the hero and decorated with drainpipes or ivy; a rough platform on castors, topped with a hangman's scaffold.

Alongside the scene dock was the workshop, full of paints and varnishes, brushes and rollers. Also, tools that might better serve as weapons than the wooden rifles and blunt swords and daggers in the armoury.

Beneath the stage, there were corridors and quiet corners, piles of timber and stage-cloth, pieces of furniture and a stretch of wall fitted with big steel hooks on which coils of rope were tidily hung.

On the dismal Monday when Maisie had accepted, almost on a whim, a job that would draw her once more into having to consider the worst of human behaviour, the darkest of human motivations, the theatre was coming back to life, emerging from its cold-weather hibernation. Led by the director, Nils van Erde, a rehearsal was in full swing on the enormous stage. Like an organism brought out of suspended animation, the hexagonal concrete bastion was beginning to thrum with life, preparing to present the paying public with the complex paradox of live performance.

'The idea,' Dorothy had told Keith during their tour the previous week, 'is to make the audience believe it's all real, then remove the mask and walk down to the front of the stage for a rapturous curtain call.'

'Yes,' Keith had replied, uncertainly.

At that moment, though, neither of them had known that reality would soon intrude on the world of smoke and mirrors, of painted sets and made-up emotion, in the most brutal and unhappy of ways.

FIVE

As it turned out, Maisie was not required to begin her unexpected job straight away. Adélaïde Amour was not 'called' at the theatre until after lunch and intended to spend the rest of her morning relaxing in her room, reading over her text and listening to the cassette-tape recordings of her songs. It was decided that Maisie would come back for her at half-past-one and they would walk up to the theatre together. In the meantime, Dorothy Dean offered to show Maisie around and introduce her to a few other members of the cast, crew and wider organisation.

'I'm trying to remain optimistic. The story of the celebrated low-life couple, Polly Peachum and Captain Macheath – the latter made famous by Frank Sinatra as 'Mack the Knife' in the popular jazz-swing classic – well, I think we can sell that. And the space,' said Dorothy, firmly, 'you have to see the space.'

There was a note of pride in her voice that Maisie found very touching. She told Dorothy about seeing Olivier in the Chekhov play, *Uncle Vanya*.

'Magical,' said Dorothy, with a gleam of nostalgia. 'He was magnetic. And the message – that we will all be saved by work – that holds true, I think.' She became business-like once again. 'Shall we go?'

'Yes, let's,' said Maisie.

Dorothy gave her a penetrating look, perhaps containing an element of doubt.

'You're taking this in your stride, it seems.'

'I hope to.'

'You're not some kind of crazed fan, are you,' she brutally demanded, 'worming your way into our lives?'

'Until the last couple of days, I had no idea who any of you were.'

'No,' mused Dorothy. 'And perhaps we don't impress you?'

'Do I need to be impressed by you?' Maisie asked.

'No.' Dorothy laughed. 'Fair enough. But do you have any theatre experience?'

'None whatsoever.' Maisie began to wonder if she ought to make an effort to seem keener, if only for the money Dorothy was offering. 'Despite my lack of experience, I have no qualms.'

'You aren't worried about entering this strange parallel community? You will find it full of wilfully heightened emotion, unnecessary crises and tantrums.'

'People are people,' said Maisie. 'At least, that's what I've always found.'

'They're people, all right,' said Dorothy, wryly. 'Mostly bonkers, in one way or another. Some pleasantly so, others not so much. I must be, too, mustn't I, to do the job that I do?'

'Whatever happens, I will try my utmost to make things run smoothly,' Maisie reassured her, 'but I won't make any rash promises. I can't offer any guarantee.'

'That's a very good summing up.' Dorothy seemed to have convinced herself. 'I think we're going to get on, Miss Cooper.'

'Call me Maisie, please.'

'If you wish. Though you'll have to call me "Miss Dean" or "guvnor". I'm afraid it's tradition. Will you mind?'

'Not in the slightest, Miss Dean.'

'Shall we?'

35

Dorothy had a large black umbrella under which they sheltered as they strode up North Street, past the Woolworths and the council offices in the Victorian assembly rooms. At the George & Dragon the owner was receiving a delivery of new barrels through a trapdoor in the pavement.

They crossed the ring-road and made their way through a large car park into the grounds of the extraordinary theatre, its hexagon of concrete ribs cantilevered out from a narrower base, overhanging the foyer and access road, looking like an alien spacecraft inexplicably set down on the edge of a provincial market town.

'We'll go in through the house,' said Dorothy. She pushed open a plate-glass door in white-painted wood and stepped through into the foyer – a broad space that followed the contours of the building, wrapping itself around three sides of the hexagon. In front of them was Door One. 'Come on.'

Dorothy pulled it open and they stepped into a small vestibule that felt cramped, like an air lock. Then Dorothy pushed through a second door and Maisie, following her, felt a change of atmosphere, from outdoors to in, from ordinary to special, from humdrum to magical. Although what she had told Dorothy was true – that she had little experience of theatre – from the point of view of an audience member, it was a world that she loved.

Dorothy put a hand on her sleeve.

'I love this moment,' she said, unexpectedly. 'Always have, always will.'

'You mean the transition from the everyday into—'

'Something different,' supplied Dorothy.

It was very dark where they were standing at the bottom of a set of about a dozen steps, but there was a soft light shining up above. Maisie peered up the steps, towards the faint glow.

'Before we go up, I want to give you a sense of the importance of this place, of the job you have agreed to take on as the theatre comes back to life after a winter of being dark. You seem a steady sort of person and I'm generally a good judge of character. I have been successful on the back of it. But, you understand, I am taking a risk.'

'It seems to me, Miss Dean,' said Maisie with a smile, 'that a greater risk was taken some time ago when you chose your director and did your casting.'

Dorothy laughed.

'Touché. Good for you. All right then. "Dark" means, quite literally, that the lights have been turned off, all except for one – usually a floor lamp of some kind with a single bulb, known as the "ghost light". What purpose would you say it serves, the "ghost light"?'

'To stop people falling through a trapdoor?'

'Yes, but more importantly, the "ghost light" is a symbol, a promise that the players will return.'

With that, Dorothy gave a brief nod and led Maisie up the steps into the huge, fan-shaped auditorium, over a thousand velvet seats rising on three sides from the projecting stage with its distinctive point, downstage centre, where she had seen Olivier stand to deliver one of his most moving speeches.

'Magnificent,' said Maisie.

'I'm glad you think so. It deserves our respect.'

'Of course.'

'And one more thing, if you don't mind?'

'Go on?'

'This theatre is an anomaly, almost a mistake, financed privately by public subscription and by jumble sales and coffee mornings, for heaven's sake. It is absurdly big and grandiose and defiantly modern, given the small, traditional town of thirty-thousand souls it's landed in. It was the first home of the National Theatre company. Did you know that? They're now in residence at the Old Vic but it's here that they began.'

'I'll take your word for it,' said Maisie.

'I'm just trying to give you a sense of the … the precarity of this adventure.'

'The thin line between success and failure?'

'Exactly.'

Suddenly, a bank of lights came on in the grid, high above their heads, and a voice shouted down from the back of the fan of seats where Maisie could just distinguish an enclosed lighting box.

'Sorry, Miss Dean, didn't know you were there. It's lamp check.'

'Never mind, Sam,' Dorothy called up. 'You get on.' She turned back to Maisie. 'That's the electrician, Sam Smithers. He's going to turn every lamp on and off, making sure we haven't lost any bulbs.'

They climbed two steps up onto the stage and walked through a set of half-painted scenery flats into a vast back-stage area where other parts of the set for *The Beggar's Opera* were being sorted and assembled by two seedy-looking stagehands, one a man in his fifties with a drooping, dolorous face, the other his blond junior. The space was lit with eerie blue light.

'This way.'

The next five minutes were extremely disorienting – though the opposite was intended – as Dorothy showed Maisie how to get about the building. Dorothy indicated the dressing rooms, pointing out the star on the door of the one reserved for Adélaïde, then down underneath the stage, in the bowels of the building, through an untidy storage area and back up again on the other side.

'So, you can pass behind the stage on the dressing room corridor as well as underneath?' Maisie said.

'Yes. It's a bit of a warren but you'll get used to it.'

'I dare say. What's left to see?'

'The green room and stage door.'

Both of these essential fragments of theatrical life were at the rear. The green room – where cast and crew could relax and socialise between rehearsals and performances – was a delightful, untidy space, and a definite upgrade on the sitting room at the Dolphin & Anchor, with seven or eight armchairs, two small sofas and two small dining tables, each with four upright chairs. There was also a catering counter to one side.

'I spend a fortune on hot meals,' said Dorothy. 'Actors are always hungry.'

'I don't suppose I might be permitted to join them?' asked Maisie, hopefully.

'Come one, come all,' said Dorothy, wearily.

That's lunch sorted, thought Maisie.

She pointed to the signed photos on the walls.

'These are past productions?'

'Some – others are just headshots.'

From the green room, they went back along the dressing room corridor to the south-eastern corner of the building where they found the stage door, which was staffed by an eager, grey-haired woman with a high-class set of pearls adorning her ruched yellow blouse. She looked up guiltily because she had been doing a crossword.

'Mrs Belt, this is Miss Cooper. She's going to be helping Mademoiselle Amour. Pass the word on, would you?' Dorothy scanned the desk. 'Where's your list?'

Mrs Belt unearthed a typewritten form with names and dates in a kind of grid.

'Here it is, Miss Dean. Are we expecting the whole company? I'm afraid not everyone is signed in.'

'Mrs Belt,' said Dorothy with exasperation, 'it is your job to sign them in.'

'But some of them came in through the front.'

'Yes, all right, but for the fire regulations, if for no other reason, we must know who is in the building at all times.'

'Yes, Miss Dean.'

'Now, we are aiming for a technical run-through at two, which will probably take us through to dinner, then we'll take it from the top for a second time this evening. If we finish before ten o'clock, I'll be surprised. Has the props truck arrived?'

Maisie recognised the change in tone as Dorothy focused fully on business. Leaving them to it, Maisie stepped out into fresh air on an area of hard-standing where three cars were pulled up – two smart ones and another rather shabby, with an elastic bungee-strap holding shut its boot. Beyond the cars were trees and grass, the car park and a few tennis courts. Beyond all that there was traffic on the ring-road that circumnavigated the heart of the old Roman town. The rain had stopped and the air felt mild. Maisie could smell the grass and there was a hint of spring, at last.

Dorothy followed her outside.

'I think I'll go back to the Dolphin,' said Maisie, 'if that's all right? Adélaïde might be glad to see me if she's expected on stage at two.'

'Good idea, Miss Cooper.'

'Maisie.'

'All right, Maisie. Watch out or everyone will be calling you "darling" and "love".'

'At home, in Paris, you have to be prepared for people to embrace you and kiss you repeatedly on the cheeks at the briefest acquaintance.'

'You didn't ever see Mademoiselle Amour perform live in her native French, did you?'

'No, I'm afraid not. I knew she existed and, of course, I've seen her on film.'

'Me, too. What do you think?'

'Magnetic. The camera loves her.'

Dorothy pursed her lips.

'Yes, but will the public?' She checked her watch. 'Look, just because you're the sort of person who takes things in her stride, don't assume everyone else can do the same.'

'What do you mean?'

'Don't put pressure on her, will you?'

'I don't see that as my job.'

'Good, because heaven knows, she might just crack.'

Dorothy turned away and went back inside. Maisie was left alone in the little parking area, wondering what she had got herself into, but glad the immediate problem of subsistence had been, for a week at least, resolved. She stood still with her eyes closed and the welcome but unexpected warmth of a little weak sunshine on her face.

As it happened, she didn't entirely agree with Dorothy Dean. It seemed to Maisie that Adélaïde Amour was quite capable of holding her own and a lot tougher than she at first appeared. From what Maisie had seen and heard in the Dolphin & Anchor, it was Nils van Erde who might be on the brink of nervous collapse.

SIX

As Maisie left the theatre, she was surprised to see Phyl Pascal walking towards her with a coffee-stained, Roneoed script of *The Beggar's Opera* in her hands.

'Maisie, good heavens. What are you doing here?'

'I've been asked to help the lead with her script and things,' said Maisie. 'She's French and I met her at the hotel.'

'I know,' said Phyl. 'I'm a patron of the theatre. They keep us up to date with everything.' She paused, then asked: 'How have you been?'

'Not too bad,' said Maisie, she thought honestly.

'Will you come back to us?'

'Not just yet, Phyl. Give me time.'

'Of course. I shouldn't have asked.'

'No, it's fine. How's Zoe?'

'She talks about you a lot.'

Maisie felt a pang of guilt.

'I'm sorry. I know she wants—'

'No, Maisie,' said Phyl. 'Don't be sorry. Take your time – but please, think of us now and then.'

Before Maisie could reply, Phyl disappeared inside the theatre, through the stage door. Maisie took a moment to breathe.

Yes, perhaps the time is coming when we can be friends.

She set off for the hotel, without feeling the need to button up her mackintosh or tighten her scarf.

All the same, I would still rather avoid calling on any favours for the time being.

Maisie realised she ought to have asked when *The Beggar's Opera* was due to open. She had an idea from the *Chichester Observer* that there was a press night at the end of the week. Was it Thursday or Friday? And had Dorothy mentioned a preview?

Maybe I'll leave the Dolphin & Anchor and find somewhere cheaper once this strange new job is over.

On reflection, there was a lot more she needed to know. The trouble was, Dorothy was clearly a woman under pressure. She only had eyes for the thing in front of her – in Maisie's case, the possibility that she might smooth the relationship with Adélaïde and help coax from her a performance of confidence and authenticity.

Another question came into Maisie's mind. How 'precarious' was the theatre? How narrow was the line between success and failure? Did she have someone she could ask, some wealthy local patron connected to Chichester Festival Theatre?

Well, Phyl was the obvious candidate. Perhaps she might ring her up at some point. In that way, she could keep the deeper emotions at arm's length.

Maisie knew that she ought to be in touch with Zoe, too. On her birth certificate, Zoe went by the surname of Richards, the name given to her as a foundling, because she had been left anonymously at the Chichester Hospital, St Richard's, abandoned just a few hours after birth. Then she had been abandoned a second time, just after her sixteenth birthday, by her foster parents, all her worldly possessions fitting in a single unhappy suitcase.

Despite Phyl having taken her in, Maisie knew poor Zoe felt trapped in the lonely village of Bunting, 'surrounded by farmers, old people and sheep', as she put it. Maisie felt a need to protect her. Might she even be able to find Zoe a job at the theatre? She had a marvellous singing voice, after all. Might there be roles for chorus members in *The Beggar's Opera* – passers-by, denizens of the taverns, street-sellers?

Perhaps not, Maisie reflected. No, she was fairly sure that was impossible. Wasn't it the case that, to perform in professional theatre, one had to be a member of the closed-shop union, Equity? Wasn't there always a big fuss about people trying to 'get their Equity card'?

But, then, a performer had to start somewhere, didn't they? Were Equity cards perhaps in the gift of the theatre management – of Dorothy Dean, in fact?

Mentally, Maisie put all that aside and thought again about practicalities. Morning and evening meals and a roof over her head at the Dolphin & Anchor until the following Monday – that was settled. In the middle of each day, she expected to be at the theatre and could, apparently, eat with the cast and crew in the green room. She would, in theory, have no additional expenses.

Feeling greatly relieved, Maisie skipped past the hotel and on into the Morant's department store. She hoped Adélaïde wouldn't have changed her mind and be fretting over her absence. She spent a few coins on a new lipstick and a better-quality shampoo than the one provided in the bathroom on the hotel corridor. She then ran back to the hotel, barely noticing the midday chime from the cathedral bell tower or the shiny black Bentley pulled up outside.

She pulled open the heavy front door and stepped into reception. The manager, a thin man whose worn blue blazer hung from his narrow shoulders as if from a wire coat-hanger, was engaged in conversation with a tall, dark figure in a beautifully cut, traditional English suit. The manager turned towards her and she took advantage of the slight pause to interrupt.

'Excuse me, has Mademoiselle Amour come down?'

'Speak of angels,' said the manager with awkward gallantry, 'and they appear.'

The tall, dark man also turned and smiled.

'Maisie Cooper, this is the very greatest pleasure. I am so pleased to see you again.'

Taken aback, Maisie smiled, realising that she felt the same.

'Mohammed, what on earth are you doing here?'

*

Despite her pleasure at seeing her brother Stephen's old friend, Mohammed As-Sabah – someone she hoped, in the fullness of time, to consider her own friend – Maisie still felt a degree of urgency over what Adélaïde might be doing. She excused herself and ran up to the first floor where the best rooms were found.

A 'Do Not Disturb' sign hung over the door handle of Adelaide's room. Maisie was sorely tempted to knock and call out: 'Are you all right? Do you need anything?' But she resisted.

Hadn't she been told she would not be needed until one-thirty to walk up to the theatre? Why would that have changed? Adélaïde was probably sleeping, wasn't she? She had a sort of feline grace and was probably capable of cat-napping more or less anytime and anywhere.

But might she wake up having forgotten the plan they had made?

Maisie walked slowly back down the stairs, wondering if she was underestimating Adélaïde. There was no reason, was there, why she should be flighty and changeable? That was just a cliché, surely, just the tired way beautiful blonde women are depicted on screen in films scripted by men.

In reception, Mohammed was waiting with his usual calm self-possession, sitting in a faded chintz armchair by the window.

He cuts a fine figure, thought Maisie.

Mohammed stood up, looking as if he had something important to say and wasn't sure when next he would get the opportunity.

'Do we have time to speak? Can I buy you something to eat?'

'I have an hour,' said Maisie.

'Splendid. Where shall we go?'

Oh, God, thought Maisie. *Where, indeed?*

Mohammed was in the habit of dining in embassies, with high-up personages from the foreign office and the bastions of international finance. What could Chichester possibly offer such a man? Also, it needed to be halal, appropriate for a practising Muslim.

'How did you know where to find me?'

'I spoke to our mutual acquaintance, Charity Clement.'

'But why are you here?'

'I came on the off chance that you might be pleased to see me,' he told her with a hopeful smile. 'And I wanted to do something for poor Stephen's memory. I hope I have not been importunate?'

'Of course not,' said Maisie, slightly thrown by how that word kept coming up. 'Charity knows we're friends. You are the most delightful surprise.'

'I am?' asked Mohammed, beaming. 'Then I couldn't be more pleased.'

SEVEN

Because time was relatively short, Maisie took Mohammed for a snack lunch at the pleasant-but-gloomy restaurant on the first floor of the Morant's department store. Mohammed was not so religiously observant that he needed to be served from a kitchen that had no contact whatsoever with inappropriately slaughtered meat, so he was able to make his choices from a reasonably wide range of items on the traditional menu. They both chose shepherd's pie which, with plenty of salt and pepper from the table, wasn't as tasteless as some Maisie had had the misfortune to be served in England.

'The trouble is, I'm spoiled by everyday food in Paris being the same as, if not better than, fancy food in England.'

'I sympathise,' he replied. 'The cuisine in Kuwait leaves a lot to be desired. Some of our most celebrated and characteristic dishes are those prepared by Bedouin travellers, suitable to be transported in camel-saddle bags over days of desert wandering. They sustain but do not delight.'

Neither of them wanted an alcoholic drink but, unexpectedly and thankfully, the restaurant served Perrier water in tear-shaped green bottles. The time flew by as Maisie told Mohammed all about what had been happening in her life. He was suitably astonished.

'You have solved another capital crime. You are becoming a professional investigator.'

'Perhaps I could do worse?' she replied, with a smile.

'One must do something with one's life.' He smiled in return. 'Shall I call you Maisie Chandler?' They both laughed. 'But what is this about a film star at the hotel?'

Maisie told the story of her unexpected morning, then checked her watch.

'Oh, it's nearly one-fifteen.' She gestured to their empty plates. 'I wish I could treat you, but…'

'I understand. It must be very difficult. Stephen left you nothing, I assume?'

'Less than nothing. Debts.'

'You know I can help. In fact, I would be pleased to help – financially, I mean. A loan, if you prefer?'

'No, thank you.'

'As you wish. There is a programme at this theatre, however, a way for them to raise money with the naming of seats. I propose to dedicate one to Stephen, as a kind of friendly memorial. I have been in touch with the general manager, Miss Dean.'

'That would be incredibly kind and generous,' said Maisie, feeling tears in her eyes.

'There is almost nothing I need that I cannot have,' argued Mohammed.

'What a lovely place to be in life,' said Maisie.

Mohammed became silent and she thought there was something else he wanted to broach. He took out his wallet, raising a hand for the waitress. Was he thinking about their inevitable next meeting? She feared he would be hoping for a kind of progression, something more than a friendly rendezvous between old friends – something with the possibility of a flicker of romance.

'Have you heard from Sergeant Wingard?' he suddenly asked, without looking up.

Maisie smiled. It was characteristic of Mohammed to use Jack's official title so as to not belittle him as a relatively junior public servant, even though he, Mohammed, had a chauffeur-driven car and important diplomatic responsibilities.

'No,' said Maisie. 'Not for a week or so. I will see him at the Bunting Manor trial, of course.'

'The trial,' said Mohammed with distaste. 'I was glad not to be called in the Church Lodge affair.'

'How did you manage that? You played a part in what I discovered, after all.'

Mohammed shrugged.

'I made a play of my diplomatic status and arranged to be in Kuwait, so was able to submit a written deposition.' He looked her in the eye. 'But that is not what I wanted to say.'

The waitress – a bony, inquisitive woman who had done her best to eavesdrop on their conversation – chose that moment to bring them their bill. Mohammed waited for her to move away, then covered it with a crisp five-pound note.

'I would like to make my position clear,' he said. 'You are often in my thoughts.'

That's a nice way of putting it, Maisie thought.

'And you in mine,' she began, but he didn't let her finish.

'I am so pleased,' he interrupted. 'I thought, perhaps—'

'But,' she insisted, 'I am very far from being able to contemplate any kind of romantic entanglement. I feel it will be some time before I am on an even keel once more.'

'Oh.' He nodded, looking disappointed. 'I have never before been dismissed as a "romantic entanglement".'

'I'm sorry. I'm making you sound like a character in a bad novel, one of those you buy from the spinners at the railway station.'

'Is a spinner a person or a thing?'

'One of those racks that you can spin and… Well, anyway, you should try one. The novels, I mean. They're incredibly predictable but great fun.'

49

'And I will recognise myself as a character in one of these "bad" novels?'

'Now, stop it. You know that isn't what I mean.'

She watched him pull himself together.

'Now it is for me to apologise. I am being boorish.'

'No, you're not. You're being delightful as always.'

'Then, as I imagine the rebuffed hero might say in one of these interesting and informative novels, I may be allowed to hope? You are sure it is not a question of preference?'

'You mean for Jack? Were he here, asking the same question, I would answer him in exactly the same words.'

Would I, though?

'Then I am satisfied, and we will meet again.'

'I hope so.' She smiled. 'I must go, but thank you for a surprisingly adequate lunch.'

'I thought so, too.' He laughed.

'You are very kind to me.'

'Being kind to you brings me the very greatest pleasure,' he told her. Then, perhaps worried he had gone too far, he apologised. 'I am doing it again, forcing my emotions on you.'

'Let's get your change.'

'There is no need for change.'

They left and the waitress ran after them because the size of the tip seemed so unlikely. Mohammed insisted it was hers to keep and they went downstairs and back outside into the street, sheltering for a moment in the alcove before the plate-glass front door because it had come on heavily to rain, sheets of grimy, grey water falling noisily from a densely clouded sky.

'We will have to run,' said Maisie.

She took his hand and they splashed, laughing, past the Post Office, past the turning into Chapel Street, and tumbled in through the heavy front door of the hotel. Dorothy was there and told Maisie that the afternoon rehearsal call had been postponed by half an hour and, in any case, Miss Amour wasn't ready. Maisie introduced Mohammed, who reiterated his intention to support the theatre in Stephen's memory.

Maisie left them and went outside to sit under the Market Cross, glad of the fresh air after the stuffy restaurant. The rain shower was passing and the streets were busy with a majority of women, the younger ones wearing Pac-a-macs and carrying see-through umbrellas, the older ones pushing upright tartan shopping trolleys. She saw a man she recognised from her childhood, Harry Farr, an elderly farm labourer fallen on hard times, wearing a seedy brown suit, picking up a few cigarette stubs from outside The Punch House, a timber-fronted public house.

Then, suddenly, there was Jack, unexpectedly emerging from the pub in his sergeant's uniform, looking brisk and authoritative. Before she knew what she was doing, Maisie jumped up and ran towards him, despite the drizzle.

'Jack, how are you?'

He turned and the impression of authority fell away.

'Hello, Maisie,' he said quietly.

She felt suddenly sorry for him – for herself, too.

'What's the matter?' she asked.

'A little trouble with underage drinking,' he told her in a voice that wouldn't be overheard by other passers-by.

'No, I didn't mean... I'm so glad to see you. We should meet.'

He sighed.

'Perhaps that isn't a good idea?' He was keeping his distance, his hands clasped behind his back. 'Unless something has changed? Has something changed – between us, I mean?'

Has it? Maisie wondered.

'I just...' she began, weakly.

He smiled. It touched her heart and she wished she'd given a stronger answer. But it was too late.

'That's what I thought,' he said. 'Let's give ourselves a chance. Maybe you're right and distance will make the heart grow fonder. Your heart, in any case.'

With that, he turned and walked away, leaving her standing as the rain came on again. After a moment of indecision – what was to stop her going after him? – she heard Dorothy Dean's voice, calling her.

She ran back the short distance to the hotel. Adélaïde was in the lobby, looking like a ghostly apparition in her floaty cotton suit, clearly not her pyjamas after all, but the clothes in which she was preparing to face the day. She had no coat or umbrella.

'There you are,' she said in French, without any trace of annoyance or impatience. 'How can we go to the theatre in this downpour? I suppose there must be taxis?' Then, unexpectedly, she added: 'Like my grandfather used to say, *il pleut comme vache il pisse.*'

It's raining like the bull pisses.

Mohammed, who had joined them, laughed and explained in his very precise French that he would be pleased to give them both a lift to the theatre as he himself had business there. His driver was waiting outside. Maisie made introductions and was amused to see Mohammed become very formal and still as Adélaïde played up to him.

'What a delight to meet a person of influence and power, someone of importance in the world,' she simpered.

The angular hotel manager helped them out to the car, holding an umbrella over them as they got into the Bentley, Mohammed in front and Maisie, Adélaïde and Dorothy Dean in the back.

'This is how I expect to be treated,' said Adélaïde, loudly. 'Is Mr As-Sabah married?' Before Maisie could answer, she went on. 'This is my joke. *Il n'a d'yeux que pour toi.*' Adélaïde translated her comment by singing, in English, in her lovely clear voice: '*He only has eyes … for you…*'

'You are embarrassing both of us,' said Mohammed quietly, smiling over his shoulder.

'What did he say?' asked Adélaïde.

'He said we're nearly there,' Maisie told her.

'*Mais non,*' laughed Adélaïde.

They were, though.

Mohammed's chauffeur pulled up in front of the theatre, more or less where Dorothy Dean had shown Maisie inside earlier that morning, and they all got out.

II

SONG

EIGHT

Dorothy Dean immediately went indoors to the foyer while Maisie watched Adélaïde take her lovely leave of Mohammed.

'You must come back and see us,' she cooed.

'I will return for the press night, if I am free,' he told her. 'For now, I have business to conclude with Miss Dean.'

Maisie and Mohammed followed Adélaïde inside where she was swallowed up by a crowd of about twenty actors, milling about in the huge foyer beneath a gallery of enormous photo enlargements, taken from previous productions.

Dorothy Dean and Nils van Erde were standing slightly apart, engaged, Maisie thought, in a not altogether friendly conversation. She hoped it was not about her sudden appointment as a kind of bodyguard to the star. She decided it probably was, however, as Nils made a beeline for her to ask several quick and probing questions about who she was and what was her background. She answered as succinctly as she could.

'And why do you think you are qualified for this strange task?'

Maisie could tell he was angry because his Dutch accent was more pronounced.

'I hope to prove my qualifications by performing the task to your satisfaction.'

Nils looked taken aback, as if he wasn't used to his underlings standing up for themselves. He beckoned to the small, square man called Micky that Maisie had seen in the bar at the Dolphin & Anchor.

NVE spoke close to his ear – on which was balanced an unlit, roll-up cigarette – then Micky climbed up on a bench seat and called out above the heads of the company in a loud, sergeant-major's voice: 'Ladies and gentlemen of the company of Beggars, not all of you signed in at the stage door this morning. Please check you have done so. Choral rehearsal on stage in five minutes, please, five minutes.'

There was a rumble of conversation in reply as Micky jumped down and disappeared into the auditorium. Just then, Maisie saw Dorothy Dean putting a possessive hand on Mohammed's arm with a look of beady interest in her eyes.

*

For the second time that day, Maisie experienced the delicious sensation of passing from the real world into one of imagination and made-up tales. She couldn't shake the fanciful feeling that it was also a shift from the temporal to the spiritual, like going into a holy place. She said as much to Adélaïde who laughed and replied: 'I am glad you didn't say that to me in English. It would sound ridiculous in English.' She shook her head. 'Even in French…'

The enormous thrust-stage, mimicking the shape of the hexagonal building, came down to a point called 'downstage centre'. Adélaïde climbed up and took possession of that very spot, standing quite still, looking very much the star.

'Maisie, I need a light on me here.'

'Right now?'

'Before everyone comes. Can you do that?'

Maisie peered up through the gloom to the lighting box at the back of the auditorium, beyond the fan of seats, thinking back to her tour with Dorothy. What was the name of the chap doing the lamp check?

'Hello, Sam?' she called. She waited a few seconds. When there was no answer, she told Adélaïde: 'Just a minute. I'll run up.'

Maisie took the long staircase, ascending two steps at a time. The door to the lighting box was ajar. Sam Smithers was a kind-looking man about Maisie's age, with a ginger-blond pony-tail. He was looking through his script, making pencil marks in the margins and consulting a large plan of the theatre's rig of lamps, laid flat across the faders and switches of an enormous lighting board.

'Excuse me, my name is Maisie Cooper. I am assistant to Miss Amour. I almost met you with Miss Dean earlier, when you were doing your lamp check?'

He looked up, seemed to come out of some kind of reverie, looked her briefly up and down and jumped off his stool.

'Gosh, you're very beautiful. I'm sorry, I was expecting my assistant.'

'Oh, well, thank you. Are you busy?'

'There are about seventy sound cues to run in tandem with lighting changes, so yes.' He smiled. 'We're going to be very busy.' He put his script down on top of the detailed map of the lighting rig. 'How can I help?'

'Miss Amour would be grateful if you could provide a light where she is standing.'

'Now?' he asked, just as Maisie had. He peered out the window. 'Downstage centre,' said Sam and grinned. 'The "Olivier point". Good for her.'

He lifted a corner of the big map and put his fingers on two adjacent faders, pushing them from zero to about seven or eight out of ten. Maisie saw two beams of warm light converge from high up in the grid on a very still white figure. At the same time, several more actors entered the stage, edging round the half-painted flats then stopping, becoming a kind of onstage audience. Others came in through the auditorium and took up positions in the front rows.

'Thank you, Sam,' said Maisie.

She left the lighting box, taking a few steps down the staircase between the seats, stopping with her hand on a rail between sections. Adélaïde was a lovely vision of austere immobility, like a clothed statue, the white cotton fabric draped becomingly over her slender body. The light was just right on her blonde hair and the strong features of her perfect face.

Then, quite unexpectedly, Adélaïde began to sing and the effect was magical – almost a definition of Maisie's fanciful idea that, climbing up into the empty auditorium, she was moving from the banal to the transcendent. Adélaïde's voice effortlessly produced the English words with only the faintest and most charming trace of her usual thick accent. It carried easily to the back of the silent auditorium and Maisie found it breath-taking.

'Can love be controlled by advice?
'Will Cupid our mothers obey?
'Though my heart were as frozen as ice,
'At his flame 'twould have melted away.
'When he kissed me so closely and pressed,
'Twas so sweet that I must have complied.
'So, I thought it both safest and best
'To marry, for fear you should chide.'

Adélaïde paused, giving Maisie the chance to remember the song. Adélaïde's character, Polly Peachum, was explaining to her venal parents that she thought it better to marry Macheath, than to give in to passion and have sex with him outside of wedlock. Maisie felt Sam's presence, coming to stand next to her.

'She's got something, hasn't she?' he said, quietly.

Maisie heard a sound of animated speech as NVE and Dorothy Dean entered halfway up the huge fan of the auditorium from one of the higher staircases. Adélaïde began again, moving a little back and forth across the stage, never leaving the pool of light cast by the two warm spots, but adjusting her position so that she addressed herself to all parts. Maisie could see the entire company was now in the auditorium, listening enraptured, like people posed for a photograph, all gazing in a single direction, as if to focus the minds of an imaginary audience on one thing alone – the lovely woman singing in a surpassingly beautiful voice to hundreds and hundreds of empty seats.

'O, ponder well, be not severe.
'So, save a wretched wife.
'For, on the rope that hangs my dear,
'Depends poor Polly's life.'

This second part of the song was in a different key and had a surprising melodic detail, like an unexpected 'blue note' in a number by George Gershwin or Cole Porter. Polly's fear, Maisie recalled, was that her mother and father would give her lover, Macheath, to the jailer, Mr Lockit, in order to touch the reward. As an inevitable consequence, Macheath would be hanged – and to lose him would mean death to Polly.

Dorothy walked along the horizontal aisle to meet Maisie, while NVE went down the stairs to stand in the first row, looking adoringly up at his star. Perhaps inspired by this, Adélaïde repeated the verse, her voice full of emotion but with, Maisie thought, a little less control, the English vowels not quite so well enunciated.

'She's bewitching, is she not?' whispered Dorothy. 'Did she tell you she was going to do this?'

61

'No. I imagine it's what she was preparing in her room. I feel bad. I thought she was just having a cat-nap.'

'Oh, no, she's a pro, in her way.'

'It shows that she's entirely capable of—'

'Theatre is about stamina,' interrupted Dorothy. 'Two-and-a-half hours a night, six nights a week, not one brief performance, however striking. We're not out of the woods yet.'

'No, Miss Dean.'

Maisie was going to ask what Dorothy and Mohammed had talked about – something in addition to naming a seat in Stephen's memory? – but she was prevented by the final note of Adélaïde's song and a great wave of cheering and applause, led by NVE, standing like an acolyte beneath the Olivier point, looking up in homage at Miss Amour.

NINE

While Maisie was taking her seat, expectant, in the stalls of Chichester Festival Theatre, wondering how the rehearsal proper might begin, Sergeant Jack Wingard was at his desk in another landmark building of that pleasant market town: Chichester police station. He was putting the finishing touches to a report on juvenile delinquency that had begun with underage drinking in The Punch House and almost ended in tragedy, with a blind-drunk sixteen-year-old being fished from the canal and resuscitated on the bank. Had the police station not been close by, and an officer trained in first aid not on hand to intervene, the teenager would inevitably have drowned.

Fred Nairn, a plain-clothes inspector, came to speak to him.

'Got a minute, Jack?' he asked.

'Make yourself a cup of tea, Fred. This is nearly done.'

Fred Nairn always had a faint air of weariness and disappointment. His premature baldness had aged him, though he was Jack's contemporary and only thirty-five years old. They had entered the force together in the same intake, fourteen years before. While Fred had progressed to inspector rank – working stints in both Horsham and Southampton before returning home to Chichester – and could go about wearing his own suit-and-tie like a civilian, Jack was still in uniform. This wasn't because Jack wasn't good at his job – quite the contrary – but because, if you wanted to get on and move up in the force, it was necessary to accept being moved around from station to station, experiencing different policing challenges.

Jack had never wanted to do that because he had his grandma at home to look after.

Did Florence need him on a day-to-day basis?

She said not, but Jack disagreed.

Jack took the paperwork out of his typewriter, separating the carbons and the copies, each one a different colour, and putting them in separate out-trays for filing.

'What's up, Fred?'

'I just need a minute to go through my report on the Bunting Manor business,' said Fred, his cup and saucer in his hand. 'You knew it better than I did. I only arrived at the last minute.'

Jack frowned. The 'Bunting Manor business' was Maisie's second involvement in a local murder and Jack had been in it almost from the start. Maisie had appealed to him for help and he, sceptical, had been slow in providing it. He wondered if she had forgiven him yet. There was no reason why she should have. He hadn't forgiven himself.

'Sure, Fred. Right now?'

'If you would.' Fred glanced round the open-plan office. Oddly, Jack thought he looked nervous. 'Just come with me, would you?'

They went out into the corridor with its unpleasant strip lighting. They found a vacant interview room. Jack was about to take a seat at the scratched Formica table when Fred Nairn stopped him.

'I'm sorry, I just wanted to get you out of earshot of the rest of the lads.'

'What is it?' asked Jack. 'Has Maisie done something to mess up—'

'No, not at all. She's been an exemplary witness.' Fred gave him a look. 'Are you getting on, the two of you?'

'She doesn't want to see me until the trials are over. She says it's too complicated and I'm beginning to think she might be right. Perhaps it's hopeless and I'm just deluding myself.'

Fred shook his head.

'Do you want my opinion?'

'If you must.'

'Despite yourself, you're smiling. You usually are whenever you think of her.'

'Yes, all right.'

'My opinion is, however long it takes, your Miss Cooper is worth it.'

'She's not "my" Miss Cooper,' Jack growled. 'Go on. What did you want to say?'

'I'm sorry, Jack,' said Fred, looking serious. 'It's your grandmother.'

'What's happened?'

'She's in hospital.'

Jack felt a hollow open up inside his chest.

'Is it a fall?'

'No, nothing like that. I've got a car ready. Barry will drive you over.' Jack left the interview room. Fred Nairn followed him out into the corridor. 'Is there anything I need to cover for you?' he called out, sympathetically.

But Jack was already gone.

TEN

The next three hours of Maisie's life were a delight. She spent them in the centre of Chichester Festival Theatre's row E, watching the shape of the play evolve in front of her fascinated eyes.

The session seemed to be run almost entirely by the small square man, Micky Petherick, apparently NVE's regular second-in-command. Much of it was accompanied by the sound of heavy rain beating noisily on the sheet-metal roof. Each time she was not on stage, Adélaïde came to sit next to Maisie, but didn't speak, indicating by gesture that she wanted to save her voice.

Because it was essentially a technical rehearsal, the actors moved from cue to cue, from scene to scene, without reciting the dialogue at anything like full volume. Their objective was to simply practise their moves. Maisie found it odd to see the shape of the play but not really hear the lines, despite the fact that she could see that they were speaking them quietly to one another, then raising their voices to performance pitch for those that marked changes in location, characters coming on or going off, and cues for songs. The stage manager barked out instructions from a marked-up script, trying to pin down aspects of positioning and pace. Now and then, something had to be reworked altogether. Between scenes, the two stagehands – the older grey-haired man and the blond youth, both wearing black trousers and shirts – moved mismatched items of furniture on and off the stage.

Perhaps, thought Maisie, *the actual pieces are yet to arrive?*

'Let's take that again,' called Micky Petherick. 'Starting positions, please.'

Prompted by the fragments of action on stage, Maisie's classroom memories of the story became clearer, beyond the central drama of Polly Peachum being in love with the highwayman Macheath and marrying him in secret, then her parents denouncing him to Mr Lockit, the jailer, for the reward. Lucy Lockit, the jailer's daughter, was also in love with Macheath and willing to help him escape – but only if she can have him all to herself.

Perhaps because her thoughts had disappeared into memory, Maisie realised with a shudder that she had seen the two stagehands before, while she was trying to get to the bottom of Stephen's murder at Church Lodge. It had been outside the theatre pub, The Bell, just before she herself had been confronted by the last moments of a dying woman's…

She shook her head. No, it would do her no good to dwell on those awful scenes.

She refocused on the action, hearing NVE's voice from the back of the auditorium where he was sitting with Sam, the lighting man, at a temporary desk set up on an old door amongst the seats, connected to the real lighting box with several thick strands of cable. Then, as an apparently defeated Adélaïde as Polly Peachum slumped down on a faded chaise longue, NVE came down close to the stage. The rehearsal continued and, now and then, he interrupted the action.

The two things must happen at precisely the same time. Once more, please.

Don't get so close. You look like you are in her lap. At least an arm's length between you on the big stage.

You forget there are people left and right. Share your performance.

Lift your chin. Tell the cheap seats at the back.

67

Each time, the actors accepted the note without comment and re-ran their lines from the previous cue to wherever they had stumbled. Meanwhile, the lights high up in the grid faded in and out and jumped on and off as different effects were tried and amended and discarded or approved. All in all, there was as much waiting as performing, as much thinking as doing.

Yes, you are wonderful, yes!

This last comment was directed with delighted emphasis as Adélaïde ran tearfully from her parents' house in fear for Macheath's life.

Dorothy Dean came to sit next to Maisie, giving her a copy of the company list.

'Thank you,' she whispered.

NVE began working on the climax to the show with the entire company on stage, including Adélaïde, who still moved with a kind of guarded self-possession, only speaking when the process required it.

'Tell me what you think?' said Dorothy quietly.

'I think it looks like a very complex ballet.'

'That's very astute. Are you sure you have no experience of show business?'

'None at all.'

Maisie waited and, eventually, Dorothy went on.

'I can say this to you because you're a stranger and it will help to get it off my chest. NVE is good at what he does, but he is, essentially, a director of theatrical pageants – spectacle, movement, rhythm, all that. I wouldn't be surprised if he hasn't thought much about character or motivation or historical context. He relies on the actors for all that. But he will make it look good.'

'Is that enough?' asked Maisie.

'Of course, it isn't,' hissed Dorothy. 'Not for us, not for the critics, either. Perhaps the audience will accept it...' She

68

stood up but immediately bent over so she could continue to speak close to Maisie's ear. 'Never repeat that, not to Adélaïde, not to anybody.'

Dorothy straightened and Maisie saw that she was smiling, as if what she had said was nothing more than everyday banter, but Maisie thought there was something much more serious behind the words. As Dorothy walked away, Maisie felt an unsettling premonition that the sequence of crimes that had begun at Church Lodge and continued at Bunting Manor was not yet ready to leave her in peace.

*

After a brief break for tea and biscuits consumed in the auditorium, the rehearsal resumed. An hour and a half later, Maisie began to feel hungry once again. Despite the rain still hammering on the sheet-metal roof, she wondered if she might be allowed to walk back to the hotel – where service began at six – for her pre-paid dinner. Happily, Micky Petherick announced just then that the green room was serving hot food to the whole company and work on stage would resume in an hour.

Maisie saw Adélaïde leaving the stage at the rear, through the set and the scene dock – she made a mental note to think of it as 'upstage' – so she went after her, feeling an odd frisson as she climbed up onto the boards, the place where nothing was real, but everything felt more real than life itself.

She caught up with Adélaïde, who was looking confused and annoyed, uncertain which exit would take her back to her dressing room.

'It's this way,' said Maisie, grateful for Dorothy's comprehensive tour.

She led Adélaïde towards the stage door hallway where the grey-haired Mrs Belt was idly filling in another crossword puzzle. They doubled back along a utilitarian corridor at the very back of the building, finding Adélaïde's dressing room right in the middle. They went inside.

The room was surprisingly spacious and Adélaïde told Maisie smugly that she had been allocated the best one. There was a large mirror with strong lightbulbs all around it, over a wooden counter. On this, Maisie saw Adélaïde's script and some essential make-up supplies. Beside the mirror, a smallish window looked out onto the rainy park.

'This room is furthest from the stage,' said Adélaïde, 'which is good but also not so good.'

'Because?'

'Because, for my cues, I am obliged to leave early and stand in the wings to be certain not to miss my entrances.'

'I see.'

'On the other hand, apart from this...' Adélaïde gestured to a speaker in the corner of wall and ceiling. 'It is quiet.'

Adélaïde was referring to the backstage relay, which communicated sound from the stage to every corner of the building. Through it, Maisie could hear a shuffling of feet and the clump and scrape of furniture being repositioned on the stage, along with low, everyday chatter.

'That's useful,' she said.

'I can't escape it,' said Adélaïde quietly. 'It reminds me that they are all better than me.' Then, suddenly, she looked up, asking sweetly: 'Would you bring me something to eat? Nothing too heavy – and not straight away. In twenty minutes. I am going to lie down and think.'

'Of course. What sort of thing?'

'Oh, it will all be awful. A plate with a little of six things, not touching each other, so I at least have a choice.' Then she sighed, glancing at a jewelled watch on her right wrist. 'The English eat dinner when children are having their teatime.'

'I know,' said Maisie, thinking of her own grown-up Parisian evening routines of *apéritif*, *dîner* and *souper* at six and eight and ten o'clock, or even later. 'Something hot?'

'There must be meat or fish – fish is better – and salad, perhaps. They cannot spoil that, as long as it is fresh.'

'I'll try and make sure it's—'

Adélaïde put a hand on her arm.

'Maisie, don't worry. You cannot do everything. Your presence has already changed things. Thank you.'

'Good, I'm glad,' Maisie replied.

Adélaïde turned away and opened her script, simultaneously removing her watch and her rings. Perhaps, Maisie thought, she was going to change into her costume. It was on hangers on hooks on the wall, protected by a dust sheet.

Maisie stepped outside and shut the door. Almost at once, she heard Adélaïde lock it on the inside. She had been politely – but summarily – dismissed. At the same time, she wondered in what way she had 'already changed things'?

Maisie followed the backstage corridor past several more dressing rooms to the green room, hearing a pleasant buzz of conversation. The door was ajar and some extra wrought-iron tables and chairs had been brought in from outside to supplement the seating. The two stagehands in their 'blacks' were drying the outdoor furniture with tea towels. It reminded Maisie of the picnic she had enjoyed with her parents, before seeing Olivier's triumph in *Uncle Vanya*, the year before they died.

A man with a self-consciously dashing air saw her in the doorway. He wore a well-cut black-and-grey tweed jacket over corduroy slacks. His eyes flicked up and down her body as he came to introduce himself.

'Miss Cooper, isn't it?'

She knew his character name already, of course, from the long and gruelling technical rehearsal.

'Good afternoon, Captain Macheath,' she said, smiling, hoping she wasn't breaking some kind of theatre taboo.

'Ha! Yes, that's me. Awful script, isn't it? Never uses three words when seventeen will do. Still, the songs grow on you.'

Maisie glanced round. Was anyone else paying attention to his rather treacherous speech? She thought not. He was speaking just for her.

In fact, as she hesitated, he took her hand precisely as NVE had done and said: 'You are a very beautiful person. Thank you for coming to our rescue. I'm Andrew and, at the end of the piece, I'm due to be hanged. Take pity on me, lovely lady?'

Was this ordinary theatre banter or, perhaps, ordinary theatre flirtation; meaningless and to be expected?

'Miss Cooper!' someone called.

The dashing Captain Macheath – Andrew, she reminded herself – dropped her hand. Maisie turned towards the voice. It was Dorothy Dean, seated at a table with several other company members. They had appropriated a few serving dishes and she and her colleagues were helping themselves from them.

'Come and sit down. You need to meet people.'

'Me, too?' asked Andrew.

'There's only one chair,' said Dorothy.

ELEVEN

Maisie sat down next to the woman playing Adélaïde's character's mother, Mrs Peachum. She was clearly ravenous, ladling some kind of stew – it smelled like goulash – onto her plate and then transferring it by soup spoon into her busy mouth. She had curly, ginger hair and a jolly moon-face that looked much more deeply lined now Maisie was seeing her off-stage. Her name was Esther Canning.

On the far side of Esther Canning – Mrs Peachum – was her stage-husband, Mr Peachum. He stood up to carve a few slices from a ham joint with a slim pocket knife, then reached across and offered to shake Maisie's hand.

'Glad to meet you. I'm Esther's husband, in the play and in real life. My name is Canning, Clive Canning.'

He spoke as if Maisie ought to know him. Was he one of those balding, barrel-shaped men popular in television comedies, like Arthur Lowe as Captain Mainwaring in *Dad's Army*, but much taller? Though she hadn't watched television in England for many years, she obliged him by replying: 'I thought I recognised you. How marvellous to work together as a family.'

Unfortunately, this remark seemed to have been the wrong thing to say and the table became rather quiet and tense.

'Eat, Miss Cooper,' said Dorothy.

'Please call me Maisie, Miss Dean.'

'Eat, Maisie.'

Having had quite a lot of shepherd's pie for lunch, Maisie found she wasn't enormously hungry after all. There was a bowl with what looked like Caesar salad. She took a modest portion, helped by a man with a very lop-sided face, rather like a clown but without benefit of make-up. Maisie wondered if he had been in some kind of accident. Just as she was thinking this, he winked and Maisie found herself laughing, as he had intended her to.

'I'm sorry,' she said. 'You play the Beggar, don't you? I haven't learned your name yet.'

'In a way, it's my show – *The Beggar's Opera*,' he told her. 'But because we didn't do many of my words this afternoon, you won't have noticed me. I stand apart.'

Esther and Clive Canning exchanged a look that Maisie didn't think was entirely benign.

'That's a very grandiose way of putting it,' said Clive.

'And in real life?' Maisie asked. 'I mean, I can't go about calling you by your fictional name, can I?'

'No,' said the Beggar. 'Only the stage manager is allowed to do that, to avoid confusion. Imagine if there was a John in the cast and a John in the show and they weren't the same person.' He did his funny wink again. 'And I am John, you see? John Hermanson, originally from Durham, later of the English Channel where my Spitfire crashed and transformed me from a promising leading man to a comic underling with a funny face – funny ha-ha and funny peculiar.'

He pulled his features into an odd, twisted smile and Maisie couldn't help laughing. He had a knack of comic timing that, she thought, probably meant he was better off no longer playing leading men anyway.

'What an extraordinary thing. How did you survive – ditching in the Channel, I mean?'

'Pure bloody-mindedness. My tiny toes still feel frozen.'

'I bet they do. Well, I'm pleased to meet you, John Hermanson.'

The table was too wide for them to shake hands so John instead turned to his neighbour and said: 'Introduce yourself, Winnie.'

'Good evening,' said a woman about Maisie's age with a voluptuous figure and long brown hair arranged in an untidy updo. 'I'm Lucy Lockit in the play.'

'The jailer's daughter?'

'That's right,' she said with a gorgeous, inviting smile. 'I'm the third corner of a wicked love triangle with Adélaïde as Polly Peachum and Andy as Macheath.'

Just then, Andrew came to join them, dragging an outdoor chair, having made himself an enormous cheese-and-salad sandwich with about a foot of French bread – the stodgy English kind, not a crisp authentic baguette. He squeezed his chair into the narrow space between Maisie and Esther Canning and everyone had to shunt round a bit. Winnie watched him with a rather possessive eye.

'Would you tell me your second name?' Maisie asked Winnie. 'I'm making an effort to get you all straight in my mind.'

'Winnie Brahms,' said the Lucy Lockit actress, politely, her attention still held by the Macheath.

There was a small pause as everyone had their mouths full. In her mind, Maisie saw the company list Dorothy had given her, beginning with the off-stage team:

Nils van Erde, director
Dorothy Dean, theatre manager
Sam Smithers, theatre electrician
Micky Petherick, stage manager
Mrs Harriet Belt, stage door

Among the actors, there was Andrew-something – she couldn't remember what – playing Macheath, then:

Adélaïde Amour, playing Polly Peachum
Esther Canning, playing Mrs Peachum, Polly's mother
Clive Canning, playing Mr Peachum, Polly's father
John Hermanson, playing the Beggar
Winnie Brahms, playing Lucy Lockit, Polly Peachum's love rival

With a clatter of her cutlery, Dorothy Dean left the table, inviting a young woman with a fragile air to take her place. Maisie had seen her on the way in, standing alone and friendless by the doors to the park outside, holding a cup and saucer and studiously ignoring the room.

'This is Kitty Farrell, the understudy,' said Dorothy.

Kitty smiled uncertainly. Her eyes seemed red, as if she had been crying.

'Which role?' Maisie asked, innocently.

'Adélaïde's understudy,' said Kitty Farrell, with a sigh.

'Oh, yes, of course,' said Maisie, realising it could be taken as criticism that she hadn't seen it straight away. 'How are you getting on?'

'I don't know,' Kitty replied quietly.

'I'm sure you're marvellous,' Maisie overcompensated. 'You do have a look of her. The right height, too. It's really very striking.'

That was no more than the truth. Kitty Farrell had the same wide-set eyes, generous mouth and clear complexion. But, where Adélaïde was appealingly pale, her understudy was diaphanous to the point of transparency.

'Kitty can sing, too,' said Clive Canning, unexpectedly.

'Not like Miss Amour can,' said Kitty.

'You are very talented,' said Esther Canning, urgently. 'Believe it, Kitty.'

'I don't have the right voice,' said Kitty, looking hopeless.

'It's not just the voice,' said Esther, her mouth full. 'It's the performance.'

'I don't have that either.'

'Course you do,' said Clive. 'Doesn't she, my dear?'

'Kitty's a star in the making,' said his wife, looking fiercely round the table. 'As long as no one upsets her.'

'Winnie, darling,' said Andrew, 'you've been rehearsing with Kitty and Liam, my understudy. You think she's doing very well, don't you?'

'Yes, Andy,' said Winnie Brahms, appearing gratified by his attention. 'She is.'

'But did you see Adélaïde?' asked Kitty. 'When she sang, *a cappella*, on the Olivier point, everyone just spontaneously cheered. I mean, what chance have I got? I hope I never have to go on. Imagine how disappointed everyone will be – the audience, the critics, NVE...'

Kitty sniffed and dabbed at her eyes.

'Now, don't say that,' said Esther, who had finally completed the arduous task of getting herself through her enormous portion of goulash. 'NVE loves you. He's absolutely delighted with you. We all are. You're going to be immensely helpful to us in rehearsals. You know Adélaïde doesn't have the stamina and you will have to step in and make it easy for us to work when she has to rest.'

There was a general murmur of approval as Esther reached once more for the ladle.

John Hermanson, the Beggar, remarked: 'NVE is very supportive – of everybody.'

Clive agreed: 'You couldn't hope for a better director for your first professional show, Kitty.'

Breadcrumbs fell from Andrew's generous lips as he nodded his head and insisted: 'Positive warmth and professionalism. Of course, I've known him more or less all my life.'

'I agree with Andy,' said Winnie Brahms.

Esther concluded what seemed to Maisie a kind of chorus by adding: 'This could be a breakthrough for you Kitty, even though it's only the understudy. NVE wants it to be.'

'I know,' said Kitty, sadly. 'I'm very lucky. Everyone tells me so. Even the voice in my head tells me so.'

The conversation moved on to matters of stage technique and timing. Maisie finished her Caesar salad and accepted a glass of water, watching the complicated interplay of affection and respect, irritation and envy.

All at once, she had an odd flash of envy herself, thinking again of her young friend Zoe, in Bunting, who could also sing like an angel and who, coincidentally, would also look the part. But Zoe was stuck in her dead-end job at the country pub, The Dancing Hare, and would never get the chance to prove it.

She stood up.

'Right,' she said. 'I'm going to take Miss Amour something to eat in her dressing room. Do you mind if I say your names aloud to fix them in my mind?' She looked at each in turn. 'Esther Canning, Clive Canning, John Hermanson, Kitty Farrell, Winnie Brahms.'

One after another, they nodded and smiled, except for Kitty who sniffed and looked away. For no good reason, Andrew stood up, making a little bow.

'In Sinatra's version, I'm Mack the Knife. According to my Equity card and, as it happens, my birth certificate, I am Andrew P Bradshaw. It has a nice ring, doesn't it? Andrew P Bradshaw. I think I sound like an actor.'

'Two syllables and two syllables,' said Esther Canning. 'It always works.'

'You sound almost sickeningly like an actor,' said John Hermanson, then took the caustic edge off his voice with his comic wink.

'Pleased to meet you, Andrew P Bradshaw,' said Maisie.

He ignored her, instead asking John Hermanson, with a smile: 'Do you need a drink, John, to perk you up or calm you down?'

John Hermanson reddened and there was an ugly little pause.

'No, thank you.'

Andrew turned back to Maisie.

'John looks down on me from the valorous heights of his distinguished war record. For myself, I was too young and all I can boast is the Sea Cadets at school and national service playing at sailors.'

'I'll have you know the Royal Navy is the senior service,' said Clive. 'A service I was honoured to serve.'

Once again, Maisie felt she had provoked a nasty undercurrent, so she slipped away, telling them: 'Thank you for being patient with me.'

She took two unused side-plates, arranging small amounts of five dishes – there weren't six on the table – such that they didn't touch, as instructed. With her early experience in hospitality, she was able to balance both in one hand. As she made her way along the corridor towards Adélaïde's dressing room, she was thinking about two things.

First, everyone seemed to like and admire NVE, Nils van Erde. So, did Adélaïde really need Maisie to protect her from him?

Her second thought was connected but independent. If, for any reason, Adélaïde couldn't go on, poor Kitty Farrell would surely be a complete disaster. The other actors had been kind, encouraging her with just the right actorly note of sincerity, but Maisie didn't think it was authentic.

Oh, and one more thing. When Kitty Farrell mentioned 'the voice in my head', did she mean that literally, or was it just a figure of speech?

79

TWELVE

While the world of smoke and mirrors at the theatre inched its way towards its first performance, Jack Wingard, Maisie's teenage sweetheart, was caught up in events that were, frustratingly, out of his control. They began with an awkward crosstown journey through traffic. Finally reaching St Richard's Hospital, he fretted impatiently in the passenger seat as Constable Barry Goodbody sought a space to park, at last bringing the police Ford Zephyr to a halt in an ambulance bay. The moment the car was still, Jack jumped out and ran indoors.

The entrance to the inpatients department at St Richard's Hospital was confusing, with signs seemingly indicating contrary routes to identical destinations. Jack asked a porter for help and there was an odd little passage of misunderstanding as Jack thought the porter was asking him: 'Which ward?'

'I don't know which,' he protested.

'No, mate, Wych Ward.' The porter pointed along a dusty, sludge green corridor. 'Down there, stairs at the end, first floor.'

Of course, thought Jack. Richard of Wych was the name of Chichester's twelfth-century patron saint, after whom the hospital was named.

Jack thanked the porter and set off, feeling clumsy in the quiet passage in his heavy constabulary boots. He took a set of winding stairs two at a time, emerging onto a landing with a north-facing window and, outside, three sinister crows on a telephone wire. The landing gave access to two wards, one male and one female, with Wych Ward to the left. He lurked in the doorway, not certain if he was permitted to enter a women's ward unaccompanied. A nurse in a pale-blue uniform and starched white bib came and rescued him.

'Are you Mr Wingard?'

'Yes. What's happened?'

'Florence is in here. Let me show you.'

Jack followed the nurse. There were six beds on either side, all enclosed by frail floral curtains, worn thin by repeated washing. His grandmother was in the last on the left, with a window alongside the head of her bed, overlooking an internal courtyard. Florence was sitting up in her winceyette nightdress with a pattern of daisies around the collar, drinking from a matching cup and saucer, the same sludge-green colour as the corridor. There was a thick bandage around her left forefinger, protected by a rubber stall.

'I told Fred Nairn there was no need,' she declared. 'What good are you here? Neither use nor ornament.'

'You be quiet, Grandma,' said Jack, turning to the nurse. 'Can you tell me—'

At that moment, the curtains were pulled back and a doctor in a white coat introduced himself, referring to Florence firmly in the third person.

'Good afternoon, Sergeant. The patient cut herself at home in her kitchen and made an inadequate dressing from a scrap of worn bedsheet and some Germolene antiseptic cream. When the bleeding wouldn't stop, she wisely called her GP's surgery. The doctor was delayed and came round three hours later, took the liberty of letting himself in and found the patient disorientated, the improvised dressing soaked through.'

He stopped, an irritated look on his face. Jack wondered what Florence had done to annoy him.

'I was not disorientated,' said Florence. 'I had just woken up.'

'Be that as it may,' insisted the doctor, 'the GP drove her here. The cut to the left forefinger was to the bone and required an X-ray. While we were waiting for the results, the patient was persuaded she might have a lie down and a cup of tea, the GP having taken the precaution of packing her night things.' The doctor looked Jack in the eye. 'You must be the grandson.'

'That's right.'

'Here.' He drew what looked like a large photographic negative from a brown paper envelope and held it up against the window. It was the X-ray. 'No nick to the bone.'

'Thank you, Doctor,' said Jack.

Florence pulled her bedclothes aside and swung her thin, blotchy legs out of bed.

'Where are my clothes? I want to go home.'

★

Jack insisted that Florence use a wheelchair to exit the building down the interminable and depressing corridors. Barry Goodbody was still parked close by the entrance on double-yellow lines. As Jack helped Florence from the wheelchair into the back seat, he thanked Barry for waiting.

'And how's your ear, by the way?' By way of reply, Barry just grimaced and readjusted the wad of cotton wool where it drooped over his ear lobe. 'Have you seen the doctor?'

'Yes, Sergeant. I have to put drops in.'

Barry drove to the Wingards' bungalow on Parklands Road and Jack helped his grandma inside, leaving Barry to return to the station. Florence slumped in her armchair by the unlit fire while Jack made tea in the small square kitchen.

When he brought it through, he saw she had elevated her left hand on a cushion.

'It throbs,' she told him, sulkily.

'Well, you shouldn't have cut a slice out of it, should you,' he told her with a smile.

'Into it, not out of it. Anyway, that knife's blunt. That's why it slipped.'

He laughed.

'Is that right? I'll tickle it up with the steel if you promise not to be so clumsy.'

'About time.'

There was a pause, then Jack asked: 'How did you hurt your head?'

'I don't remember,' said Florence, looking small and unhappy.

'You hated all that, didn't you?'

'They treated me like an old woman,' she told him with a sigh.

'I expect they did.' He winked. 'Do you want me to go and arrest them?'

'I wish you would. It should be a crime, "speaking in a baby voice to an adult".'

'Or "excessive niceness to a senior citizen".'

'Exactly.'

'Not that doctor, though,' said Jack. 'He was very straight-forward.'

'I'd already given him a piece of my mind.'

'I thought you must have. He looked on best behaviour.'

'Something of that.'

Florence drank her tea and Jack went to find her a biscuit. When he came back, she looked serious.

'It's true, what I told them. I was asleep, Jack. I wasn't lightheaded or fainting. The doctor came in and found me dribbling on my cushion and jumped to conclusions. He's an old fool.'

'How old?'

'Nearly as old as me.'

They both laughed.

'Anyway,' said Jack, 'it was all for your own good. Better safe than sorry.' The doorbell rang. 'Are you expecting someone?'

Florence put a hand to her mouth.

'Oh, in all the drama, I forgot.'

'Forgot what?'

'It's Mrs Pascal, from Bunting.'

*

Florence asked Jack to make yet another cup of tea – this time for her visitor – then sidled through to the kitchen and told him to return to work.

'I'll be fine, look. Here's Mrs Pascal to watch over me and I think we'll need some privacy.'

Jack protested but, eventually, he left, and Florence returned to the living room. As she related the drama of her day, she felt pleased to have an opportunity to study the woman who had been so important to Jack's last big investigation – and important to Maisie Cooper, too, the woman Florence intended her grandson to marry.

Phyllis 'Phyl' Pascal was an interesting specimen. She was, by all accounts, a rich woman, but she dressed in what appeared to be a husband's or an older brother's cast-offs. Her face was wind-burned and healthy looking, but her eyes were sad. It was the kind of sadness that didn't make you want to say: 'buck up'. It was the kind that might easily make you miserable yourself.

Florence enjoyed their chat about the unpredictable weather, the depressing lateness of the spring, the unhappy countenance of the crops, the unreliable fertility of sheep and the inevitable unreliability of buses. After about twenty minutes, though, she still had no real idea why Phyl was there.

'Now, there must be something you wanted to ask me. Is that right?' she asked. 'Or to tell me?'

Phyl seemed on the point of denying it, then said: 'Have you seen Maisie? Maisie Cooper, I mean?'

'No, dear.'

'Why not?'

'Should I have?'

'Perhaps not. It's just … I haven't either. I wonder, how is she living?'

Florence took a moment before she answered.

'Jack says she's at the Dolphin & Anchor. I expect she's keeping herself to herself, you know, with all she's seen and all she's had to face.'

'For example?' asked Phyl, tersely.

'Well, murders. Don't you think that's enough?' Phyl nodded and there was another pause. Florence added: 'You must be still feeling the shock, too, with everything that happened in Bunting.'

'I suppose.'

There was another silence and Florence dunked her biscuit. Phyl Pascal seemed to come to a decision.

'Is your Jack giving up on her – on Maisie, I mean?' she asked abruptly.

'I wouldn't know, I'm sure.'

'I expect you think I'm meddling?'

'I don't think a thing, yet. Why do you ask?'

'I do have the right,' said Phyl, defensively. 'At least…'

85

Florence sipped her tea, thinking that this really was the most extraordinary conversation. She decided to engage a little more enthusiastically.

'What else did you want to know?'

Phyl shifted awkwardly in her armchair.

'I owe Maisie something and...'

'Yes?'

'I can't see how to get her to take it.'

*

Later that afternoon, as Jack's shift ended, he returned home to the pleasant bungalow on Parklands Road with Chinese food from the take-away – sweet-and-sour pork balls, egg-fried rice, chow mein and free prawn crackers because he and Florence were regular customers. As they sat down to eat with *Nationwide* on the television but the sound turned down, his grandma told him about Phyl Pascal's inconclusive visit.

'And then she left?' he asked with a frown.

'She did.'

'Straight away? Not another word?'

'No, she ended up giving me chapter and verse on their family drama – how she had an affair with Maisie's father, her own sister's husband, and that Maisie is actually her child.'

'That's right,' said Jack, sighing. 'It's just another damn thing.'

'More trouble between you and Maisie, you mean?'

'I do.' He pointed with his fork. 'Do you want that last pork ball?'

'No, you have it.'

He took it, aware of her watching him.

'There's nothing to be done till Maisie feels she's ready, Jack. And, look, she's got Mrs Pascal wanting something from her, too, that perhaps she doesn't want to give. You're better off leaving her be for the time being.'

'I know.' He put down his fork. 'Or perhaps for ever.'

'Don't be ridiculous,' said Florence. 'You'll not do better, not anywhere, not ever. And I'll tell you another thing. You look peaky,' she told him.

'So do you.'

'Never mind me. You could do with a change of scene, a change of ideas.'

Jack pushed back his chair.

'You know what? That's an excellent idea. I think you're right.'

THIRTEEN

Back in the generously proportioned star dressing room overlooking the park, to Maisie's surprise, Adélaïde emptied both small plates. Then they heard the tannoy calling five minutes for the resumption of the onstage rehearsal, the sound crackly and indistinct.

'I think it said they're going to start again at the very beginning of the play.'

Adélaïde shrugged.

'They will come for me if they need me.'

Hearing footsteps, Maisie put her head out into the corridor and saw the stage manager, Micky Petherick, knocking on the adjacent dressing room door. It opened and John Hermanson came out in full costume and make-up as the Beggar – a dirty red tailcoat, breeches in filthy brown, laddered stockings and buckle shoes with preposterous tall heels. On his head was a top hat that looked like someone had sat on it. His make-up was severe – thick, dark lines in the creases in his funny face, red rims to his eyes, dark lips. Maisie found it rather disconcerting. It seemed to have completely hidden his natural comic charm, but perhaps it would look all right from 'out front'.

John read her thoughts.

'It's NVE's idea. I'm supposed to be playing against type. I'm to try my best to be funny even though I look like the Devil himself, driving the characters on to tragedy.'

'Five minutes was the call, Mr Hermanson,' said Micky Petherick. 'That'll be three minutes, now.'

'All right, Petherick.'

'Do you need Miss Amour?' Maisie asked.

'We're going from the top, so only need the Beggar and Mr and Mrs Peachum – Mr Hermanson, here, and Mr and Mrs Canning,' Micky replied, shaking his head. 'If we get on well, we'll arrive at Polly Peachum before we're all allowed home, but I wouldn't bank on it. The Boss is in a bate, but it wasn't me who told you.'

Micky bustled away and Maisie went back into Adelaide's dressing room. John sidled in behind her.

'Aren't I pretty?' he cooed, fanning his fingers either side of his face, like a child pretending to be a sunflower.

'*Imbécile*,' said Adélaïde, laughing.

Incredibly, under his repellent make-up, Maisie thought she saw John blush. Then he coughed theatrically and swung away, calling back over his shoulder: 'My public awaits!'

'He is in love with me,' said Adélaïde. 'It is dull and it is sad because he is otherwise so amusing.'

Adélaïde shrugged again. Maisie wondered if it was an affectation – that she did it because it was an expected characteristic of her French-ness.

'Well, if you're not on stage, what can I do to help?' Maisie asked.

'I listen,' said Adélaïde, 'and I practise.'

She stood and reached a long arm up to the speaker in the angle of ceiling and wall and turned the dial, increasing the volume, then bent over her script.

There were only two chairs. Adélaïde sat in an upright one, leaning a pale arm on the counter beneath the illuminated mirror. Maisie took the other, a low armchair-like seat whose foam gave little support. She leaned back, aware of the metal frame against her shoulders, listening to the bustle over the tannoy – mostly Micky Petherick chivvying his stage crew and then, finally, calling: 'Positions, please.'

89

The play began with John Hermanson's voice, raised in self-pitying – but commanding – introduction.

'If poverty be a title to poetry, I am sure nobody can dispute mine. I am myself of the company of beggars…'

*

Despite the difficulty of the language and the obscurity of some of the archaic references, Maisie found it mesmerising. After a few speeches, though, she realised there was a second sound in the dressing room. Adélaïde was reading along, very quietly, practising her English by trying to copy and keep up with the performance from the stage. Just then, as Maisie watched her, Adélaïde stumbled over a difficult phrase and threw her script on the floor.

'I cannot say the words. I trip and I trip again.'

Maisie picked up the text. The front page was slightly torn.

'It must be frustrating,' she said, 'but your singing was wonderful.'

'Yes, you have told me my singing is good. I know this.'

Maisie put the script back on the counter. On stage, someone had gone wrong and the performance had broken, the voices muffled and distant from the speaker.

'Try again?' she suggested. 'I think they are going to go back to the beginning.'

Adélaïde shook her head.

'Read it to me. Perhaps a woman's voice would be better.'

Adélaïde turned the tannoy down so they could only just hear it and Maisie did as she was asked, speaking the Beggar's lines very clearly.

'You have a pleasant timbre,' said Adélaïde. 'Find my first scene and read my lines from that, too.'

Maisie was used to being given peremptory orders by her Paris *patronne*, the redoubtable Madame de Rosette, but she was beginning to wonder if a full week of Adélaïde's sulky bossiness might wear a little thin. All the same, she dutifully turned the pages, found the place and read aloud:

'I know as well as any of the fine ladies how to make the most of myself and of my man, too. A woman knows how to be mercenary. We have it in our natures. If I allow Captain Macheath some trifling liberties, I have this watch and other visible marks of his favour to shew for it.'

'That was good. Now you are better than me,' said Adélaïde in a sullen voice. 'Read it again, then I will try.'

Maisie did as she was asked, then handed the script over. Adélaïde recited the same lines without looking at the page, involuntarily giving them an odd foreign intonation, making even easy words sound awkward.

'I am terrible,' she said and threw the script on the floor for a second time.

'Look, why don't you listen again. I'm sure you can do it.' Maisie picked it up again and re-read the first sentence. 'Now, your turn.'

Without looking at the page, Adélaïde repeated it with the same awkwardness.

'You're not catching the right rhythm,' said Maisie.

'Because I am very bad,' she said. 'This was a mistake.'

Maisie had a flash of inspiration.

'I think the problem is that you've learned your script by heart, on your own, which is incredibly professional, but it also means you've been hearing it in your head and reinforcing the wrong intonation. But there must be a way to fix that. When you were singing, it was so lovely.'

'Yes, yes, I was good then and I am bad now. I can sing but I cannot talk, perhaps? Is that so unusual? It is like the opposite of the early musical film stars who could talk but not sing. So, they had other women record their numbers.

But I cannot do this. I must be alone on the huge stage and a thousand people will laugh at me.'

More than a thousand, thought Maisie.

'But you have hardly any accent when you sing,' she insisted.

'How does this help?' said Adélaïde. 'I cannot sing my lines.'

'Actually,' said Maisie, 'why not?'

Adélaïde opened her mouth to argue but Maisie held out the script encouragingly and, after a pause, Adélaïde took it.

'I tell you this is foolish,' she said.

'Perhaps stand up?' suggested Maisie. 'You usually sing standing up, don't you?'

Adélaïde got to her feet in a single graceful movement, instinctively adjusting the fall of her clothes as she did so. There was a momentary pause, then Adélaïde flicked some kind of mental switch and became a different person. She put her head on one side as if an interesting thought had, at just that moment, come into her head, then opened her lovely mouth and sang, in a fluid improvised tune:

'I know as well as any of the fine ladies
'How to make the most of myself
'And of my man, too.
'A woman knows how to be mercenary…'

As she completed the paragraph, Maisie told her: 'Now, do it again, but in your speaking voice, retaining the music of the language.'

Adélaïde hesitated for a moment then, with the same convincing inclination of her head as a sort of trigger, she spoke the words:

'I know as well as any of the fine ladies how to make the most of myself and of my man, too. A woman knows how to be mercenary…'

When she had finished, Maisie realised that she had been holding her breath.

'That was marvellous.'

'It was better,' admitted Adélaïde.

'Marvellous,' Maisie insisted. 'Can you do it again?'

'One moment.' Adélaïde listened to the distant tannoy. 'Oh, they are going to take the beginning again then go on to the end when the Beggar is to complete the play. I am not needed so, yes, let us do more.'

*

For Maisie, time began to pass both slowly and quickly. In one respect, the minutes crawled by, with Maisie astonished at the level of concentration required to work closely on the archaic text. Then, when she looked at her watch, having reached the end of Polly Peachum's second scene, she was amazed to find it was nearly nine o'clock in the evening.

'You're doing very well,' she said.

'I am not tired,' said Adélaïde, 'but I must not overwork. I will return to the hotel.'

'They won't want you on stage?'

'The understudy can do it. I will walk in the fresh air. The evening now is dry, I think?'

Maisie glanced through the small gap in the curtains. It was true – the window-glass had no trace of rain.

'Shall I come with you?'

'Miss Dean will come with me. You should watch and learn the play so that you can help me more tomorrow. We will begin after breakfast. Shall we say seven o'clock?'

'That's very early.'

'I was born in a Breton fishing family. We wake before the sun.'

'Won't that be a sure way to strain your voice?'

93

'Perhaps.' Adélaïde nodded. 'In the restaurant at eight o'clock.'

Maisie accompanied Adélaïde to the stage door. A call was relayed over the tannoy. A couple of minutes later, Dorothy Dean appeared, pushing her arms into the sleeves of a slightly-too-small waterproof jacket.

'This one,' said Adélaïde, pointing at Maisie, 'she is like a gift from God.'

Without any other preamble, Adélaïde spoke some of the lines they had practised.

'Well, I never,' said Dorothy when she had finished.

'I am good, yes?' asked Adélaïde.

'You are,' said Dorothy, emphatically.

Adélaïde pushed open the door and swept outside. Before she followed her star, Dorothy surprised Maisie by giving her a hug.

'Keep this up, Maisie Cooper, and you've a job for life.'

FOURTEEN

Once Dorothy had left, Maisie took Adélaïde's dirty plates and cutlery back to the green room. No one else was there, not even the woman who had served the food. Everything had been washed up and put away. On one of the tables was a half-complete Airfix model of a Spitfire fighter plane and she wondered whose hobby that might be. Someone introverted who liked to keep themselves to themselves when they weren't acting? John Hermanson, perhaps? No, surely it would bring back unhappy memories.

Here, too, the stage relay could be heard. Micky Petherick called for Polly Peachum, Adélaïde's role – obviously, Kitty would go on and understudy in her absence – and for her parents in the drama, Mr and Mrs Peachum.

Maisie decided to go out front and observe. She entered the auditorium discreetly in a dark corner right at the back, finding a flip-down usherette's seat from which to watch Esther and Clive take Kitty through a complicated, dialogue-heavy scene in which it became clear that Polly Peachum truly loved the anti-hero Captain Macheath, but her parents were determined to turn him in for the reward.

Could Kitty ever be any good, Maisie wondered? Might she perhaps be more engaging on television where the camera could hold her in close-up and reveal the nuances in her expressions? Her technique definitely wasn't 'big' enough for the enormous thrust stage.

There were a few other actors on stage playing unnamed roles, including Liam Jukes, a wirily handsome young man

95

who she recognised as Andrew's understudy for Macheath. There were no performance notes from NVE, no technical advice from Micky. Maisie wondered if that was a deliberate decision, not to stop the flow. All the same, the scene had very little energy. Yes, she could hear the lines, but they sort of evaporated in the huge space, leaving no lasting impression.

Then, everything changed as three other actors came on: the voluptuous Winnie Bradshaw as the love-rival, Lucy Lockit; John Hermanson upstage and prowling as the Beggar; Andrew P Bradshaw looking very pleased with his dashing highwayman's costume, a thigh-length red jacket and a lovely silvery waistcoat underneath. Esther and Clive became expansive, their gestures growing more theatrical as their voices carried more easily to Maisie's distant corner. She wondered if the Cannings had been moderating their performance to Kitty's subdued level.

Micky Petherick called a reset and Maisie saw Winnie draw Andrew coquettishly aside for an indiscreet dalliance up behind the set. Esther and Clive, she noticed, went to congratulate – or perhaps reassure – Kitty, but she broke away like a frustrated teenager. They followed, Esther putting a hand on her arm, Kitty dabbing at her eyes with the inevitable hanky. Then Micky instructed the company that they were going to practise a song.

'The movements are complicated,' said NVE, 'but they must be measured, precise, like a formal dance.'

The dance included almost the whole cast and more performers climbed up out of the stalls. Maisie counted twenty-one actors, in total, most of them now wearing complete or almost-complete eighteenth-century costumes. As NVE detailed a long series of movement instructions, her mind drifted.

For a few minutes, in her imagination, Maisie was back in her attic apartment on the Place des Vosges. Then, she was downstairs at a café she liked where street cleaners dropped in at ten o'clock each morning – four hours into their working days – for a glass of white wine and an espresso coffee. From there, her thoughts led her, dreamlike, to Phyl Pascal's 'big house' in Bunting, climbing down the ladder-like stair to the basement to choose a dusty bottle from Phyl's wine rack. That led Maisie back to a burning farmhouse and a memory that she wished she could find a way to forget – and a feeling of regret that she had pushed Jack so far away.

*

With applause from NVE, the skilfully choreographed song came to an end, jerking Maisie back to the present. Micky announced: 'Last on tonight's agenda – fight call. Let's make this a good one and be away before ten.'

The ladies of the company left the stage, Kitty moving quickly, without a word to any of the other actors, although Maisie thought Esther tried to catch her attention. Soon, only the gentlemen remained. Maisie glanced at her watch. It was nine-forty and the actors looked tired.

The fighting was stylised and, Maisie thought, very effective. NVE directed it like a kind of dance, beating a rhythm by clapping his hands, adding first one actor then the next, until a whole ballet of slow-motion combat emerged from the confusion. Now and then, someone made a mistake, but they pressed on, stumbling to a climax.

'Not bad but let's do it one more time from the top,' said NVE.

'The spacing is so much wider than the Drill Hall,' said Andrew.

'It's hard to get where you need to be in time,' said Clive, for once in agreement, mopping his brow.

'You are doing very well,' said NVE. 'We begin again.'

The atmosphere in the theatre became more intense as NVE accelerated the rhythm. The men were all sweating, their faces fixed, but they made it through to the end with no major hiccups.

'One more,' shouted NVE.

'Seriously, though,' called back Andrew, good humouredly, fanning himself with the tails of his dashing highwayman's riding coat. 'Let us catch our breaths.'

'A count of ten,' NVE called back. 'Keep that energy.'

The actors resumed at an even quicker tempo. The Beggar, John Hermanson, didn't take part, but he prowled around them, banging on the floor with his stick as they lunged and swerved, kicked and punched. John's stick and the stamping of the actors' feet were designed to reinforce the rhythm, rising to a noisy climax.

'Magnificent,' shouted NVE once they had finished. 'Triumphant.'

'God,' said Clive, his hands on his knees, 'that was almost too much.'

'Invigorating,' said Andrew, but his chest was heaving.

'You are a master, NVE,' said John. 'Bravo.'

'You are all extraordinary,' replied the director. 'Thank you, thank you.' He turned to his assistant. 'That's it.'

'Whole company, eleven o'clock tomorrow morning, please,' shouted Micky. 'Now, let's all turn in, for God's sake.'

★

Maisie didn't want to get caught up with any of the actors so she slipped away, remembering to sign out at the stage door. Mrs Belt was nowhere to be seen but the typed list was lying on the desk. While she was there, she noticed a board with hooks for spare keys, labelled with numbers and functions, such as 'wardrobe' and 'boiler room'. One of the hooks was labelled 'pass key', which Maisie thought showed a lack of concern for security.

She hurried back through the quiet streets to the hotel, intending to go straight up to bed. Passing through the lobby, however, she noticed Dorothy Dean in the bar, talking to someone who had his back towards her but she recognised regardless. She went in.

'Mohammed,' she said, 'you're still here. Did something happen?'

'Yes, something delightful.' He stood up politely and brought over a chair from another table. 'Miss Dean has invited me to take an interest in the production. The transfer to the West End is virtually assured.'

'No, no, I won't have that,' said Dorothy. 'Not assured. Nothing in this business is assured. But there's a good chance.'

Maisie sat down, glancing round the room. There was no one else from the company present. They could speak without fear of being overheard.

'With Adélaïde in the lead?' she asked. 'You believe she's up to it?'

'A star is a star,' said Dorothy, nodding. She reached for a cut-glass tumbler of whisky and water. 'She's a story we can tell.'

'It seems very risky,' said Maisie.

'I am aware of the risk, Maisie,' said Mohammed with a complacent smile. 'But it is exciting, too, like trying to predict the future. And not actually risky if you only wager what you can afford to lose.'

'And the frisson of potential failure is always alluring,' said Dorothy. She drained her glass. 'We live on the edge and that's how we like it.'

She sat back and Maisie wondered if it was alcohol or the lifeline of Mohammed's investment that made her less tightly wound.

'You know your own affairs best, Mohammed,' said Maisie.

At that moment, the hotel manager came to ask if anyone wanted another drink as he would be closing the bar shortly, at ten-thirty. They refused. Mohammed went on: 'I intend to sleep as my chauffeur drives me back to London. I will return for the press night performance.'

He took his leave. The hotel manager draped tea-towels over the handles of the ale pumps. Maisie felt becalmed and alone.

'Off to Bedfordshire for me,' said Dorothy, lurching over to the bar to leave her whisky tumbler. 'Miss Amour tells me you have an early start tomorrow. It really is very remarkable.'

'What is?'

'How, in almost every way, the success or failure of *The Beggar's Opera*,' said Dorothy, 'has come to depend on Maisie Cooper.'

FIFTEEN

As Maisie climbed the stairs to her disappointing room and Dorothy made her way to what was, doubtless, a much nicer one – and Mohammed began to doze in the back of his chauffeur-driven Bentley – at the theatre, the elderly volunteer Harriet Belt believed that everyone had signed out.

The process was not a completely reliable one. It depended on everyone playing the game, taking responsibility and, well … on the stage door keeper taking a professional interest, too.

As it happened, Harriet Belt was not a professional. She was well off – as might be guessed from her smart ruched blouse and genuine pearls – and had close connections to several other Chichester institutions, including the hierarchy at the cathedral, another landmark building whose denizens enjoyed dressing up for their performances. Because she was unpaid, it was difficult for management to complain whenever she did her work shoddily – which was often. The same issue applied to one or two of the volunteer ushers, content merely to take part in the Chichester Festival Theatre adventure in lieu of financial reward. But, because there wasn't currently an audience, there were no ushers in the building and their amateurishness was not yet a problem.

As Maisie had left the theatre, Harriet had been in the green room, imbibing a nip of brandy as the hour was late and she had become cold, sitting still with her crossword. Returning to the stage door in a rush, she had done her best to tick off all the actors and crew, then given up and signed everyone out, whether or not she had actually seen them file past. They had all gone by in such a rush, anyway, talking and laughing, the men sweaty from their exertions, the women neat and well turned out in their street clothes. And several had run back in to pick up something they had forgotten and then run out again. She hadn't made a note of which ones.

Yes, she thought, *everyone's gone. Probably.*

Harriet tidied her desk and silenced the ringer on the telephone. The last thing she had to do was hand over to the nightwatchman, a young man who enjoyed making Airfix models as a way of passing the interminable hours of darkness. His name was Keith Sadler and he was eighteen years old, though he looked only sixteen. He arrived at the stage door with his eyes vague and his hair uncombed and greasy.

'You look very seedy, young man,' said Harriet Belt. 'You know you have to make your inspections according to the schedule.' She pointed to the overnight book on the desk. 'Look at the gaps you left last night.'

'I did them all, I just forgot to sign.'

'Did you call the fire station when you were supposed to?'

'Of course I did, but I don't see why I have to.'

'Because theatres used to be a fire risk with canvas sets and hemp ropes and all the rest of it. And limelight and sparks.'

'But it isn't like that anymore,' said Keith with the impatience of youth for the established practices of days gone by.

'No, that's true, especially not in a new theatre like this one. But did you go to sleep in the green room?'

'I did,' admitted Keith. 'Will you tell?'

'Indeed I won't,' said Harriet indulgently, patting her set grey hair. 'I don't know why you want all this money anyway.'

Actually, Keith had told Harriet that he had plans to travel, specifically to Los Angeles, the home of the movie industry.

'I'll be all right tonight,' said Keith, yawning. 'I've brought an alarm clock for my rounds.'

'You don't want to get a reputation for slackness.'

'No one works harder than I do,' said Keith, aggrieved.

'I know, dear. You're a good lad. I suppose your parents must be very proud.'

Keith thought about his dad who had wanted him to follow into the family business of painting and decorating, not 'spending every hour God sends at the pictures'.

'I hope so,' he said.

Harriet put on her dramatic camel-hair overcoat and left. Keith bolted the door behind her and yawned for a second time.

His first duty was to carry out a circuit of the building. He had a predetermined route, including the foyer, the auditorium, the backstage areas and the basement. He found nothing amiss and only one desk lamp left on in Fort Knox.

Foolish, he thought. *That room of all rooms should be locked.*

He extinguished the lamp and retired to the green room where he had left his Airfix model, sitting down with a weary bump. He set his alarm clock – a bulbous metal affair with two ringers on top like bicycle bells. Then he levered the lid from a tiny pot of brown enamel paint, selected a clean brush and began painting in some of the camouflage pattern on the fuselage.

Soon, however, he felt too tired to continue. He cleaned his brush and lay down on the bench seat, sleep soon overtaking him.

*

While Keith dozed, dreaming of Hollywood and the Oscars, luscious steaks in noisy restaurants on 'the strip', whatever that might mean, someone else was in the building, someone who knew the routine of the theatre and who had discovered over the previous few nights that Keith was in the habit of sleeping through his shift, neglecting his rounds.

Had Keith been awake and heard the sound of them moving about, he might have formed his own ideas about why the intruder was there. He had a good brain and a lively imagination.

Perhaps they had a creative purpose to staying late, a need to experience the theatre in solitude and, in that way, make it more fully their own, nourishing their understanding of the play.

Perhaps they might be a member of the company who wanted to save money on digs. There were places that were warm and dry to sleep, hot water on hand in the dressing rooms, left-over food in the green room.

Perhaps they had practical work to do, sewing costumes or painting scenery. A show was like a pregnancy, after all. There was no way to delay the arrival of the audience. Whatever else happened, that date was immutable.

The intruder waited for time to pass, allowing Keith to fall profoundly asleep. Finally, at a little after half past one, they padded along the corridor in their socks to the green room and looked in.

Had the night been brighter, with moon and stars visible in the sky, they might have noticed a shaft of light glinting on the shiny alarm clock alongside the plastic model parts and paints on the table.

But it wasn't. The sky was cloudy.

The intruder turned away, moving silently through the backstage corridors towards the room popularly referred to as Fort Knox, more or less opposite John Hermanson's dressing room and not far from Adélaïde's. This was the one that contained sensitive financial information and, more importantly, a safe with a combination dial and a large keyhole. Normally, because the season had not yet begun, the safe would contain only a modest float in notes and coins, but not today.

What was more, because Miss Dean had been abruptly called away to escort Miss Amour back to her hotel, the door to Fort Knox had inadvertently been left open.

It was very dark inside so the intruder turned on the desk lamp under its green glass shade. The key was in the keyhole of the safe. The intruder crouched down, turning the dial four times, picking out four numbers, as they had seen Dorothy Dean do earlier that day in order to deposit a thick wedge of banknotes handed over by the Arab gentleman with the words: 'A down payment of five hundred pounds to secure the investment.'

The handle wouldn't turn. The combination the intruder thought they had memorised was wrong.

The intruder sat back on their heels, visualising Miss Dean's hand on the dial. Left, right, left, right. What must it have been?

The intruder was someone who knew the history of this particular theatre. They thought about numbers and dates.

Could that be it?

They leaned in and turned the combination dial once more – left, right, left, right – then turned the handle with a clunk.

There it was, the year the theatre opened: 1962.

The intruder opened the heavy metal door, reached in and closed a greedy hand around the thick wedge of fresh banknotes, bringing them briefly to their nose, smelling their distinctive aroma, so different from used currency. This was the odour of wealth and the intruder wanted oh-so-dearly to be wealthy. They felt it almost like a physical ache.

As well as the unprotected wedge of cash, there was a heavy cash box with sharp corners. The intruder picked it up and gently shook it.

Yes, there was money in there, too – not much, perhaps, but worth taking after all. How tough could it be to get inside, given time and, perhaps, a few useful tools?

There was a momentary pause.

Where might I find some useful tools?

*

At two minutes to two o'clock, Keith woke with a stiff neck just before his alarm, meaning it never actually rang, meaning that the intruder got no warning that the nightwatchman was awake.

Blearily, Keith yawned.

'What a life,' he said quietly, as if he was the hero of his story, as if his efforts were being filmed in becoming close-up. 'Duty calls.'

He flipped the little arm that silenced the ringers and, with an effort of will, dragged himself upright, turned on his torch and shambled away to the nearest toilet. He did his business then washed his hands and dried them on the scratchy paper towels.

*

In the dock area behind the set at the back of the stage, the intruder picked up a chisel from a work bench.

Was it heavy enough to break into the cash box? Perhaps. But not right now. It would make too much noise.

The intruder found a screwdriver and began prodding at the lock. Heavy though it was, the cash box didn't seem very sophisticated. Maybe the mechanism could be forced?

*

Three-quarters of the way through his regulation tour of the building – navigating with his torch, through the foyer and into the auditorium, up onto the stage, through the set and into the dressing room corridor – Keith found the desk lamp had been left on in the management office.

Didn't I turn that off?

He flicked the switch, re-emerged into the corridor, walked to the end and took the steps down to the dusty basement.

*

The intruder gave up on trying to force the lock. Might there be keys somewhere? Maybe at the stage door? Mrs Belt might need petty cash now and then?

*

Keith completed his inspection of the basement then took the stairs up towards the stage door area to sign the book and confirm that he had done his duty.

*

The intruder heard the footsteps approaching just as they were about to draw the bolt and step out into the night, free and clear. But no. Someone was coming and it was too late and there was nowhere to hide.

How had this happened? Why wasn't the stupid boy asleep like last night and the one before that?

The stage door hallway was triangular in shape, so the intruder retreated to the darkest corner just as the night-watchman appeared from the basement stairs, bleary-eyed and yawning.

Perhaps it will all be fine, the intruder thought. *Perhaps, if I stay very still, he won't glance in my direction. He'll simply do whatever it is he's here to do and then potter back to the green room without noticing.*

The intruder watched the nightwatchman using his torch to light the counter so that he could sign some kind of register, then return the biro to a mug containing three or four others. Then the boy sighed and stretched and turned and, by chance, the beam caught the intruder full in the face.

*

'Oh, sorry, I didn't know you were here…' Keith began.

Then his eyes went to the heavy cash box in the intruder's hands.

Blimey, he thought. *It's a heist.*

Befuddled with sleep, he wanted to say something clever, like a hero would in a movie, but nothing came out of his mouth. Then the heavy cash box came crashing down and he never said anything ever again.

*

The intruder stood for a few seconds, irresolute, thinking about what they had done. The boy was on the floor. He had collapsed from the blow but seemed to be breathing, as blood ran freely from his nose. The intruder had aimed for the top of his head, but the boy had flinched back and the corner of the cash box had caught him full in the face and…

The intruder kneeled down, the cash box still tensely held in two white-knuckled hands. The boy was breathing. There were bubbles in the blood on his lips. And he was a witness.

Might he not remember, though? Might the sudden blow give him – what was it called – amnesia?

Perhaps. Perhaps not.

The boy's eyelids flickered and then opened. His eyes, vague at first, became more focused and he raised a weak hand. It looked like he wanted to speak.

What did he want to say?

Please, don't.

Something like that?

The intruder sighed. This wasn't the plan. This wasn't how it was supposed to play out.

The boy lowered his weak hand and shut his eyes. The intruder was pleased. It made it easier, not being looked at.

The head lolled to one side. The intruder raised the cash box high in the air, then brought it down with as much force as they could muster, muscles and gravity working as one, a pointed metal corner spearing deep into Keith Sadler's fragile temple.

SIXTEEN

The next morning, Maisie came down to breakfast a little before eight and found herself on the edge of a storm. The manager of the hotel was there, looking very bony in his shirt sleeves, confronting the chef.

'But what can I do? He simply isn't here.'

'Would you like to tell me how I'm supposed to simultaneously cook the breakfasts and serve the breakfasts? That would be clever.'

'All right, Chef. You've made your point.'

'And I've my prep to begin for lunch and who's going to help with the deliveries?'

'What do you want me to do?'

'Get me someone else.'

'I don't have anyone reliable. You know how long it took to find Keith.'

'Reliable? That's a joke, now, isn't it?'

The manager noticed Maisie's presence.

'Good morning, Miss Cooper. Forgive us. A little local difficulty.' He turned back to his colleague. 'I will help,' he said. 'It's the best we can do. Come on, now, let's pull together.'

'Then why are we talking about it?' retorted the chef and stomped off through the swing door into the kitchen.

'Has something happened?' Maisie asked.

'The boy,' said the manager.

'Keith?' said Maisie.

'He's not here. He's not turned up.'

'Is that unlike him?'

'Completely unheard of.' He sighed. 'Anyway, needs must.'

Maisie had a sudden inspiration.

'I know someone who might be able to help.'

'Someone you can recommend?'

'She's only sixteen but she's very good. She's been virtually running The Dancing Hare pub in Bunting for the last six months.'

That was a slight exaggeration, but it was true that the publican had relied on Zoe to keep the wheels turning while he drank. Since the Bunting Manor drama, though, Ernest Sumner was a reformed character, and his fiancé Jenny was pitching in as well. Zoe had been sidelined.

'Will you let me have a phone number?' said the manager. 'She won't be able to serve in the bar, but she can help out with meals.'

'I will.'

'Thank you. Now, what would you like?'

'Two poached eggs on brown toast, butter not margarine.'

At that moment, Adélaïde came in, wearing a casual suit of turquoise wool – long, straight trousers plus a matching round-neck jumper with a white collar. The manager stood up rather straighter, sketching an ingratiating smile.

'I will have sardines with no sauce and brown toast,' Adélaïde said, without preamble. 'Butter not margarine.'

'Yes, Miss Amour. Straight away.'

As the manager followed the chef through the swing door to the kitchen, Maisie and Adélaïde both served themselves coffee from the filter jug on the side table and sat down.

'We will speak in English and begin shortly in my room.'

'That's what I thought,' said Maisie.

Adélaïde took both sugar and cream in her coffee and had drunk two cups by the time the manager returned with their plates. Either he or the chef had taken a little extra trouble, decorating their dishes with a dusting of finely chopped parsley. They ate with appetite then went upstairs.

Adélaïde's room was, in comparison to Maisie's, enormous. Not only did it have a huge, king-sized bed, there was also a sitting area with two armchairs and a desk, over which Adélaïde had spread what looked like the entire contents of her wardrobe. It was a little chilly with the double doors open onto the balcony that Maisie knew was directly beneath her own window. The lovely white pyjama-like clothes Adélaïde had worn the previous day were hanging in the damp breeze.

'So many people smoke. It clings to the ... what is the word?'

'To the fabric,' said Maisie.

'I shut it now.'

She did so and flicked the switch on a two-bar electric radiator set in the fireplace. Soon the elements began to glow.

They spent the next two hours working as they had in Adélaïde's dressing room – Maisie reading in a strong clear voice, Adélaïde sweetly singing the lines, then speaking them while attempting to retain a sense of the music of the language. It didn't come as easily as it had the previous evening, but it was good enough progress to convince them that their earlier success wasn't a fluke. At ten o'clock, Adélaïde ordered coffee.

'You think I can do this?' she asked, persisting with English.

'I do,' said Maisie.

Adélaïde shrugged. 'Can I believe you? You are paid to say it.'

'I suppose I am paid to support and help you, but not to lie, I hope.'

Adélaïde smiled.

'You are clever – *vive*. How would I say "*vive*"?'

'I suppose "quick-witted" would be a good translation.'

'What is "witted"?'

'Your wits are your thoughts, your ideas, your ability to work things out.'

Adélaïde nodded.

'You are clever to work things out. You have solved crimes.'

Maisie blushed, simultaneously feeling foolish for doing so.

'How do you know that?'

'The boy Keith in the bar. The one who is not here this morning. Yes, I overheard the shouting. He showed me in the newspaper. All the old newspapers, they are in the room for watching television that smells of tobacco and old milk.'

'Oh,' said Maisie.

'You don't want to talk about this? It is exciting, no?'

Maisie didn't answer straight away. A kind of slideshow ran through her memory: blood on a damp pavement; a body face down in a stream in the woods; a burning building.

'I suppose,' she said, 'it might be an exciting story to tell if it hadn't happened to people I knew.'

'Some of them deserved it, I think?'

Maisie was taken aback.

'How much did you read? What did Keith tell you?'

'Your brother was murdered. Whoever did that, if it was me, I would…' She made a gesture, miming tying a rope and pulling it up sharply like a noose. 'But I would get away with it, I think.'

'Because you would be quick-witted enough for no one to find out?' said Maisie, smiling indulgently.

Adélaïde laughed.

'No, I would do it in a passion and I would leave many clues.'

'Then how would you get away with it?'

'The judge would love me and understand. The jury would be on my side.'

113

Maisie laughed, too.

'I'm not sure that's how it works.'

There was a knock on the door. Maisie went to answer. It was Dorothy Dean. She was wearing a different suit, grey this time, still slightly too small. The expression on her face was hopeful.

'Shall we walk up together? The weather is fine. How are you getting on?'

'We progress,' said Adélaïde. 'We come down.'

★

Maisie found the manager to give him the telephone number of Bunting Manor so he could call Zoe, then she, Dorothy and Adélaïde went outside.

The weather was dry and it was pleasant walking up North Street. Maisie saw Mr Chitty, an older man in a brown warehouse coat who ran the bike shop – someone she considered an ally. He was adjusting a saddle for a customer on the pavement. She still felt a little guilty about how Mr Chitty's grandson had been dragged into the Church Lodge investigation.

'Good morning, Mr Chitty, you're looking very well. How's Nicholas?' she asked.

'On fine form,' said Mr Chitty, wiping his hands on an oily rag. 'Am I to understand that you are on your way to the theatre? I recognise your delightful companion from the newspaper. Is it a suitable show for a young person?'

'Perhaps, perhaps not,' said Adélaïde, 'that depends on the quick-witted of the boy.' Mr Chitty frowned and Adélaïde mirrored him. 'I have used the expression in the wrong way?'

'No, I quite see what you mean,' said Mr Chitty.

'We mustn't dawdle,' said Dorothy Dean. 'If Miss Cooper gives me your name, I will make sure that you are sent tickets.'

'As it happens, I have taken a small advertisement in the programme. I believe I will be invited.'

'God, yes, of course you have,' said Dorothy, looking at the sign above the shop. 'Chitty's Cycles, I remember now.' She turned to Maisie and Adélaïde, sounding like a headmistress. 'Come along now.'

They walked on and Maisie took the trouble to tell Adélaïde how well she was doing one more time.

'And it's developing your general conversation, too. You seem to have much less of an accent.'

'But I must always have some accent,' said Adélaïde with a sly look. 'It is my charm.'

Maisie laughed.

'Perhaps you're right.'

They arrived at the theatre at the same time as a dozen other members of the company, all gravitating to the extraordinary concrete and glass building from their digs throughout the town. Maisie said hello to Micky Petherick and he told her that the stage crew had been in from eight o'clock, working on the set.

'I'm looking forward to seeing what you've done,' she told him, and he looked pleased.

One or two of the actors had a rather bleary air and it turned out, as Maisie had expected, a good number of them had stayed up late at The Bell, the theatre pub just across the road. Winnie Brahms was wearing dark glasses and leaning on the back of an outdoor chair. Liam Jukes, Andrew Bradshaw's understudy, was complaining about the lumpy mattress and unaccustomed pillow in his lodgings. Andrew himself was telling anyone who cared to listen that he travelled with his own pillow and was therefore guaranteed rest.

'In any case, I'm what they call an "elite sleeper". I only need five and a half hours a night to be fresh. Then, a dab of *eau de Cologne* on the temples, eye drops for sparkle and I'm ready to face the day. I promise you, I will always be first in.'

'Would you just calm down?' pleaded Clive Canning. 'I'm perfectly ready to face the day but perhaps not, at top volume, ready to face Andrew P Bradshaw.'

'Well said, Clive,' murmured John Hermanson who had appeared at Maisie's elbow. 'What's that you have there?'

'Oh, this?' Clive put down a cardboard box on one of the outdoor tables and, from a nest of scrunched up newspaper, took out a trophy, shaped like an obelisk, made of high-quality engraved crystal.

'Good heavens, is that what I think it is?' asked John.

'Yes,' said Clive's wife, Esther, with enthusiasm. 'A lifetime achievement award, no less, from the Academy.'

'Congratulations, old boy,' said John. 'Bravo.'

'It arrived at my digs this morning,' said Clive. 'I am exceptionally moved at the recognition from my peers—'

Micky Petherick – unaware of what they were all talking about – interrupted by shouting: 'It's time to go to work.'

Once everyone was indoors, NVE made a speech of congratulation to Clive and everyone – except Andrew, Maisie thought – enthusiastically clapped. Then, there was a warm-up call requiring the whole company on stage. Adélaïde took no part, sitting beside Maisie in the stalls, murmuring her lines to herself as the other actors breathed in and out to NVE's rhythm, and hummed and sang and stretched.

The warm-up took place in a fug of paint fumes. The early start Micky had made with his team had transformed the set. In addition to some very realistic painted effects, new elements had been added – a fireplace, a landscape painting in a battered gilt frame, several bits of more appropriate furniture. Upstage centre were wide, warehouse-style doors and, behind them, a *trompe-l'oeil* vista – an optical illusion – giving a clever impression of seedy streets between damp buildings, with litter on the cobbled ground.

The rehearsal proper began at half past eleven. Adélaïde was on for much of it and Maisie thought she saw the other actors responding warmly to the improvement in her performance. That said, Adélaïde pitched her voice quite low. Eventually, NVE called out to her: 'No one can hear you at the back, darling.'

'There is no one at the back,' Adélaïde replied.

'But there will be.'

'They will hear me when it is time,' she replied composedly, continuing at conversational pitch.

At one of the breaks to refocus a light, the wardrobe mistress, Beryl Vere, asked for permission to 'borrow' Adélaïde for a fitting. NVE agreed. They went backstage but Adélaïde's dressing room was too crowded for three people, plus the voluminous skirts that the wardrobe mistress wanted Adélaïde to try. Maisie made for the green room for more coffee and found Kitty Farrell practising with the other understudy, Liam Jukes. She told them that they made a very handsome couple.

'Not as handsome as Adélaïde and Andy,' said Kitty, making Maisie wonder about her relationship with Andrew Bradshaw. The only other person to call him 'Andy' was the very-attentive Winnie Brahms. 'But I suppose I'll just have to soldier on.'

'We both must,' said Liam. 'God, it's better than my last job in stage management. Come on. Let's read it again.

NVE clearly isn't going to find any time for us to work together on stage.'

Maisie noticed that Clive's 'lifetime achievement award' was now in pride of place in the centre of the dining table.

'I'm very ignorant,' she told them, 'living in France. I suppose that's a big deal?'

'It is,' said Liam. 'And Clive feels it very, very deeply.'

Maisie poured another coffee for Adélaïde. On her way backstage, she noticed that Dorothy Dean was there, talking intently to a prematurely balding man in his thirties and recognised him as Inspector Fred Nairn of the Chichester police. Maisie put Adélaïde's coffee on the counter beneath the mirror in the dressing room and then squeezed back out past Beryl Vere into the corridor.

'Is there a problem?' she asked.

Dorothy and Inspector Nairn were in the doorway of Fort Knox while someone inside was busy taking flash photographs.

'Is there a problem?' repeated Dorothy, exasperated.

'Good afternoon, Miss Cooper. How are you?' said Fred Nairn.

Dorothy burst out: 'That damn boy's robbed the safe and disappeared.'

'Now, Miss Dean—' Nairn began.

'The one from the hotel,' Dorothy ploughed on. 'I knew, when I realised he already had a job, that it was a damn foolish idea to take him on and I should have known better, but there was no one else worthwhile who applied. Now look what he's done.'

'We don't know for certain,' persisted the inspector, 'that anything of the kind has occurred.'

'Do you mean Keith?' asked Maisie.

'Obviously we mean Keith. Who else could it be?' said Dorothy. She turned back to the police officer. 'Where is he though?'

'Yes, that's a good question,' said Nairn, 'and the police will do their best to answer it.'

'I need to call our insurers.'

'I'm sure you do, but not from this room. We have still to take prints and so on. And I'd like to ask you one or two more questions.'

'You'll have to wait.'

Dorothy stomped away towards the stage door area where, Maisie supposed, she would find another phone and another office.

'Miss Cooper, do you think you might be able to help?' said Nairn, sighing. 'The young man had two jobs. Did he have debts, do you know?'

'I have no idea,' said Maisie. 'I barely knew him, and he seemed little more than a child.'

'Fair enough. By the way, have you heard about Jack Wingard, Miss Cooper?' asked Nairn, unexpectedly.

'What about Jack?'

'His bit of trouble?'

Maisie felt a lurch.

'What's happened?'

'Nothing serious, but his grandma was in hospital for a nasty cut and a fainting spell. Well, she is an old lady,' Nairn added. 'Comes to us all.'

'Poor Florence. How did it happen?'

'Storm in a teacup, apparently, but he's taken her away for a day or two.'

'That's a relief.' Maisie smiled. Then she thought about the second part of what Nairn had said. 'They've both gone away?'

'That's right.'

'Where have they gone?'

'New Forest,' said Nairn, as if no further details were necessary. 'To give his grandma a break.'

'That sounds lovely,' said Maisie, feeling disappointed.

Another officer emerged from the management office, his hands full of camera equipment.

'Would you excuse us, Miss Cooper?' asked Nairn.

'Yes, of course.'

Maisie left Inspector Nairn to his investigations, unhappy that Jack had left without telling her.

She returned to the star dressing room. Adélaïde was still busy with the wardrobe mistress, so she drifted back to the green room. Kitty was still there, but with Andrew instead of Liam. Maisie soon worked out that Andrew had been backstage when the police arrived and was relishing the story.

'So, when Micky Petherick came in early to paint the set, the stage door was not even bolted. Vandals could have got in and done all kinds of damage. I suppose he just made a run for it. He broke into the safe and got away with everything, the cash box and the money that the Arab man gave Miss Dean and it's a great hoo-ha because he's disappeared. He's probably gone to Portsmouth and escaped on a ferry.' Andrew stopped when he noticed Maisie was there. 'Did you hear any of this?'

'No, I don't know anything,' said Maisie.

'That's right, though, isn't it?' Kitty insisted. 'He wasn't at the hotel where he ought to have been this morning? I heard NVE talking about it. Of course, I wouldn't know. I don't get a hotel room. I've got a bed little bigger than a cot in a damp upstairs bedroom and an old woman as landlady who thinks we're still living under rationing.'

It was the most animated Maisie had ever seen Kitty. Was it because of the story she was telling, or because she had Andrew all to herself for once?

'Miss Cooper is an aficionado of crime,' said Andrew to Kitty, before turning back to Maisie. 'Young Keith told me all about you, before he legged it.'

'I didn't think you were staying at the Dolphin?' said Maisie.

'I came in for a drink the other night. You were there, sitting quiet and sensible in a wing-backed armchair with your newspaper. I had a look at that, too. It was full of your doings,' he said with a wink.

'I suppose there aren't very many secrets in theatre,' said Maisie lightly.

'Oh, you'd be surprised,' said Kitty, putting a possessive hand on Andrew's arm.

He put his own hand over hers, smiled and said: 'You are a delightful child.'

Kitty frowned.

No, thought Maisie, *that was not the response Kitty was looking for.*

Then Micky Petherick put his head round the green room door.

'All on, if you please.'

III
PLOT

SEVENTEEN

Maisie hated prying. She hated being the subject of gossip. She hated having got into the inquisitive habit herself. She hated to see other people's lives picked over. It made her want to shout: 'Just stop it. This has nothing to do with you.'

In every break from rehearsals on that interminable day, she had to endure the multiple provocations of actors and crew discussing Keith and his robbery and disappearance. That would have been bad enough, but they also wanted to talk about her 'track record' solving crimes, and her connection to the mysterious gentleman whose cash it was that had been stolen. The unwelcome questions were posed in the green room and in the corridors, in the aisle between the seats and the stage – even, on one unhappy occasion, on her way back from the toilet.

Maisie tried to stay close to Adélaïde who remained isolated and self-possessed, quite uninterested in what she dismissively referred to as 'this drama without consequence'. She lounged, very decoratively, in the plush tip-down seats. She, alone among the company, had been allowed to rehearse wearing her own clothes, rather than her eighteenth-century garb.

What might the costume be like once she put it on, Maisie wondered? She hadn't really paid attention in the dressing room. Something to show off Adélaïde's exceptional figure, probably. Perhaps NVE knew that keeping her in her street clothes helped make Adélaïde more relaxed. Certainly, the edge of anxiety Maisie had recognised on their first meeting had almost entirely disappeared. Adélaïde was becoming so much more confident in her own performance, but might there be something else to it? Was it the fact that Maisie's presence had done its job and provided a shield from…?

So much had happened that Maisie took a moment to think back to what she had been told. Who was she to protect Adélaïde from? She made an effort to remember Adélaïde's exact words.

It seems I am to be pawed at and fawned over by an old man who believes himself to be a god, in his own way, a god of the theatre with a 'unique vision' which, in the end, is just to put the beautiful woman opposite the handsome man and have them take their time over falling in love.

Then she had said something else.

Then the leading man, who resembles the director in a way, believes that he must take advantage of me if the director does not.

Wasn't there more than a hint, there, that NVE was a manageable problem, but that Andrew, the leading man, was the issue?

The action on stage was progressing smoothly, so the rehearsal didn't distract from Maisie's memories. She thought back to the scene she had overheard from her hotel room window, the voices rising from the balcony in Adélaïde's vast quarters. Was there any chance that it hadn't been Nils van Erde engaged in a clumsy attempted seduction – an enterprise that had, Maisie thought, been physically rebuffed?

No, NVE's voice was much too distinctive to be mistaken, his Dutch accent clearly audible in those moments of deeper emotion.

Maisie acknowledged that she looked down on NVE because of the presumptuous way he had taken her hand at the foot of the hotel stairs, but might that just have been because she was unused to theatrical behaviour? Everyone else seemed delighted with him – at least, if she could take what they said at face value.

The same could not be said about Andrew P Bradshaw. Everyone seemed to look at him askance: John Hermanson because Andrew had made a point of trying to rile the older man; Dorothy Dean trying to exclude him from the lunch table in the green room; Winnie Brahms wanting his attention – perhaps being in love with him and Maisie didn't think that was likely to end well. There had also been something about the fact that the Cannings were husband and wife. Discovering that for the first time, Maisie had replied: 'How marvellous to work together as a family.' The remark had made everyone at the table quiet and tense.

She roused herself to pay more attention to the stage. None of this was any of her business.

★

Because the company was a large one and the sequence of scenes was complicated, they ate their meals in shifts so that the work remained continuous. As a result, the green room never became really busy because they were never all in there at once. Eventually, though, the long day approached dinner time and people started talking about a 'proper break'.

Maisie was aware that Adélaïde hadn't left the auditorium since her costume fitting. She finally insisted on bringing her some freshly made tuna and salad cream sandwiches. Adélaïde thanked her and went to the back of the seats to consume them in private.

The crew took advantage of a longer pause to reset the stage and, surprisingly, Dorothy Dean came to apologise to Maisie for her brusqueness in the corridor. She spoke low but didn't really need to as there was no one else in earshot and those that were anywhere at hand were busy running their lines, adjusting their costumes and discussing the details of their performances.

'There was no need for me to get so cross. It's going to be fine,' she said. 'The insurers will cover it. There's nothing we did wrong. The boy had good references.'

'From the Dolphin?'

'He'd been an office boy at an estate agent, too, and they thought very highly of him. They're astonished at what he's done.'

'Wasn't he very young to already have two jobs?'

'He was eighteen with big dreams,' said Dorothy with a frown. 'I still can't quite believe it of him.'

'I suppose he was sort of obsessed with the film industry,' said Maisie doubtfully.

Dorothy sat down.

'God, that's a point. Maybe he's on a plane halfway to California. How much would that cost?'

'I'm afraid I don't know.'

'Something like five hundred pounds, if I remember rightly. There's a coincidence. Do you think that's likely?'

'Perhaps,' said Maisie, trying to visualise young Keith 'on the run' as a criminal and safe breaker. 'Wouldn't he need a visa?'

'Maybe he already had one? Maybe he's been planning this for some time?'

'But didn't you say you only took him on for the season when you re-opened the building last week? And Mohammed's money turned up out of the blue so he couldn't have been planning—'

'Yes, all right.' Dorothy bit her lip, impatiently. 'Do you think that rather typecast policeman will think to find out if he has a passport? You know him, don't you?'

Maisie sighed.

'Yes, I do know Inspector Nairn. If it helps to reassure you, I can tell you that I have a close friend in the police force who has great respect for him.'

'Do you?' asked Dorothy, clearly fishing for more information.

Maisie changed the subject.

'The money was in the safe, wasn't it?'

'Yes,' said Dorothy.

'Was it locked?'

'Clearly it was locked.'

'How? With a key?'

'A key and a combination.'

'Then how was the money stolen?'

Dorothy looked shifty.

'The key was in the lock. There's not usually very much in there and the building's patrolled and…' She sighed. 'I suppose I've got into lazy habits. Ten years we've operated with not a sniff of unpleasantness.'

'I see. So, the key was in the lock, but there was still the combination, wasn't there? How would Keith have known what it was? How could anyone have known? Did anyone else have access?'

Dorothy shrugged.

'Micky. He sometimes needs petty cash.'

'And he's someone you know to be honest?'

'Absolutely.'

'Anyone else?'

'No one.'

Maisie paused, trying to visualise the safe.

'Could someone have seen you or Micky opening the safe? You know, looking over your shoulder when you opened it to deposit Mohammed's money. Was anyone else there, actually in the room, who might have been able to peep at what you were doing and memorise the combination? Would it be visible from the corridor if the door was open?'

'How would I know any of that?' said Dorothy with an edge to her voice.

'But it might have happened? You can't say for sure that it didn't?'

'No, I can't.'

Maisie knew the police would focus on who had been in the vicinity at that crucial moment. Then she had another idea.

'Is the combination a memorable number for some reason? Is it something somebody might be able to guess?'

'I'm not sure this is getting us anywhere,' said Dorothy brusquely, standing up. 'The money's gone and the boy's gone and that's the end of it.'

Maisie felt sure Dorothy felt guilty that the combination she had chosen was easily guessable.

'How much did Mohammed As-Sabah agree to invest, Miss Dean?' asked Maisie.

'I'm not sure I should—'

'He's my friend, after all. Was the five hundred a down payment on a much bigger sum?'

There was a pause.

'Five thousand,' said Dorothy, 'but I didn't tell you that.' She walked away.

Well, thought Maisie, *apparently Mohammed could afford to lose five thousand pounds on a whimsical investment in a new production of an old musical that seemed based on rather shaky foundations – the unlikely conversion of a French film star into an English theatre actress.*

At that moment, the rehearsal resumed. Kitty appeared in full eighteenth-century costume, in Adélaïde's role as Polly Peachum, and Maisie realised that was the answer to the question of what Adélaïde was to wear – a white blouse with a blue waistcoat over it, and a very full skirt.

Maisie went to sit in the front row and watched the action more closely for a few minutes. She decided that Kitty was giving a much better performance, though she still wondered if the young woman had the personality to engage a large audience.

Just then, Adélaïde returned. She had changed, at last, and was wearing the same clothes. Close up, Maisie saw that the white blouse was made of silk and that its three-quarter length sleeves stopped, becomingly, well above the wrist. The blue waistcoat was tightly fitted and shimmered because it was made of satin. Adélaïde's full skirt trailed on the ground and her feet were bare.

Maisie's gaze went from Adélaïde to Kitty. Adélaïde was picking at a thread on her sleeve, her mind elsewhere. Kitty was on stage, in full flow. Yet it was Adélaïde who drew the eye. Both women were wearing the very same costume tailored to an identical cut. On Kitty, it overpowered. On Adélaïde, it celebrated.

While Maisie was lost in these thoughts, something happened on the stage that she missed. All at once, voices were raised and fingers pointed. For some reason, Clive was furious with Andrew, and Kitty was in tears and being comforted by Esther. John Hermanson was lurking upstage and, Maisie thought, looking for someone with whom to share an acerbic aside. NVE sat immobile in the gloomy auditorium, in the middle of a row about halfway up, simply watching, doing nothing to help or hinder the crescendo of carefully phrased insults.

'I have never respected the Bristol training and I see now that I was right to take that view,' said Clive.

'That's so unfair,' said Winnie.

'Just because you're on the telly, Clive, doesn't mean you're better than everyone else,' said Andrew.

'A reputation must be slowly, painstakingly built, and is easily,' insisted Clive, 'oh, so easily lost.'

'Quite the contrary if you ask me,' said Andrew. 'Just stand still and let the camera do the work.'

'Stop it, both of you,' said Kitty, through her sobs.

'Pay no attention, dear,' said Esther.

'Isn't it hard enough?' Kitty wailed.

'Just concentrate on your own performance,' said Esther. She waved a hand dismissively at the men. 'God knows, you can't rely on any of them.'

'I'm glad, NVE,' called out John Hermanson, 'to stand apart. Thank you for protecting me from all this with your impeccable casting. The Beggar needs no ally on the stage. As narrator, he needs only to be friends with his audience.'

Once more, Maisie picked out NVE. She thought, from the stage, that he might well be invisible to the actors, dazzled as they must be by the lights. John hadn't been looking in quite the right direction. She, however, could see the expression on his face – one comprised of satisfaction and excitement. She found it unsettling, almost unnerving. This was real human emotion on the stage, not acting.

Then she saw NVE nod and she began to wonder if, somehow, while she had been talking to Dorothy and then thinking about Adélaïde's costume, he had somehow contrived this upset, this drama, for his own purposes. Was he one of those people who thrive on conflict, who believe that unhappiness is a useful motivation, that discord and destabilisation bring greater and more focused efforts?

Surely not. Hadn't everyone been extremely complimentary about the whole rehearsal process?

Yes, they had. But, as the actors continued to snipe at one another, she realised that, even at the time, she hadn't quite believed it.

He's very supportive – of everybody.

You couldn't hope for a better director for your first show, Kitty. Positive warmth and professionalism.

Change the inflection slightly and every one of those remarks might have sounded sarcastic, overblown.

And what had Kitty Farrell replied?

I'm very lucky. Everyone tells me so. The voice in my head tells me so.

At that moment, NVE jumped up and clapped his hands.

'Everyone goes outside for a breath of air. That is an order, not a request. Twice round the building and back in. You have ten minutes.'

'Ten minutes,' Micky Petherick repeated in his powerful voice. 'Working lights.'

Up at the back, Sam the technician confirmed the instruction: 'Workers.'

Additional lamps came on and the whole auditorium was illuminated, not just the stage. The result was rather like turning on the neon lighting at the end of a school disco, the harshness sending everyone scurrying for the cloakrooms and their coats and the exits. The onstage actors left by the shortest route, up through the newly painted set and out through the dock. A few others, plus Dorothy and NVE, left the auditorium and headed down into the foyer. Micky Petherick followed them. Maisie and Adélaïde were left quite alone.

'I thought I would love this,' said Adélaïde in French. 'But it is the worst decision of my whole life.'

'It can't be that bad,' said Maisie.

'What do you know? You are a stranger. This,' Adélaïde said, waving a hand at the stage, 'was the drop of water to make the vase overflow. Now, nothing is certain, except disaster. Do you not feel it?'

'That's a very fanciful idea. Feel what, exactly? Wasn't that just a routine blow-up of the sort that must be ten-a-penny in the theatre.'

'No, it was not.'

Adélaïde turned to look Maisie in the eye. Maisie was astonished to see that her lashes were wet.

'*Qu'est-ce qui ne va pas, Adélaïde?*' she asked, quietly.

What's wrong?

'*Tout.*'

Everything.

'I don't understand.'

'I have one chance to be more than candy for the camera, and all this will make me fail.'

*

In the end, Maisie decided that it would be best to try and distract Adélaïde by getting her to practise her lines. She obeyed, meekly. In any case, soon the company was back and the rehearsal resumed in an atmosphere of slightly forced bonhomie.

'Workers out,' called Micky Petherick.

The auditorium became gloomy, the stage took on its special glow and the now-familiar lines floated out into the enormous space. Maisie saw for the first time some fragments of other scenes she remembered from the classroom at Westbrook College with Jack: Andrew P Bradshaw, as Macheath, in a tavern, surrounded by women of dubious virtue, then betrayed to Mr Lockit, the keeper of Newgate prison; Winnie Brahms, as Lucy Lockit, the prison-keeper's daughter, complaining to Macheath that he has broken his promise to marry her; Kitty, understudying as Polly Peachum, telling Lucy that Macheath is already married to her; Lucy helping him escape; Macheath recaptured and sentenced to be hanged; Polly and Lucy becoming allies, each wanting – for their own selfish reasons – to save Macheath's life.

Because she was quite close to the action, Maisie could see that the actors weren't quite looking one another in the eye.

Instead, they focused on their opposite number's shoulder or neckerchief or collar – even looking past them, their gaze fixed on the scenery or on nothing.

Was this a sort of shared decision to proceed at a less elevated pitch of emotion, avoiding eye contact in order to lower the stakes? Or was it because they didn't dare confront their seething enmities?

The rehearsal was rather plodding, perhaps because of the come-down from the bust-up. Then NVE said that Kitty was doing very well but that would be all for the time being. Kitty exited quickly through the set, looking rather crushed, and Adélaïde went up on stage to join the action.

Adélaïde's presence immediately gave an entirely different sort of energy to the scene.

She really does have a rather special kind of magic, Maisie thought.

Maisie looked across at NVE. He was slumped in his chair, a look of intense satisfaction on his fleshy features.

Yes, she thought, *I'm sure that's what it was. He manipulated that whole drama in order to get a reaction, to upset the equilibrium and then allow Adélaïde – who he must have known would stand apart – to become the still point at the centre of the play, a focus for all the competing emotions.*

The scene progressed, building in a series of waves to a steady but compelling climax, ending with Adélaïde singing a simple, old-fashioned tune, her voice carrying apparently effortlessly to every corner of the vast space, all the other actors – named characters and bystanders – spread across the stage, moving in a clever pattern, following her rhythm, swapping places, sharing their presence with all three sides of the audience, but watching her, rapt and attentive.

Then, unexpectedly, as Adélaïde found a spot at the very centre of the boards, she switched from singing to speaking the final lines, her voice clear and steady, just a trace of accent giving colour to the almost-threatening words, the adult-child Polly determined to defy her parents' wishes:

> 'No power on Earth can e'er divide,
> 'The knot that sacred love hath tied.
> 'When parents draw against our mind,
> 'The true-love's knot, they faster bind.'

As the last note of the accompaniment faded, there was a pause, almost as if the music continued in the silence, but felt rather than heard. Maisie glanced over at NVE. He, too, was completely still.

What was he doing? Waiting to see who broke the spell?

Then Micky Petherick shouted: 'Bring it in.'

Nobody moved as the two mismatched stagehands pushed a rough scaffold through the big opening between the two warehouse doors – a platform surmounted by a gantry from which descended a rope, coiled and knotted in the shape of a hangman's noose.

Then all the lights went dark.

EIGHTEEN

When, after a few moments of blackout, the working lights came back on, dispelling the magic, the actors were all smiles.

It was rather touching, Maisie thought, the way everyone forgot their upsets and disagreements and wanted to applaud Adélaïde's performance. The Cannings were first to congratulate her, taking her hands, one each, and talking over one another.

'A gift, that's what it is. I've always said so,' Clive boomed.

'You must save it up now for the actual performance,' said Esther.

'A special ability shared by very few,' insisted Clive.

'It's inside you. Now, we all know it,' said Esther. 'Nurture it. Keep it safe.'

The Cannings released her, allowing Andrew to come close and sketch a Regency bow.

'*Mes hommages*,' he said in a reasonably good accent.

My respects.

Winnie ran over and took Andrew's hand.

'Lovely, Andy, wasn't it?' she said.

Andrew smiled rather uncomfortably.

Kitty had come round from behind the set and was sitting nearby in the stalls.

'What chance have I got,' she said – for the second time that Maisie knew of – with a bright but brittle laugh. Maisie thought she was making a considerable effort to keep the mood light. 'I ask you, really?'

John Hermanson called out: '*Brava, cara,*' switching the compliments to Italian, then he repeated the last two lines of Adélaïde's song in his strong bass voice:

'*When parents draw against our mind,*
'*The true-love's knot, they faster bind.*'

NVE stood up in his seat in row E and called out: 'John, that's an excellent idea – the distance between your voices, you know, the musical distance. That could be very strong. You, the Beggar, the narrator, joining Polly in her tragic pilgrimage – commenting upon it in your *basso profundo* while she speaks in her lovely contralto with a charming trace of her seductive accent. Adélaïde, my sweet, what do you think? You say it and John sings in the bass beneath you. Can we try it again?'

'I will not do it now,' said Adélaïde simply. 'I will go to reflect and try to hold the magic of this moment in my mind.'

Maisie smiled, thinking what a preposterous and self-centred statement that was. Then she realised no one agreed with her. They all recognised that Adélaïde had been wonderful and approved her desire to slip away.

'Would you like me to come with you?' Maisie asked.

'I will go on my own to find a place where it is quiet and I can be alone.'

'She wants to be alone,' said Kitty Farrell and laughed again, unhappily this time. 'I'm sorry, I didn't mean to go all Garbo.'

'Really, Kitty,' said Esther Canning with a titter. 'Behave yourself.'

Adélaïde turned upstage and walked away beyond the set, through the wide warehouse doors, past the noose and the painting-in-perspective of miserable slum streets, out of reach of the atmospheric lighting.

'Never mind,' said NVE crossly. 'Kitty, you know it, don't you? John, let's try.'

Liam Jukes, Andrew's wiry understudy, stepped forward from the group of bystanders.

'Do we have time for me to run it as Macheath?' he asked.

'Not now, Liam,' said NVE.

Maisie watched with interest as the close of the scene was replayed with Kitty at the centre of the complex blocking, singing the same song to the same tune, but without the extra something – the 'magic' – that had made Adélaïde's performance so special.

All the same, NVE's idea was a good one – John far upstage, his deep voice seemingly created for his role as the Beggar, a sinister counterpoint to Kitty as Polly Peachum, expressing determined defiance.

'That will do,' said NVE. 'That's how we'll block it. Liam, run the lines with Kitty at some point. John, find a moment to rehearse in private with Adélaïde, would you?'

'Oh, yes, he'll probably find time for that,' said Andrew.

'Yes, love, I will,' John replied. 'Is that so strange?'

The rehearsal resumed, moving on to a scene Maisie hadn't seen before, with Kitty still taking Adélaïde's place. Stage crew brought in a handcart that became an important prop – the vehicle in which the condemned man would be taken to the scaffold.

The whole thing seemed to go a little better. It was essentially a stylised combat between Polly Peachum and Lucy Lockit – a combat in words, not physical fighting. Winnie's performance was sprightly and witty, and the scene became, oddly, a kind of seduction, the two women circling one another, becoming temporary allies. Without any of the men around her, Kitty began to make something of the potential of her physical presence, enhanced by the bright satin waistcoat and flowing skirts.

'Lovely, Kitty, keep that up,' said NVE.

'We don't need those men, do we?' said Kitty.

'No, we don't,' said Winnie, but her eyes sought Andrew where he lounged in the stalls.

Micky called the next scene. Time passed and there were no more upsets. Then there was another blackout and a scene change.

The rehearsal resumed at the start of act three with a montage of action: pickpockets and beggars in the streets; hawkers with baskets of fruit and flowers; a minor character attacked with a stick and robbed; an arrest and a stylised hanging. The sequence was accompanied by a discordant soundtrack, taking the pleasant tunes of the incidental songs that punctuated the show and twisting them into a very effective change of mood, creepy and unsettling.

Maisie thought back to her original impression of the production and the presumptuous comments she had shared with Dorothy Dean – that NVE was directing the play as a kind of superficial ballet. She felt ashamed of her ill-informed judgement. She could now see that, with all the paraphernalia of lighting, costume and sound, the choreographed action was immensely effective.

With a tinge of reluctance, Maisie got out of her seat and exited through the upper doors at the back of the auditorium, rounding the foyer to the door that led backstage, looking briefly in at the green room. Adélaïde wasn't there so she tried the dressing room.

Not here either?

Maisie hesitated. Why would Adélaïde have left the door unlocked with her things – a necklace, two rings, her personal make-up and so on – laid out on the counter beneath the mirror? Was it just inattention or did actors generally feel so safe in the theatre that they believed themselves out of reach of any danger?

But there's just been a robbery.

Adélaïde's street clothes were on the low foam chair, her outdoor coat on a hook on the back of the door. Maisie followed the dressing room corridor to the stage door. The elderly volunteer, Harriet Belt, was once more on duty, her eyes on a copy of the local newspaper.

'Good evening,' said Maisie.

'Miss Cooper, how are you? Aren't you a celebrity?' She tittered. 'Of course, not a celebrity like the actors, but you're in the papers just as much as they are. More, perhaps. You've made quite a name for yourself.'

'Mrs Belt, might you happen to know where Miss Amour is? Did she go outside?'

'I've no idea.'

'Don't you keep a watch?'

'There's been lots of ins and outs – props and furniture and things. And I've been taking calls,' said Harriet. 'People always ring up the stage door when the box office is closed. They think I can help, but I can't.'

Maisie nodded, glancing round the dusty, triangular hallway. Without her coat, Adélaïde could have gone for a short walk, but not very far and not for very long. Maisie opened the door and looked outside. The air was damp and the breeze from the southwest was chilly on her cheek. For some reason, the night felt threatening. She shut it again.

'Mrs Belt, where might one go for a little peace and quiet in this busy building?' she asked.

'To be alone with one's thoughts?' Harriet clarified, reminding Maisie of Kitty and her Garbo comment. 'Perhaps the lower corridor where the storage rooms are?'

'Yes,' said Maisie. She gave Mrs Belt a smile, not wanting to reveal her anxiety. 'Good idea.'

Like the rest of the building, the staircase to the lower floor was concrete. Unlike the impressive public areas, however, the basement had a look of never having been quite finished. The edges of the steps were sharp, and the walls of the sub-terranean corridor were rough to the touch. The ceiling was low, only eight inches higher than Maisie's five-foot-eight, and was lit with nasty neon strips, giving it an unfriendly, dungeon-like air. In the angle of wall and ceiling were the omnipresent relay speakers, communicating the continuing action from the stage.

First, Maisie tried a locked door labelled 'Armoury', then found the corridor opened out on the left into a large, unlit space that her sense of direction told her must be directly under the stage. This open area was broken up by the dark shadows of four pillars and was at least twenty paces across.

Hesitating in the opening, she heard movement and won-dered if it might be a rat or a mouse. Hadn't she seen bait boxes in several places, containing anti-rodent poison?

She felt with her hands round the walls on either side of the opening, at last finding a light switch. When she pressed it, there was a delay and she thought at first that it wasn't working. Then two more neon strips came on, both blink-ing and flickering, creating an effect something like a strobe, jumbling her impressions.

Maisie's mind struggled to piece together the fragments of what she saw: bits and pieces of furniture; several standard lamps; two dining chairs with raffia seats; three rolled car-pets; a stack of stage curtains, folded in a pile.

And someone kneeling on the floor, their wide, eighteenth-century skirt spread out like a puddle.

In front of that kneeling figure, Maisie could see the pale face of a boy that she knew to be eighteen years old, though he looked no more than sixteen, a boy who would now never see nineteen. Blood was matted in his hair and a lot more of it soaked into his shirt, just his head and shoulders visible, the rest of him shrouded in one of the dusty stage curtains.

'Adélaïde?' said Maisie.

'*C'est le garçon de l'hôtel?*'

'Yes, it's Keith, from the Dolphin & Anchor.'

'*Pourquoi il est là?*'

'I've no idea why he's here in this room, but he's in the building because he had a second job as nightwatchman in the theatre. Didn't you know?'

As she said it, Maisie realised that Keith must have disturbed the robber who had taken Mohammed's money from the safe. And now he was – well, was he dead? He certainly looked dead. In any case, it was awful to think that everyone had assumed that he was the perpetrator of the theft when all the while…

'I told you everything was wrong,' said Adélaïde.

Maisie was following her own train of thought. Had Keith been lying down here all day, slowly expiring, while everyone went about their business, unaware…

'People said he robbed the safe and ran off with the money in the middle of the night,' said Adélaïde.

Blinking in the awkward, uneven light, Maisie bent down, drew Keith's arm from beneath the curtain and gently held the boy's cold wrist, waiting in vain for perhaps half a minute for an unlikely pulse.

'Come, Adélaïde. We must get away from here.'

Maisie helped the star to her feet and, when she turned, Maisie saw, for the first time, the blood on Adélaïde's hands and the stains smeared across the satin breast of her tight-fitting blue waistcoat.

NINETEEN

Maisie knew it was important to get Adélaïde away from what her experiences of two other murder investigations had taught her to refer to as the 'crime scene'. She also knew she had to try and make sure that the evidence – if there was any evidence – was not disturbed or destroyed. The blood on Adélaïde's hands should be examined. The bloodstained waistcoat would have to be set aside.

'Where do I go?' asked Adélaïde, in a small voice.

'To your dressing room. Come with me,' said Maisie firmly.

Looking round the low-ceilinged basement, Maisie realised there were marks in the dust on the floor, as if something heavy had been dragged across the room.

'Why do we stop?' asked Adélaïde.

'Come this way.'

Maisie led her round the outside of the pillars, along the walls. At the opening into the corridor, she looked back.

Yes, there's clearly a trail where the floor has been polished almost clean.

Maisie made the obvious deduction. Whoever killed Keith had done so somewhere else in the building, then dragged him down here to be concealed in a pile of old curtains.

What was the significance of the hiding place? That the person who committed the crime was a member of the company? That they knew the building?

Not necessarily. It wouldn't take long for someone to locate this quiet corner, even without turning on the neon lights that otherwise might have given away their presence to anyone passing through the park late at night.

But had it happened late at night?

Yes, of course it had – because the nightwatchman had been on duty. That was why he was dead – because he had discovered the robbery and tried to intervene.

'I don't want to stay here,' said Adélaïde.

'No, of course not.'

Maisie took Adélaïde back upstairs, past the stage door where Harriet Belt spoke to them, but Maisie didn't quite hear what she said. It sounded something like: 'What on Earth has happened?'

'I'll come back in a moment,' she called back.

Once seated at her mirror in her dressing room, Adélaïde became aware of the bloodstains on her clothes.

'*Ah, mon Dieu,*' she said.

Maisie helped her by undoing the buttons on the waistcoat. Remarkably, the white silk blouse underneath seemed unmarked. She folded the waistcoat over on itself and put it aside at the far end of the counter.

'What shall I wear now?' Adélaïde asked. 'I want to change.'

'Perhaps not yet. The police may want to see you first.'

'But there is a mark here.'

It was true, after all. There was blood that Maisie hadn't noticed on one of the three-quarter length silk sleeves.

'Wait here.'

Maisie ran to the wardrobe room.

'Might you have something Miss Amour can wear while eating,' she improvised, 'so she doesn't get anything on her costume?'

'Yes, gladly,' said Beryl Vere, and found Maisie a man's shirt in a smallish size in white cotton. 'This won't be used in the show.'

'Thank you so much.'

145

When Maisie got back to the star dressing room, she found that Adélaïde had already cleaned her hands with cold cream. Half-a-dozen unpleasantly smeared paper towels crowded the bin. She helped Adélaïde into the shirt, kneeling in front of her and doing up the buttons.

'He was dead,' said Adélaïde simply. 'There was a rat. That was why I found him. I like rats. If you live on boats or by the sea, there are always rats. There was a sound and the fabric, that was the word you taught me, the fabric was moving. I went to see and lifted the fabric. It was a curtain. You saw that. The rat was licking the blood but it ran away.'

Maisie folded the blouse and put it on the counter with the waistcoat.

'Would you like a drink, Adélaïde?' asked Maisie. 'Something to buck you up?'

'Yes, please. Bring me something.'

Once again, Maisie hurried from the dressing room, closing the door behind her. She found gin, whisky and brandy in the green room, on a tray on the sideboard, next to the knife block with its six sharp, serrated blades. Not knowing which would be best, she poured a finger of whisky and a finger of brandy into two separate glasses and returned.

Adélaïde still hadn't moved but, for the first time since they had returned from the basement, she met Maisie's eyes.

'This has happened to you before,' Adélaïde said. 'That is why you are calm.'

'I don't feel calm,' said Maisie.

'You know murder.'

'Stop it, Adélaïde.'

Maisie put down the glasses and glanced at her watch. How much time had passed since she had slipped out of the auditorium unseen, via the stairs at the back of the seats?

Barely any time at all – just six or seven minutes. But how long had Adélaïde been on her own?

Adélaïde picked up the two glasses and sniffed them.

'I prefer brandy,' she said, and knocked it back in one. She grimaced. 'But I will drink both.' She put down the brandy glass and sipped the whisky. 'You must tell Miss Dean. You must tell the police.'

'Don't worry about any of that.'

'You have a friend in the police?'

'If I go, will you be all right?'

'There is nothing for me to do but wait to answer their questions. There will be many questions. I will try to be "quick-witted".' Adélaïde smiled. 'There, I have used it correctly, haven't I?'

Maisie wondered if Adélaïde was pleased at the idea that she would soon become the centre of attention, as the person who discovered the body. Then she frowned and told herself not to be so unkind.

'I'll run and start sorting things out, but only if you're sure?'

'I am sure,' said Adélaïde.

Maisie went first to Fort Knox, but found it locked. Whether that was because Dorothy had left the building or was in the auditorium, or because the police had sealed it, she didn't know. She went on to the stage door.

'Mrs Belt, could I use your telephone, please?'

'What for?' she asked, her eyes keen for information.

'And could you tannoy a call for Miss Dean to meet me here, if she's still in the building, that is?'

'Oh, I think she might be. Have you seen her go out?'

'Why would I have seen her?' asked Maisie, shortly. 'Never mind.' She remembered Dorothy coming to the stage door area to make her call to the insurers. 'Isn't there another office I can use?'

147

'There's the board room,' said Harriet doubtfully.

'That would be perfect. This is a private conversation, Mrs Belt. It is extremely important.'

Apparently convinced by the firmness of Maisie's tone, Harriet Belt lifted a hatch in her counter.

'Come through here.'

Maisie soon found herself in a well-appointed meeting room with a long, teak table and a set of matching wooden chairs. She sat down at one end.

'I can manage, thank you,' she said pointedly.

'Of course,' said Mrs Belt and stepped outside, quietly closing the glass door.

Maisie pulled the telephone towards her, composing 999 on the rotary dial. The operator answered after two rings, wanting to know the nature of the emergency.

Maisie opened her mouth to speak, then changed her mind and hung up. She had had dealings with the emergency services before. Her memory of the calls was that the process was surprisingly laborious. It would be wiser to go straight to the local police station that would, inevitably, be the one asked to respond. She knew the number by heart because, of course, it was Jack Wingard's work number.

She dialled. It rang five times, then a youngish voice answered with a trace of the local accent, on an upward inflection as if asking a question.

'Chichester police?'

'Good evening.' Maisie glanced again at her watch. It was well after nine o'clock. Who would be on duty? It would depend on the shift pattern. 'There's been an incident at the Festival Theatre. Could I speak to Jack Wingard?'

'Sergeant Wingard is not on duty,' said the voice.

Maisie remembered what Fred Nairn had told her – that Jack and Florence had gone away to the New Forest for a few days.

'No, of course. This is Maisie Cooper. Who am I speaking to?'

'Constable Goodbody, Miss Cooper,' said the voice.

Oh God, thought Maisie.

She hadn't made many enemies since she had been back in Sussex, but the ferret-faced Barry Goodbody was one of them.

'Could you put me through to Fred Nairn, please?'

'What is the nature of the enquiry?' prevaricated Constable Goodbody, infuriatingly.

Maisie took a breath, trying not to become angry.

'I would prefer to speak to him directly.'

'What about?' he asked, rudely.

Maisie gave up on remaining calm.

'Listen, Barry, you've been an unnecessary obstruction in at least two investigations that I know of. Do you really want me to have to complain about you getting in the way for a third time?'

There was a pause and Maisie wondered if she had gone too far and made things harder. Probably, yes, in the long run. Wasn't it always a mistake to lose one's temper? Then there was a sequence of dull clicks and another voice came on the line.

'Nairn, here.'

Maisie repeated her opening gambit, word for word.

'Good evening. It's Maisie Cooper here. There's been an incident at the Festival Theatre. Can you come straight away?' Maisie noticed that Harriet Belt was standing outside the glazed door to the meeting room, brazenly eavesdropping. Maisie spoke very close to the receiver. 'It's about Keith.'

'What did you say, Miss Cooper?'

'Keith, the nightwatchman.'

'I didn't quite catch that. The line seems very quiet.'

Maisie spoke a little more distinctly.

'I don't think he could have committed the robbery, inspector.'

'Now, you haven't gone sleuthing and got yourself caught up in another local drama, have you?' asked Nairn patronisingly. 'Barry Goodbody told me you sounded upset.'

'What did you just say, Inspector?'

'Well, it would be quite the coincidence.'

'I realise that, Inspector Nairn,' Maisie snapped. 'And I hope you agree that your constable, whose reputation for incompetence precedes him, should be encouraged to show me – and perhaps other members of the public – a little more respect.'

'Yes, all right. He's not our best, not by a long chalk. Now, what important clues have me and my boys missed?' he asked, with a chuckle. 'Why couldn't Keith Sadler have committed the robbery?'

'Because he's dead.'

TWENTY

Once Maisie had given Inspector Nairn a clear digest of all she knew, his attitude swiftly became apologetic – almost deferential.

'Did you discover the body, Miss Cooper?'

'I was second to the scene.'

'Is the location secure?'

'No, but people don't go there much. It's a large, open space – a storeroom under the stage.'

'Would you wait there for me, please,' he asked, 'and make sure that no one else approaches?'

'I will do my best. Goodbye.'

She hung up. Harriet Belt was still on the other side of the glazed door and Dorothy Dean had finally responded to the tannoy. Maisie gestured for her to come in.

'What on Earth's going on?' asked Dorothy. 'Not another theft, is it, from one of the dressing rooms? Tell me it isn't Adélaïde's room? That would just about put the tin hat on it.'

Maisie shut the door and turned her back on it.

'Miss Dean, it's nothing like that, but it isn't good news. Adélaïde was down in the lower corridor, practising her lines and taking a break from the stage. Perhaps you know there was a bit of a bust-up earlier?'

'A little bird told me.'

'Well, she needed some solitude and, quite by chance, she came across something…'

Maisie stopped, wondering why the words were so hard to pronounce. Because they were so preposterous, perhaps?

'What did she come across?'

'The body of the nightwatchman, the poor young man, Keith Sadler.'

'What?'

'He's dead,' she reiterated, as if it were possible to miscon-strue the words 'the body'. 'Would you go downstairs, to the under-stage storeroom, and stand by the door – I mean, the opening, there isn't a door, as such – and make sure no one else goes in? The police are on their way. I want to check on Adélaïde.'

'Yes, of course.' Dorothy opened the door and impatiently confronted the stage door keeper. 'Mrs Belt, please go back to your desk. The police will be here shortly. Can you man-age to wait there and direct them?'

'Yes, Miss Dean,' said Harriet Belt, her eyes widening.

'Do not move from that spot, Mrs Belt. Do I make myself clear?'

Maisie wondered how much Harriet had heard, then she found out.

'It's murder as well as robbery, then?' she asked.

'That remains to be seen,' said Dorothy, crossly, lifting the hatch in the counter. 'Not a word to anyone,' she insisted.

Maisie and Dorothy went in opposite directions – Dorothy down the stairs to the basement level and Maisie along the dressing room corridor. She stopped, however, and looked back.

There it is again, a wide swathe of the dusty tiles, polished and shining as if something heavy has been dragged across them.

Regretting that she couldn't be in two places at once, Maisie hurried away and found, to her dismay, that the dressing room door was open and Adélaïde was nowhere to be seen.

★

Maisie had still not found Adélaïde by the time Inspector Nairn arrived. She met him out of doors in the car park, in order to briefly converse in semi-private. Nairn was accompanied by two scene-of-crime experts in drab raincoats, both carrying official-looking bags, one of whom was the man Maisie had met coming out of Fort Knox. She reassured Nairn that someone was guarding the scene, then told him about her deduction of what must have occurred.

'The theatre is unoccupied all winter and there's a layer of dust on almost everything. You can see marks on the tiles of the stage door hallway and then towards the stairs. I don't know that you'll be able to see anything on the steps themselves because the concrete's very rough, but you definitely can in the under-stage storeroom. Adélaïde will have walked across those marks. I did, too, when I went in and found her. I'm sorry about that. On the way out, though, we walked round the edge of the room.'

'Thank you. That's very helpful and clear. Anything else?'

'Well, from all that, it looks like he was killed in the stage door lobby, doesn't it? Then, whoever did it maybe fetched an old curtain to wrap him up and drag him into a dark corner. Do you think it might have been someone that he knew? I mean, someone who came to the door and knocked, and Keith let them in?' Nairn didn't answer so Maisie continued her own train of thought. 'He was the only person left in the building, after everyone was signed out. It's a relief to think he wasn't the thief. I rather liked him.'

Inspector Nairn gave a nod to one of his two officers, a tall, bony man with round glasses.

'Go into the hallway, there, Tindall, and have a shufti. Keep to the edge.'

'Yes, sir.'

The man took a large torch from his bag and went inside. Maisie shivered, not from the cold but from a feeling of tension. All her muscles seemed tight. She made an effort of will to relax while, behind the slot window in the door, she could see the beam of the powerful torch inspecting the space.

'Did you know him well?' asked Nairn. 'In fact, would you mind telling me how it is you're here in the theatre at all?'

'I was asked to help the leading lady, Miss Amour, who is French and needed coaching with her text.'

'By chance, like?'

'Actually, yes. We happen to both be staying at the Dolphin.'

'You're not a theatre person, then?'

'No.'

'How do you find them?' asked Fred Nairn, with an unexpected smile of encouragement. 'Your reading of the characters involved in the Bunting Manor business was very sound. This lot seem to have big personalities. Hard work, are they?'

Maisie didn't feel like smiling. An image of Keith's white, bloodstained face under the harsh neon lights was too vivid in her mind.

'Not hard work, exactly,' she said, 'but draining.'

'I can imagine. Now, young Keith Sadler. You knew him because…?'

'We spoke a few times at the Dolphin & Anchor. I don't recall seeing him about the theatre last night, before we all left. It was my first day.'

Nairn turned away to peer in through the slot window in the door. Maisie wondered aloud if she had over-reached herself in presenting him with her deductions. He turned back, looking grave.

'We're not fans of coincidence in the police, Miss Cooper.'

Maisie's heart sank.

'You mean my involvement in two murder investigations.'

'But there's a lot of people with cause to feel grateful for your insight and prompt action. I'm glad to have this opportunity of telling you.'

'Thank you. You don't have an address for Jack in the New Forest, or a phone number, perhaps?' asked Maisie, abruptly.

'I have the name of the hotel back at the station. I'll share it.'

The officer called Tindall came back outside.

'Blood on the whitewashed walls, guvnor. Not much and low down. There might have been more but it was wiped away by the perpetrator trying to cover their tracks. It would be easy to miss some of it. The hallway's a kind of awkward triangle and the light isn't that good.'

'Direction?' asked Nairn.

'More or less downwards, about knee height, but maybe flinching away.'

Tindall jerked his head in imitation of what he meant. Maisie swallowed. He and Nairn were coldly beginning to reconstruct the murder by the way Keith's blood had spattered the paintwork.

'How tall was young Keith?' Nairn asked her.

She frowned, making an effort of memory.

'I would say about five-foot-four. That was part of the reason why he looked so young.'

'Just to confirm,' said Nairn with a glance at her sensible flat shoes, 'three or four inches shorter than you?'

'Yes, I would say so.'

'Downward blow,' said Tindall, lifting his torch above his head in two bony hands and bringing it down, as if on the head of his victim.

'All right, Tindall,' said Nairn, impatiently. 'We're not making a movie out of it.'

'No, sir.'

'I don't know if this matters,' said Maisie, 'but, actually, Keith loved films. He read all the magazines and…'

She stopped, not sure why she had begun.

A uniformed officer arrived. Inevitably, it was the ferret-faced Barry Goodbody. Maisie noticed he had a wad of cotton wool sticking out of his right ear.

'Stay here, Barry,' said Nairn. 'We're going inside. Tindall and Wilson will look after backstage and downstairs. Meanwhile I'll get everyone together and have a little word. We'll have to corral them somewhere. We don't want people tramping about all over the place.'

'Yes, sir. No one in or out,' said Barry, standing to attention.

'What's the best way to get everyone assembled, Miss Cooper?' asked Nairn.

'You can use the tannoy. Most of the company and crew are in the auditorium anyway.'

'And who can help with the tannoy?'

'Mrs Belt, the stage door keeper.'

'Right, let's get on with that then.'

TWENTY-ONE

The call was made and Maisie escorted the inspector to the stage. Meanwhile the two forensics officers, Tindall and Wilson, went to the basement 'for a first shufti at the crime scene'.

Maisie and Nairn entered from upstage, through the set. The atmosphere in the auditorium was febrile. Kitty Farrell, Winnie Brahms and Liam Jukes were on stage, sitting on the furniture from the play, as if interrupted in the delivery of a scene. The rest were in the stalls. The working lights were on, meaning everything had an unpleasant, bleached-out appearance.

Inspector Nairn asked the three actors to go down into the stalls to sit alongside NVE, Micky Petherick, Sam Smithers and other members of the cast and crew. They did so more or less reluctantly, unused to being bossed about by an outsider in their own jealously guarded professional space. Dorothy came in from one of the aisles, presumably relieved to have been sent away from guarding the body by either Tindall or Wilson. She sat slightly apart.

Showing a strong natural understanding of how to dominate an audience, Nairn took up a position downstage centre. He raised a hand and everyone became still and quiet, wondering what he might be about to say.

'I am Inspector Nairn of the Sussex CID. I work out of Chichester station. We've been called in to respond to an incident whose details I am not yet at liberty to share. This is

157

all very upsetting and inconvenient, I'm sure, but first things first. Can anyone tell me, is everyone present and correct?'

'I can.' Micky Petherick stood up and looked round, now and then glancing at his call sheet. 'All except one,' he finally said.

'Someone's missing?' asked Nairn.

Maisie's heart sank.

'The leading lady,' said Micky. 'Miss Amour.'

'No,' came a very clear voice from the back of the stalls, the darkest corner. 'I am here.'

Nairn put a hand to his eyes to shield them from the working lights.

'I understand you might have some important information for us, Miss?' he called.

'*Oui*,' said Adélaïde and the word sounded like little more than an exhalation.

'And Miss Cooper was with you?' Nairn insisted.

'I was there just after,' said Maisie.

There was a pause as everyone in the stalls looked at one another and then back at Maisie. She knew what they were thinking – at least, she thought she did – that she was a kind of Jonah, bringing bad luck to the theatre. Ever since she'd been back in Sussex, bad luck and trouble had followed her around like the albatross that followed the doomed ghost-ship in Coleridge's poem *The Ancient Mariner*.

Maybe they're right.

'Miss Amour,' said Nairn to the figure at the back of the stalls. 'Would you mind coming a little closer?'

Adélaïde made her way slowly down through the seats to the lip of the stage. She stopped and looked up at the police officer, patient and docile, looking very lovely in her flowing skirt, into which she had tucked her man's white cotton shirt, not looking very different from how she had appeared in costume. It seemed to take Nairn a few moments to find an appropriate next remark, as if he was trying to recapture a forgotten memory. He held out a gallant hand to help Adélaïde up onto the boards.

'*Merci*,' said Adélaïde quietly.

Just as Maisie was beginning to think that Nairn was out of his depth and was going to say something gauche, he pulled himself together.

'Of course,' he said, smiling. 'I remember now. I've seen you in the pictures.' He laughed. 'I'm sorry, I was trying to place you and it's always annoying to a police officer to have a memory of a face and not to be able to put a name to it. You were in that one set at the seaside.'

'In Saint-Tropez,' said Adélaïde. 'It was called *Sirène*. That is "mermaid".'

'Yes, very nice, too.'

NVE's voice came strongly from the stalls.

'Perhaps Miss Amour would have sprung more readily to your memory, Inspector, had she been dressed – or rather undressed – as she mostly was in that film?' NVE left a pause for Nairn to locate him with his eyes. 'This is all very marvellous that you are a fan of the cinema, but shouldn't we be getting on?'

'I agree,' said Dorothy from the other side. 'Do let's get on but also, Nils, let's not interrupt.'

'I'm sure we all want to help,' said NVE.

'I'm sure you do,' said Nairn, without asking who it was who had spoken. He turned back to Micky Petherick. 'I'll send someone,' said the inspector, 'to get a full list of names and addresses. You can provide that?'

'You can take this one,' said Micky, holding it up.

'Good. And your role is…?'

'Assistant to the director,' said Micky. 'And stage manager and anything else that needs doing. Micky Petherick.'

'Thank you, Mr Petherick.'

Behind Micky, Maisie saw NVE bridle that the inspector was paying him no attention. She wondered if she ought to tell Nairn who he was – until now the most important person in the room – but she didn't get the chance.

'Right, ladies,' said Nairn, looking from Maisie to Adélaïde and back again. 'Perhaps the best thing would be for us to go backstage and take your statements, then you can show me the place.'

He stopped and gave them both a look that meant: *No need to tell everyone else where we're talking about.*

'But what place?' called out Esther. 'What's happened?'

'Yes, I agree,' said Clive. 'Is that too much to ask?'

'I agree, too,' said Winnie. 'Don't you, Andy?'

She was sitting next to Andrew but he didn't reply. He looked very still and observant, Maisie thought.

'Does it matter?' asked Kitty. 'I suppose we'll know in the end.'

'Kitty, dear,' said Esther, urgently. 'Come and sit by me.'

After a tiny but noticeable pause – undoubtedly Nairn would have clocked it – Maisie watched Kitty get up and, with ill-concealed reluctance, make her way towards Esther.

'You are noticing, perhaps,' called out NVE, 'how much our dear Kitty resembles Miss Amour. They are equally beautiful and are wearing similar costumes. Kitty is Adélaïde's understudy.'

'I see,' said Nairn without inflection. 'How remarkable.'

Kitty finally took her seat and Esther clasped her hand.

John Hermanson spoke quietly but, still, in his carrying actor's voice: 'A mother's love is a wonderful thing.'

Maisie frowned, suddenly struck by how little she knew these people. Was that right? Had she missed that? Was Kitty Farrell in reality Esther and Clive Canning's daughter?

'Could I have that list of yours right away, Mr Petherick?' asked Nairn.

'No problem,' said Micky, sidling out of his row and coming down to the lip of the stage, passing the paper up.

The inspector scanned the names. As he did so, Maisie glanced round the company. Not only did she not really know them, she felt oddly at home on the stage with Nairn and Adélaïde, as if the three of them made a team, separate from the rest of the cast and crew, secure in their roles, knowing their lines, while the audience – Esther and Clive and Kitty, Winnie and Andrew, John, Dorothy, NVE and the rest – had yet to work it all out. Sometime soon, they would applaud, and she and Adélaïde and Nairn would leave the theatre and return to real life.

'Have you lost your lines, Inspector?' called NVE, his words in tune with Maisie's thoughts. 'I'm afraid we don't have a prompt book to help you.'

Nairn had been glancing into the stalls, cross-referencing with the names on Micky's cast list, perhaps leaving a deliberate pause to see who might next speak, looking for clues – perhaps a nervous tension or an inability to sit still.

'I'll make this as quick as possible,' he suddenly said, very crisply. 'You can all use the WCs in the foyer, if you need to, but otherwise you must remain here. Miss Cooper, will you lead us backstage?'

'Why backstage?' called NVE.

'How intriguing,' said John in his deep bass.

'Yes, what's happened?' Esther repeated in a rather shrill voice.

'Please, tell us,' Clive begged.

'I'm afraid I can't discuss it at this point,' said Nairn.

'But that's not fair,' said Winnie. 'Tell them it's not fair, Andy.'

Just then, however, Harriet Belt's foolish voice came over the auditorium loudspeakers.

'By orders of the police, no one is to go backstage and especially not down to the basement. There's a dead body.'

Nairn raised his eyes to the grid in exasperation.

'Yes, a body,' he said, quietly.

'Should I come with you?' called Dorothy.

'Not just now, Miss Dean,' said Nairn.

'It's Keith,' announced Harriet's disembodied voice, in a tone that seemed to imply that no further explanation was necessary.

'Ladies,' said Nairn, 'shall we?'

Maisie led Nairn and Adélaïde upstage through the set, leaving behind a loud buzz of excited speculation.

TWENTY-TWO

Maisie led Adélaïde and Nairn to the dressing room corridor. Adélaïde stopped outside her door.

'I cannot look at him again,' she said, quite calmly. 'I will not go to the basement.'

'You will have to, eventually, you know,' said Nairn.

Adélaïde seemed to weigh him up.

'Now? You insist?'

Nairn returned her gaze. Maisie wasn't sure what he saw there.

'No,' he conceded, 'perhaps not right away.'

'Thank you, Inspector. Maisie is employed to protect me. Her task, in this moment, is to accompany you to see the dead person so that I do not need to.'

'In what way is Miss Cooper paid to protect you?' asked Nairn, looking interested.

'From life, from trouble, from complications. It is not a difficult idea.'

Adélaïde turned away and went to sit at her mirror.

Maisie thought Nairn would have liked to probe further, but his eye alighted on the wastepaper bin under the make-up counter.

'What's that?' he asked, placidly.

'What is what?' said Adélaïde.

Nairn bent over the bin.

'It looks like bloodstained paper towels, to me.'

'Adélaïde had blood on her hands,' said Maisie, 'and she cleaned them with make-up remover.'

Nairn looked from one to the other.

'Yes,' said Adélaïde. 'That is what I did.'

'You watched her do this, Miss Cooper?'

'Yes.' Maisie frowned and shook her head. 'No, I didn't, not exactly. I ran out to get something else for Adélaïde to wear because her costume blouse and waistcoat were blood-stained, too. They're there, on the shelf.'

'I see. No, don't touch them, if you please. I'll send Wilson to collect them.' He turned back to Adélaïde. 'You didn't take it into your head to clean blood from the floor of the stage door hallway or the wall while Miss Cooper was busy elsewhere?'

'When would I do this?' asked Adélaïde, dismissively.

'Inspector,' Maisie explained, 'we came back from the basement and just breezed past the stage door. I didn't want anyone to see. We didn't stop for a second. Mrs Belt can tell you.'

'I'm not sure Mrs Belt would be my first witness if I was looking for absolute certainty,' said Nairn. 'Right, Miss Cooper, I take it you've no objection to showing me—'

'Let's not waste any more time,' Maisie interrupted.

She led him along the corridor, feeling frustrated. She was beginning to lose patience with Adélaïde. First, she had twice disappeared without telling Maisie where she was going. Now, she'd taken it into her head to tell Nairn that she, Adélaïde, needed some kind of bodyguard and that she, Maisie, was fulfilling that unlikely function.

Maisie paused halfway down the stairs to the basement.

'Can I just mention something in confidence?' she asked, looking up at him.

'Nothing you say to the police is ever "in confidence",' said Nairn, gently. 'You know that.'

Maisie sighed. He was rather looming over her, two steps above.

'All right. I just want you to understand that this whole sequence of events was completely unpredictable.'

'Go on.'

'There was apparently some trouble earlier in the rehearsals, while they were still working in London, before they came down to Chichester, with somebody – perhaps more than one man – making unwanted advances to Miss Amour. Then Adélaïde's assistant had to return to France for some reason, leaving them in the lurch. She and Miss Dean, the producer, asked if I could act as coach to Miss Amour and, at the same time, sort of stick with her, making it hard for anyone to—'

'To get too forward,' said Nairn, interrupting in his turn. 'I quite see that. It makes a good deal of sense if there's a Lothario in the company who won't take no for an answer. Who was it – the mouthy director or the one at the back, sitting all quiet and unassuming?'

Maisie thought back to the cast and crew, dispersed in the stalls. Nairn was sharp. He had recognised the director and also noticed the unobtrusive Andrew P Bradshaw, not saying a word.

'How did you know NVE was the director?'

'Oh, that wasn't particularly clever. His face was on the front page of the *Chichester Observer* when the season was announced and, as I said to Miss Amour, a policeman makes a habit of remembering faces. Anyway, he also had that look about him – wondering why he wasn't in charge anymore.'

'That's very perceptive. And Andrew?'

'That's the silent actor?'

'Yes, Andrew P Bradshaw. He plays the leading man – Macheath is his character name – opposite Adélaïde.'

'Well, you saw for yourself, most people were talking, weren't they, one to another, and some of them calling out. He was very self-possessed.'

'Yes,' said Maisie, 'he was, wasn't he.'

'And he didn't seem very inclined to answer the appeals from that rather luscious piece sitting next to him. He was watching everyone – and us, of course.'

'I don't think he would have been paying much attention to me,' said Maisie.

'Don't you?' asked Nairn. 'Anyway, if he's the leading man, he'd have plenty of opportunity in the playing of their scenes to get up close and personal with Miss Amour.'

Maisie thought about the passages she had seen rehearsed. If there had been any funny business, she'd missed it.

'I suppose he would.'

'You mentioned they'd been rehearsing in London. When did everyone come down?' Nairn asked.

'To Chichester? I've been at the Dolphin & Anchor all week and at least a couple of them, including the director, arrived last Thursday or Friday. It's only a couple of hours on the train.'

'And probably longer in a car. There are three parked outside.'

That's right, thought Maisie. *Two smart ones and a bit of a wreck. Who does the wreck belong to?*

'Others are in digs,' she went on, 'but a few came to the Dolphin for a drink on Saturday and again on Sunday.'

'The same ones?'

'I'm afraid I don't know.' Maisie frowned, annoyed with herself. 'Maybe the same ones, maybe different ones, drifting in and out over the course of the weekend. I'm sorry I can't be more precise. I wasn't really paying attention to them at that point. I mean, there was no reason…'

Maisie felt herself flush as she thought back to NVE taking her hand, propositioning her. Ought she to tell Nairn about that? If she did, would it get back to Jack?

'Something else?' asked Nairn.

Maisie shook her head, uncomfortable that they were still poised awkwardly, halfway down the stairs.

'No, it's just all catching up with me. Shall we?'

'All right,' said Nairn thoughtfully. 'Just as you prefer.'

★

'So that's it,' Maisie concluded, twenty minutes later.

She had given Nairn word-portraits of the company, as well as describing all she had seen and done since joining them. And, of course, she had once more gone over how she found Adélaïde kneeling over the body.

'Did you get Miss Cooper's statement down, Tindall?' asked Nairn.

The tall bony officer in the little round glasses nodded and shut his notebook.

'Yes, sir. And, if I may say so, an exemplary summary, Miss Cooper.'

The three of them were standing in the opening from the starkly lit corridor, looking across the dingy, dusty space, between the heavy pillars, to where the body of Keith Sadler still lay, wrapped in a faded stage curtain, with a corner decorously draped across his face. The neon lights had stabilised and were no longer flickering.

'There seemed to be a lot of blood on his shirt front as well as in his hair,' said Maisie. 'You've covered him up now, but did I mention that?'

'He was struck more than once,' said Tindall, 'on the temple and in his face. Most of the blood will have come from a nosebleed, I'll wager, and that was probably first, though the doctor will give us chapter and verse.'

'Would you mind,' said Maisie, unable to prevent her imagination from queasily visualising how it might have happened, 'if I went back to see how Adélaïde is getting on?'

167

'No, I think that's about all we'll need for the moment. You'll sign a fair copy of your statement before you go home?'

She felt herself sway slightly and tried to pull herself together.

'Home would be Paris,' she said ruefully. 'I wouldn't still be in Chichester if it weren't for the Bunting Manor trial taking an age to come to court.'

'It's not been that long, in point of fact,' said Nairn carefully.

'No, I'm sorry.' Maisie sighed. 'That's what the solicitors tell me. And none of that is your fault. I'm just beginning to feel I must be some kind of Jonah, bringing bad luck wherever I go.' She looked at her watch. 'Good heavens, it's nearly eleven.'

'Yes. You're looking very pale. When did you last eat something?'

Good question, thought Maisie.

'Don't worry, Inspector. I can find something in the green room and then I will wait for you with Adélaïde.'

'Let me come with you.'

Nairn took Maisie's arm and led her back up the stairs. Her head was swimming. He sat her down in the dressing room with Adélaïde who had already raided the green room, carrying away a dinner plate of cocktail sticks – trios of Edam cheese, celery and cherry tomatoes – plus a few curling sandwiches. Adélaïde had changed out of her costume and was wearing her woollen turquoise suit. She also had her coat on, as if on the point of leaving.

To Maisie's relief, she was able to sit quietly and nibble some of the snacks for ten minutes while Nairn spoke briefly to Tindall then took Adélaïde through the events that Maisie had already described – 'just for corroboration, you understand'. Finally, as Maisie was beginning to feel drowsy, Nairn shut his notebook.

'I have that all down. If you wouldn't mind, I will pop into the hotel just after breakfast tomorrow. Will that do? Shall we say at ten?'

'We will be working,' said Adélaïde.

'Do you think so?' asked Maisie. 'Doesn't Keith's murder change things?'

'Why not work? There is the show. It must go on. We have the press night soon.' Adélaïde shrugged. 'All this, it has nothing to do with us. It is a common theft and a violence. People have paid for their tickets. We must give them the spectacle.'

I suppose that's right, thought Maisie.

'In that case,' said Nairn, 'I will hope not to disturb you for any longer than it takes for you to read and sign your statements. Now, I imagine you are keen to get to bed. Can I drive you?'

Adélaïde stood up.

'No, it will be better to walk. Come, Maisie. We are free.'

'But don't you need us on stage to speak to the others?' Maisie asked.

'I sent Wilson to turn them out some time ago,' said Nairn. 'No one else is left. As far as we know, none of them went anywhere near the body. If anything else comes up, we will know where to find them.'

*

It was a good idea to walk, Maisie reflected, as they crossed the car park, the fresh air doing her good. Adélaïde kept silent and Maisie was quite content to walk alongside her without speaking. As they passed the George & Dragon public house on North Street, they heard music from within. Then the door opened as a jolly couple exited, making their way home. There was a fiddle band inside, playing a reel.

'*Mais c'est une chanson bretonne*,' said Adélaïde.

It was true – the band was singing a folk song from Brittany about 'strange days' when the wolf and the fox and the weasel sing together in the fields, and the mare eats all the cut hay in the summer pasture.

'*When winter comes, she'll be sorry,*' sang the vocalist.

They walked on, Adélaïde singing quietly to herself.

'You do have such a lovely voice,' said Maisie.

'Everyone sings where I come from.'

'Folk music like that?'

'Like that, perhaps.' Adélaïde shrugged. 'But closer together, the notes, so that they are almost…' She searched for the right word in English. 'They are blue notes,' she said, 'like in jazz, but they are all blue notes.' She laughed. 'I cannot explain it, even in French, I don't know.'

Maisie laughed, too, because the discussion of Breton folk music seemed like such an innocent release.

'Let us sit,' said Adélaïde.

They walked on to the Market Cross, the medieval landmark at the junction of the four cardinal streets of the city, north, south, east and west. Sheltered by the ancient buttresses, the circular stone bench around the centre column was dry but cold. The streets were quiet and still. A few yellow streetlamps lent definition to the mature trees on the cathedral green, the pleasant Georgian façades opposite.

'Do you know what happened?' asked Adélaïde.

'No,' said Maisie. 'How could I?'

'I was not involved in any way. I want you to know this.'

'Obviously you weren't.'

'You say that but you are polite, so it is inevitable that you will agree.' Adélaïde sighed and closed her eyes. 'I feel something bad.'

'Are you ill?'

'No, I mean I have been feeling something bad. I told you. That is why I wanted you with me. That is why I complain to Miss Dean.'

'Well, you can relax, now,' said Maisie. 'The bad thing has already happened.'

'Perhaps,' said Adélaïde, in a whisper. '*Si seulement c'était vrai.*'

If only that were true.

IV

CHARACTER

TWENTY-THREE

The next morning, Maisie was down for breakfast at seven-thirty. She had set her alarm early, hoping for a few minutes to herself and intending to avoid the rush when the kitchen got busy while simultaneously, in Keith's absence, being understaffed. She was just moving to her usual table, wondering whether the hotel would know that their barman had been murdered, when someone excitedly called her name.

'Maisie, this is wonderful. Thank you.'

She turned. It was Zoe, Phyl Pascal's sixteen-year-old ward, slamming down a tray of pats of butter, then almost running towards Maisie, enfolding her in her young arms.

'Glad to see you, too,' said Maisie. 'That was quick work.'

'What a brilliant idea,' said Zoe. 'The manager rang me up at Phyl's. Ernie doesn't need me at The Dancing Hare. He only kept me on because he's kind, but we were basically under each other's feet, now he's not upstairs on his own, drowning his sorrows.'

'Leaving you high and dry, though?'

'Phyl was going to find me something on her land.'

Maisie smiled.

'This is better, though?'

Zoe nodded, enthusiastically.

'This is better. And Phyl agreed. And the manager's given me a room.'

'You're staying here? That's a bonus.'

Zoe pulled a face.

'It's a horrible garret in a kind of annex overlooking the boiler vent. It comes out of my wages, but I don't care.'

'You've wanted to get away from the village for ages.'

'I absolutely have.'

'But, actually, how are you?' Maisie took Zoe's hands in hers. 'I wish I could have protected you better from—'

'Don't you dare, Maisie. You were amazing.'

'I wish I'd been quicker to—' Maisie protested.

'Maisie, trust me. I'm totally fine.'

'I'm glad.' She paused. 'Did the manager tell you I'm helping at the theatre? You must come and see the show.'

'Love to,' said Zoe. 'And another thing. I've decided to change my name.'

'Back to Richards?'

'No, why would I want a foundling name?' said Zoe, with a serious expression. 'Look, I hope it's okay. And Phyl said it was a good idea. She's basically my mother, now,' said Zoe, with a shy look.

'You've taken her name?'

'In the process of taking it. I went in to see Charity Clement and she says they can draw up the deed.'

'I see.'

'You don't mind, do you?'

'Why should I mind?' said Maisie.

'Well, because it's your name, in a way. Phyl's your mother.'

'Birth mother,' said Maisie, uncomfortably. 'She didn't bring me up. Anyway, "Zoe Pascal" is a lovely name. In fact, it makes you sound like an actor. Esther Canning says: "two syllables and two syllables always works".'

'Who's Esther Canning?'

'She's in *The Beggar's Opera*.'

'You're sure you couldn't care less, though? You have a greater right—'

'That's enough,' said Maisie. 'Phyl found you and looked after you long before I was in the picture.'

'I don't want—'

'Please,' said Maisie. 'It's a perfect plan.'

At that moment the manager came in from reception, also keen to thank Maisie for bringing Zoe in to fill the breach.

'She worked last night's restaurant shift, too. Very good, very organised and professional.'

'I'm so pleased,' said Maisie, smiling.

Two other hotel guests – not theatre people – came in and Zoe went to take their order, quickly and efficiently, before disappearing beyond the swing doors into the kitchen.

'I have high hopes,' said the manager. 'She has the right stuff, in my opinion.' Before he went about his business he added, with a dismissive shake of the head: 'Not like Keith Sadler.'

Well, Maisie thought, once the manager had gone, *that makes it pretty clear that no one on the staff of the Dolphin & Anchor yet knows that poor Keith has been the victim of a murderous attack.*

She drank her first coffee, enjoying watching Zoe work and sharing an occasional smile, and wondering what she really thought about Phyl giving her name to Zoe. She was surprised to discover that it made her feel warm inside, as if she was acquiring more family, rather than being supplanted.

At seven-forty-five, Adélaïde came in and they each placed their food order. Zoe gave Maisie a tiny shake of the head to indicate that she didn't want to be introduced as a friend, that she just wanted to get on with her work.

Maisie and Adélaïde didn't discuss the drama of the previous evening. In any case, not long after eight they had finished their sardines and poached eggs and were back upstairs in Adélaïde's room, working.

As Maisie had hoped, it turned out the singing cure was so effective that – counter-intuitively – Adélaïde barely needed to use it anymore. She could now recite her text with a sense of the music of the language already present. The method Maisie had stumbled upon had definitively tuned her in to the eighteenth-century dialogue.

All the same, now and then, Adélaïde continued to sing her lines to herself, but mostly under her breath. The bulk of the assistance Maisie was now able to give was what Adélaïde called in French '*donner la réplique*', to *give the reply* – meaning to read in the other parts.

Inspector Nairn came to interrupt this process, as promised, at ten o'clock. They met him in the television room that smelled, as Adélaïde had said, of tobacco and stale milk.

'I hope you both slept well,' he told them, politely.

'Like a log,' said Adélaïde.

'Yes, thank you,' said Maisie. 'Do you have our statements?'

'I do.'

They read them over and signed them. Nairn seemed disinclined to leave.

'Would you have time for one or two more questions?'

Maisie looked at Adélaïde who nodded, though she looked displeased.

'Where would you like to begin?' Maisie asked. 'What didn't we cover last night?'

'I would like you to tell me more about the people involved in the play – the people working in the building.'

'Why?' asked Adélaïde.

'Because,' explained Maisie on Nairn's behalf, 'they are the most likely perpetrators.'

'Murders,' explained Nairn, 'are not exclusively committed by people known to the victim – but very often they are. In addition, this crime is related to a theft of property that

178

required a certain amount of knowledge of the building, of the goings-on.'

'Do you agree, though,' asked Maisie, 'that this must have been an unplanned murder?'

'Why would you say that?' asked Nairn.

'Two things. If I were to steal, I would want to get straight away, not get caught up in further complications. And the method of assault – wouldn't you say it looked rather haphazard?'

'We haven't determined the weapon, Miss Cooper.'

Maisie had spent some time thinking about this.

'But it was probably the cash box, wasn't it? The thief must have had it in his hands when poor Keith came upon him. If the patterns in the dust and in blood on the wall of the hallway are a good guide, it happened just as the thief was about to make their escape. He used the weapon he had to hand.'

'You are very "quick-witted", Maisie,' said Adélaïde, her eyes widening. 'I did not see any of this,'

'You found the body, Adélaïde. You were in shock.'

'And you are experienced,' Adélaïde replied.

Maisie frowned. The same remark had been made several times recently. What had Andrew said? That she was *an aficionado of crime*. She didn't like it, but she couldn't argue that it wasn't true.

'The location is important, yes,' said Nairn, rubbing a hand over his prematurely bald head. His rim of hair – what was left of it – was very fine, and strawberry blond in colour. 'You may be right about all that. And, as we say in the force, crime causes crime. One bad deed leads to another, if you see what I mean.'

'It will be important for you to discover,' said Maisie, 'who knew that the five hundred pounds was in the safe and who had the opportunity to see Miss Dean operating the combination lock, who might have discovered the code.'

'Yes.'

'Or got it from the stage manager.'

'No,' said Nairn. 'As it turns out, Mr Petherick hasn't had occasion to open the safe.'

'But he knew the combination,' insisted Adélaïde.

'Yes, but he maintains he hasn't shared that knowledge with anyone else.'

'Does he have big need of money?' asked Adélaïde.

'Miss Amour, we are becoming side-tracked.' Nairn focused on Maisie. 'Now, the cash that was put by in the safe, I understand you know the gentleman who provided it, Miss Cooper. Mr Al-Sabah?'

'Mohammed As-Sabah is an old friend, probably my brother's oldest friend. He came to Chichester to see me and to do something charitable in Stephen's memory – naming a seat at the theatre. We had lunch. By chance, he also met Miss Amour and he gave us a lift to the theatre because it was raining. Miss Amour and I went into the auditorium to work, and Mohammed remained with Miss Dean in the foyer. I imagine she made a strong case for investment in the show.'

'Yes, that's all very clear.' He frowned over his notes. 'I have Al-Sabah, but you call him As-Sabah. Did I make a mistake?'

'Not exactly,' said Maisie. 'It's a linguistic thing about how certain sounds are elided in Arabic. It's written "Al" but it's pronounced "As" because the next word begins with an "S". It's rather complicated,' she finished, weakly.

'I see. And, according to Miss Dean, your friend went to the management office with her and was present when the cash was placed inside the safe. Where were you at that point?'

'As I said – in the auditorium, both of us,' said Maisie.

'How many people are there in the company, altogether?'

'Myself and twenty-one,' said Adélaïde. 'It is necessary that we fill the stage. In the script, there are roles for thirty or more.'

'And that's managed by doubling up with different costumes and so forth?' Nairn sighed.

'It would be better with one actor for every character,' said Adélaïde. 'That is how it would be in a film.' She shook her head, contemptuously. 'Someone comes on in a different hat, but everyone knows it is the same actor. Why is it like this in the theatre?'

'And, as far as we're concerned,' said Nairn ruefully, 'it doesn't make our jobs any easier.'

Maisie felt sympathy for the inspector.

'I can see that the idea of nearly two dozen actors in a variety of outfits must seem difficult to pin down. You are interested in precise movements around the building. All I can say is that everyone was in the theatre at the moment Mohammed put the money in the safe and Miss Dean locked it, but there was a lot of back and forth from the stage to wardrobe for costumes and to the green room for snacks and so on.'

'I see. And backstage staff? What can you tell me about them?'

'Well,' said Maisie, visualising, 'there are two members of stage crew who also double as set builders and painters. I don't know if that's usual, but it makes for a compact team. Mr Petherick runs their activities. I'm afraid I don't know their names.'

'I do,' said Nairn, tapping his notebook.

'Then there's the wardrobe mistress. Her name is Beryl Vere. She wafts in and out, "borrowing" an actor here and there. There was a lot of that. She has a helper, a girl who never seems to leave their room, ironing and darning. And then there's Sam who runs sound and lights. He's working completely on his own and seems run off his feet.'

'Sam Smithers is a good man. I know him from church,' said Nairn. 'He's supposed to have an assistant but apparently he's gone home with the flu.'

'This is why every change to the lighting takes so long,' said Adélaïde with what Maisie recognised as an actor's impatience with the technical paraphernalia of theatre.

'So, you can't help me there,' said Nairn in a resigned voice.

'You mean,' Maisie clarified, 'about who knew the money was there? You – or rather your men, Wilson and Tindall – must have asked everyone to account for their movements?'

'They did. Except for those minor roles, everyone was everywhere, apparently,' said Nairn with a discouraged expression. 'And no one seems at any point to have known the precise time.'

Maisie smiled.

'Time by the clock changes in the theatre. The outside world sort of disappears.'

'As it's meant to do, I imagine.' Nairn wrote something down and turned over a leaf in his notebook to a new blank page. 'What can you tell me about the play? I borrowed a script and had a look last night, but I must say it didn't hold my attention.'

'A theatre script,' said Adélaïde, 'is not a book. It requires a different way of reading.'

'I dare say I'm not equipped,' agreed Nairn. 'All the same, how would you describe it?'

'Well,' said Maisie, 'I'd say it's about corruption.'

'No, Maisie,' said Adélaïde, 'it's about love.'

'Yes, it's about love, but thematically it's a satire on corrupt officialdom and poor people bending the law to get by.'

'I don't understand,' said Adélaïde. 'You talk too fast.'

'Please go on,' said Nairn.

'The heart of the play is, as Adélaïde says, a love story, between her character, Polly Peachum, and the rogue, Captain Macheath. That develops into a love triangle because Macheath is also entangled with Lucy Lockit who is the daughter of the jailer. He oversees the jail in which Macheath will be locked up and, perhaps, hanged, if Polly Peachum's parents, Mr and Mrs Peachum, give him away to the police for the reward.'

'That's very clear.'

'But, when it was written, theatregoers would have understood that the characters were commentaries on powerful people of the era. I'd have to check but I think it was about 1730. At the same time, it wasn't considered a "serious" play. I mean, it tells its stories with songs as well, almost seventy of them, most of them popular songs borrowed from other sources with the words changed to fit.'

'So,' said Nairn, writing furiously, 'it's a social satire and a love triangle but rather like a music hall production in the way it tells the story.'

'That's very well put,' said Maisie. 'Just to give you an example, there's a song about Tyburn Tree, which was, I'm sure you know, a place where criminals were executed by hanging, and it's sung to the tune of "Greensleeves", which some people maintain was composed by Henry VIII. At the time of *The Beggar's Opera*, it's already a well-known tune and maybe two hundred years old.'

'Thank you.' Nairn didn't write all that down, Maisie noticed. 'Now, I skipped to the end of the script,' he admitted. 'The Beggar finishes the play and this Macheath, he gets away with it and it all ends happily?'

'It does,' said Maisie, 'but only in a way. You see, the love triangle isn't resolved and, at the last, as well as Polly Peachum, played by Adélaïde, and Lucy Lockit, played by Winnie Brahms, four other women turn up, all with a claim on Macheath – a better claim, in fact, because all four of them have a child by him – and the last thing he does is to ask his jailers to take him to the scaffold and hang him because it's all too much and he can't cope with the responsibility and the nagging. I suppose it's a joke.'

Adélaïde added: 'He says "tell the sheriff's officers I am ready". The audience will laugh, I think.'

Nairn's pen remained poised above the page.

'Now that I've got something I can hold on to from the story, I would very much like a rundown of the actors who play these characters.'

There was a knock at the door. It opened and Dorothy put her head round.

'I have a taxi to take us to the theatre—' She stopped, seeing the police officer. 'Excuse me.'

'Miss Dean,' said Nairn, 'I wonder if I might keep Miss Cooper for, perhaps, another half an hour? Then I will bring her to the theatre myself. Would that be all right?'

'Why?' asked Dorothy.

'Routine enquiries, Miss Dean.'

'Well, it's rather up to Miss Amour.'

'Adélaïde, will you be all right—?' Maisie began.

'If it is not for very long,' said Adélaïde, magnanimously getting to her feet, very much the *grande dame*. 'Yes, I will agree to agree.'

'Adélaïde, you are wonderful,' said Maisie, laughing.

Nairn was smiling into his notebook.

Dorothy and Adélaïde left and Maisie shut her eyes, beginning to assemble her impressions of the actors into a coherent set of *dramatis personae*.

*

Half an hour later, almost to the dot, Maisie thought she had exhausted everything she had seen and heard from the cast and crew of *The Beggar's Opera*. Nairn had filled perhaps a dozen pages of his notebook and was looking a little overwhelmed.

'Can I ask you,' he said, 'how you learned to do this?'

'I'm not sure what you mean.'

'Well, Jack told me you were a remarkable witness with a finely tuned sense of character, but I have to admit I thought he was overdoing it because…' He paused. 'To speak frankly, because he's a close friend of yours. Is that fair?'

'I hope so,' said Maisie.

'You and I had dealings over the Bunting Manor business, and I appreciated your clarity.'

'Yes?' Maisie said, not sure where this was going.

Nairn tapped his notebook.

'This, Miss Cooper, this set of character studies, the relationships, the things that you have chosen to tell me and the way you've connected it all – it's better than my best man would have laid it out.'

'Thank you.'

'So, how did you—'

'I don't know,' interrupted Maisie, shortly. 'And, to tell you the truth, much as I appreciate the compliment, I wish I'd never been put in a position to discover that I'm good at understanding why people do awful things.'

Maisie took a breath and drained her cup of cold coffee.

'Fair enough,' he said finally. 'I can see why you might resent the cards life has dealt you. All the same,' he told her, 'you play them like a master.'

Maisie sighed. She supposed she ought to thank him again, but she didn't want to. She didn't want to think any more about poor Keith Sadler. She just wanted to go back to the theatre and sit in the dark listening to actors reciting made-up lines from made-up stories, where everything was imaginary and no one would ever be brought to justice or have to go to jail for their crimes.

In real life, though, she thought, *if I have anything to do with it, somebody will.*

TWENTY-FOUR

Having dropped Maisie at the theatre, Fred Nairn drove back into the centre of Chichester and parked behind Marks & Spencer so he could walk to Forbuoy's, the tobacconist near the Cross.

When he emerged with his packet of Old Holborn rolling tobacco and some liquorice papers, he stood for a moment, looking up at the sky.

There was a patch of blue up there, enough to make a sailor a pair of trousers, as his wife was fond of saying; his mother-in-law as well, from whom his wife had no doubt picked up the habit. Not enough blue, though, to convince him that the spell of bad weather was over.

Sure enough, before he moved on, a cloud came scurrying in and cut off the momentary warmth.

Nairn strode back to his car, a Mark II Jaguar that he had bought to celebrate his promotion to inspector. With two small children at home, it was the only place he ever felt entirely sheltered from life, somewhere no one could get at him and he could be at peace with his thoughts.

That said, on the telly, the baddies always seemed to drive Mark II Jags. Still, that wasn't real life, was it?

He got in, relishing the leather seat that had allowed itself to be shaped to the exact form of his body, enjoying the warm sheen of the walnut dashboard, the pleasant smell of lubricating oil. He turned the key and, of course, the engine started the first time. He drove away, feeling pleased with himself and his life choices. But, by the time he reached the police station and parked in a spot out front from which he could see the canal, his mood had changed.

He sat with his hands on the wheel, thinking about the job that lay ahead of him: correlating the movements of all the theatre people; cross-checking their statements with the period when the producer, Miss Dean, had accepted the five hundred pounds in cash from the Arab gentleman; interviewing everyone a second time, looking for corroboration or contradiction; then, laying it all out in some way that would make it possible to explain his interpretation of these details to his impatient superintendent.

Even then, it might not boil down to a single individual because there might be no definitive answers. More than one person might turn out to have been unseen and unaccounted for at the key time. Plus, there was the stage manager who, despite his admirable attention to detail in his work, seemed pretty vague about everything that he wasn't directly responsible for.

Nairn got out of the Jag and allowed the heavy door to shut under its own weight. The rain began falling, so he hurried inside, briefly nodding to the desk officer who told him: 'Sergeant's back.'

He stopped.

'Wingard?'

'That's right, Inspector. Just. Not on duty but he asked me to tell you.'

'That was quick. What's up?'

'Didn't say.'

*

Jack Wingard had been at the station for just five minutes. He was looking at a large cork board on which just a few pieces of paper had been pinned, his eye drawn inexorably to Maisie's name.

'Hello, Fred,' he said.

'How did you know I was here?' asked Nairn, entering the room behind him.

Jack gestured.

'I saw your reflection in the window.' Jack shook his colleague's hand. 'You seem to be mobilising a lot of resources for a petty theft.'

'Yes, well, there's more to it than that.'

Jack listened, appalled, as Nairn gave him an overview of the surprising story of how Maisie had been taken on as assistant to Miss Adélaïde Amour, then the theft and, finally, the discovery of the body of the young nightwatchman. Jack's mood darkened with each thing he learned.

'Poor Maisie. This really isn't fair. How is she, Fred?'

'A remarkable young woman,' said Nairn. 'The more I see of her, the more I think so. Hang on a minute, though. You were supposed to be away for the rest of the week, weren't you? You've not put your uniform on. It's not your grandma again, is it?'

'No, nothing like that.' Jack smiled, shaking his head. 'It was nice enough in the New Forest to start with, but it rained for the whole twenty-four hours we were there and, when it came to it, there wasn't going to be that much to do without a car.'

'If you went for a promotion, like I told you to, you could afford a car – a nice one,' said Nairn.

'Never mind that,' said Jack. He didn't feel like explaining for the umpteenth time why he was happy to remain a uniformed sergeant. 'First thing this morning, I found her on her knees in the hotel garden, weeding the borders.'

'Your Florence?'

'Yes.'

'Weren't you at the Balmer Lawn? Isn't that quite posh? How did the management take to her, grovelling in the shrubberies?'

'Not well.'

'What had got into her?'

'She told the head gardener the rain had brought the weeds rushing up out of the ground and she couldn't bear to look at them. He told her he had a professional team of his own. That was when I found her, telling him: "If you do, and I can't see any evidence of it, they're not on top of things like they ought to be." How's that?'

Nairn laughed.

'I can hear it clear as day. She's a card and no mistake.'

'I got her indoors and sent her upstairs to put on some dry tights as hers were wet from where she'd been kneeling in the grass. Lo and behold, she was down again fifteen minutes later, in reception, with her little bag packed, ready to leave.'

'She wasn't?'

'She told me she wanted to go home and weed her own borders and, to tell you the truth, I wasn't disappointed.'

'You wanted to get back home yourself?'

'That's right.'

Nairn nodded. 'And see what Miss Cooper's been up to?' he suggested.

Jack was saved from answering by the arrival of a colleague, come to fetch Nairn for a matter of routine. Jack sat down, his eyes unfocused. On the scenic train journey back from the New Forest, his grandma had dozed off, giving him time to think.

Since Maisie had come surging back into his life, everything had changed. He had been transformed from a placid man of routine and moderate habits, without ambition or grand projects for the future, into someone who thought often about tomorrow, who dreamed of making a home with a woman with a clear complexion and short curly hair, serious eyes and a ready smile. And he seemed to be in the habit of smiling for what he thought was no reason.

But, of course, there was always a reason, the same one each time. His thoughts had, yet again, drifted back to the first and last girl he would ever love.

No, not 'girl'. That was one of the things that made Maisie so special. You couldn't think of her as a 'girl'. She had far too much independence and strength of character for that.

Nairn returned and Jack paid close attention as his colleague took him through everything that had so far been accomplished and the next steps he had planned. As he did so, Jack watched Nairn put a few more pieces of paper on the huge cork board, including a company call-sheet that he said the stage manager, Micky Petherick, had given him – a complete list of all the performers and backstage crew. Nairn also pinned up a plan of the theatre, showing the layout of the foyer, the auditorium, the stage door area, the dressing rooms, wardrobe and the management offices. There was a second drawing for the basement level where the body had turned up.

'And it was the star who found him?' asked Jack. 'What was she doing down there?'

'You won't be surprised to hear that I asked her that question myself. I'm very far from having received a satisfactory answer.'

'She told you she was just looking for somewhere quiet to be on her own?' Jack guessed.

'More or less.'

'And Maisie was second on the scene?'

'Yes,' said Nairn, 'but only because she's responsible for looking after Miss Amour. Isn't that a damn stupid name, by the way?'

'Maisie wasn't doing some investigating of her own?' Jack asked, with a worried frown.

'As far as I can see, without the French lady going down there, your Maisie wouldn't have had any call to visit the basement at all.'

'She isn't "my" Maisie,' muttered Jack.

'You wish she was, though,' said his colleague and friend.

Jack ran a finger down the cast list.

'There're a lot of these buggers, aren't there?'

'There are,' said Nairn. 'Twenty-two actors and getting on for round about a dozen more staff. And I'll tell you something else. These aren't all their names. I mean they are their names but—'

'These are stage names,' Jack interrupted. 'In their passports and their cheque books, it might say something different.'

'Exactly. For the time being, though, we'll go with these.'

Nairn went on to explain the unresolved question of who had seen the money deposited in the safe.

'It's not just whether they knew it was there,' agreed Jack, 'but also whether they could have seen Miss Dean turning the combination dial and memorised what they saw.'

'Precisely,' said Nairn. 'From the statements we've collected, it can only have been one of the leads or the management. All the second-string actors were busy on stage for a choral rehearsal, but the main actors and the director and so on were in the neighbourhood.'

'Easy to guess, the code? Even if you hadn't seen it?'

'If you know the history of the place.' Nairn explained that it was the year the theatre opened, 1962. 'Then there's Mr As-Sabah and the how and why and what he might know. I'll have to be on to him. It was his five hundred quid.'

Nairn told Jack the detailed story Maisie had given him about how Mohammed had become involved.

'How come he had five hundred pounds in cash in his top pocket?' asked Jack.

'I don't know. Perhaps from his own private oil well? He's supposed to be back for the press night at the end of the week. Have you got something extra for me about this character?'

'No,' said Jack, carefully. 'I've nothing against him except for the fact that he's rich, educated, multi-lingual, handsome and at least as interested in Maisie Cooper as…' He stopped, realising he was going a bit far, standing in the open-plan office. 'Well, you know what I mean.' There was a pause while Jack got his thoughts together. 'Tell you what, Fred. How would it be if I took the rest of the week off, as planned, and no one needs to know I'm back?'

'When you say "no one", you mean Miss Cooper?'

Jack nodded.

'I'll help Grandma get on top of her weeds and just come in and speak to you at the end of the day or whenever is convenient and you can run things past me. Perhaps I'll be a help, not a hindrance,' he added, humbly.

'Don't pretend you're not at least as quick on the uptake as I am, Sergeant Wingard,' said Nairn, smiling. 'Obviously, I'll be glad to have another pair of eyes on the board.'

They both looked at the sparse information so far collected.

'This will fill up pretty quick,' said Jack. 'There's too damn many of them.'

'You can say that again,' said Nairn.

Jack shook his head.

'Think about what Maisie's walked into since she's been back in Sussex, Fred. I don't like it. Don't forget, crime causes crime.'

'I know that. I told them. But look, there's nothing to worry about here. Maisie's a bystander, Jack. She's not involved this time. It's just a robbery that went bad, that's all.'

'Course it is, Fred,' said Jack. 'I see that. But, all the same, by God, I wish she was out of it.'

TWENTY-FIVE

While Inspector Nairn was buying his Old Holborn from the tobacconist near the medieval Cross, Maisie was looking at the three cars outside the stage door. One – a bottle green Rover – she thought belonged to Dorothy Dean, because she could see management paperwork on the front passenger seat. The second one was a royal blue Triumph TR6 convertible – a very desirable motor indeed. Peering in through the driver's window, she could see almost 80,000 miles on the clock. Though it was fitted with a standard UK registration plate, it had a GB sticker on the back, making her wonder if it might belong to NVE for use back in the Netherlands.

The third car, the one whose boot was held closed with a bungee strap, was a Morris Minor in a colour that Maisie thought should be described as 'diarrhoea brown', though it was probably listed as 'café crème' in the brochure. As well as the defective boot, there was rust at the bottom of the doors and the chrome of the bumpers was eaten through in several places. One of the rear brake lights had been repaired with transparent red tape, indicating that whoever it belonged to couldn't afford proper repairs.

Or maybe they're just frugal, thought Maisie. *That's not a crime, after all.*

Before going back inside, she peeped in through the slot window to the stage door hallway. Harriet Belt was there, of course. So was Barry Goodbody. Harriet had him sitting in her chair and was – surprisingly – doing something to his ear. Maisie pushed the door open.

'Miss Cooper, there you are,' said Mrs Belt. 'That's handy.'

'Has someone been asking for me?' Maisie asked.

'No, dear me, no. I just mean, with all that's going on, it's good to know where everyone is and how they're doing.'

'I suppose it is,' Maisie agreed.

'Now, have you heard?'

Maisie dearly wanted to leave. Barry Goodbody was looking at her, red faced, with something bordering on hatred in his close-set eyes as Harriet held his head at an angle, the dropper from some kind of medication held poised between the first finger and thumb of her right hand. But she found she wanted to know the news more.

'Have I heard what?'

'That Arab man's gone abroad.'

'Has he?' asked Maisie, feeling a lurch. Jack gone and now Mohammed, too. 'Where?'

'To Paris, to the embassy. His embassy,' Mrs Belt clarified, as if that was suspicious in itself. 'No smoke without fire, is there? And, if he's making a run for it, there must be a reason.'

Maisie thought Mohammed had probably gone abroad to escape the possible taint of scandal.

'I don't think travelling to Paris on national business,' she said, 'is "making a run for it". Mr As-Sabah is an important member of the Kuwaiti diplomatic staff.'

'Is he now?' said Harriet. 'Do tell.'

'Mrs Belt,' said Barry, 'could you please—'

'Yes, what am I thinking?'

Harriet squeezed the medication into Barry's ear then put the dropper back into the neck of a dark-brown medicine bottle. Barry found the wad of cotton wool on her desk and packed it tightly into his ear.

'That's better,' said Harriet, with a foolish laugh.

Maisie hurried away along the dressing room corridor, past wardrobe and Fort Knox and John Hermanson's room, and knocked on Adélaïde's door. There was no answer, and it was locked. She paused for a moment, listening to the tannoy. It sounded like another choral rehearsal for the minor characters – many voices singing in unison. Then she heard some solo lines and deduced that the principals were also involved – some of them, at least. John Hermanson seemed to be leading the rehearsal, which wasn't surprising. He was clearly very musical.

Maisie walked on to the far end of the corridor and stopped outside the green room. She could hear voices from the far side of the door. It was slightly ajar.

'Well?' someone shouted. 'What do you say?'

Maisie could only just catch the faint reply.

'Don't be such a prig, Neil.'

The other voice came loud and clear into the corridor.

'A prig? But you're clearly out of your mind. Nothing I have been able to say has made any difference. Not one woman, not two, but three. And that is on top of your debts – debts that I have done my best to help you to pay because of our relationship. But there are limits. If you are determined to waste your talent and alienate everyone you have ever worked with, that is for you to decide but, believe me, you have exhausted my patience. You have reached the end of your rope. I wouldn't be surprised if Dorothy tells me to sack you. What will you do then?'

If there was an answer from the other voice, Maisie didn't hear it. After a second or two, a door slammed, probably the one that led outdoors onto the theatre terrace. Then there were footsteps coming towards her, so she hopped back.

NVE came storming out, his eyes on the ground, swearing to himself in Dutch, not noticing her presence. Once he had disappeared through the door into the public foyer, Maisie went quickly into the green room and over to the terrace door. Who had NVE been reading the riot act to? She had an idea, but she wanted to be sure.

She opened the door to the terrace and looked left and right. No one. She was too late.

She ran back, following NVE through into the foyer, hoping to catch whoever it was coming in through one of the public doors. There, though, she discovered that the choral rehearsal had concluded and the entire company was milling about in their cumbersome eighteenth-century costumes and wigs, getting ready for a photocall.

*

Maisie watched the work of the photographer for a few minutes, wishing she had opened the green room door, if only for a fraction of a second, to witness whatever was going on with her own eyes. Her job was to protect Adélaïde. She suspected that NVE's tirade had something to do with his female star and hoped it hadn't been preceded by something that had happened while she wasn't at her post.

It's not my fault Fred Nairn needed an extra half-hour of my time, she told herself.

Maisie returned to the green room. In the centre of the dining table was Clive Canning's lifetime achievement award, shaped like a graceful obelisk in crystal. On a table in the corner was an alarm clock and the Airfix model of a Spitfire fighter plane. No more work had been done to it. A fine paintbrush had been left in a container of thinner, the bristles bent over and damaged. There was also something on the floor.

Maisie bent down and picked it up. It was the propeller, a very light piece of plastic, three points radiating from a tiny central hub. She supposed it must have been swept onto the dingy carpet by the draught from the slammed door.

She put it on the table, alongside the half-painted fuselage. Next to the model was a piece of newspaper. Idly, she picked it up and opened it out. It was the article about Adélaïde from the *Chichester Observer*. Around the photograph of Adélaïde's lovely face, someone had drawn a circle of hearts pierced with arrows.

Maisie smiled.

What a funny, childish thing to do.

Then, with a sinking of her heart, she realised. The Airfix model must have belonged to poor Keith Sadler, and this was his newspaper cutting, a symbol of his innocent unrequited love for a film star.

The door swung open behind her and the woman who served food in the green room came bustling in with her heated trolley.

'Don't mind me, dear. I'll be ready at twelve as usual.'

'No, I mean yes,' said Maisie, then she fled.

★

It was a horrible sensation, knowing she was right – feeling absolutely convinced that she must be right – when there was still a remote possibility that she was wrong.

Maisie was in the basement corridor where no one much went. She was standing in the opening into the under-stage area, looking into the gloom from which Keith's body had been removed.

She wasn't looking for clues. She wasn't so foolish as to think that she was better at crime scene investigation than Nairn's forensics team, Tindall and Wilson. She just needed somewhere to stand and think and breathe.

She went and sat down on the bottom step of the stairs that led up to the stage door, close to where she and Nairn had had their awkward, up-and-down conversation.

If it was, indeed, Keith's Airfix model, what did that mean?

Nothing. It had nothing to do with the safe or Mohammed's money or the bad luck of running into a murderer.

Or did it?

Perhaps, but Maisie couldn't see how.

She leaned back against the rough concrete wall, thinking about possible connections. Her two previous involvements in murder investigations had taught her that, with patience, it was possible to think one's way to a solution, as long as one had enough facts, enough clues as to character and motivation.

Or, if not a solution, one could develop an understanding of what was and what wasn't relevant.

Was that possible now?

She didn't think it was. She didn't feel that she knew enough – that anyone knew enough. Not her, not Nairn, not...

She wanted to say 'Not Jack' but Jack had disappeared, just when she needed him most.

Her hands were dusty from leaning on the steps. She stood up and rubbed them on her hanky. As an idea began to form in the back of her mind, her gestures slowed.

'Yes,' she said aloud.

Decided, she ran up the stairs to the stage door. She was pleased to see that Constable Barry Goodbody was outside in the car park, not lurking in the hallway.

'Mrs Belt,' she lied, 'Miss Amour has misplaced her dressing room key. Could you help? I wondered if your pass key might get me in?'

'I don't know.' Harriet turned and looked at the key board, blinking as if seeing it for the very first time. 'I suppose it might.'

'I'll just run along with it, shall I? I won't be a moment. I expect she just took the lock off the latch and shut the door, leaving her key on the make-up counter.'

200

'Yes, yes, I quite see. And the star mustn't be contraried or vexed, must she,' said the elderly volunteer with an attempt at a girlish twinkle.

Maisie held out her hand.

'If you would?'

'Here you are.'

Maisie took the key and ran along the upper corridor. She went past Adélaïde's dressing room to the next door but one. The key turned easily in the lock and she slipped inside, closing it softly behind her.

It was a depressing room, she thought, though it was hard to say why. It smelled of tobacco, as she had expected it to. The window was open a crack and the air felt damp. The street clothes on the hangers on the hooks on the left-hand wall – a pair of corduroy slacks, a greyish-white shirt – were poorly looked after, threadbare at the cuffs with other marks from wear and imperfect washing.

On the make-up counter were a small white bottle of eye drops and a leather make-up pouch, as well as a quarter bottle of scotch. The whisky bottle hadn't been opened. She sniffed the drinking glass. It had been used only for water. The whisky was perhaps for a special occasion, not a regular indulgence.

On the back of the chair, at an angle to the mirror, was a nicely cut jacket in black-and-grey tweed. With a feeling of revulsion – for herself and for the untidy pockets she was rifling – she quickly laid out the contents on the counter: a comb; a stub of pencil; some hard-to-read handwritten notes on a scrap of theatre notepaper; a packet of ten Silk Cut cigarettes; a box of Swan Vesta matches; a filthy hanky; a cheque book containing a sheaf of betting slips, all of them torn half through to indicate that they were losing wagers; a car key.

Feeling still more like she was doing something criminal, Maisie leafed through the cheque book. It was well kept with a balance recorded on every stub. Each one she looked at, coming closer and closer to the present day, was inscribed with a higher and higher number.

Sadly, the numbers were all preceded by a minus sign.

She put the miscellaneous objects away again, making sure to return them all to the correct pockets.

What had she learned?

Firstly, she thought she knew whose car was rusting through at the sills, with a boot that was only held closed by a bungee strap, because she now knew for certain that Andrew P Bradshaw was a gambler and that he appeared to be in serious debt.

Second, she was almost certain that Andrew had been the subject of NVE's tirade in the green room.

Third, she felt sorry for him.

TWENTY-SIX

Maisie returned the pass key and thanked Harriet for her co-operation.

'Please don't tell anyone. Adélaïde hates the idea people might think her disorganised.'

'No, of course. You found it then?'

It took Maisie a moment to catch up with what Harriet meant.

'Yes, her key was on the counter, like I thought.'

Maisie made her way round into the foyer and found the company still busy with the photographer. She went into the auditorium where the stage was lit as if for a daytime scene, but with no one about. She took a seat to one side, thinking about NVE's tirade – about being personally let down, about having protected Andrew, if it was Andrew.

But who else could it be? The key phrase, surely, was: 'Not one woman, not two, but three.'

Wasn't it obvious that NVE was talking about the women in the company that Andrew was carrying on with – or that he had sought to carry on with – and therefore offended in some way?

Who were they?

Andrew was clearly in some kind of entanglement with Winnie Brahms. And it was an entanglement that Maisie thought he would probably like to escape from, not that Winnie appeared to have noticed, given that she didn't miss an opportunity to play up to him.

And previously? Adélaïde?

At some point in London – probably more than once – Andrew had tried it on with Adélaïde and had, like NVE, been rebuffed. She thought he must have gone quite far – how far? – because his behaviour had led to Adélaïde becoming properly angry and threatening Dorothy with leaving the production.

In Maisie's opinion, that wasn't an insignificant threat. Making a success of Polly Peachum on the big stage meant a lot to Adélaïde. She wouldn't have raised the possibility of throwing it all away without strong cause.

Then, there was the third woman, whose story seemed more complicated. Maisie believed she knew who that was, too.

Before she could explore the idea, her train of thought was interrupted by activity on the stage. It was Micky Petherick and his team of stagehands in their black shirts and trousers. They were wheeling on the mobile scaffold, the gantry from which Macheath was due to be hanged, and were looking down at the boards for the marks that told them where exactly the structure should be positioned. It was made of heavy timber, but moved quite easily on its casters, with five rough steps up to a platform about four feet above the level of the stage. In the centre of the platform were the two hinged panels of a trapdoor.

Once it was correctly positioned, Micky went round the four corners, treading on the brakes on the casters to make sure it could no longer move. Then he climbed up to inspect the mechanism, the older grey-haired stagehand hauling on a lever at ground level.

The trapdoor crashed open, the two panels swinging down on their hinges, clearly visible to the audience in the gap between the platform and the stage, thudding into the solid framework. Maisie heard Micky's voice telling his team:

'That seems to be working nicely. Where's the bloody sign, though?'

The younger blond stagehand passed it up. Micky took it and attached it to the crossbeam of the scaffold, between the heavy post and the far end where the noose was tied. It was a panel of rough wood. On both sides had been scorched in rough letters: 'Tyburn Tree.'

'Now let's get on with checking the safety,' said Micky. He called up to the lighting box. 'Sam? You there?'

There was a pause then Sam Smithers – who was, Maisie remembered, a co-congregationist with Fred Nairn at a local church – came out of his lighting box right up at the back.

'What do you need?' he called.

'Give us the dawn state from the hanging, would you, Sam,' Micky shouted.

Sam moved down through the seats to where he had temporarily set up his lighting desk on an old door as a table. The lighting changed from the daytime wash of warm light, most of it coming from directly above, as if it was midday, to something colder and much more oblique. Maisie slipped out of her seat and made her way to the front row, admiring the way Sam had combined blue light for night and a few rays – hardly any, in fact – of horizontal yellow-orange to suggest the sunrise. The faces of the men on the stage became sinister, deeply shadowed.

'Let's go again,' said Micky. 'I'll be Macheath. I weigh about the same. He's taller but I'm wider. You clip me in.'

Maisie felt a frisson of anxiety as Micky put his head in the noose. One of the crew passed him a harness that he stepped into and pulled up over his jeans, securing it round his waist. The other stagehand clipped a safety line to the back of the harness, connected high up on the heavy post. Then the two black-shirted helpers climbed down and stood back.

'All set? Everyone clear? You don't want to get hit by the panels of the trapdoor when they swing open.'

Everyone took an extra step away. Maisie felt herself shrinking unnecessarily into her seat in the front row. This was going to be a very effective and nerve-wracking moment in the climax of the play.

'Does anyone remember the line?' asked Micky.

None of the stage crew did.

'Is it: "Tell the sheriff's officers I am ready"?' said Maisie.

'Blimey,' said Micky. 'I didn't know you were there.'

'I'm sorry. Am I doing the wrong thing? Is this private?'

'No, of course not. You're one of us now. Have you been learning it, though?'

'I know the play from school. And someone mentioned it the other day.' She had an odd reluctance to say it was Adélaïde who had quoted it. 'But isn't it supposed to be funny? You know, with Macheath being ironic, saying hanging is better than all those women wanting a piece of him? With this slant light, surely, it's going to be very macabre?'

'That's how the Boss wants it.'

'And Macheath is actually going to be hanged on stage?'

'Not "actually" hanged, but the director's playing against the laugh.'

'It looks very dangerous.'

'It isn't,' said Micky confidently. 'Otherwise, I wouldn't be putting my head in the noose, would I?'

'How does it work?'

'Someone pull the lever,' he called.

The older stagehand did as he was told. The trap opened with a clunk beneath Micky's feet and the two heavy panels swung away beneath him on their hinges, thumping into the framework below. Micky remained suspended in mid-air, having fallen only about six inches, caught by the line they had attached to the back of his harness, the noose slack around his neck. He waved his arms, as if he was swimming.

'*Oh, I do like to be beside the seaside*,' he sang, and Maisie laughed.

'Well, that works,' called Sam. 'Nice one, Micky.'

'It doesn't look much now,' said Micky, 'but once we adjust the rope precisely for Mr Bradshaw's height it will look, from out front, like it's been pulled tight. Then he'll jiggle about a bit, you know, struggling for a few seconds, jerking the rope, then we go dark.'

Micky and the stage crew tried the trapdoor twice more, shortening the noose and applying some oil to the mechanism of the lever, then kicked off the brakes and wheeled the whole contraption off-stage again, through the wide warehouse doors, just as the company came filtering in from the foyer.

Adélaïde came to join Maisie in the front row, wearing her costume but with a new waistcoat in a slightly different satin – a rather lovely burgundy colour. Maisie supposed that Beryl Vere had worked all through the night to make it as a replacement for the bloodstained one taken away by the police.

Maisie looked round for Kitty and saw that both Adélaïde's and Kitty's outfits were now completed with elbow-length gloves in soft chestnut leather. Kitty was still wearing the blue waistcoat. Would that be a problem? No, of course not. The whole point of Kitty's understudy role was that she would never be on at the same time as Adélaïde.

'How was this morning,' Maisie asked, 'before the photo-call?'

'The same,' said Adélaïde.

'I was worried that I was away too long.'

Adélaïde gave her a dazzling smile.

'You are so kind. It is almost a shame that you should have to live amongst us.'

'You mean the "rogues and scoundrels" of the theatre?' Adélaïde laughed lightly.

'I do,' she said, but her eyes looked worried. 'The press night is almost here,' she went on. 'This photocall makes it real. I am terrified.'

Fair enough, Maisie told herself. *But there's something else as well. I'm sure of it.*

TWENTY-SEVEN

Watching the rehearsal that afternoon, Maisie's first thought was: *Adélaïde has nothing to worry about. She's shown enough times that she has that special something to command the stage. The only issue will be whether she has the stamina to last the whole run of eight shows a week.*

As the rehearsal progressed, her second thought was: *How far they've come.*

Maisie had changed position in the auditorium because she was interested to see Sam Smithers at work on his lighting board. His assistant – the one who had been off with flu – had finally made it in to work and was sitting nearby with a reel-to-reel tape recorder, responsible for the sound cues. Kitty Farrell was close at hand and Maisie took advantage to try and build the young woman up.

'You really think I'm all right?' whispered Kitty. 'You don't think I'm going to let everyone down.'

'Concentrate on yourself, on your own integrity and professionalism,' advised Maisie, *sotto voce*, 'and I'm convinced of it. You must feel that, in your heart of hearts?'

'When I hear you say it,' replied Kitty, timidly, 'I think I do.'

In a way, this run-through was like a grown-up version of the first rehearsal Maisie had attended, the difference being that the actors hardly needed to stop at all. By four-thirty they had completed almost the whole show. All that was left was the hanging scene.

The way NVE had organised the climax was to make sure that everyone was on, all twenty-two actors, including four minor female cast members carrying bundles of swaddling clothes to give the impression of Macheath's multiple illegitimate children. They progressed to the point where Macheath was about to mount the scaffold, then NVE clapped his hands and everyone stopped, holding their positions.

Micky climbed up onto the scaffold and Maisie took a moment to recognise him. He was in costume, in a shabby coat and breeches of brown velvet, presumably so that he could take responsibility for the fake hanging, coming on as if he were a member of the cast, setting the harness and verifying the correct length for the rope.

Andrew P Bradshaw climbed up beside him in his long riding coat with his long silvery waistcoat underneath. Because both the riding coat and the waistcoat were slit up the back, held together with Velcro, it was possible for Micky to get at the harness Andrew was wearing underneath and attach it to the safety line. They tried it a couple of times, making sure Andrew's body masked what Micky was doing from the audience. NVE got the other actors to make sure their own actions drew attention away from them.

While all this was going on, Maisie contemplated what would happen if the harness failed. Andrew would fall through the trapdoor, perhaps hurting himself – twisting or even breaking an ankle. Then she saw Micky pulling on the noose.

No, of course, that wouldn't happen because Andrew's head would be in the noose.

'Sam, isn't this dangerous?' asked Maisie, quietly.

'In what way?'

'What if something goes wrong with the safety line or the harness?'

'That's why they keep checking it.'

Maisie watched them doing exactly that.

'A noose is such a sinister shape.'

'It isn't actually a noose,' said Sam. 'It just looks like one.'

Yes, of course, Maisie realised. *That was why Micky was pulling on it, to show that it wasn't a slipknot, that it would never pull tight around the neck of the actor.*

NVE clapped his hands again.

'Reset, please,' said Micky.

The actors all stood up a little straighter, each one finding their own trigger movement to return to their roles. Andrew climbed down off the scaffold and went upstage, so he could be brought in by Mr Lockit of Newgate Prison, his hands bound behind his back, through the warehouse doors with the slum-vista beyond. Sam made a tweak to the lighting – the 'dawn state' – blue with a few rays of slant sunlight.

'Go,' called Micky.

Suddenly, everyone was in movement. Upstage, standing on a barrel, John Hermanson as the Beggar was making a speech from the very end of the play about needing to tie everything together and provide the audience with a proper resolution to all the narrative questions, and Maisie realised that NVE had changed the order of events in the script, so that the 'hanging' would be the very last thing to occur.

John's lovely bass voice stopped and one of the minor actors began beating a slow rhythm on a drum as Andrew was brought forward to the scaffold. The women in the company sang a reprise of the Tyburn Tree song, to the tune of 'Greensleeves', but very high and insistent, turning on the spot like dervishes. Andrew climbed up and Maisie only noticed what Micky was up to with the safety harness because she had seen it rehearsed. All the other 'business' would definitely distract the real audience.

Micky climbed down, leaving Andrew alone on the trap door. Throughout all this action, Adélaïde and Winnie were standing together, distraught, as Polly Peachum and Lucy Lockit, Macheath's lovers, holding one another's hands as if sharing their grief for the man they were both about to lose. The four mothers of Macheath's illegitimate children made their own mute appeal and Andrew spoke his final line – the final line of the play in NVE's re-working.

'Tell the sheriff's officers I am ready.'

Micky pulled the lever and the trap door opened. The two heavy panels swung down and thumped against the frame below the platform. Andrew dropped about eight or ten inches and was caught by the harness. Andrew jerked his shoulders and legs, twitching and grunting. Maisie knew he was safe, but for a few seconds she couldn't believe it. His acting was so convincing that Maisie almost believed she should run down to the stage to save him.

Then Sam punched the master cut-out on the lighting board and everything went dark.

*

How long did the darkness last?

When, at last, it was over, Maisie wished she had counted the seconds. All she knew was that, when Sam turned on the working lights and NVE stood up out of his seat to say 'well done', she had been holding her breath.

Up on the scaffold, Andrew was laughing as Micky swung him away from the trapdoor opening and helped him to stand on tiptoe to one side. The two stagehands ran on from backstage to reset the trapdoor. Micky unhooked the harness and, at a word from NVE, called out: 'We'll take the director's notes now, please. All on.'

To start with, the actors milled about, looking for somewhere to perch. When it quickly became clear that most would end up cross-legged on the floor, NVE said: 'Other way round, Micky. Actors in the stalls, director on stage.'

Two minutes later, everyone was settled and NVE was sitting on the edge of the scaffold, his legs swinging, with a copiously marked-up copy of the script in his hands, the heavy post and cross beam above him, the noose almost directly above his head.

*

Later on, looking back, once she had separated it from everything else that happened, Maisie felt privileged to have been present, seeing at first hand the extraordinary combination of generosity, professionalism, attention to detail and creative integrity shown to even the most minor of the performers.

NVE began by saying that he was very pleased, that there would be no more changes of any kind, that the rehearsals from this point on would serve only one purpose – to practise what they had learned, nothing more.

'Just before we go on,' said Andrew, 'to start at the end, was the drop enough? I thought perhaps it could have been longer. I mean, did it look like anything from out front. It needs to be shocking, doesn't it?'

'It does need to be shocking,' said NVE, 'and you need to play your part with much less desire to excite the audience's sympathy. I have told you, Andrew, you are not a "goodie" in this play.'

'Yes, all right. I'll make him sharp as a tack, bitter as gall and devious as a fox,' said Andrew.

'Or a rat,' said Kitty.

Yes, thought Maisie. *Kitty Farrell must be the third actress to have made complaints about Andrew P Bradshaw.*

'But is the drop enough?' Andrew insisted.

'You don't want to hurt yourself, Mr Bradshaw,' said Micky. 'How was the harness?'

'It was fine,' Andrew laughed. 'If you're worrying about my man parts, Micky, you'll be pleased to hear that they remain in fully functioning working order.'

Winnie tittered ingratiatingly and Andrew gave her a wink.

Kitty said: 'Oh God, must we?'

'If Micky says it's safe,' said NVE, 'and you're sure, Andrew, we can lengthen the drop.' NVE looked round. 'Miss Cooper, are you about?'

Maisie raised her hand.

'Up here.'

NVE found her with his eyes, up by the lighting desk.

'You've not seen it before. What did you think?' he asked her.

'I found it very shocking and convincing,' she told him.

'Fine,' said Andrew. He didn't turn round in his seat to look at her. 'If Miss Cooper is the oracle, I bow to her greater wisdom.'

'I will start with the prologue,' said NVE. 'There was a problem upstage left, wasn't there? What happened?'

*

The notes session lasted for more than an hour and, throughout NVE's notes, Maisie remained in her seat by the lighting board. At each query, the relevant actor or actors responded, asked for direction, nodded and promised to bear the note in mind. Because the rhythm of the notes was steady and unhurried, she found it an excellent backdrop to organising her thoughts, analysing the characters of the principal actors, their enmities and alliances.

She began with Adélaïde's resentment at both NVE and Andrew. Both men had made life difficult for Adélaïde by assuming that she would want them to make love to her. She thought that Andrew's advances had all been made in

London because she had seen no evidence of them in Chichester. NVE, on the other hand, had propositioned Adélaïde at the Dolphin & Anchor, perhaps as a result of their relative isolation, being the only two members of the company – plus Dorothy, the producer – who had been lodged in the more expensive hotel rooms, rather than digs around the town.

If the two men were rivals for the affection of Adélaïde Amour, they were also in thrall to her, almost. There was no show without the star, as Dorothy had said, more than once.

For a minute or two, Maisie was drawn out of her reverie as NVE's notes moved on to act two with a sequence of complimentary remarks. Maisie heard Adélaïde thank him for one particularly warm approval, reinforcing the impression that Adélaïde was only being given positive notes and wondered if the other actors might find that grating.

'Don't you agree, Dorothy?' said NVE.

Maisie saw that Miss Dean was in the stalls, close to the stage on the left of the auditorium.

'I think we have a hit on our hands,' said Dorothy, warmly.

NVE resumed his notes, turning a page in his copy of the script.

Maisie began to wonder – assuming the other actors took Adélaïde's star-billing in their stride – if Adélaïde might be resentful of Dorothy Dean? The first time Maisie had met the two women, they had been utterly at loggerheads and, Maisie thought, Dorothy hadn't seemed very willing to take Adélaïde's complaints seriously, except insofar as they threatened the smooth running of the production.

And how much money did Dorothy Dean have riding on the show? Was the theatre in trouble in some way? It had earned no money over the long winter months, obviously. And Dorothy had been very quick to buttonhole Mohammed and tap him for additional funds. Was that normal? Didn't it seem a little amateurish?

The trouble was, she didn't really know. In the odd bubble of the theatre, with the exciting but intimidating finishing line of the press night so close at hand, she was no more than a callow ingénue.

Thinking of money, her mind went back to Andrew and what NVE had shouted at him in the green room, when he thought he was speaking in private because the whole company was in the foyer for the photocall.

And that is on top of your debts – debts that I have done my best to help you to pay because of our relationship.

What relationship? Friends? How long had they been friends? Oh, yes, Andrew had mentioned it at the lunch table in the green room.

Nearly all my life.

Was that theatrical hyperbole? In any case, it would surely place them both at theatre school together in Bristol. That was definitely where Andrew had trained. She knew that because Clive Canning had been so dismissive of it.

I have never respected the Bristol training and I see now that I was right to take that attitude.

Could NVE have been there as well?

'Sam,' she whispered. 'Do you know how NVE and Andrew know one another?'

'I don't, sorry,' he whispered.

The thought of Clive Canning brought Maisie back to the family relationship between Clive and Esther and Kitty. Maisie was sure now that Kitty was their daughter. Did they know that Andrew was the reason Kitty kept bursting into tears – that it wasn't just because she feared being a poor understudy for the star? Maisie remembered what she had said, back at that first lunch in the green room.

How marvellous to work together as a family.

Maisie's innocent remark had caused them all to become quiet and tense.

NVE's notes moved on to the song whose last verse Adélaïde had decided to speak with the Beggar singing in his deep voice in the background. It prompted Maisie to consider John Hermanson's clear antagonism towards Andrew, focused on Adélaïde once more. Adélaïde had told Maisie that John loved her and seemed annoyed at the idea, as if it was a foolish and unnecessary complication. John, though, hadn't importuned Adélaïde, as far as Maisie knew.

NVE's notes were moving on quite quickly, now. Maisie moved down the stalls to sit closer to Adélaïde. Because the working lights were on, everyone was starkly lit and, from her new position, Maisie was able to compare Esther's bone structure with Kitty's.

There was a resemblance, she decided, although Esther's symmetrical features were softened by age and her love of good wholesome food. Kitty was five or six inches taller than Esther, but that height could easily have been inherited from Clive who was probably six-foot-one, as well as being very round about the middle.

There was a brief note for Winnie Brahms as Lucy Lockit, something to do with the moment when Macheath was being taken into custody by her father, the jailer. Winnie got up out of her seat and sidled along the row to find herself next to Andrew.

'Like this?' she asked, and put her hands either side of Andrew's head, pulling his face onto her bosom.

'Oh, God,' said Kitty.

'Love it, darling,' said NVE. 'Love. It.'

Maisie sighed. How had Fred Nairn described Winnie?

That rather luscious piece.

Maisie supposed it was true. Winnie was curvaceous and smiley and seemed to be all the time in movement, as if constantly engaged in some kind of mating display – and always with a sole aim.

Andrew P Bradshaw, again.

Winnie flopped back in the seat next to him and rested her head on his shoulder. Andrew brushed her untidy updo away from his face.

Ten more minutes passed before the notes session at last drew to a close. Andrew once more asked if the drop on the rope could be made longer to increase the visual impact. NVE told him to discuss it with Micky and find a moment to try it out, but to take no risks.

And that was it. The time was just after five-thirty. The company was dismissed until five to seven, what Micky called 'the half'.

NVE concluded the meeting with:

'Curtain-up at seven-thirty – although there is no curtain, because of this enormous thrust stage – then we will perform, from first line to last line, without stopping, except for an interval of fifteen minutes, as if it was an actual show in front of Chichester's most assiduous theatregoers.' He took a breath. 'You're all going to be wonderful. You know it. I know it. We're going to practise and keep our level, our focus. For all of you, this production will become a reference point in your careers – a production you can all look back on with pride. People will say: "*The Beggar's Opera* at Chichester? Were you in that?" And you will modestly reply: "You've heard about it? How kind." For myself, I absolutely couldn't be more pleased.'

There was a round of applause and NVE jumped down from the scaffold. Before he could leave, however, another short speech was made.

'On behalf of the company,' said Clive Canning, pompously, getting to his feet and turning left and right to take in his fellow thespians, 'might I take this opportunity of thanking you, NVE, for your inspired and sensitive direction, for the welcome afforded to us by this remarkable theatre, for the magnificent and eerie set, the dramatic and expressive lighting, the clever and evocative costumes. Finally, might I wish my colleagues, every last one of them, all the good fortune that their integrity and the truth of their performance merits.'

He sat down. There was a little chorus of approval – 'oh, yes' and 'hear-hear' and 'seconded'.

Taken at face value, Maisie was thinking, *that was a nicely phrased compliment. But what about those members of the company – that one particular member of the company, perhaps? – that Clive Canning didn't believe merited 'good fortune' for the 'integrity and the truth of their performance'?*

V

SPECTACLE

Twenty-Eight

At Chichester police station, it was towards the end of the regular working day as well, not that all activity would cease. That was a similarity between police work and the business of theatre. While there was work to be done, no one would go home.

Jack arrived, in plain clothes rather than in uniform because he wasn't officially on duty. Whereas Maisie had focused her mind on character and motivation, Jack's first instinct was to discuss opportunity – both for the theft and for the murder. Inspector Fred Nairn looked grumpy.

'I seem to have reached a dead end,' he said. 'Several of them.'

'Go on,' Jack encouraged him.

'The statements we've taken and the evidence we've gathered points to everyone and no one. The only concrete thing we've got,' said Fred, 'I mean the only definitive evidence that emerges from the mess, is a print.'

'A fingerprint?' asked Jack, interested.

'No such luck.' Nairn pointed to two photographs on the cork board. Jack leaned in to get a better look. 'This is where Keith Sadler's body was hidden,' said Nairn, pointing at the left-hand image.

In the stark light of the camera flash, it showed the basement storage room, containing two standard lamps, two dining chairs with raffia seats, three rolled up carpets and a stack of stage curtains, folded in a pile.

'The print comes from one of these bits of furniture?' Jack guessed.

'Yes.' Nairn pointed to the right-hand photograph, a brightly lit close-up of a timber shaft, dusted to reveal its clue. 'From one of the standard lamps.'

'Because the murderer moved it in order to get at the curtains,' Jack suggested.

'Presumably.'

'While still in a rush, full of adrenaline.'

'But thinking clearly enough to put on a glove,' said Nairn wearily. They both examined the right-hand photograph. 'It's leather. Pretty high quality, I'd say. Kidskin. Unique in its own way,' said Nairn, hopefully. 'I mean, what's a finger-print? It's the mark left by your skin.'

'Good enough to present as evidence?'

'If we find the glove, yes. There's plenty of precedent.'

'Yes,' said Jack, 'the grain of the leather, the creases from use… But the issue is being able to prove ownership of the glove. I mean, let's say we found it stuffed in a dark corner in the theatre or in a bin in the car park.' He paused. 'Have we checked?'

'Yep. Nothing.'

'Okay, but say we found it somewhere, then we'd have the problem of not being able to prove that said owner was wear-ing it at a particular time—'

'The moment of the murder,' cut in Nairn, 'after midnight on Monday.'

'And now it's Wednesday evening and—'

'All right,' said Nairn. 'Don't rub it in. *Tempus fugit.*'

Jack ran his finger down the cast list, pinned up in the cor-ner of the cork board.

'Time flies, indeed. Who do you fancy, Fred?' he asked.

'Well, the car someone drives is usually a pretty good indi-cation of how they're doing – financially I mean.'

'Yes, I thought that, too. And there's two nice ones and an old banger. Anyone else come down by car?'

'No, the rest all took the train and walked or got a Dunnaways taxi to their digs. But I know what you're getting at. You want me to say for certain that it's one of this lot.' Nairn gestured to the cast list as Jack had done. 'You want me to say that it couldn't have been an outsider and I'd like to, but you can't exclude your Maisie's idea that young Keith Sadler might have opened the door and let someone in.'

'Not my Maisie,' said Jack once more. 'Is there any chance Keith could have seen the moment when the money was put in the safe?'

'You mean that he was in on it and had a partner who then did him in?'

'Or someone came upon him by accident, carrying away the loot, and did him in.'

'Snatched the cash box out of his hands and used it to knock him down and out?'

'Yes.'

'But what would they be doing there, if it was a chance meeting?' argued Nairn.

'Well, it brings us back to the theatre crowd. They've got reasons for being in the building, haven't they, when no one else has, even late at night? But what about my question? Did Keith see the business with the safe?'

'No.'

'Sure and certain?'

'On the morning in question,' said Nairn in his courtroom voice, 'Keith Sadler worked his breakfast shift, then was busy with prep for lunch and deliveries at the hotel. He was nowhere near the theatre at the time Miss Dean was depositing Mr As-Sabah's down payment in the office safe. I'd say the odds of it being an outsider are long.'

'If you'd been the one to kill the nightwatchman, you wouldn't want to be carrying him away across the car park in full view. You'd look for a dark corner to hide him and—'

'Yes, all right,' said Nairn. 'You and I have been over all that.'

There was a pause as they scanned the evidence.

'What's your plan, then?' asked Jack, at last.

'I've been hoping to see someone come into the theatre with a new fur coat or something.'

'Having spent the money, you mean?'

'Exactly. I asked Barry to keep an eye out at the stage door, but he's not seen anything.'

'No new watches or necklaces? He might have missed something like that.'

'I told him to keep a sharp eye. I know he's let you down in the past, Jack, but he's doing his best. That kid he pulled out of the canal would be dead without him.'

'Oh, I know,' said Jack. 'It's only because I think he's got the making of a good copper that I've been trying to get him to understand what's required.'

'Attention to detail, working when you're tired.'

'Respect for authority, respect for the job, respect for the public.'

'He's got a long way to go, then,' laughed Nairn.

'He has.' Jack smiled. 'But he didn't deserve the ear infection he picked up from the stagnant canal water.'

'Do any of us,' asked Nairn, 'get precisely what we deserve?'

'Not at first,' said Jack, almost to himself, looking at Maisie's statement, pinned up just beneath the cast list. 'But maybe in the end.'

TWENTY-NINE

Back at the theatre, as the cast dispersed from the stage – Adélaïde going to rest in her dressing room – the atmosphere changed.

There was an end-of-term feel about the place, Maisie thought. But why was that? Shouldn't it be the opposite, a start-of-term feeling? Weren't they all about to try and put on a complete performance for the first time, albeit to an empty theatre?

She supposed it was because of what NVE had said, that there would be no more changes, no more cuts or additions, that the script and the moves were set. Now, it was just a question of practising – and they had time to get it right.

Micky came to sit by her in the front row.

'All right, then?'

'Very well, thank you.'

There was a pause and Maisie wondered if she was keeping Micky from anything. They were the only ones left in the auditorium.

'Am I in the way, here?' she asked.

'No,' said Micky. 'Not at all.'

Maisie realised that she would be helping Micky take a break if she stayed where she was for a chat. She asked him about the schedule for the next two days.

'Performance tonight, as live,' he said, 'as you heard. The Boss doesn't like us to call it a dress rehearsal. He says we've been dressed most of the week, so there you are. Then we all go to our digs. The cast will mostly sleep in late while me and my boys crack on, then notes at eleven, followed by a slow lunch and maybe practise a couple of things, then all on stage to walk it through in the afternoon.'

'What does "walk it through" mean exactly?'

'You've seen it a couple of times. It's something the Boss likes to do. He's very protective of the actors' voices – their energy, too. Look at Miss Amour. She can duck out whenever she feels like it. I bet she's got it in her to last the course. Still, the Boss wants to take care.'

'Hence the understudy always being available.'

'Yeah, poor little Miss Kitty.' He shifted in his seat. 'Anyway, walking it through, that's essentially a performance to one another, making sure the lines and the moves are all solid, like practising a golf shot.'

Maisie was good at golf – though she had never really taken to it because four hours always felt like a very long time to be chasing a little white ball – so she knew what he meant.

'You mean "grooving" the performance.'

'So that it becomes second nature. Then everyone will have time for a bit of a kip or a walk in the fresh air before the press night performance in the evening.'

'Yes, press night is tomorrow, Thursday,' said Maisie, counting the days in her head. 'Already.'

'Have you lost track?'

'I don't know how you do it,' she laughed. 'Time is very relative inside this building.'

'Do you think?' said Micky, looking like he thought she might be mentally deficient. 'Then, Friday, the call will be two o'clock to walk it through once more, nice and quiet but full pace, getting ready for the second performance – always a tricky one – in the evening.'

'And each time the call will be "the half" at five to seven? Why is it called the "half"?'

'We call "beginners" five minutes before the show goes up. That's when the actors have to find their positions – in the wings or on stage, ready for lift off. They need to be in the building thirty minutes before that, so the half is half-an-hour plus five minutes.'

'I see. And "goes up" because of the raising of the curtain?'

He nodded.

'Which in this case, we do not have.' He looked round, twisting in his seat. Maisie thought he was making sure they weren't overheard. 'You've been a boon,' he told her, quietly.

'I have?'

'God, it was ructions each and every day up in London. I don't know exactly what you've done, but it's worked.'

It crossed Maisie's mind that Dorothy had perhaps asked Micky to come and thank her like this. What he was saying was more or less exactly what she and Dorothy had discussed at their first meeting, back at the hotel.

'I'm not sure I know either,' she said, 'but I'm glad.'

'I suppose it's two things, isn't it? Firstly, you've helped with the lines. Anyone can see that, but I reckon she would have got there in the end. The Boss said so and I've never known him to be wrong.'

Maisie wasn't sure that was true as Adélaïde had been on the point of giving up. But out loud, she agreed: 'She's very good now, isn't she?'

'Second, there's you being with her, like a force-field.'

'Really?'

'It wasn't just one. We had Mr Hermanson mooning about after her. You'd not know it now, but he'd fallen for her in a big way.'

'John "mooning about"?' said Maisie. 'That seems unlikely.'

229

'He was like a puppy dog, couldn't take his eyes off of her, telling her she was wonderful. Painful to watch, it was. And then, whenever Mr Bradshaw was making his play, Mr Hermanson would go red and froth at the mouth.'

Maisie's mind was busy trying to recast John Hermanson as a lovesick suitor.

'But John doesn't take anything seriously,' she said at last. 'He's a sort of detached cynic.'

'Don't you believe it. He's got hidden depths, you know, and uses them in his performance, of course. He's what people call "a fine actor". That usually means a fruity voice and some old-school mannerisms but, in his case, I can go along with it. He's got something in the way he delivers it.'

'He's very listenable,' said Maisie.

'He used to be a drinker, you know, till not long ago. Almost did for him. This is his comeback. He needs to make a success of it.'

'I had no idea.'

'Positively begged the Boss for the opportunity. Fireworks, though. He's been dry for, what, eighteen months? But he's still got the temper.'

Maisie thought she had perhaps underestimated the intensity of the emotions that she had been shielding Adélaïde from.

'And he wasn't the only one?'

'After Miss Amour? No, it was all three of them.'

'So, Andrew and John – who else?'

'Then there was his nibs,' said Micky.

'Mr van Erde?'

'Yeah, that,' Micky laughed. 'Now, don't get me wrong. I'm as big a fan as you can get. I've been with the Boss twelve years and never a dull moment, but at the same time…' He shook his head. 'The public love his stuff. Yeah, he's the business.'

'So why do you laugh?'

'Just between you and me and the gatepost, his name's Neil, and his surname's not quite his mother's.'

'I don't follow.'

'Van Erde means "of the Earth", doesn't it, in Dutch. He made that up. His mother's Dutch and so it's fair enough he should take her name, van Ende, with a letter n, but he didn't like that. So, when he signed up with Equity, he gave it a little tweak.'

'Does anyone else know this?'

'Mr Bradshaw knew him back then. Very close, they were. Him it was who told me.'

'Is it a secret?' asked Maisie. She knew from recent experience that even very old secrets had a way of making themselves known. 'Would NVE be upset if it got out?'

Micky shrugged.

'The Boss would hate it, no question, but lots of them change their names.'

'To be memorable on the poster?'

'And they don't always get it right. Winnie Brahms?' Micky laughed. 'Who told her that was a good idea?'

'So, NVE made advances to Adélaïde?'

'Course he did. Way of the world, isn't it?'

Perhaps, thought Maisie, *but I wish it wasn't.*

'Did John know? Was he angry with NVE?'

'I would say coldly angry. You must have noticed the chill.'

Yes, thought Maisie. *That was true.*

'And Andrew?'

'Jealous as a viper.'

'But Andrew was the biggest problem in Town?'

'Terrible. Always the same, that one.'

'So why does NVE cast him? Doesn't he realise what he's like?'

'You'd think he would by now,' said Micky.

'Does Andrew have some kind of hold over NVE?' asked Maisie, feeling rather melodramatic. 'Or is there a debt between them?'

'I wouldn't be surprised. And, if there was, Mr Andrew P Bradshaw would play it for all it was worth. You can trust me on that.'

'You don't like him?'

'I can't stand him. If I could get him out of our orbit, me and the Boss, I'd do it like that.' He snapped his fingers. 'And the poor kid, he was after her from day one.'

'You mean Kitty?'

'Yeah, little Miss Farrell. She's too fragile for this business, but maybe she wouldn't be if she hadn't let Mr Bradshaw twist her round his little finger.'

Maisie wasn't surprised at Andrew's predatory behaviour – or with Kitty being his prey – but she was struck by the vehemence of Micky's tone.

'I see.'

'And he's putting the whole production at risk. Do you know how many jobs that is?' asked Micky, punching a heavy right fist into his left palm.

'The whole production?'

'Upsets right and left.'

'Have I understood correctly,' Maisie asked, 'that Esther and Clive Canning are Kitty's parents?'

'That's right.'

'What did they think – of Andrew toying with their daughter?'

'The parents got wind of it, of course, with Miss Farrell weeping in corners and looking side-eyes. Mr and Mrs Canning confronted Mr Bradshaw and weren't inclined to let it lie, though Miss Farrell asked them to. I reckon she still thinks there's a chance Mr Bradshaw will come back to her.'

'She couldn't be pregnant, could she?' asked Maisie.

Micky paused, judiciously.

'What would you say?'

'The thought only just came into my head,' Maisie answered.

'If she is, only she would know.'

'Of course. It would only be a few weeks. Might he have promised marriage?'

Micky laughed.

'Mr Bradshaw was never going to invite Miss Farrell up the aisle. There was no chance of that. Anyway, in the end, the pot boiled over and it was Mrs Esther Canning who went for him, pulled his hair and gave him a shove. Then Mr Canning piled in and he's a big bloke, so Mr Bradshaw left off.'

'Left off what?' said Maisie, confused.

'Taking advantage of Miss Farrell.'

Maisie frowned.

'If that's right, Andrew didn't cast Kitty off. Clive made him leave her alone. Do you think Kitty resents her parents' intrusion into her life?'

'It doesn't matter, does it? Mr Bradshaw's already moved on.'

'To Winnie.'

'To Miss Brahms,' said Micky, laughing again. 'Oi, look out.'

Maisie looked up at the stage. The two stagehands were coming on with Andrew and he appeared to be talking to them about the mechanism of the scaffold and the fake hanging.

'That bastard again,' said Micky. 'He's everywhere. I'd better go and see what he wants.'

THIRTY

For ten minutes, Maisie watched Micky, Andrew and the stagehands setting and resetting the special effect of the fake hanging, adjusting the length of the rope, lengthening the drop as Andrew had requested.

'You don't want the noose to take your ears off, Mr Bradshaw,' Micky warned.

'No, I don't. But I do want it to pull taut.'

'I know, I know.'

They tried it one more time.

'So, Miss Cooper,' called Andrew, 'you're the oracle, it seems. Did that work?'

'I think it was better, yes.'

'Good,' said Andrew. 'At least someone's on my side.'

Maisie said nothing. With all that she had learned, she was definitely not on Andrew P Bradshaw's side.

'While we're here,' said Micky, 'the only thing I'm worried about is getting you out of the noose and off the safety line for when we come out of blackout for the applause. I counted it in my head earlier on and I made it we were dark for seven seconds. We might manage it, but it will be tight.'

'Well, let's ask Sam to keep it black for a bit longer,' said Andrew.

Maisie left them to it, exiting the auditorium into the foyer. She went backstage to the green room. It was almost full, with a lively buzz of conversation from actors playing minor roles, without great responsibility, who were simply glad to be there, well-fed at the theatre's expense, making the most of their gainful employment.

She didn't stop, though. She wanted to make sure Adélaïde was happy, resting in her dressing room. As she approached, she was concerned to hear a man's voice, raised in anger. She hurried to open the door, ready to intervene.

It was John Hermanson, standing in the middle of the room, waving a bottle of whisky, already in costume but without the awful make-up.

'It's a bloody provocation and I won't stand for it. I'm going to the management.'

'What's happening?' Maisie asked.

'That bastard,' said John, and he flopped down onto the uncomfortable foam armchair. 'Don't worry, Miss Cooper. I'm not making a scene. I mean, I am, but you and Miss Amour are quite safe.' The whisky bottle was in his lap, cradled in his two hands, like something precious. 'Here, take this away, would you? I don't know if I'm more tempted to drink it or smash it over his bloody head.'

Maisie took the bottle and Adélaïde reached out a long arm for it.

'Let me keep it. I may need it to mix with lemon juice for a grog later in the run. Then, at least, it will serve.'

'I don't understand what's happened,' said Maisie.

'That bastard Bradshaw left it in my room to taunt me.'

Maisie thought back to what Micky had told her – that John Hermanson had been a drinker with a terrible temper. And she remembered seeing the untouched bottle in Andrew's dressing room when she had been snooping.

'But why would he do such a horrible thing?'

'Because it's what he's like.'

'Andrew is jealous because John loves me,' said Adélaïde, simply, 'and I love him, too, but not in the same way. Yet, we are still friends.'

'There's no way you could be friends with him,' said John, 'after what he's done.'

'You mean trying to take advantage of Kitty?' asked Maisie. 'Did you know this, Adélaïde?'

'He tried the same with me,' Adélaïde shrugged, 'but I am strong, and I am aware of a man's weakness.'

'He walked with a limp for two days afterwards,' said John with a smile of satisfaction. 'I wish NVE hadn't stopped Clive giving him the beating he deserved.'

Maisie frowned.

'What about Winnie Brahms? Does she know all this about him?'

'Winnie came late,' said John. 'She had a telly thing, so she missed the worst of it. By the time she joined the rehearsals at the Drill Hall, there was just the aftermath, the simmering discontent, and everyone doing their best to move on and make a great show. And people are discreet.' He shook his head. 'Not always. I mean, we're theatre, so we gossip, but, when the show is on the line, people tend to do their best to brush things under the carpet.'

'Because a lot of jobs depend upon it,' said Maisie, echoing what Micky had told her.

'Exactly.'

'I still don't understand why NVE casts Andrew if this isn't news to any of you,' said Maisie.

'What do you mean, "still", Maisie?' asked Adélaïde. 'Who have you been talking to?'

'I got the impression they'd worked together on and off for a long time,' Maisie prevaricated.

'They have,' said John. 'God, they even look alike.'

'They are brothers,' said Adélaïde, unexpectedly.

'You're joking.'

'No,' said Adélaïde.

'But yes, of course they are,' said John, sitting forward. 'That explains everything. Tell us more.'

'It came up. That is all.'

Maisie put her hands to her mouth.

'Adélaïde,' she said, 'of course, I heard you both.'

'What do you mean?'

'I overheard you. I didn't mean to. He was in your room at the hotel and your balcony is below my window. I think it was last Sunday. You and NVE were arguing – I mean, you were trying to send him packing. I was on the point of coming downstairs to interrupt and knock on the door or something. But now I remember what he said. "Am I not better looking than my brother?" And you told him he wasn't and he said he'd protected you from him – the brother, I mean – and you said—'

'I said "Not even",' cut in Adélaïde. 'He did not protect me from Andrew – hanging around me when I was not rehearsing, touching my arm, touching my hair, wanting to walk with me to my London hotel – a hotel I paid for, not the company, because the one chosen by Dorothy' – she pronounced it 'Dorothée' – 'well, it was more like a hostel for students.'

'You paid for your own accommodation in London?'

'I am rich. I am a star,' said Adélaïde, 'in the cinema.' She shook her head. 'But in Chichester there is nothing that can be done. The Dolphin & Anchor is the best there is, it seems, and it is no better than...' Again, she switched to French. *'Médiocre.'*

Maisie, defensive about her home town, felt they were getting off the point.

'Andrew repeatedly propositioned you and you had to keep rebuffing him?'

'Rebuffing?'

'Pushing back, turning him down.'

'Yes.'

'Up to the point where you—'

'Kicked him in the goolies,' interrupted Adélaïde with a broad smile. 'John taught me to say this.'

'So NVE's name is Bradshaw,' said John, laughing. 'Well, that branding isn't as good as Nils van Erde.'

'No, John,' Adélaïde explained. 'Their parents separated. Nils was raised in the Netherlands by the mother with one name and Andrew in England by the father with another.'

Maisie didn't tell them that Micky said NVE's name was actually Neil or the clever tweak he had given to his surname.

'Anyway,' said John, 'that explains why NVE puts up with him.'

Maisie thought about the losing betting slips she had seen in Andrew's room.

'He's short of money, though,' she said. 'And he has that terrible old rusting car.'

'I don't think so,' said Adélaïde.

'Yes, that coffee-coloured Morris Minor.'

'Oh, no,' said John. 'Andrew's is the sports car. He wouldn't be seen dead in anything less.'

'Whose is the one that's falling apart?' asked Maisie.

'NVE's,' John replied. 'He says: "It gets me from A to B – I need nothing else." It seems reliable enough.'

Maisie wondered if that was true. Morris Minors had a pretty dreadful reputation. Did Andrew have such a hold over NVE that the English-raised brother was bleeding the Dutch-raised brother dry and he couldn't afford a decent car while Andrew swanned about in his convertible?

'The time passes,' said Adélaïde. 'You should get ready, John. You have your make-up still to do.'

'All right.' He stood up. 'He hasn't also upset you, Miss Cooper, has he?'

'Upset me?' said Maisie, thinking about her first meeting with Andrew, and the heavy-handed flirtation at lunch in the green room. 'No.'

'Good.' John turned to Adélaïde. 'You know how good you are, Adélaïde. I don't need to repeat it.'

'*Merci*, John.'

He made a little bow and left the room, closing the door quietly behind him.

'You never told me quite how bad things got,' said Maisie.

'No,' said Adélaïde.

'You should have, don't you think?'

Adélaïde sighed.

'*J'en suis désolée*,' she said.

'No, there's no need to apologise,' said Maisie, realising this wasn't the moment for recriminations, however mild. Adélaïde had a first 'as live' performance to give. 'John's right. You are terrific, the heart of the show, and it's going to be all that you dreamed. After tomorrow night, people are going to consider you an accomplished stage actress as well as a film star.'

'Oh, Maisie,' said Adélaïde, with a fierce intensity in her grateful gaze. 'I hope so. I would give anything.'

'I know you would,' said Maisie. 'And it's as good as done.'

As she left the dressing room, Maisie wondered what Adélaïde would do to anyone who stood in her way.

THIRTY-ONE

Feeling in need of a little fresh air, Masie went out into the tiny car park. The evening was damp but a warm front must have rolled in because the air was heavy and the chill had gone.

There were the three vehicles. She now knew that the old banger was NVE's, the royal blue sports car was Andrew's and the third one, the bottle-green Rover, was Dorothy's. She wondered why they were always there. Was parking difficult at the hotel? Probably. She hadn't seen any spaces, and it was right in the crowded centre of the city.

A short distance away, on the grassy area that separated the theatre from the main car park, she saw Constable Barry Goodbody sitting rather slumped on a bench.

Aren't you supposed to be on duty?

She went back inside and asked Mrs Belt.

'Oh, poor boy, he has vertigo, you know. He can barely stand up straight. It's his ears. Ears are tricky.'

At that moment, John came along the corridor, ready to take up his position for the opening. Maisie smiled at him and he nodded but didn't speak. He disappeared into the wings. Adélaïde came along quickly afterwards.

'When I am not on, I will watch the whole show from the wings. You can be in my dressing room, if you wish.'

'Thank you.'

Maisie was grateful for Adélaïde's invitation. She felt she had rather had enough of watching *The Beggar's Opera* for the time being – and she didn't want to be drawn into any more confessions or arguments.

Adélaïde's dressing room was unlocked with the key on the counter, the bottle of scotch alongside Adélaïde's script. Maisie raised the volume on the tannoy, pulled Adélaïde's chair close to the armchair so she could put her feet up, and prepared to turn the pages along with the disembodied voices from the stage.

*

For Maisie, the next hour and a quarter – the time it took to play the first half – was like time out of time. The process of reading along was completely engrossing, while also permitting her mind to wander in memory during the passages she knew well from seeing them rehearsed multiple times.

It took her back to the classroom at Westbrook College, she and her classmates sitting in rows, with the job of reading aloud Polly Peachum's dialogue and songs, hearing Jack's warm voice from two rows ahead of her, feeling a connection that meant something more than their years.

Why had she not allowed that connection to re-establish itself? It was there. She couldn't deny that. He had told her he felt it, and she knew that she did, too.

So why not?

At first, it had been the confusion and upset of the investigation into her brother Stephen's death. Then it had been her wounded pride – knowing she had done the wrong thing and that she needed his help to put it right, while also wanting nothing more than to go home to Paris, in a hurry to get back to work and pay her bills and live her own life, not the one poor Stephen had unintentionally bequeathed her. Then she had become entangled in the tragedy at Bunting Manor, defying Jack's express request for her not to get involved, and even going so far as to question a witness by pretending to be a police officer.

The voices from the tannoy stopped and she realised time had flown by and it was the interval. She glanced at the script, seeing the instruction 'Blackout' at the foot of the page. Beneath that was a message or a note that Adélaïde must have written for herself.

'*Tu ne peux faire confiance à personne.*'

You can't trust anyone.

Was it a note for herself, for Adélaïde Amour, star of screen and – as Adélaïde fervently hoped – stage? Or was it intended as a reminder of Polly Peachum's predicament in the drama?

The door opened and Clive Canning looked in, very imposing with his height and his round belly, almost filling the opening.

'Oh, I just wanted to tell Miss Amour that she's going great guns. Pass it on, would you?'

'I will.' She watched him hesitate. 'Is there something else?' Maisie asked.

'It's hard to do the right thing, isn't it? I mean when it's close to your heart and all that.'

He gave her a quick nod and disappeared, presumably to his own dressing room. Almost at once, Esther, his wife, replaced him in the open doorway.

'Adélaïde not here?'

'She said she was going to watch the whole thing from the wings. Do you think I should take her anything?'

'Oh, I expect there's enough men circling to provide her with anything she might need.'

Esther's tone was caustic and unpleasant. Maisie didn't answer at first, but it made her wonder if she was neglecting her duty: 'Perhaps I should go and find out and—'

'Did Clive come looking for her?' Esther interrupted, brutally. 'I saw him in the corridor so I expect he did. There isn't one of them who can see her for what she is.'

242

'And what's that?' asked Maisie coldly, unable to help herself.

'A man-stealer.'

'That's not my impression. You might say that I was employed in part to make sure that nothing of the kind took place.'

'What?'

'Just what I said.'

Esther looked round to make sure she wasn't overheard.

'You mean you were to stop her making eyes at each of them in turn,' she hissed with an unhappy smirk on her fleshy features.

'No,' said Maisie. 'Absolutely not. You have entirely misunderstood. I mean part of my job has been to protect her from unwanted advances.'

'Pah,' said Esther. 'She stole Andrew away from my Kitty. Then she chucked him over after leading him on and now he's taken up with Winnie who only wants him for what she can get. What do you say to that?'

'I'd rather not say anything but, in my judgement, Kitty is better off without him. I can't say about Winnie – I really don't know her – but Adélaïde refused his advances in any case.'

'Says who?'

'Isn't it obvious?'

There was a pause, then Esther said: 'I'm going to ask him.'

'What, Andrew?' said Maisie. 'Surely not. Not during the run-through.'

'No,' said Esther, subsiding slightly. 'Let's get that over with first.'

In her turn, she abruptly disappeared.

Laurence Olivier's pre-recorded voice came over the tannoy, telling the company and the absent audience that the play would resume in just three minutes. Maisie had missed her chance to see if all was well with Adélaïde who would now be about to step back on stage. She sat quietly with her eyes on the open doorway. After the two-minute call, she heard urgent voices in the corridor, just their tone, then Clive and Esther Canning went by. She saw them for only a second, hearing six hissed words before they were gone.

'...confront him again.'

'And tell Winnie...'

Maisie got up and shut the door, then made herself comfortable for the second half.

★

Maisie found it hard to concentrate: perhaps it was the interruptions during the interval; perhaps it was because she had been sitting still too long; perhaps it was because the memories of her school days felt like memories of loss.

She became restless and, in the end, decided to go round and watch the last twenty minutes from the back of the auditorium.

She found a spot far back in the most distant seats. The stage was lit with the warm light of noon. The actors were assured, in control. She realised she was smiling.

Yes, it had been the most wonderful stroke of luck to find herself in the Dolphin, to meet Adélaïde, to compliment her singing, to be invited to assist...

Oh, she thought. *For a minute there I completely forgot about poor Keith Sadler.*

She sat down, internally admonishing herself for allowing the boy to have utterly vanished from her consciousness. She owed him a debt, as well, in a way. Wasn't it Keith who first alerted her to who the 'theatre people' were? What had he said about Adélaïde?

She's a doll. She's gorgeous, but they say she can't act for toffee.

Maisie had asked him who said that.

My film magazine. I buy it at the railway station.

It had turned out that 'they' were quite wrong. Adélaïde was very good indeed – commanding, drawing the eye with her performance as well as her statuesque beauty.

The action on stage reached the final crescendo, leading to what was a frivolous happy ending in the original script, but which NVE had shaded with darkness by changing the order of events. As dawn broke and the rhythm accelerated, the Beggar, John Hermanson, made his final speech about needing to tie everything together and provide a proper resolution to all the narrative questions. Then Macheath, Andrew P Bradshaw, was brought forward.

It seemed silly to think of the empty theatre as 'hushed', but that really was the impression Maisie got as Micky mounted the scaffold in his disreputable brown velvet suit, while all the other actors performed their distracting 'business' and he attached Andrew to the safety line.

Micky climbed down, leaving Andrew alone on the trapdoor. The four mistresses stepped forward in mute appeal. Andrew spoke the final line that, to Maisie, had begun to sound so ominous.

'Tell the sheriff's officers I am ready.'

Micky pulled the lever, the trapdoor opened, Andrew fell and seemed to be stopped only by the noose pulling tight around his neck, choking him. Maisie half rose as he twitched and grunted, struggling with his hands bound behind his back.

Then the theatre went dark.

Maisie counted the seconds – one, two, three, four, five, six, seven – not daring to breathe. In the auditorium, a few hands clapped to give the impression of an audience in raptures – presumably NVE, Dorothy, Beryl the wardrobe mistress, Sam Smithers and his assistant, perhaps the stage crew.

The lights came back on with Andrew Bradshaw still attached to the safety, laughing and calling out.

'We said give us ten seconds, Sam.'

'No, that will be too long,' said NVE. 'You must manage it more quickly.'

★

Maisie didn't wait to see if NVE would insist on practising there and then. She went back round to the dressing rooms and discovered Adélaïde already in the process of changing out of her eighteenth-century costume. Maisie stood with her back to the door so no one could come in and interrupt. Adélaïde put on her coat.

'*Allez*.'

They left the theatre, signing out in Harriet Belt's book at the stage door, loomed over by Constable Barry Goodbody who looked sickly but was, at least, upright.

The muggy evening was dry. They crossed the car park and the ring-road into North Street. As they went past the George & Dragon, Adélaïde began quietly singing the Breton folk tune they had heard the previous evening. She kept it up all the way to the lobby of the hotel when she turned to Maisie and said: 'Once would be enough for me.'

'I beg your pardon?'

'Once would be enough. I need only to do this once – for people to see that I am capable, that I am not just the mermaid who undresses nicely for the camera.'

'Oh, you mean one excellent live performance, then call it a day.'

'Yes, I wish, sometimes,' said Adélaïde with a sly smile, 'that we could do the press night and the applause, then walk away.'

'But theatre is about the relationship with the audience – and the audience is a different set of individuals every night. That's where the beauty is, don't you think?'

246

'Not for me.'

Maisie frowned.

'You can't mean that.'

Adélaïde became apologetic.

'I have depressed you. You have fallen in love with the theatre. I thought so. That is my fault,' she added complacently, 'but trust me, if I could walk away with a few good reviews and never venture on that stage again…'

'In the end,' said Maisie, 'this is no more than a stepping-stone for you.'

'*Je ne comprends pas.*'

I don't understand.

'Like in a river, so you can get across to the other side without getting your feet wet.'

'Yes, a stepping-stone to the future.' Adélaïde gave Maisie her brightest smile. 'And the future will soon be here, and I will be free.'

★

Alone in her cramped room, Maisie discovered not one but two letters, pushed under the door. The first was in a reused envelope with the previous address crossed out and a note in the top left corner: 'By hand.'

She peeled off the Sellotape that had been used to reseal it. Inside was a single sheet of good quality writing paper, covered on both sides in a dramatic, untidy hand, with the address of Bunting Manor embossed at the top.

Dear Maisie
Thank you for thinking of Zoe. I came to see her at the hotel this afternoon. She seems very happy. I was sorry when she left but that seems to be my lot these days.

*I hope you are happy, too. Zoe told me all about what's
been happening at the theatre. Gossip spreads quickly in a
small town, as you know.*

   *Maisie, I'm worried about you. It isn't fair that you
should have to face another investigation. I hope you have
the sense…*

The word 'sense' was crossed out and replaced with 'will be
able'.

*I hope you will be able to keep your distance. It isn't your
business. I don't think I could stand it if…*

There was another crossing out, illegible this time, then a
final paragraph.

*If you discover anything, however trivial, leave it alone
and just tell Jack. Like me, he has your best interests at
heart.*
Your 'aunt' who loves you,
Phyl

Maisie sighed, feeling an ache of loneliness, the paper dan-
gling from her fingers. Why had she felt so certain that she
needed time alone? Phyl only wanted to make up for her
mistake – albeit her affair with Maisie's father, Phyl's sister's
husband, had been an enormous error.

I should call her, Maisie thought, *just as soon as the show has
opened.*

Then she realised that Phyl, as a patron of the theatre, would almost certainly be at the press night the next
evening.

All right, I'll cross that bridge when I come to it.

248

The second letter was in an ancient envelope, yellowed with age and closed with a gummed flap that peeled away at the slightest touch.

It was from Jack, which surprised her, because Fred Nairn had told her that Jack was away in the New Forest. The message was short and to the point.

My dear Maisie
I don't know why I can't ever find the right words each
time we meet. If you need anything, at any time, day
or night, you have only to call. I hope we might find a
moment to talk – perhaps after the press night? Phyl's got
tickets for Grandma and for me.
All my love
Jack

Maisie pressed the letter against her chest. It felt almost as comforting as Jack being there with her, promising to stand by her and protect her from harm.

But not quite.

THIRTY-TWO

While Maisie and Adélaïde, very wisely, were preparing for bed, Andrew P Bradshaw was outside The Bell, a pint of mild-and-bitter in one hand and a Senior Service cigarette in the other. Because he was thus occupied, he had no way of physically mollifying Winnie Brahms.

'You've made a fool of me, Andy. An utter fool.'

'No, darling. We've had a bit of fun, that's all.'

'No, I haven't. I've been used – and you lied to me.'

'How did I lie?'

'What did I tell you? "I don't want to start anything if you've been carrying on with anyone else in the company." And you promised you hadn't.'

'I told you, Adélaïde gave me the brush off, but you can't blame me. You can't blame any man. I mean, look at her.' He shook his head and quickly added: 'And look at you, too. You're irresistible. Come here—'

'I will not "come here". And what about taking advantage of the kid?'

'Who told you that?'

'Esther.'

'Stupid cow.'

'How old is she, Andy?'

'She's eighteen.'

'Only just,' snapped Winnie. 'But she's a child, all the same.'

'Winnie, I broke it off when I saw you and I knew what was good for me – a proper woman.' He took a last drag on his cigarette and dropped it on the ground, crushing it underfoot. He tried to take hold of her hand. 'You know you're special to me, don't you?'

Winnie squirmed away so that she was on the far side of one of the outdoor tables.

'How am I special?'

'Because you're you,' said Andrew with what he hoped was his most endearing smile.

It didn't work.

'I know all about you, now. Esther told me. Clive told me. They're in there now.' She gestured at the warmly lit pub window. 'Sitting with Kitty while she weeps.'

'You don't want to believe what Esther says. I never went too far.'

'Says you.'

'Yes, says me.'

'And you think I should believe you?' retorted Winnie, contemptuously. 'There's the show to think about as well. You're a piece of work, Andy Bradshaw.'

Andrew took a sip of his pint of mild-and-bitter and thought briefly about putting down his glass, taking hold of her and kissing her, whether she wanted him to or not. Winnie perhaps saw the dawning intention in his eyes.

'No, you don't,' she said, skipping away and re-entering the pub.

Andrew lit another Senior Service and sat down on a bench. It was slightly damp from all the rain earlier in the day, but he didn't care. He looked up at the sky and thought about fine fillies – both the actual human women he couldn't get enough of, and the kind that came romping home at ten-to-one, if you were lucky, and paid out ten quid for a one-pound stake.

He'd had a lot of the former, lately, and not enough of the latter.

Behind him, the door opened. He turned and saw Winnie come out on the arm of NVE.

'Nils is walking me back to my digs. It's on the way to the hotel anyway.'

'Is he now?' said Andrew, with a leer. 'Are you looking to take advantage of my cast-offs, brother?'

'Are you drunk?' asked NVE coldly.

'No,' said Andrew. 'Sober as a judge – and more used to being judged than judging.'

'Why did he call you "brother", Nils?' asked Winnie.

'Pay no attention to me,' said Andrew, before NVE could answer. 'Aren't we all brothers under the skin? And, if not brothers, then everybody's darling? Why shouldn't you be Neil's darling, after you've been mine.'

'Stop it, Andrew,' snapped NVE. 'I warned you this morning that you are running out of rope. I can tolerate no more.'

'Rope again? Do you enjoy watching me being hanged, over and over again?'

'I mean it.'

'But you don't want your secrets shared, do you, Neil?'

NVE shook his head.

'I don't care. I tell you frankly, it no longer matters. I used to think that it would, but not anymore. I have protected you because my mother asked me to, knowing that Father was not a good man, that he would not raise you as a child should be raised, with respect and love. For those reasons, I have tried to protect you, for her sake, but no more.'

With that, NVE turned away, Winnie still clinging to his arm, glancing back over her shoulder, giving Andrew a look that seemed to mean: *What was all that about?*

Andrew smiled and winked, and he could see it was all she could do not to smile in return.

No, thought Andrew, *it isn't necessarily over with Winnie. I might be able to get her back onside, if I play my cards right.*

Andrew drained his glass and stood up.

What now, however? He had intended to share Winnie's bed but the circumstances...

He went over to the pub window, peering in. There were Esther and Clive Canning, one either side of their daughter. Kitty seemed very small between her fat mother and her roly-poly giant of a father. But she was lovely, wasn't she? And young enough to be malleable. He was sure that Kitty, too, could be brought back onside. He was the star, wasn't he, the male lead, the hero, whatever NVE said. It was Macheath's charisma that carried the show and, though he would have liked to play the role more sympathetically, it was quite a wheeze NVE had come up with to give him the tag, the last line, dying as the final act in the drama.

Esther and Clive got up to go to the bar, leaving Kitty alone on the bench seat.

Andrew knew that just around the corner from The Bell was a development of new houses in a small estate called Somerstown – modern maisonettes with built-under garages and white wood panelling. Kitty was staying in the second one on the left.

Yes, that was where he might sleep tonight.

Just at that moment, Kitty glanced up at the window. He smiled and gave her a wink.

He saw the hesitation in her eye, the fact that she wanted to look away, but also didn't. There was wariness coupled with desire – not desire for him, he knew that.

Desire for first love to be real.

He nodded and gestured with his thumb, meaning he would be waiting for her when, finally, she left the security of her parents' supervision and came outside.

She frowned, then nodded in reply.

253

THIRTY-THREE

On the following morning, Thursday, the day of the press night, Maisie woke at a civilised hour for the first time in she couldn't remember how long. She luxuriated in her bed, reaching out an arm to tug aside the ill-fitting curtains in her tiny room, seeing a pleasant patch of blue sky with a few drifting white clouds.

'Well, that's an improvement,' she said aloud.

She checked her watch. The time was eight-forty, not actually slovenly but she thought it would be best if she pulled herself together. They had all been 'called' at the theatre at eleven o'clock for notes on the previous evening's dress rehearsal.

Happily, the shared bathroom on the corridor was free and she was able to run a shallow bath and get back to her room without having to speak to any other guests. In the breakfast room, she was delighted to see Zoe.

'How are you getting on?'

'Work is really tiring,' said Zoe.

'That always comes as a surprise to teenagers,' said Maisie. 'Do you have the energy to bring me some breakfast?'

'Will you tip?' asked Zoe with a grin.

'You'll have to wait for the end of the week,' laughed Maisie. 'By the way, has Adélaïde been in?'

'I took her up a tray.'

'Good,' said Maisie, but with a slight edge of concern. 'Was she all right? Did she ask for a tray because she's unwell? Did you speak to her?'

'No, I just left it outside.' Zoe put her head on one side. 'Are you trying to fix her life like you've tried to fix me?'

'I've succeeded, haven't I?'

'You will have when you find me a job in Paris, not Chichester.'

'Go on with you.'

Zoe disappeared through the swing door into the kitchen while Maisie served herself some coffee. Her two unexpected letters were in her handbag. She would have liked to re-read them, but didn't want to do so in public.

The poached eggs, when they came, were nicely cooked and they had been allowed to drain properly so the toast wasn't soggy. Maisie ate with gusto. As she was getting up to leave, Zoe told her: 'Phyl and I will be there this evening. You won't snub her, will you?'

'Why would you say that?' Maisie protested.

'It would be so nice if you could be friends again.'

'Don't worry, Zoe. Everything will come right in the end.'

Maisie went back upstairs to brush her teeth and tidy her room. She couldn't leave the bed unmade, even though she knew it was the chambermaid's job to do it. Then she went downstairs to read the paper in the television room.

The windows onto West Street were both open, so the air didn't feel quite as trapped or the room smell quite as much of cigarette smoke and stale milk. The *Chichester Observer* was on the table – it was a weekly publication, and it was the newest edition, in the shops the previous day. The front page was mostly about the opening night of the Chichester Festival Theatre season: the expected crowds; the glamorous actors and actresses; the hopes for a bumper crop of tourists bringing prosperity to the town.

Alongside all this optimism were two other articles about bitter local planning disputes. Maisie ignored them and looked inside.

Page three carried an interview with Adélaïde, which bore a striking similarity to the one Maisie had read in the movie magazine that Keith Sadler had recommended. She supposed it was syndicated and the local journalist hadn't bothered to make much effort to rewrite it. Maisie put the paper aside and went to the window.

Yes, it was a little breezy, but the improvement in the weather meant it should be possible for the first night audience to enjoy drinks out of doors – before the show, at least. By the interval, it would be cooler.

She went downstairs and drifted to the threshold, looking out towards the cathedral green, not really knowing why she was there.

Then it came to her. She had been infected by the theatre virus. She was anxious – full of energy with nothing to spend it on.

In an effort to rid herself of her nerves, she went out for a walk, not bothering to return to her room for a coat or an extra jumper. She was chilly at first, but soon the exercise warmed her and she enjoyed her circuit of the old city walls. When she got back to the hotel, Adélaïde was in reception, wearing mustard yellow trousers with a wide leg, a crisp powder-blue collared shirt and a dark-blue polka-dotted neckerchief at her throat. She carried a long woollen cardigan over her arm.

'How are you?' asked Maisie.

'I told you last night,' said Adélaïde, in a small voice. 'I was terrified before. What is more than terrified?'

'Petrified?' suggested Maisie.

'Yes, that. Let's go before anyone talks to us.'

Adélaïde pushed her arms into her long cream cardigan and found some enormous sunglasses in the pocket. She put them on. They covered at least half of her face.

'You look like a film star, now,' said Maisie, smiling.

'It is easier to be private,' said Adélaïde.

They set off, walking briskly through the town. Then Adélaïde decided she didn't want to be early.

'Where can we go?'

Maisie took her through the iron gates in the flint wall of Priory Park where a groundsman was mowing the cricket pitch.

'This is the most English thing I have ever seen,' said Adélaïde. She gestured to the priory itself, standing isolated in the midst of the grass. 'What is this?'

'It's the chapel of a twelfth-century Franciscan monastery. Later on, it was used as a courtroom. Some very famous smugglers were tried in there and sentenced to death by hanging.'

'Hanging again, like Andrew,' said Adélaïde.

'Well, like Macheath,' said Maisie.

'If you prefer.'

Adélaïde climbed the park mound, following the tarmac path in a spiral to the top. Maisie followed.

'Did you like growing up in Chichester?'

'I grew up in a village a few miles out of town. It was indescribably dull.'

'Our fishing village was dull at the time, but now I look back and I think: "That, at least, was real." You know?'

Maisie thought Adélaïde was going to say something else. When she didn't, Maisie decided to ask her own question.

'Why is it so desperately important to you to make a success of this show, Adélaïde? You're already a star. I expect – I mean, I know, because you've told me – that you're rich.'

'Because, in the films, it is not me, the thing that is famous. It is what I look like.'

Yes, thought Maisie. *That makes sense.*

'But you know what you're worth,' she argued. 'Is it good for you to be bothered about what others think?'

'That is what actors do.' Adélaïde laughed, then led Maisie back down the mound. As they turned a corner in the spiral path, she pointed and asked: 'What is that grass?'

'Behind the hedge? That's the bowling green.'

'Like *pétanque?*'

Maisie laughed, too.

'Much more sedate and well-kept. You can play *pétanque* on any old stretch of dusty gravel. Bowling needs a perfect lawn.'

'Ah, you English and the perfect lawn.' Adélaïde sighed. 'That is all. We have done it. The time has passed and it is the moment to worry once more. Shall we go?'

They walked up through the car park to the theatre. Maisie wondered how she would cope if she had to endure auditions and first nights and all the rest of it. Badly, she decided. She needed to live life on her own terms, to be in charge of her own destiny. It was probably something to do with having become an orphan at quite a young – albeit adult – age.

And because her brother was dead, too, of course.

Arriving at the stage door, Maisie tried to shake off her sudden funk and in they went, signing the book and making their way into the auditorium. The scaffold was still centre stage and NVE took the notes session sitting on its edge, the actors in the stalls, as before. NVE was true to his word, only picking up on things that hadn't gone according to the established plan, not meddling or tweaking. In any case, most of what he had to say was complimentary.

To John: 'I love that deep bass voice under Adélaïde's lines. That was very good.'

To Clive and Andrew and several of the other men: 'The fight is very exciting, now, exactly how we worked it.'

To Winnie: 'You absolutely gave yourself to him, darling. Can you keep that feeling and do it again tonight? You like it better doing it that way, don't you?'

'I will do my best,' Winnie replied with a sharp look at Andrew.

Maisie wondered what had happened. Some kind of rift, she thought.

At the end of the notes, Dorothy Dean stood up and made a speech on behalf of the management, thanking everyone for their efforts, telling them that they shouldn't worry, but...

'The future of this theatre and everyone who works in it is in your hands.'

Everyone laughed and Dorothy joined in, though she looked a little strained. Finally, she announced that a special lunch would be served in ten minutes – in other words at twelve-thirty – in the green room. Because the weather was fine, some more outdoor chairs and tables had been retrieved from the store and set out on the grass in the sun.

'That's all,' said NVE. 'I love you all.'

'Whole company,' shouted Micky Petherick, before everyone got a chance to leave, 'in costume not make-up, walk through for moves and lines at two, if you please.'

*

The following hour was delightful. Adélaïde ate a small salad with roll-mop herrings and new potatoes, then slipped away to her dressing room for some peace and quiet. Meanwhile, Maisie got the chance to mingle with the rest of the company, including some of the secondary and minor role actors whom she hadn't much spoken to, including the wirily handsome Liam Jukes whose strong features and dark hair meant he could pass for older than his years.

'It must be a big responsibility, understudying Andrew as Macheath. Will you go on, do you think?' asked Maisie.

'God, I hope I do ... and I hope I don't,' said Liam.

'You mean you'd love the chance, but you don't want anything to happen to Andrew to make it necessary?'

'Exactly,' said Liam. 'But also, I've had no proper rehearsal time. I mean, Kitty's been on pretty much every day, including down here in Chichester. I've not run it on its feet since London.'

'Tough for you,' said Maisie, sympathetically.

Just then, Dorothy came into the green room, red-faced and storming. She marched straight to the corner table where Andrew was sitting on his own, having swept the bits and pieces of poor Keith's Airfix model back into their box and put it on the floor. He had a glass in front of him with at least a finger of whisky in it.

'Of all the selfish, self-important, self-destructive things to do,' hissed Dorothy.

'Give it a rest, Dottie,' said Andrew, without looking up. 'You think you're in charge but you're not. Without us you're nothing.'

'Jesus Christ.' She turned and saw Maisie. 'Where's Liam?'

'Er, I was just talking to him. I think he's gone outside. Can I help?'

'Will you go to my office and see what you can do?'

Without giving any kind of explanation, Dorothy swept out of the French windows onto the grass and buttonholed Liam Jukes.

Not knowing what to do for the best, Maisie left the green room and went quietly along the dressing room corridor, past Adélaïde's door – which was shut – and John Hermanson's door – also shut – and paused outside Fort Knox.

There was an unmistakable sound of sniffling from within. Maisie turned the handle and slipped inside.

It took a few moments to adjust to the dim lighting. Only the desk lamp under its dark-green glass shade was on. Kitty was sitting on an oak swivel chair – like the one Maisie had used in the board room when she called the police station – with her legs drawn up and her chin on her knees. She was rocking from side to side, making the chair twist left and right, her eyes tight shut.

'What on Earth has happened, Kitty?' said Maisie.

The sniffing suddenly stopped and Kitty opened her eyes. 'Why have you come?'

'I've no idea. Miss Dean asked me. I didn't know what to expect. What can I do to help?'

'Nothing. There's nothing anyone can do. I'm so ashamed.'

Kitty began properly crying, her shoulders heaving and her chest lurching with each sob, an awful plaintive keening filling the office.

'But you poor thing. What in heaven's name is it?' Maisie quietly closed the door, worried that Kitty would disturb Adélaïde or John on the other side of the corridor. She went round the other side of the desk, put her hands on Kitty's shoulders and twisted the chair to face her.

'Kitty,' she said, kindly, giving her a little shake. 'That's enough, now. You need to be strong.'

Oddly, after a few seconds, it worked.

'Yes,' said Kitty, 'I'm being ridiculous.' She unfolded her legs and arms and sat up sensibly, leaning her elbows on the desk, almost as if she was about to make a presentation to a business meeting. 'This is just what it's like for a woman in the theatre. I should have expected it. My mother's told me often enough.'

'Told you what?' asked Maisie.

'What to look out for.'

'Do you mean men who want to have sex with you?'

'I let him come back with me,' said Kitty. 'I took pity on him. He said it was all a mistake and he'd only gone with Winnie because I'd made him so unhappy by rejecting him. Did I reject him? I didn't think I did.'

261

'Your parents certainly warned him off but, if you want my opinion, I think Andrew was just toying with you.'

'No, he wasn't. It was me that he wanted, but, you know, "a man must go with a woman", isn't that what Kipling says in *The Mary Gloster*?'

'I don't think the dying hero of that poem is meant as a moral guide,' said Maisie.

'And Winnie's a man-eater. Anyone can see that.'

'I don't think she is,' said Maisie. 'She's just a very attractive woman who likes to feel desired.'

'I almost think she's on my side, somehow. Do you think that's possible? She told Andrew she would get him fired over what he did.'

'We're getting off the point. You invited him back to your digs, is that right?'

'He told me he was too tired to go back to his own place and he was worried about his performance with the press night coming up and everything on his shoulders and he would sleep better next to me in bed. It sounded romantic.'

'Why didn't he go to his own digs?'

'I don't know. Because he knew mine were right behind the pub?'

'All right. Go on.'

'We talked and talked and I thought I'd made him feel better. Then, I suppose my landlady heard us and she came upstairs with a rolling pin, like in a ridiculous Benny Hill sketch, and she literally chased us down the stairs and out of the house into the street and all the neighbours' lights came on and their doors opened and they were looking at us and pointing and … it was so shameful.' Kitty leaned back, looking utterly defeated. 'It will be in the papers. My reputation is ruined.'

'Had either of you undressed?'

'No.'

'Then, I don't think that's true,' said Maisie. 'People won't necessarily jump to conclusions and, in any case, I'm not sure public morals were so very badly offended if that's all.'

'No, not my personal reputation, my professional reputation. It's like Dad says, that's something that takes years to build and can be thrown away in an instant.'

'But you're young and beautiful and talented, Kitty. And life is long. Who knows what triumphs you might accomplish? What happened next?'

'Andy just ran off, leaving me to face the music.'

'What did you do?'

'I begged my landlady to let me back in. I told her I had nowhere else to go and, in the end, she let me.' Kitty gave Maisie a small smile. 'It was actually a very good performance from me as a "wronged innocent".'

Maisie smiled, too.

'Well done, Kitty.' Maisie opened her arms and Kitty stood up and allowed herself to be comforted. 'That was a horrible experience, and you did very well to cope.'

'I know,' said Kitty, close to Maisie's ear.

'So, there's no need to be hiding and crying and nothing more to worry about.'

'Except,' said Kitty, very quietly, 'Mum says she's going to kill him.'

THIRTY-FOUR

For Maisie, the next hour or so took on a kind of nightmare quality, with people plotting in corners, surging out and arguing and the men almost all coming to blows in every possible permutation. Dorothy returned to Fort Knox and begged Kitty to come to the auditorium. Kitty agreed, but only if Maisie would keep on holding her hand. They entered from behind the set and found Micky and the stagehands testing the scaffold mechanism without bringing it forward onto the stage proper. When Micky put his head in the fake noose and one of the crew actioned the lever, it worked beautifully, but Kitty put her hands to her face and begged them to stop. Then they were all interrupted by the whole cast filtering in, putting down scripts and extra jumpers on the tip-up seats in the front row. Maisie took Kitty a little further away and sat her down.

What was clear from the broken snatches of conversation was that different people were in possession of different facts, but everyone knew that "something" had occurred to destabilise the production. Adélaïde, Maisie noticed, had taken a position as far upstage as was possible, without actually disappearing behind the set.

'Darling, has something else happened?' said Esther Canning when she noticed her daughter in the stalls with Maisie.

'What is it now, for God's sake,' said Clive. Then, when he saw his wife's frown, he added: 'My dear girl.'

Dorothy Dean stated categorically that it would be a good idea for Andrew to stand down and for Liam Jukes to play Macheath.

After a moment of absolute silence, NVE was immediately up in arms against it – not, he said, on the strength of Andrew's character, but because Liam was unprepared.

'Are you sure?' asked Dorothy.

'I am.'

'Well, I would like to know for certain. Andrew has done something entirely beyond the pale.'

'All right,' said NVE, as a chorus of voices demanded to know exactly what Andrew had done. 'Let's try it. Liam, we'll take the scene leading up to the kiss, Macheath and Lucy.'

The other actors stood back to allow Lucy Lockit – Winnie Brahms – and Liam Jukes – as Macheath – to perform their most important love scene.

Maisie felt nothing but sympathy for the poor young man. He stumbled over his lines and, when it came time to grasp Winnie in his arms and kiss her in the throes of unquenchable passion, Andrew laughed immoderately in the stalls. NVE told Liam he looked like 'a fishmonger unhappy to be holding a three-day-old fish'.

Uncertain who had offered him the greater insult, Liam said he was prepared to fight them both, at the same time, if necessary. That simply made Andrew laugh more, so Liam stormed off to the shared dressing room for the minor male actors, promising he would not emerge until curtain-up – "and damn the walk-through". That led to a strong exchange of views between NVE and Andrew in which everyone present learned a few disconnected details of the hidden relationship between them.

'So, NVE, or should I say Neil,' said Clive, 'you've foisted this popinjay Andrew Bradshaw onto us purely on the strength of a family connection that you have been devious enough – wise enough? – to conceal?'

'There's no need to make a whole bloody speech, Canning,' said Andrew.

'My name is Nils,' said NVE.

Clive demanded to know why the understudy was being tried out at all and, when it was finally revealed to him by his wife what had happened the previous night in his daughter's digs, he flew at Andrew and it took the combined efforts of Micky, John and NVE to hold him back.

Throughout all of this – and the many more sallies and flurries that followed – Maisie sat as still as she was able, holding Kitty's hand, wishing all these over-grown children would act more like grown-ups and recognise who the real victim was in these dreadful circumstances. In the end, it was Dorothy Dean who settled matters.

'There's no point in trying to do this afternoon's run-through, NVE. I don't want any more upset. Andrew, did you drink that stupidly large scotch you poured yourself?'

'I thought about it, but I changed my mind. My name is not Hermanson, you see.'

'Don't tempt me,' said John, menacingly. 'By God, I'll help Clive next time, not hinder him.'

'Be quiet, John,' said Dorothy. 'What I'm asking is this, Andrew. Can you go on as Macheath at seven-thirty this evening?'

'Of course I can, if I'm allowed.'

'And you won't let yourself or any of us down? You won't put at risk so many jobs, great and small?'

Remarkably, Maisie thought she saw evidence in Andrew's eyes that Dorothy's words had hit home, but he mocked her in reply, by singing: '*All things bright and beautiful, all creatures great and small…*'

'I insist, Andrew,' the manager said, doubling down. 'Can you go on? Will you do your best to make up for all the damage you've done?'

'Absolutely all the damage?' Andrew asked. 'No, I can't promise that but, with respect to the show, I will play my unsympathetic part and die as instructed as darkness falls.'

'Right,' said Dorothy, slowly turning in a circle and gesturing to the whole company. 'I'm sure I don't have to remind you that you are all under contract to this theatre, to this management. More than that, your responsibility, your artistic responsibility, is to the paying public, over a thousand of them, plus two-hundred-odd great and good of theatre, this world we work in because we love it, remember, however tricky it might sometimes get.' She turned to Kitty who had gasped. 'No, I'm not dismissing or diminishing what has happened, but I beg you, Kitty, to trust that I will not let it lie. Please, can we get through this evening's performance then think again?'

Esther burst into speech, clinging to her husband's arm.

'We will never forgive you, Andrew.'

'Neither will I,' said Dorothy and Maisie thought it had the absolute ring of truth.

'I don't believe I've asked you to,' said Andrew.

★

Maisie left Kitty in the care of her parents – for whatever that was worth – and went up on to the stage to look for Adélaïde. She found her behind the scenery, looking at the scaffold with its macabre sign declaring in scorched letters that it was 'Tyburn Tree'.

'How many of us would be glad to see him really hanged?' she asked quietly.

'Don't say that,' said Maisie.

Adélaïde shrugged.

'*Il faut regarder les choses en face.*'

'I am looking at things as they are,' Maisie argued. 'I'm just suggesting that, as there was a murder in this building the other day, you shouldn't just blithely start suggesting ways of committing another one.'

'You are talking too fast again but I understand your meaning. Let us go.'

'To your dressing room?'

'No, to the hotel. You will help me with my lines. I must read them through. My brain expects it. That was the plan and…' She shrugged again. 'It is how I am.'

'Fine. Actually, yes. If we stay here, we're almost bound to find ourselves caught up in more upsets.'

'Good. But one other thing. You know the wardrobe lady, the one with the name of a jewel?'

'Beryl.'

'I asked her to find a dress for you. When your friend comes this evening, he will see you dressed as a woman and not a schoolteacher, at last.'

'I think I'll be fine as I am.'

'At the press night? I don't think so,' insisted Adélaïde.

She led Maisie to Beryl Vere's wardrobe room where a remarkable garment was briefly displayed, tried on and judged satisfactory – by the wardrobe mistress.

'You look as good as the actress who wore that dress on stage last season,' said Beryl.

'Thank you.'

As Maisie struggled to undo the zip, she noticed Clive Canning in the corridor, talking heatedly with Adélaïde, but too low for her to hear.

'A picture,' said Beryl, delightedly.

Adélaïde came back in.

'Keep it on,' she exclaimed.

'No,' said Maisie firmly. 'I don't want to walk through town dressed like a…'

'Like a woman?' said Adélaïde. 'All right. We will take it to my room. When we return for the half, you will change alongside me.'

'If you insist,' said Maisie.

As they walked back to the hotel, with the clock in the cathedral bell tower chiming three, Maisie wondered who Adélaïde had meant when she said: 'When your friend comes this evening.'

Well, Mohammed, of course. Adélaïde didn't know Jack and Maisie supposed she didn't know about the change of plan.

On reflection, thought Maisie, *I'm glad Mohammed has made himself scarce. If the show goes well, Adélaïde will be busy being congratulated and Jack and I can find a moment, just for ourselves.*

Thirty-Five

Back at the hotel, Maisie helped Adélaïde read through all of her scenes, speaking aloud the lines of every character except Polly Peachum. It made her feel rather queasy. There really wasn't anyone – not one fictional person – that she thought she could like or admire.

She found this odd because, from the classroom back at Westbrook College, she had a memory of a jolly romp.

Could it simply be NVE's reworking of the ending with Macheath getting his – deserved or not – comeuppance?

Once that was done, Adélaïde said she would like to rest so Maisie made her way to her own room to find her birthday books, setting her trusty travel alarm for six-ten.

She picked up the volume she had already begun – the one called *Opening Night* that was set in a theatre. The other evening, she had read for an hour or so before putting it aside, because at that point in the narrative the murder still hadn't taken place and she didn't find the story very compelling. Now, though, she became fully engrossed in the characters. When, finally, there was a death more or less on the middle page – leaving the rest of the book for the detective to work out who did it and why and how – she stopped reading for quite a different reason.

It struck too close to home.

Sitting up on her narrow bed, her back against the hard wooden headboard, looking out of the window at the city trees that were slow to come into leaf because they lived in shadow on the north side of the hotel building, she thought through the people she had met.

First, there was Adélaïde, of course – voracious for success, to prove herself, outside of the world of cinema that she had already conquered, desperate to be seen as an actress, not just a...

A what? A clothes horse?

Second was Dorothy Dean, a woman of pugnacious drive and efficiency, but with an extraordinary pressure on her shoulders – keeping alive the dream of a major theatre in a provincial city that wasn't really big enough to sustain it. And a theatre that was closed for half the year.

Third was NVE, a director whose career had only ever known success, whose delightful patterns of movement and song and speech and dance engaged and thrilled audiences. But, also, someone who had made two dangerous casting choices – his secret brother who had brought poison into the company and a film star without stage credentials that he had pursued as a sexual conquest.

Next was poor Kitty Farrell, a fragile ensemble player, raised to the important position of understudy for the star by the accident of her physical appearance – and because Adélaïde was incapable of working with the stamina of a trained theatre professional throughout the gruelling rehearsal process.

Then there were the Cannings, at the same time protective of and ambitious for their daughter, impatient with her frailty, smothering her with their love.

Standing a little apart was John Hermanson, the reformed alcoholic, needing this production to go well in order to get his career back on track, and Winnie Brahms, another 'wronged woman'.

Finally, Andrew P Bradshaw, a bitter ladies' man whose predatory sexual behaviour seemed to give him no satisfaction except, Maisie supposed, a fleeting physical release. Someone who had managed to turn everyone against him, too.

On the bed in her cramped hotel room, Maisie had been holding her birthday copy of *Opening Night* in her lap. She looked again at the page. In parallel to the murder investigation, there was a love story, a young actress who had joined the fictional company almost by accident – just as she had been drawn in on Adélaïde's whim.

I hope it's a happy ending, she thought, with a smile.

She shut the book and put it aside, her logical mind considering some more 'characters' from her own story: Micky Petherick, devoted to his 'Boss', resentful of Andrew's destabilising influence; Harriet Belt, a silly, self-important woman who might have prevented Keith Sadler's death, had she done her stage door job properly; Sam Smithers, quiet, reliable, one of the people whose modest livelihoods depended utterly on the theatre and who had no involvement – as far as she knew – in any of the on- or off-stage drama; Liam Jukes, like Kitty an ensemble actor as well as the understudy for Macheath, a young man living on the edge of his nerves, terrified at the prospect of going on in a role for which he seemed quite unprepared but which others would kill for.

Kill for.

What a foolish expression, thought Maisie. No one would kill an actor simply for the opportunity of going on in their place.

Then, without really being aware of how it happened, she scooched down in the narrow bed, turned on her side, her eyes still on the window, but gently closing, the light fading as she drifted into sleep.

*

Woken by her alarm, Maisie jumped off the bed and went to wash and brush her teeth in the shared bathroom on the corridor. Then she hurried to knock on Adélaïde's door.

Getting no answer and hearing no sound, she tried the handle. It turned and, very gently, very slowly, she pushed the door open.

The curtains were drawn and there was an exceptional stillness in the room.

'*C'est l'heure*, Adélaïde.'

It's time.

There was no answer so she crossed the room, taking care not to bang into anything in the gloom, and half drew the curtains. The light of early evening slouched in reluctantly from a pink and grey sky.

Maisie approached the wide double bed. Adélaïde was lying on her back, as if in state, her head making a tidy depression right in the centre of her feather pillow.

'Adélaïde?'

Maisie leaned in. Had she taken a sleeping pill?

'All is well,' came the sweetly accented voice, 'I am awake.'

'Thank goodness,' said Maisie, 'I thought I was going to have to throw a bucket of cold water over you. I'll wait for you downstairs.'

In the lobby, Maisie found the hotel manager busy behind the reception desk, typing the menu for the evening meal.

'Miss Dean called to say she has arranged a car for you. It is already here.'

'Oh,' said Maisie. 'Is it raining?'

'No, I think it is simply a consideration for the importance of tonight's performance.' He got up and came out from behind the dark wood of the reception counter. 'Is it permitted to wish a star good luck? When she comes down, I mean?'

At that moment, Adélaïde was already descending the stairs with her habitual poise and grace.

'Thank you.' She approached the hotel manager and put her hands together in front of her breast, as if praying. 'You have been very kind.'

273

'We do our best, I like to think—' he began.

'Come, Maisie. We must hurry,' said Adélaïde, dismissing him in full flow.

Outside the hotel, in the fading evening sunshine, Adélaïde was delighted to find they had been sent a car, even if it was only Micky driving Dorothy's bottle green Rover. They both got in the back seat.

'All set?' said Micky, and away they went.

The short journey took only five minutes, despite the streets being busy and the car park already filling up. Quite a few people – perhaps twelve or fifteen folding tables – were eating chilly picnics on the lawns surrounding the theatre.

Micky parked close to the stage door and Adélaïde hurried inside, not wanting to be caught by the autograph hunters – two rather seedy-looking men in drab, shapeless garments.

Maisie was about to follow Adélaïde inside when she saw something that made her cross. It was Constable Barry Goodbody, talking to a tramp who had been rootling through a waste bin. She felt like going over to tell the policeman to leave the poor man alone. Wasn't it bad enough that he had to look for food among general waste? Then she saw Barry fish a few coins out of his pocket and hold them out and she chided herself for jumping to unkind conclusions.

Then something odd happened. Barry wasn't simply giving the tramp money. He wanted something in return. Annoyingly, Maisie couldn't see what it was.

Adélaïde called out from just inside the doorway: 'Come, Maisie, or we will be late after all, and you must put on your dress.'

★

A little later, at ten to seven, almost the 'half', Maisie was backstage with Adélaïde, sitting on the uncomfortable foam

274

armchair in the 'star' dressing room, wishing her all the best for the opening night of the Chichester Festival Theatre season. Adélaïde was wearing plain make-up that enhanced the contours of her face. But beneath her foundation and blusher, her skin was very pale.

'You have shown me,' Maisie insisted, 'shown everybody so many times that you have the charisma to command the stage.'

'*Merci, mon amie*,' said Adélaïde and Maisie realised it was the first time Adélaïde had called her a friend.

Maisie grinned.

'There's only one thing left to say.'

'There is?' Adélaïde asked.

Maisie left a deliberate tiny pause, then she used the traditional rude French expression for wishing good luck, the equivalent of the archaic English phrase 'break a leg'.

'*Merde*.'

'Thank you, Maisie,' Adélaïde replied, delightedly. 'You have helped me so much…'

Adélaïde's voice drifted away and Maisie felt she had stayed too long, that it was time Adélaïde was left to herself, to gather her thoughts and get ready for the enormous audience. Dorothy had told her the show was sold out with a full complement of reviewers from all the most important newspapers.

Maisie left the dressing room and made her way to the green room. Harriet Belt was there, all on her own, taking a dainty sip at a small glass of brandy.

'Oh, you've caught me,' she said foolishly. 'Always about this time – just the one.' She drained her glass. 'I'll be off. No peace for the wicked.'

Harriet left and Maisie sat down at the lunch table, nervous of going out into the lobby where she might see Phyl – and Zoe, of course – and Jack and his grandma, Florence.

I'll just wait another minute.

She took a deep breath. It was surprisingly quiet in the green room and she had an odd impression that something was missing. She traced a pattern on the worn wood of the dining table, thinking back to her first few hours in the building, arriving in this very room, sitting in this very spot, eating a Caesar salad and trying to learn everyone's names, to understand their relationships.

Why had she felt the need to do that?

Well, because it was a habit of hers. It wasn't just the two police investigations she had assisted with – it was how her mind worked.

She had a brief daydream in which she became a different person and used this skill, this way of thinking and understanding of character to become a playwright, to write something that was about to be performed on the Chichester Festival Theatre stage to an audience of twelve hundred knowledgeable theatregoers and a dozen possibly jaded critics.

She shuddered and smiled.

'How absolutely terrifying,' she said aloud.

She looked around the spacious room – the comfortable chairs, the photographs on the walls, the heated trolley empty of food. Was that normal? Were none of the actors able to face anything to eat on this special night?

Once again, she felt gratitude that Adélaïde and Dorothy – each for their own reasons – had invited her into this closed and special world.

She checked her watch. It was five-past seven.

She stood and smoothed down her dress. It had a rather loud pattern and was not at all the sort of thing she usually wore. There was a mirror on the left-hand wall for actors to check themselves before they made for the stage and she went and stood in front of it, turning to either side.

No, this isn't me, she thought.

She had to admit, however, that Beryl, the wardrobe mistress, had chosen well from the rail of dresses from past productions.

'Most of the men will be in black tie,' Beryl had told her, 'and the women in long dresses. This will do nicely, I think.'

Maisie had tried it on and, of course, if had fitted her like a glove, Beryl's experienced eye making sure of that.

'Don't you think it's a little…'

'You look lovely,' Beryl had told her.

'It's quite tight, though.'

'That's what a dress feels like when it fits,' Beryl had insisted.

'It's quite loud, too. Don't you think I look like I've been wall-papered?'

'It's a copy of a Balmain,' Beryl had told her, scandalised. 'It's the height of fashion.'

Well, thought Maisie, *it's too late now. I can't go back to my everyday suits and sensible flat shoes.*

She turned back to the door and noticed a scrunching under her feet. She raised the hem of her dress to see what it might be, and gasped. There, on the worn carpet, were the smashed fragments of Clive Canning's lifetime achievement award.

How had that happened? Could it have been an accident?

No, not a chance. The crystal obelisk would never have broken into so many pieces simply by falling the short distance to the floor. And there, on the edge of the seat of one of the heavy wrought-iron chairs brought in from outside, the paintwork was freshly chipped.

Someone has destroyed it on purpose, in anger or in spite. Does Clive know? If he doesn't, what will he do when he finds out? Or Esther or Kitty, come to that?

THIRTY-SIX

Maisie picked up all the fragments of Clive Canning's award and collected them together on a large dinner plate, knowing that Jack would advise her to leave well alone. But, surely, this wasn't a matter for the police?

That done, she went out into the backstage corridor and approached the pass door into the foyer. She could hear the hubbub on the far side: an excited audience preparing to enter the imaginary world of the play; to see the set for the first time; to experience the atmosphere created by the design, by the lights; to see old friends and wave to them across the stalls…

She hesitated, with her hand on the door handle, feeling absurdly apprehensive.

What's wrong with me, she wondered? *I'm not the one who has to go on and sing and dance and recite and create a spectacle for twelve hundred strangers.*

Steeling herself, she pulled the door open and stepped through into the crowd.

★

As it turned out, the pre-show chatter was much less of an ordeal than Maisie had anticipated. It was a pleasure to see Mr Chitty and his grandson and she talked to them for five minutes about the bike shop and Nicholas' school and the preparations for the Chichester city fête. Then Jack came up with a broad smile and asked her if she might want a drink.

'Thank you. I'd like a glass of white wine, with ice, if there is any.'

He walked away to join the scrum at the bar, leaving her feeling foolish that she hadn't refused, in order to enjoy his company. Meanwhile Florence, Jack's grandma, told Maisie the story of their aborted trip to the New Forest.

'I couldn't stay there knowing what was happening back at home,' said Florence.

'What was happening back home?' asked Maisie, who was still watching Jack.

'Why, the weeds, simply leaping out of the soil. It's spring you know – or it would be, if the rain could ever stop.'

'It has, hasn't it?' said Maisie, distracted.

She glanced round. It was a lovely evening. All the same, time was moving on and most of the audience was indoors, crushed into the foyer. She caught sight of Fred Nairn across the crowd, climbing the stairs to one of the upper entrances with a woman in a camel-coloured fur coat with very severely set hair. They were arm in arm and Maisie guessed that she must be his wife.

Jack came back with a glass of white wine for Maisie and a very pale, dry sherry for Florence.

'How has it been?' asked Jack. 'It must have been horrible for you.'

Maisie frowned.

'Horrible…?' Then she blushed, Of course, Keith Sadler. 'Oh God, isn't that terrible. I'd forgotten for a moment, with all the pressure and nerves of the first night. That's the second time it's happened.'

'You've become a thespian, dear,' said Florence.

'Have you been working, Jack?' Maisie asked. 'Do you know where Inspector Nairn's investigation has got to?'

'No, I've taken the week off.' He smiled at Florence. 'I decided to spend my holidays at home with my best friend.'

'Get on with you,' Florence replied. 'He's gone in every day to ask Fred what he's been doing and to know you're all right, Maisie.'

'Stop it, Grandma,' said Jack.

'Well, you have.'

Maisie looked from one to the other, thinking she ought to feel embarrassed, but she didn't. Jack looked very handsome in his dinner jacket with his bright white shirt and correctly knotted bow tie. The noise of the crowd receded. She felt an urge to take his hand and thank him for worrying about her, to step closer to him in her long, figure-hugging evening dress…

Then the moment was lost as Charity Clement and her solicitor-husband, Maurice Ryan, came to join them.

'This is very exciting,' said Charity.

'Cor-blimey, don't you polish up well,' said Maurice, standing back and taking in Maisie's appearance. 'What an outfit.'

'I don't think it's the outfit that you're looking at, Maurice,' said Charity.

Maisie did her best to join in the general chit-chat but, inside, she felt she had missed an important opportunity for a more intimate moment with Jack.

Maybe later, after the show…

A bell rang and Laurence Olivier's pre-recorded voice came over the tannoy: 'Ladies and gentlemen, please take your seats as the performance will begin in ten minutes.'

Charity and Maurice went off to find the right door. Florence left Maisie and Jack alone in order, she said, to powder her nose, but Maisie thought she was just being discreet.

'Maisie,' said Jack, 'are you, though? All right, I mean?'

The crowd around them was thinning out. There was no one close by to overhear.

'Inspector Nairn must be close to deciding who killed Keith Sadler,' she said quietly. 'Is there nothing you can tell me?'

Jack frowned.

'I will trust you to be discreet. It wasn't an intruder. It was one of the principals or management. No one else had an opportunity to see the combination or even to know the money had been deposited.'

'Fingerprints?'

'Everybody's fingerprints are more or less everywhere, including yours. And people know to wear gloves.'

'Of course.'

Florence came back from the bathroom and she and Jack entered the auditorium. Maisie was about to climb the foyer stairs to the upper entrance, because her seat was halfway back, when Zoe came rushing up with Phyl Pascal in her wake.

'Phyl was late,' said Zoe. 'Her stupid Land Rover's playing up again. Would you believe she hasn't replaced it?'

'Hello, Maisie,' said Phyl, looking worried. 'I hope this isn't too much, that you don't mind I'm here. Did you get my note? I almost rang the hotel to talk to you but—'

'No, of course it's not too much,' said Maisie. The emotion she had been feeling for Jack seemed to transfer itself to Phyl – or was it just sympathy for Phyl's haunted expression? 'Come here.'

Maisie opened her arms and Phyl hesitated before stepping into her embrace. To Maisie's surprise, Zoe grasped them both tightly, saying: 'Is it all over, at last, all the drama?'

Maisie released them and took a step back.

'No, the drama's about to begin,' she said lightly.

'You know what I mean,' said Zoe. 'I mean between you two.'

'Don't push,' said Phyl, quietly, rubbing her weather-beaten face with a rough, farmer-woman's hand. 'These things take time.'

'How much time?' asked Zoe with all the impatience of youth.

'Phyl,' said Maisie, 'how about you come and have lunch with me tomorrow? You'll find me at the hotel. Let's have a good talk.'

'Yes, please, I'd like that very much,' said Phyl, breathily. 'I'm so sorry.'

'You don't have to be sorry anymore. That's all past.'

'I am, though,' insisted Phyl.

The bell rang again and Olivier's voice told them that only one minute remained. Phyl and Zoe turned away, moving quickly so as not to be late. Maisie watched them go, thinking that yes, perhaps, it was time finally to draw a line under what Fred Nairn called 'the Bunting Manor business'.

Then she pulled herself together, put down the glass of wine she had barely tasted, climbed the stairs and went into the dim auditorium.

★

The first half of the show went by in a blur and was over much more quickly than Maisie had expected. She had been given a seat alongside Dorothy and NVE, halfway up the stalls, near the end of a row so that the director and manager would be able to slip away as soon as the applause began for the interval. About two-thirds of the way through, in the midst of a song, Dorothy whispered to her: 'Andrew is doing a good job. They all are, don't you think?'

'Do you mean: "Is the audience aware of all the upset between the cast members?" I'm sure they aren't.'

The first act came to a close to a delighted ovation.

'Would you like to come behind?' asked Dorothy.

'No, thank you. Adélaïde said not to. I'll stay here.'

The audience began its half-time shuffle, some people on their way to the toilets, others looking for their pre-booked drinks, still others remaining stolidly in their seats, reading their programmes.

'Why would you do that?' asked a voice. Maisie looked up. It was Sam Smithers, the chief electrician. 'The programme is always full of clues as to what's going to happen, even if it's just naming characters that haven't yet appeared. They should wait till they get home.'

'Well, I suppose it's habit,' said Maisie. There was a pause as they watched the big scene change. Micky and his mis-matched stagehands busy with furniture and mobile flats. 'How do you think it's going?' she asked. 'Or shouldn't I ask that because it's tempting fate.'

'It's very good,' said Sam. 'Adélaïde is breathtaking.'

'And the rest? The story's coming across? I mean, it doesn't seem complicated to me, but I know it. Maybe that's why people are looking at their programmes?'

Sam gestured to the audience.

'I'd say they're going with it. If they don't quite get it, they're trusting the fact that it will all come together in the second half.'

At that moment, Micky and the stagehands completed their change and left the stage to a warm round of applause from the audience members who had not left their seats.

'Got to go. No peace for the wicked,' said Sam before he took the steps up through the seats to the lighting box two at a time.

Maisie stood up to stretch her legs, still feeling a little self-conscious in her dramatic dress, and glanced round the auditorium. Over to the right-hand side, in the middle of a row, she could see Fred Nairn and his wife eating ice-creams in tubs. Charity and Maurice were not far away. Maurice gave her an enthusiastic thumbs up.

In the most expensive seats, in the centre of row D, she saw Zoe and Phyl Pascal. She watched long enough for them to become aware of her gaze and they both glanced back, Zoe with her little wooden spoon in her mouth and Phyl making the shape of the words 'thank you'.

Maisie nodded and smiled. Zoe and Phyl turned away.

Down in the front row, her eyes found the group that had been her target all along. There was Mr Chitty alongside Jack's grandma on one side and young Nicholas on the other. Beside Florence was an empty seat, then Jack returned from the lengthy ice-cream queue and sat down, passing the tubs he had bought along the row.

Dorothy came bustling back.

'All good. No upsets. No complaints. Everyone on the money.'

'Good news,' said Maisie, wondering if it was always the producer's job to check at half-time that the cast was pulling together as a team.

The warning bell rang and Laurence Olivier's voice once more gently chided the audience back to their seats.

'Here we go again,' said Dorothy.

'Is NVE coming back?' asked Maisie, seeing his empty seat. 'Or will he watch from backstage?'

Just then, the director emerged from the stairwell. He glanced round the house and Maisie thought she caught a hint of excitement in his eyes. He also thought it was going well.

NVE came towards them, then veered away to speak to one of the critics, a man with a salt-and-pepper beard with a notebook on his lap. Maisie was surprised to hear them discussing not *The Beggar's Opera* but quite a different show – a Stephen Sondheim musical called *Company* that had been playing at Her Majesty's Theatre in the West End since January.

'Good for another six months, if you value my opinion,' judged the critic, self-importantly. 'But one never knows.'

'I'm glad to hear it,' said NVE. 'I have friends in that production.'

Maisie, Dorothy and NVE took their seats. NVE leaned across Dorothy to whisper an explanation.

'You can never talk about the show you're actually watching to a critic. You might upset them if they get the impression that you're telling them what to think. Better to compliment something for which they've already given a good write-up and hope some of that rubs off on yours.'

He sat back. The house lights dimmed and the second half of *The Beggar's Opera* got underway with the kaleidoscopic street scene of pickpockets and vagrants, hawkers with baskets of fruit and flowers, a passer-by attacked with a stick and robbed, the thief arrested and subjected to a stylised hanging, bringing the Tyburn Tree scaffold on stage for the first time.

Maisie smiled. The audience was, once again, rapt. Even though the minor character hadn't actually put his head in the noose – even though the hanging had been more like a dance than a realistic representation of capital punishment – it had brilliantly set up what she knew was to come.

NVE's carefully crafted climax, culminating in the shocking death of Andrew P Bradshaw as the anti-hero, Macheath.

THIRTY-SEVEN

Just before the final scene of the play, in quite a noisy change of location with off-stage incidental music, Maisie was aware of NVE slipping out of his seat and away down the staircase to the foyer.

'Where's he going?' she whispered to Dorothy.

'He wants to come on for the curtain call as director,' she hissed in reply.

On stage, the familiar waves of tension and drama waxed and waned then waxed once more, building in energy and poetry to John Hermanson's final speech as the Beggar.

The scaffold was brought forward and Maisie noticed much sooner this time the figure of Micky Petherick, square and solid in his brown velvet suit.

Andrew, his hands bound behind his back, climbed up onto the platform. Micky followed and there was the planned flurry from all the other actors as he attached the safety line. All the same, Maisie felt her chest tighten and smiled to herself.

Really, she thought, *there's no way I could be an actor. I feel it all too deeply, every time it happens.*

Micky climbed down and Maisie glanced round the auditorium. The audience, too, was still and tense. Some of them perhaps knew the play's normal 'happy' ending and were excited or intrigued to see the alterations NVE might have made. Others, who had neither read nor seen the play previously, were simply carried along with the drama of a man alone with his neck in a hangman's noose, about to pay for his sins.

'Tell the sheriff's officers I am ready,' said Andrew, his voice perfectly pitched between arrogance and self-pity.

Micky took hold of the lever and looked up at Macheath in his long red riding jacket and silvery waistcoat.

The pause before Micky pulled the lever seemed longer than before. Maisie wondered if, while she and Adélaïde had been resting back at the hotel, NVE had got the actors together and slightly changed the timing.

Then Micky hauled on the lever and the trap door opened, both panels swinging down and thumping against the framework as Andrew fell, apparently only stopped by the noose pulling tight around his throat as he twitched and struggled and gurgled.

Then, as planned, everything went dark.

Maisie counted the seconds. Not seven or eight, but a full ten seconds of blackout, during which the audience gave a collective gasp, collected themselves, then burst forth in a cataract of delighted applause, some of them immediately on their feet, obscuring Maisie's view of the stage.

The lights came back on for the curtain call and Micky was still struggling to get Andrew down from the rope and – unlike in the last rehearsal Maisie had seen – Andrew wasn't laughing. Then Micky was calling out something she couldn't hear because of the applause and, between the heads of the people in front of her, she caught a glimpse of the two stagehands running on and the company standing back from the scaffold, edging away, Adélaïde and Winnie still clinging to one another in what was meant to be their shared fictional grief.

And, in that moment, Maisie knew – without the slightest hesitation or doubt – that the fiction had become reality.

Then, incredibly, Jack Wingard was on the stage, jumping up from the front row of the stalls. As the ovation ceased and the audience stopped clapping, the noise replaced by a low buzz of uncertain, confused conversation, she was able to make out what Jack was shouting.

'Bring the set forward. Make a screen. Play *The National Anthem.*'

*

While Maisie was still trying to process what had occurred, craning her neck to see between the audience members standing in front of her, perhaps the most alert person in the whole theatre was Sam Smithers – or maybe his assistant, still suffering from flu symptoms but quick on the uptake. *God Save the Queen* began its drum roll, broadcast loudly over the public address system.

As was customary, those audience members who weren't already on their feet stood up. Maisie wanted to get to the stage, but it was impossible. Some people – who perhaps hadn't realised that a real-life drama was unfolding and who had bought tickets at the ends of rows in order to be able to slip away quickly to the crowded car park – began to leave. The steps down between the seats were already crammed with shuffling people.

Because she was quite high up in the auditorium, Maisie could just see Liam and the two stagehands dragging elements of the set forward – the flats that represented the walls of buildings in eighteenth-century London. They positioned them in front of the scaffold, closing off from view what was happening on the platform – the awful on-going struggle to lift Andrew up and release him from the strangling noose.

The final chords of the anthem sounded and the audience's voices rose in a wave of speculation. Maisie realised that Dorothy had somehow got away, perhaps through one of the upper doors, and that Fred Nairn was attempting to fight his way down through the crush.

'Police, let me through,' he was shouting, making painfully slow progress towards the stage.

Then she heard a calm, authoritative voice over the loud-speakers and she realised that, cleverly, Dorothy hadn't tried to leave the auditorium but had run up the steps, between the seats, to the technical box at the very back in order to make an announcement.

'Ladies and gentlemen, due to an accident in the final scene of the play, we would ask you kindly to leave the theatre in an orderly fashion. There is no cause for alarm. Thank you for your understanding. I repeat, kindly leave the theatre. Meanwhile, if there is a doctor in the house, could they please make themselves known to the company?'

The announcement had the desired effect. The dribble of patrons slipping away became a flood, flowing down the aisles and out of the exits to the foyer. Maisie stayed where she was, seeing Fred Nairn finally reach the stage and climb up, just as Jack emerged from behind the scenery. The two policemen exchanged a few words then Fred exited, running, upstage. He crossed paths with NVE, entering, looking confused. Jack went to meet him, taking hold of his arms, shaking his head. NVE struggled to be released, but Jack wouldn't let him go.

Maisie looked round the stage. She saw Esther and Clive Canning standing in a little group of their own with Kitty, who was in costume as a flower seller in the final scene, an insignificant member of the ensemble. Maisie saw John Hermanson approach Jack and NVE, helping the director away.

It was all horribly grotesque. Had it been real, the hanging was the kind of event that actual historical members of eighteenth-century society would have flocked to see.

Had it been real…

Maisie saw Barry Goodbody run on from backstage in his heavy constabulary boots, heading directly for the scaffold

289

concealed behind the flats. Jack followed as Liam Jukes emerged, looking sweaty and breathless and Maisie wondered if he had been giving Andrew CPR, pumping his chest to try and restart his heart. Two men, each with short grey hair, climbed onto the stage from different directions and Maisie assumed they must both be doctors, offering their help. One of them dithered, not knowing what to do. The other slipped in through a narrow gap in the flats.

The area of the auditorium around Maisie's seat had finally cleared. There were only a hundred or so audience members left, dawdling around the lip of the stage, wanting to catch a glimpse of the real-life drama that had overtaken the fiction. Fred Nairn came forward and told them in no uncertain terms to leave.

'Move along quickly, if you please, ladies and gentlemen. Don't dawdle.'

Dorothy came down from the lighting box with Sam. They stood close to Maisie, asking one another questions.

'Something must have happened to the safety line, right?' suggested Sam.

'Who checked it?' Dorothy asked.

'Micky did that, didn't he?'

'Did he change it himself – the drop, I mean? Wasn't it longer?'

'They all decided. Could he have done it deliberately?'

'You mean, could he have tried to kill himself?' said Dorothy.

'He was pretty ashamed of what he'd done, wasn't he?' Sam offered.

'No, he wouldn't ruin the show at the same time, would he?'

'I wouldn't put it past him. You've met him, haven't you?'

None of those, Maisie thought, *is the right question.*

Dorothy and Sam followed the last few audience members down to the lip of the stage. The house lights were on, as well as the lighting for the curtain calls. Following the usual routine at the end of each evening's performance, the ushers began filtering into the auditorium to clear the empty ice-cream tubs and sweet wrappers from between the seats. Dorothy called out to them in a loud voice:

'We will tidy the theatre tomorrow. That will be all for this evening, if you please.' Reluctantly, the inquisitive ushers began to sidle away. 'Hurry along now,' Dorothy insisted.

Having not moved, Maisie was alone in her row, looking down on the remnants of the tragedy of *The Beggar's Opera*. She saw Jack emerge from behind the flats once more. He had taken off the jacket of his dinner suit and undone his bow tie. It hung down his shirt front. As she watched, he took out his cufflinks and rolled up his sleeves, his eyes darting this way and that.

Masie frowned. Where was Adélaïde?

Scanning the enormous stage, her eyes found Winnie in a cluster with Clive, Esther, Kitty and several minor characters. Liam was there, too, telling them, she was sure, what he had done, that he had tried to bring Andrew back from the brink. NVE was out of sight. She supposed he had been allowed behind the flats to see for himself what had happened to his brother. Adélaïde had gone.

Then she realised that Jack was looking for her – looking at her, in fact.

Their eyes met and she went down the stairs between the seats to meet him just below the Olivier point. He came down and took her arm, leading her away so they could speak quietly without being overheard.

'They are still trying, but I think he's gone.' Maisie was speechless. Jack continued: 'I need to speak to you. Fred and I need to speak to you. Will you tell us what's been going on?'

'Of course. Inspector Nairn knows most of what I know but—'

'First of all, who organised this stage effect?'

'The fake hanging?'

'Yes.'

'Well, the director, Mr van Erde, the stage manager, Micky Petherick, and the actor himself, Andrew Bradshaw.'

'Right. And who was responsible for checking that the safety line was properly attached?'

'That would be Micky.'

'Did you see it in rehearsal? Did they take it seriously? It seems to me a haphazard sort of contraption.'

'Yes, they did, many times. It seemed absolutely secure. Why?'

'Because it wasn't.'

VI

SPEECH

THIRTY-EIGHT

Maisie wanted Jack to clarify what he meant.

'When you say "it wasn't", do you mean the hanging wasn't properly rehearsed or the line wasn't securely attached?'

'The latter,' said Jack. 'Now, please, just give me a quick overview of all you've seen and heard.'

As succinctly as she was able, Maisie gave Jack a run-down of the events of the previous twenty-four hours. Mean-while, instructed by Fred Nairn, Micky Petherick assembled the whole company and crew in the audience seats. Maisie reached the end of her recital. Jack thanked her then spoke briefly to Fred Nairn. In turn, the inspector raised his voice.

'Ladies and gentlemen, if I might have your attention.' He waited for quiet. 'This is all very distressing, I'm sure. Some-thing has occurred and we will have to keep you all here for the time being. I'm sure this is the last thing you want to do, to sit about not knowing what to think, while we go about our routine, but I'm afraid we have no choice in the matter.'

At that moment, two paramedics came on stage with a wheeled stretcher. The more decisive of the two grey-haired doctors from the audience emerged from behind the flats and said in a clear, emotionless voice: 'It's over. He's gone.'

There was a deadly hiatus as everyone waited and watched. The stagehands replaced the flats upstage, revealing the scaf-fold. Andrew was on the floor alongside, his face covered by Micky's brown velvet coat. Micky helped the paramedics move Andrew's corpse onto the wheeled stretcher and was about to follow them and the two grey-haired doctors off when Jack told him: 'No one may leave the stage except the medical professionals, if you please.'

'All right,' said Micky, 'keep your hair on.'

'How does this scaffold move? Is it on casters or something?' Jack asked.

'That's right.'

'Take off the brakes, would you? But don't touch anything else.' Micky used the toe of his shoe to flick up the catches that prevented the casters from rolling. 'Now come round by me,' said Jack, 'to this front edge and we'll push it upstage.'

Nairn instructed the stagehands to collect all the chairs that had served in the play and arrange them in a circle. Barry Goodbody was sitting on the floor, his hands on his knees, looking as though he too had played a part in the resuscitation effort. Nairn spoke to him. He nodded, stood up straight and took out his notebook.

'Mr Petherick,' said Nairn. 'Is everyone here?'

Micky glanced around.

'Well, to coin a phrase, I've already told you that – all except one.'

Nairn looked confused but Maisie knew what Micky meant. The answer was the same as it had been after the discovery of Keith Sadler's body.

'What are you talking about, Petherick?' said Nairn.

'The leading lady,' said Micky. 'Miss Amour.'

'Does anyone know where she might be?' asked Jack.

'I think she left the stage,' said Maisie, from the front row of the stalls. 'Would you like me to check her dressing room?'

There was a pause. Maisie looked from one policeman to the other. She thought Nairn was biting his tongue, leaving Jack to decide.

'You go, Fred, would you?' he finally replied. 'Do you need someone to show you?'

'I know where it is.'

Nairn strode away upstage.

'Miss Cooper, would you join the company, please?' said Jack. 'And the rest of you from the audience seats, climb up and join the circle, if you would.'

Jack gave Maisie his hand to help her up and she took it, feeling suddenly anchored. Then he led her to an empty chair and she felt a tinge of regret as he moved away.

'As my colleague has already mentioned,' said Jack in a loud, clear voice, 'this is undoubtedly a very distressing time for you. Not only has your colleague met with...' He seemed to correct himself. 'Not only has he died, but the triumph of this evening's performance has been snatched away from you.'

'Oh my God, the party, the caterers,' said Dorothy, who was sitting on the edge of a green room dining chair, looking utterly squashed.

'Miss Dean, isn't it? My colleague will send them away,' Jack told her. 'Now, I have to give you all a warning, but I don't want you to become unduly concerned by this. It is more by way of a reminder. This is an official police investigation and anything you say will be taken down and may be used as evidence in a court of law. I would be grateful if, for the time being, you would simply sit quietly and wait for us to begin collecting statements without discussing what may or may not have occurred. Speculation – especially speculation without knowledge of the facts – is usually in vain, always unsettling and may prejudice our enquiries.'

At that moment, Tindall and Wilson, Fred Nairn's colleagues, came on stage. Jack went and spoke to them, giving them instructions to dust and photograph the scaffold. Simultaneously, Fred brought Adélaïde back into the auditorium. She was wearing her street clothes – the mustard yellow trousers, crisp powder-blue collared shirt and dark-blue polka-dotted neckerchief. As she walked, she was pushing her arms into the sleeves of her long woollen cardigan.

'I would like to sit with Maisie,' she said.

John Hermanson, in his awful make-up and disreputable stained and threadbare costume, stood up and gave her his seat – a battered chaise longue from the Peachum's dwelling. Adélaïde draped herself decoratively across it.

'*Merci*,' she said.

John went and found an empty chair next to Dorothy.

Jack informed the company and crew that Constable Goodbody and Detective-Sergeants Tindall and Wilson would remain on stage and would take down anything of substance that anyone said.

'In the meantime, I will have to ask for a little patience. Inspector Nairn and I need a moment to take stock. Miss Cooper, would you accompany us?'

It was phrased as a question, but Maisie knew she had no choice. She led the way to the green room and, once there, went straight to the sideboard and poured herself a very small brandy, knocking it back in one. Then her hands idly straightened the cutlery tray and the knife block.

'This is becoming routine for you, Miss Cooper,' said Nairn, with a clumsy attempt at lightness.

'Shut up, Fred,' said Jack, protectively.

'I didn't mean anything,' said Nairn.

'I know you didn't,' Maisie told him. 'Shall we sit?'

'Maisie, I'm so sorry,' said Jack. 'This must be the last thing you could possibly want. It's the worst luck. Could you repeat, though, what you told me about the last twenty-four hours, going into a little more detail?'

'Of course. I know the form.'

They went to sit in the corner of the green room, with Maisie on the bench seat where she assumed Keith Sadler had sat with his Airfix model. The box had been knocked on the floor so she picked up the pieces. The propeller was broken and she looked in vain for the lost rotor.

'Maisie?' said Jack.

'I'm sorry. I was thinking about something else.'

'Something important?'

'Keith Sadler. This is his model. I suppose he used it to pass the time when he was nightwatchman. It's been here ever since he… It's rather sad, isn't it, that someone's broken it?'

'Yes,' said Jack, sympathetically. 'People underestimate how much sadness surrounds a murder. It's not all excitement and drama and a puzzle to solve.'

'It's not all "the game's afoot",' said Fred Nairn, quoting Sherlock Holmes. 'It shouldn't be glamourised.'

'But we don't need to tell you that,' said Jack. 'Now, if you would, can you just go over what you told me, so we're in full possession of the facts, as you understand them?'

Maisie recognised with a sinking feeling Jack's adoption of his constabulary voice, formal and impersonal. She told her story for a second time, interrupted regularly by questions – things she knew but the two officers needed explained. Eventually, once she had told them about the overnight scandal of Andrew being caught by a puritanical landlady in Kitty's digs and its public and private aftermath, they were up to date, to the point where she and Adélaïde had left the building.

'So, you know nothing of what happened between… When did you say?' said Nairn, looking at his notes.

'Adélaïde and I left the theatre a little before three. We went straight to the hotel together. We returned around ten to seven.'

'And Miss Amour was with you all this time?'

'She was with me on the journey each way and for the first hour back at the hotel. We practised her lines. She practised, I mean, and I read in the other characters.'

'How did she seem?' asked Nairn.

'Like an actress full of nerves but rather subdued because of all the upset. This performance was extremely important

299

to her – to her sense of self-worth and to her career. She resents being thought of as a clothes horse, you know, as mere decoration – something for the camera to dwell upon. She was desperate to make a success of her role.'

'You say "desperate"?' said Nairn. 'That's quite an extreme word.'

'All right, "very keen",' if you prefer,' said Maisie. 'I don't mean she would…'

She stopped, thinking about what Jack had said about speculation.

'What is it?' asked Jack.

Maisie frowned.

'I'm sorry, I'm worried I'm going to start seeing things where there's nothing of importance.'

'Don't worry. We're used to sifting the wheat from the chaff.'

'And, as witnesses go, Jack,' said Nairn, 'Miss Cooper is the *crème de la crème*, wouldn't you say?'

'I would.' Jack nodded, encouragingly. 'So, you were with Miss Amour constantly from when you left to when you returned?'

'No,' said Maisie. 'When we had finished reading through the lines, I went back to my room and read one of my birthday books for a while. Then I dropped off. It's all been quite draining,' she finished apologetically.

'Leaving Miss Amour alone?'

'Yes.'

'And you saw her again…'

Maisie thought back, picturing the darkened room.

'At six-twenty, maybe six-twenty-five. She was sleeping.'

'When would you have completed your readthrough and left her?' asked Nairn.

'Well after four – maybe twenty-past?'

'But enough time for Miss Amour to have returned to the theatre then come back again for you to discover her two hours later, apparently sleeping in her bed?' insisted Nairn.

'That's ridiculous.'

'It was you who said she was desperate, Miss Cooper.'

'One thing at a time, Fred,' said Jack, frowning.

'I'm sorry. I didn't mean to—' Nairn began, then added: 'I don't want Miss Cooper to misunderstand the direction in which our questions are leading.'

'It's fine,' said Maisie. She dropped her eyes to the Airfix model again. 'Oh, I forgot to tell you.'

She got up and showed them the smashed lifetime achievement award whose crystal fragments she had collected on a large dining plate and the fresh chip to the paint on the cast-iron chair.

'And you don't know how that happened?' asked Jack.

'I'm sorry, I have no idea. I only discovered it just before curtain-up and coming to find you in the foyer.'

Saying this, Maisie remembered her fond wish that she and Jack would find time to be alone together at the after-show party and – she had hoped – get their relationship back on an even keel.

There's no chance of that now. This will set us back again. Soon, he's going to hate the sight of me.

She realised that Jack and his colleague were discussing what to do next.

'You're thinking of questioning them together?' Nairn asked.

'I am,' Jack confirmed. 'We won't have enough officers to prevent them huddling in corners and connecting their stories. Don't you agree?'

'Yes,' said Nairn, 'I think I do. I reckon it's probably the best way to confront their different versions of what happened

– perhaps the only way to get a clear timetable for the crucial times between three and seven.'

'Because that's when someone detached the safety line?' asked Maisie.

'Something like that,' said Jack. 'As you say, Mr Petherick was seen checking it before the aborted rehearsal.'

'And later?'

'That's one of the things we need to find out. If it was my show,' said Jack, 'I would have checked it last thing before letting the audience into the building.'

'Or in the interval?' suggested Nairn.

'Good point,' said Jack. 'Maisie, the scaffold was used earlier than the finale, at the beginning of act two, but no one actually put their head in the noose.'

'What a memory you have, Jack,' said Nairn.

Maisie visualised the sequence.

'No, at that point it was just the focus of a kind of stylised dance. No one could have tinkered with it then. And it stayed on in full view after that.'

'Yes,' said Nairn. 'I thought at the time it was a very effective stage element.'

'Like a threat,' said Jack. 'And no one else climbed up until Mr Bradshaw and Mr Petherick right at the end.'

'But it was a very busy show,' said Nairn, 'if you know what I mean. That could have distracted anyone from seeing any interference.'

'Except I was in the front row,' said Jack, 'just a few paces away.'

'How was it done?' Maisie asked.

After a pause, Jack told her: 'The safety rope was almost cut through, leaving only a few threads to hold it in place.'

'With a knife?'

'Any kind of good-quality blade would have done it. We'd better go. We've left them alone long enough.'

'But,' she said, her eyes back on the Airfix Spitfire, 'there's still the question of Keith's murder. You know, without him, I don't think I would be here. It feels dreadful that his death has somehow been superseded.'

'No, it hasn't,' said Nairn, unexpectedly. Then he surprised her by adding: 'Not at all – and, for that, we have to thank the excellent work of Constable Barry Goodbody.'

THIRTY-NINE

As they made their way back to the stage, Maisie asked what Inspector Nairn meant, but he said he couldn't tell her straight away. She returned to her upright chair next to Adélaïde's chaise longue, and Jack took centre stage, with Nairn standing to one side, behind the actors.

Jack began by describing – only in general terms – the pattern of the day. He was quickly able to ascertain that the two stagehands had left the building when the company had been dismissed after all the upset.

'At that point, where was the scaffold?' Jack asked.

The stagehands conferred then confirmed it had been at the rear of stage, ready to be brought on.

'And where did you go?'

It took a little while to get them to admit that they had gone to The Bell where the owner was in the habit of serving them outside of lawful licensing hours.

'We'll have to have a word with your accommodating publican,' said Fred Nairn.

After a few more questions, Jack established that NVE and Dorothy, between them, had made an effort at calming nerves and settling such disputes as could be settled.

'And who supervised all the departures?' asked Jack.

'I was at the stage door with Mrs Belt. Your constable was there, too,' Dorothy added, glancing at Barry Good-body.

'And every ensemble member left.'

'No, I didn't say that. It was every member of the ensemble except for the two most important understudies, Kitty Farrell and Liam Jukes.'

Jack glanced round the circle, easily picking out Adélaïde's cover.

Liam raised his hand.

'I was asked if I might be able to stand in for Andrew,' he said. 'I didn't know why at that point, and I didn't like to ask. I know almost nothing about what's been going on. I stayed in my dressing room – I mean, one of the shared men's dressing rooms – and read over my lines. I mean, Macheath's lines.'

While Liam spoke, Maisie contemplated him.

Yes, she thought, *there's something nervy and overwrought in that wiry young man. Would that be enough to make him kill for the role? Surely not. But why, then, had he been so keen to tell everyone that he was incapable of going on?*

'That must have been a terrifying but enticing prospect,' said Jack, sympathetically, and Maisie wondered if he was trying to get Liam to reveal something he might regret. 'I wonder how you felt at the sudden challenge?'

'It was ridiculous,' said the young man. 'I told NVE. I told Miss Dean. I simply haven't rehearsed.'

'So, you wouldn't have gone on?' Jack asked.

'I didn't say that,' snapped Liam. 'I just mean, no one should have expected too much from me. But, of course, I would have stepped up. I could have had the script behind the set, you know, for between scenes, and the others would have helped me.'

'We would,' said Esther and Clive simultaneously.

'Oh, yes, we're just one big happy family,' added John, with heavy irony.

Jack asked Dorothy to confirm which actors had been signed out.

'That's easy. As I said, all of the ensemble members aside from Kitty and Liam left. They stayed, as did most of the leads – Andrew, John, Esther, Clive and Winnie...' She glanced round the circle. 'Micky you remained in the building, didn't you, love?'

'Yep.'

'Sam, where are you?'

'Here, Miss Dean,' said Sam Smithers. He was the only one without a chair, sitting on the floor. 'I went to The Bell with the crew but I came back after half an hour for the lamp check and so on.'

'Yes,' said Dorothy, 'of course you did.'

'And me,' said NVE. 'The gentlemen of the police will want to know that I remained in the building.'

'Right,' said Jack. Then, rather impressively Maisie thought, he went through the names without checking his notes. 'The people who stayed were Miss Dean, Mr van Erde, Mr Bradshaw, Mr Hermanson, Mr and Mrs Canning, Miss Brahms, Miss Farrell, Mr Jukes, Mr Petherick, Mr Smithers. No one else?'

'Well,' said Dorothy, 'and Mrs Belt.'

'Of course. But no caterers or support staff, no front of house, anything like that?'

Dorothy shook her head.

'No, the open sandwiches for the audience were prepared over the road in a building set aside for that purpose and the ushers and so on came later.'

'Wardrobe?'

'Beryl and her girl went into town to eat. I saw them go and met them on their way back in, just before the half.'

'The food for the green room?'

'I stopped it. The trolley's empty. I didn't want anything to interrupt our attempts at reconciliation,' she reiterated with a rueful expression. 'Had anyone wanted anything, I would have fetched it myself from the kitchen across the way. But I...'

Her voice drifted off and it was, Maisie thought, only the fact of her managerial authority over the theatre that made it clear that she was thinking and that no one should interrupt.

'Earlier on, when it happened...' Dorothy stopped and swallowed. 'You referred to an accident.'

'No, Miss Dean,' said Nairn.

'You did. I'm sure.'

'You are mistaken.'

'I distinctly remember—' she began.

'It was you,' quibbled the inspector, 'who said the word "accident" when you made your wise announcement from the lighting box.'

'Well, anyway, you seem to be saying that you don't agree it was an accident,' said Dorothy. Then she changed her inflection to turn it into a question. 'Are you suggesting it wasn't an accident?'

'It was not, Miss Dean.'

'Then it was...'

Dorothy stopped and Maisie felt suddenly very sorry for her. She knew what it felt like to be confronted with the word that no one wanted to say and to have no choice but to pronounce it, making it real.

Then a thin hysterical voice spoke up.

'Someone has to say the word,' bleated Kitty. 'Don't they?'

'Yes, Miss Farrell,' said Jack. 'You will all have to face it.'

'If it wasn't an accident,' said Kitty, grasping her mother's arm, 'it was murder.'

307

FORTY

Clive Canning got to his feet. With his height and bulk, he looked impressive in his eighteenth-century long-coat and breeches, his buckle shoes with ridiculously tall heels.

'This is really too much. I'm afraid I haven't learned your names, as you have ours,' he began, 'and I apologise for that. But surely the proper form is for you to dismiss us collectively, taking individual statements later on? It's very late. We are all exhausted, not least our daughter.' His eyes took in Esther and Kitty. 'She has had as much as she can reasonably be asked to take and I beg you, as a father – you are perhaps a father yourself, one of you…'

Clive left the rhetorical thought hanging.

'My husband is right,' said Esther. 'You can't possibly question all of us at the same time.'

'Would you be good enough to retake your seat, Mr Canning?' said Jack, in a tone of complete authority. Clive subsided onto his upholstered dining chair. 'Thank you.' Jack looked round the stage. 'As you have perhaps deduced, the key time in this investigation is the period from the beginning of this afternoon's aborted rehearsal and somewhere around ten to seven, when the company reassembled. While we were attempting in vain to resuscitate Mr Bradshaw – and I must thank Mr Jukes and Constable Goodbody for their sterling efforts – I was able to establish that no one could have approached the scaffold without being observed by a member of the stage crew after this time. We have since confirmed all this from your statements, here on this stage. Plus, the scaffold mechanism was tested around two o'clock, before the aborted rehearsal, with Mr Petherick's head in the noose.'

'And here I am,' said Micky with a sour grin.

'Please don't interrupt unless you are asked a direct question,' said Jack.

'All right. Keep your hair on,' said Micky for a second time. 'But you keep circling round my involvement and...' Micky kissed his teeth and sat back. 'Never mind.'

'Thank you.' Jack resumed: 'I was going on to explain that our enquiries have led us to the inescapable conclusion that the safety line was deliberately damaged, such that it could no longer be relied upon to arrest Mr Bradshaw's fall, and that this must have occurred between when Mr Petherick and the crew tested it soon after lunch, and ten to seven, from which point such a manoeuvre could not have been undertaken without being observed. It follows, as I am sure you all appreciate, that only those members of the company who were in the building during that period could have had the opportunity.'

His eye picked them out in turn. As he did so, Maisie saw them look at one another – the tight family unit of the Cannings and Kitty; NVE and Dorothy isolated and – in some ways – friendless; the other actors displaying various degrees of suspicion or caution.

'So,' said Nairn – and, from outside the circle, his unexpected voice came as a shock – 'everyone else can leave.'

*

It took a little while. The two stagehands, especially, seemed reluctant to depart. Perhaps, thought Maisie, uncharitably, they were unwilling to leave a scene of real-life drama, like drivers who slow down irresponsibly as they pass the scene of an accident.

309

No, not an accident, she reminded herself.

Eventually it was done and Jack enlisted the help of Clive and John to move the chairs into a smaller circle, including seats for himself and for Nairn, on opposite sides. Goodbody, Tindall and Wilson sat further back, towards the edges of the stage, notebooks in hand.

'I notice you were limping just then, Mr Canning,' said Jack, once everyone was settled. 'Is that a long-term injury?'

'No, I hurt myself.'

'This afternoon?'

'Yes.'

'Could you explain to me how?'

'Well, it wasn't clambering about on the scaffold, I can tell you that.'

'So, how did you hurt yourself? Is it your ankle?'

'What difference does it make whether it's my calf or my big toe or my buttock?' shouted Clive unexpectedly.

Micky laughed and John stood up.

'I'm not sure of the form,' he drawled, 'but, perhaps I can help dear Clive out? Would it help if we stood to make our pronouncements, if we have pronouncements? Or perhaps we could pass round my staff as a talking stick and only contribute when holding it?'

'No, I don't think there'll be any need for that,' said Jack. 'Did you have something to add?'

'Yes.'

'Would you like to tell us?' asked Jack, patiently.

'Would I like to? No. But it is clearly my duty.'

John stopped, sitting back down and adjusting his costume with finicking movements.

'I am glad to hear you understand your duty, sir,' said Jack, stolidly.

'Well, it was like this. Not long after Miss Amour and Miss Cooper left, I was mooching about the stage door hallway. It faces south, you know, and the sun was out and I was thinking about going for a walk. Then I changed my mind because Dorothy and NVE wanted us all to kiss and make up, though I had, obviously, nothing to reproach myself for.'

'Mr Bradshaw made a habit of taunting you,' said Jack, 'on the strength of your recent recovery from alcoholism.'

John took the interruption in his stride.

'If you are intending to dress that up as a motive for murder, you will be disappointed.'

'And he mocked your devotion to Miss Amour.'

'John is a friend, that is all,' said Adélaïde.

'Thank you, my dear,' said John. His eyes – looking both angry and hurt – slid from Adélaïde to Maisie. 'I see Miss Cooper has brought you intimately up to speed with our goings-on.'

'Please continue,' said Jack, ignoring the reference to Maisie. 'You acknowledge your resentment of Mr Bradshaw?'

'Yes, I resented him and his horrible goading ways, but no more than that.'

'I see. And the stage door hallway?'

'Yes, well, I stayed in because I'd been asked to and I was weary of all the rigmarole of signing out and signing in and, in any case, the ladies were already out of sight across the car park, so my prey had escaped me.'

'You mean you intended to spend the afternoon with Miss Amour and Miss Cooper?'

'Seeing the rehearsal was cancelled, I thought—'

'That was very kind of you, John,' said Adélaïde, 'but we had no need of company.'

'As I perceived,' said John.

'And then?' asked Jack.

'Why are you making such a meal of this, John?' shouted Clive. 'Spit it out, man.'

'I am merely setting the scene.'

'You are trying everyone's patience,' said NVE.

'The truth is,' said Clive in a loud voice, 'I wanted to confront that scoundrel Andrew P Bradshaw. And I still blame you, NVE. You brought him into the company, knowing the man that he is … that he was, God rest his soul, though a soul such as his cannot hope of finding rest.'

Maisie wondered if Clive had, at some point, played a bishop or a monk and still enjoyed the sonority of those ecclesiastical cadences. There was a digression during which the story of NVE's family connection was unpacked and everyone – including the police officers – ended up in full possession of the facts. Jack seemed happy to let the conversation flow.

'So, he was my brother,' NVE summed up. 'And raised unhappily by our unkind father while I was loved and cherished by our gentle mother, and that experience made him less than the man he might have been. I felt, as you must all appreciate, sorry for him, that I drew the long straw and he the short, that I was nurtured and he neglected, set a bad example of independence and cruelty while I was taught to do my best to be good.' NVE's eyes held a kind of appeal. 'But Andrew was a good actor,' he said pleadingly. 'He deserved his part in the show, in our show. You all saw him this evening. Despite the upset—'

'Upset!' cried Kitty.

'Yes,' went on NVE, very quickly, 'I know "upset" is a very small word for what happened, but please let me just say, in my own defence, whatever else I have done wrong or failed to do to protect you all, Andrew gave a wonderful performance this evening.'

He sat back and Maisie wondered who would speak next. NVE's self-defence seemed an extraordinary sleight of hand, deflecting everyone's attention. But from what?

'Miss Farrell,' Jack resumed, 'you take exception to the use of the word "upset". Would you like to tell me why?'

'How would you like to be paraded in front of all your neighbours in the middle of the night?'

Jack left a pause, his eye travelling from Kitty to Esther to Clive.

'Perhaps we should step away for a moment and you can tell me exactly what you mean.' He stood up. So did Clive. 'No, Mr Canning, please rest your injured leg or foot or buttock, as it may be. We won't be long. Mrs Canning, would you accompany us, please?'

Esther got up and she and Kitty, clinging to one another, exited upstage, followed by Jack and Nairn.

★

Time slowed to a crawl. When Maisie checked her watch, she was surprised to find that only four minutes had passed, rather than the fifteen or twenty she had expected. When the two police officers and the two women finally came back, Kitty seemed much calmer for having told her story and Esther appeared reassured – perhaps by having been given the opportunity to stand by her daughter. It was rather touching how much of a unit they now looked. It made Maisie think about how misfortune and danger can unite people, if they only have the courage to face things together and ask for one another's support.

Nairn retook his seat while Jack remained standing.

'I would like to reiterate my thanks for your patience,' he said. 'We are making progress.'

'Towards what?' said NVE.

'Towards understanding,' said Jack.

'Oh, very good,' said NVE, sarcastically.

Unexpectedly, Jack turned to Winnie.

'Miss Brahms, what was your relationship to the deceased?'

'I had none, Inspector Wingard.'

'Sergeant Wingard,' said Jack, automatically. 'But you and he—?'

'Oh, yes. We had a fling, that was all.'

'Were you aware that he had already formed an attachment to Miss Farrell?'

'No, I joined the company late and had no idea. He played me for a fool.'

Jack paused, weighing up his next question.

'The liaison meant little to you?'

'It meant as much as any other,' said Winnie, a rather hard smile on her pretty face. 'Do I shock you? You must realise the world of the theatre doesn't necessarily follow the moral code of a provincial cathedral city.'

'I am not shocked nor am I making any kind of judgement on the morals of the theatre, though I am bound to say that murder transgresses more or less any ethical code, wouldn't you say?'

'Yes, I'm sorry. Go on.'

'I am trying to discover, to speak plainly, whether you felt betrayed, horrified or perhaps even relieved when, this afternoon, you learned of the commotion Mr Bradshaw's behaviour caused for Miss Farrell.'

'All of the above,' said Winnie. She turned to Kitty and Esther who were still clasped together. 'I really am very sorry. It was just a bit of fun, me and Andy. If I'd known…'

Winnie lost her way and looked rather desperate. Maisie felt a rush of sympathy for her.

'Go on,' said Jack.

'He told me,' Winnie resumed to Kitty, 'that he found out you were a virgin and broke it off, that he wasn't that sort of man. That was his story, and I had no reason not to believe it. I knew you were upset, but I thought it was because he'd chucked you, love. I'm so sorry.'

Unlike much of what she had heard since the end of the play, Maisie thought that Winnie's voice held a tone of authenticity and truth – that she had nothing to hide. Jack seemed to agree.

'That all seems fairly clear,' he said.

'Hang on a minute,' said NVE. 'May I be permitted to ask a question? Three questions, in fact.'

'Go ahead,' said Jack, once more giving Maisie the impression that he was happy for the circle of witnesses and suspects to speak out, perhaps giving themselves away in the process. 'Please.'

'*Primo*,' said NVE pedantically, 'why is the sergeant asking the questions when there's an inspector present? *Secundo*, have we simply forgotten about John and his mooning about after Adélaïde in the stage door hallway and how that connects to Clive and his limp? And, *tertio*, what about Keith Sadler?'

FORTY-ONE

An excited buzz broke out, several conversations starting all at once. Maisie smiled to herself to see Jack quietly take a seat and listen. Eventually, however, the members of the theatre company all realised they were being overheard and faded away into silence, rather like an audience when the director comes on before a show to announce an illness in the cast – comprehension and sympathy mixed with disappointment at the absence of the star.

'I'll take the first question,' said Nairn. 'Sergeant Wingard is an experienced investigating officer and, in my judgement, the ideal person to lead this phase of our inquiry.'

'Thank you,' said NVE. 'I thought for just a tiny moment that it might have something to do with a pre-existing relationship Sergeant Wingard has – with Miss Cooper, for example.'

'What you thought on this topic, Mr van Erde, is not material to this investigation,' said Nairn. 'Perhaps you should refrain from commenting on matters that don't concern you.'

'You say it doesn't concern me?' said NVE. 'He was my brother.'

'I simply meant that the conduct of the investigation doesn't concern you,' replied Nairn weakly.

'Really,' said Maisie, 'it couldn't matter less. Yes, I do have what Mr van Erde calls a "pre-existing relationship" with Sergeant Wingard, but I am no more than a bystander in this investigation. My presence is a complete accident.'

'There's that word again,' said NVE. 'Accident.'

'That's enough,' said Jack, abruptly. 'Mr van Erde, if I have to detain you elsewhere to prevent any more interruptions, I will. Do you understand?'

'I do. In your turn, do you understand—?'

'To take your second question,' said Jack, not allowing NVE to elaborate, 'we have not forgotten about Mr Hermanson's offer to elucidate the circumstances of Mr Canning's injury. Moving on to your third question, I am happy to inform you that the issue of Keith Sadler's death has been settled to the police's satisfaction.'

*

The company's response to this remark, Maisie felt, made a contrast with all the answers given to questions about Andrew P Bradshaw. His death seemed to have affected nobody very deeply, except perhaps for Dorothy – who was worried for the show – and NVE who claimed a deep well of feeling or, perhaps, responsibility for his wastrel brother. Keith's murder, on the other hand, seemed to excite a proper sense of loss for a young life cut short.

'Barry, would you fetch Mrs Belt and then we'll hear your evidence? Lock the outer door while she leaves it unsupervised.'

'Sir,' said Constable Goodbody, leaving.

Jack stood in silence, apparently waiting for Barry's footsteps to recede. Then it became clear that he was content to stand in silence until the constable returned.

In the pause, Maisie thought how different this confrontation was from the one that she had organised – and dominated – in Church Lodge, like a scene in a classical whodunnit, determined to play her cards in such a way that those with any guilt around her brother's death might give themselves away. She had briefed Jack on what she wanted to say – all that she had discovered and all she had deduced but could not prove – and he had supported her and let her take the lead because he believed her and, perhaps, thought that her emotional connection might help entice a confession.

This was very different. To start with, she was only a bystander. She wasn't asking the questions because she wasn't in possession of the full facts. For example, what did Barry Goodbody and Harriet Belt know that she didn't?

Maisie glanced round the circle. Liam looked as though he might bolt or burst into tears. Dorothy was next to him, speaking in a low voice, telling him about his responsibility to the show as Andrew's understudy.

Good heavens, thought Maisie. *She means for them to perform again tomorrow night.*

To Dorothy's left, Micky was leaning back in his chair, his feet crossed at the ankles, his arms folded across his chest, his eyes shut. Was he faintly snoring?

Between Maisie and Micky was Adélaïde, her legs curled up under her on her battered chaise longue like a cat. She yawned and glanced at Maisie – Maisie nodding encouragement, Adélaïde smiling a warm, self-satisfied smile. Maisie said: 'I'm sure this will soon be over.' Then she heard footsteps – heavy boots and the clip-clop of a woman's heels on the echoing stage boards.

'Good,' said Jack. 'Come into the circle, Mrs Belt.'

Harriet Belt twittered ineffectually as she sidled in, weaving between the chairs of John Hermanson and the family group of the Cannings.

'I told your constable, and I'm happy to tell everyone else. I don't believe I have anything to be ashamed of. One's eyes can't be in every direction at once, can they?'

'No, Mrs Belt,' said Jack, 'they can't. Now, would you tell me what you told Constable Goodbody?'

'Yes, I will.' Her eyes darted round the circle, looking rather furtive. 'If I could… I feel a little… Might you fetch me a chair?'

Barry lifted one high over Clive's head and passed it into the circle. Mrs Belt sat down.

'Thank you. Now, what were you asking?'

'On the night of Keith Sadler's murder,' said Jack, 'you were on duty as the company went home?'

'The theatre can't function without volunteers. It grew out of the local community and it needs the local community to keep it going.'

'And there was quite a lot of going in and going out. Is that right?'

'Well, people forget things,' she said, her eyes flicking from one company member to another. 'Mr Hermanson came back in for his script.'

'Is that right, sir?' asked Jack mildly.

'Perhaps,' said John. 'How would I remember?'

'It was only a few days ago.'

'Days in which a good deal has happened.'

'True,' said Jack. 'Anyone else, Mrs Belt?'

'Miss Farrell was back and forth looking for somebody.'

'Why shouldn't I look for somebody?' asked Kitty, looking hunted.

'Was it Mr Bradshaw you were looking for, Miss Farrell?' asked Jack.

'Yes, it was,' Kitty shouted, with a glance at her father. Maisie wondered if it was guilt or defiance. Kitty went on: 'I wanted him to walk me home. That's all right, isn't it? It was a long day and I'd been shown up for what I am – a poor imitation of the original.' She gestured to Adélaïde without looking at her. 'No offence. It isn't your fault,' she said, though her tone suggested that it was.

'*Il n'y a pas de quoi*,' said Adélaïde.

319

'She says it doesn't matter,' said Maisie, automatically softening Adélaïde's tone of voice with her own.

'But Mr Bradshaw,' Jack continued, 'had told you that the relationship between you was over. Isn't that right?'

'Yes, I told you that when we went off with mum.'

'What was the reason? Would you mind clarifying that for everybody?'

'Yes, I would mind. It was personal.'

Clive Canning half-stood.

'This is a grossly unprofessional—'

'Sit down, Mr Canning,' said Jack. Clive subsided like a punctured balloon. 'Was it, Miss Farrell, because he had learned your family ties to Mr and Mrs Canning – something he hadn't previously known – and that you were inexperienced in romantic liaisons?'

'Oh, there's no need,' said Kitty, almost shouting, 'to beat about the bush. He didn't know they were my parents when we started rehearsals but, of course, he found out when... Well, when they looked out for me. Then, when he found out I had no experience of, well, sex, he didn't want anything to do with me because...' She stopped for a second and took a kind of sobbing breath. 'Winnie was much more what he was looking for.'

'I'm sure I don't know what you mean,' said Winnie.

'She means,' said Jack, stolidly, 'that you were much more likely to entertain a physical relationship with Mr Bradshaw. Was that the case?'

'I believe I've already told you, not that it's any of your business,' said Winnie.

'In a case of murder, everything is our business.'

'Whose murder?' asked John, abruptly, his face still disfigured by his unsightly make-up. 'Andrew or the nightwatchman?'

'Yes, who says Andrew was murdered? I'd like to know, too,' said Clive. 'But I don't expect any kind of answer. You're damned if you speak and you're damned if you don't.'

'Mr Hermanson,' said Jack. 'I realise that this is very distressing for you – the loss of your colleague.'

'I'll manage,' said John.

'And you, too, Mr Canning, given the humiliating experience suffered by your daughter. But we have no choice but to pursue the facts wherever they may lead. As a man of the world, you must understand that?'

'Well, yes, of course I do,' said Clive.

'We were glad at first to speak to Miss Farrell and Mrs Canning in private but, in the end, police work cannot be discreet or polite.'

'It's your duty, sir,' said Clive, apparently mollified, 'like the play and the audience are ours.'

That's an odd way to look at it, thought Maisie.

'May I say something?' asked Adélaïde, unexpectedly.

'Please do,' said Jack.

'Mrs Belt was saying who came back in, who it was, I suppose, who killed the barman of the hotel. What was his name, Maisie?'

'Keith,' Maisie replied. 'Keith Sadler.'

'And Mrs Belt, she told us that John and Kitty were both in and out and they have told you their reasons,' persisted Adélaïde. 'There was another?'

'Well, yes,' said Mrs Belt. 'I was coming to that. It was when I was helping the constable here with his medicine. It's not easy to put drops in your own ear. Anyone who's tried it will know that's true. And the fact is, he swanned out and then popped back for his Optrex because, he said, there was hay fever about and it stopped the itching.'

At that moment, Maisie knew what the stage door keeper was about to say. After all, she had seen the small white conical bottle herself.

'But the constable wasn't in the theatre on the night in question,' said Jack, quietly.

'No, I don't mean the constable was there. It was afterwards, helping Barry put in the ear drops that reminded me of the eye drops,' said Mrs Belt. 'And I told Barry about it and he immediately saw the importance.'

'I would like to know,' said John, 'why your constable mooches about with a frankly unsavoury wad of cotton wool in his obviously infected ear.'

'Constable Goodbody is highly qualified in first aid and was instrumental in saving a life,' said Jack. 'He pulled a drunken teenager from the canal, resuscitating him on the bank. The infection came from the stagnant water. You will read about his heroism in the paper next week. Although not on the front page. That will likely be reserved for … these events.'

Maisie felt bad. She'd had no idea what Barry had done and, like John, had felt faintly disgusted.

'Yes,' said John, unperturbed, 'I see. Congratulations, Constable, on your bravery. I see now why the inspector relied on you to try and bring Andrew back from his deserved quietus.'

Barry Goodbody said something Maisie didn't hear, some embarrassed noise in his throat, but simultaneously Jack was asking: 'You say Mr Bradshaw deserved his "quietus", Mr Hermanson?'

'I do.'

'Might you tell me why?'

'If you wish.' John sat up straighter on his chair, readjusting his legs with a sigh. Maisie wondered if stiffness was another lasting effect of ditching his Spitfire in the Channel. 'It has already come to light that he goaded me, repeatedly, for my abuse of alcohol in a previous life – eighteen months ago, if absolute candour is required – even going so far as to leave a bottle of scotch in my dressing room to taunt and tempt me.'

'Yes, we are aware of that,' said Jack.

'I expect you are,' said John with a glance at Maisie. 'It may not mean much to you, but he was also a ham, a wildly melodramatic actor that NVE would never have cast without the fraternal bond so recently vouchsafed to us.'

'Talk about hams,' said Kitty spitefully, but John went on.

'Yes, I am aware that the same criticism could be levelled at me,' he said. 'But then, there was something Andrew was that I am not. Two things, in fact.'

'And what are they?' asked Jack, as if he was merely making polite conversation.

'Well, to take them in reverse chronological sequence, as it were, this would be the second thing. I am not, have never been – at least not yet – a victim of murder.'

John left an actor's pause so that the impact of his line could be fully felt by his audience.

'And the first thing that you are not?' asked Jack, mildly. 'The one that came earlier in the chronological sequence?'

'Isn't that obvious?' asked John.

'Oh, stop prevaricating,' said Esther Canning. 'Just spit it out.'

'None of you wants to chip in?' asked John.

'I believe we would all prefer you to say aloud what you believe you know, Mr Hermanson,' said Jack.

'Well, all right then, if you insist. Unlike Andrew...' He stopped again, picking out the director with his gruesome eyes. 'I'm sorry NVE, this must be very painful to you?'

NVE was sitting on the other side of Winnie Brahms. He was unnaturally stiff, Maisie realised, and had been throughout.

'I agree with Esther,' said NVE. 'Say what you have to say and then shut up.'

'Fair enough,' said John. He turned back to Jack. 'I have been neither a victim ... nor a perpetrator.' He looked at Mrs Belt, a dramatic intensity in his red-rimmed eyes and hideously lined face. Maisie saw the poor woman flinch. 'That was what you were about to say, wasn't it – that you eventually realised that Mr Bradshaw came back into the theatre and never left.'

'Well, yes,' said Mrs Belt. 'That is what I was about to say, but I'm afraid I've not understood anything else.'

'If he came back in,' said NVE, 'and didn't leave, then my brother was the—'

'Yes,' interrupted John, in his impressive bass voice. 'Both the murdered and the murderer.'

FORTY-TWO

'It was surprising to me that he was so punctual,' said NVE, a little later, when everyone had caught up. 'That had never been his habit.'

Maisie remembered Andrew talking outside the theatre.

A dab of eau de Cologne on the temples, eye drops for sparkle and I'm ready to face the day. I promise you, I will always be first in.

'So, he didn't have anywhere to stay?' asked Kitty.

'Of course, he did,' said Dorothy. 'Digs were allocated to him, but I suppose he didn't take them up.'

'In order to pocket his *per diem* allowance,' said NVE.

'He was always badgering to stay with me,' said Winnie, 'but that would have put me in bad odour with my landlady and I've got the whole season here, and it's nice where I am.'

'I wish you'd told me,' said Kitty.

'I'm sorry, love,' said Winnie. 'I would have if I'd known he was going to try it on with you, too. There's no question of closing, Miss Dean, is there?'

'Oh, no,' said Liam, as if the idea was absurd. 'Winnie, darling, we must come in early tomorrow to run it together. Adélaïde, will you? Or Kitty?'

'It was a breach of the insurance,' said Dorothy, abruptly, 'staying the night in the building. What if something had happened and the place had burned down? We wouldn't have been covered.'

'But it didn't,' said NVE.

'But it might have,' shouted Dorothy. 'Your brother, for God's sake, cast against my wishes and—'

'And against mine,' said NVE sharply, then stopped, as if caught out in a lie.

'That's interesting,' said Jack, after a pause. 'Why would that be?'

'Because I am a very shallow man, wedded to my image of myself,' sighed NVE, raising his chin and attempting to give an impression, Maisie thought, of an aristocrat approaching the guillotine, determined to be brave. 'I didn't want our relationship to come out, my disastrous father from whom Andrew's misfortune saved me, my mother who agreed to toss a coin to decide which son each was to take...' He stopped and looked at the boards of the stage. 'And changing my name,' he said quietly. 'I don't know why it meant so much to me...'

'This is barely relevant, Sergeant,' said John. 'And it is ground we have already covered. Shall I go on?'

'Please do, sir,' said Jack.

There was a pause as John gathered his thoughts. The silence stretched out. Maisie thought about Andrew's gambling debts and the awful lengths they had driven him to.

'During the interval of tonight's performance, I saw Andrew follow Winnie into her dressing room and I thought: "Well, that's not my business." It gave me the opportunity, however, to go to the stage door and borrow the pass key. Isn't that right, Mrs Belt?'

'Yes.'

'The pass key, Mrs Belt,' said Dorothy, severely, 'is for management or for the fire brigade, not for handing out willy-nilly.'

'Excuse me,' said Maisie, persisting in her white lie. 'Just to be clear, I borrowed the pass key the other day as well. Adélaïde's key was locked inside her room by mistake.'

'Thank you for your honesty, Miss Cooper,' said Jack. 'Please, go on, Mr Hermanson.'

'Well, I knew that Andrew was in the habit of locking his dressing room door,' said John, 'and I had the idea of putting back the bottle of whisky – you know, the one with which he had taunted me? I fetched it from where I'd left it with Adélaïde and, in Andrew's dressing room, on the make-up counter beneath the mirror, I saw his car key, singular, and I thought to myself: "How does he get into his digs?" And for some reason, it made me wonder: "Is he sleeping in his car?" And I followed that up with another question: "Is he skint?" Did you know—?'

'The police are aware that Mr Bradshaw was an unsuccessful gambler,' said Jack.

'I wonder how,' mused John, with another penetrating glance at Maisie.

'Yes, John,' she replied, 'it was I who told Jack, Sergeant Wingard, earlier this evening, after the ... after Andrew was pronounced dead.'

'And how did you know?' asked NVE.

'I expect she overheard him asking me for an advance on his wages,' said Dorothy.

'He did?' said NVE. 'Did you refuse?'

'Obviously.'

'That must have been,' said NVE, sadly, 'not long before I told him that I would no longer support him. We drove him to this.'

'To what?' said Dorothy.

'To suicide,' said NVE. 'He has killed himself on stage in front of an audience of over a thousand people. That would be in character – to ruin my production and create a ridiculous melodrama, to make himself the centre of attention.'

No one replied.

'None of this speculation,' said Jack, eventually, 'is relevant. Please, continue, Mr Hermanson.'

'Well, yes, there I was,' said John, 'with eight minutes till I would be called for the second half. I picked up his car key and went out through the stage door, intending to tell Mrs Belt that I needed the fresh air, but she was so busy with her crossword that I passed like a ghost. Once outside, I opened the driver's door of his rather dainty Triumph and said to myself: "A child couldn't sleep in here, surely?" I opened the boot in order to see if there might be some blankets secreted therein, perhaps a feather pillow for his troubled head. I really don't know why, at that moment, I didn't think of him sleeping in the theatre. Then I saw it.'

John stopped as if troubled by the memory.

'Yes?' said Mrs Belt who was leaning in on the edge of her chair in the centre of the circle. 'What did you see?'

'The cash box,' said John.

'Did you touch it?' asked Jack, sharply.

'I did not.'

'Did you interfere with it in any way?'

'No.'

'It all slotted into place then – his sleeping in the theatre, the opportunity that would have afforded him to steal the money from the safe. I suppose the moment when he asked for his advance coincided with the visit of Miss Cooper's mysterious benefactor, allowing him to observe the combination.'

'I will thank you to cease goading Miss Cooper, Mr Hermanson,' said Jack coldly. 'Let me be clear. At the interval of this evening's performance, you discovered the cash box in the boot of Mr Bradshaw's car. You saw, I imagine, the blood on one corner, where it was driven into Mr Sadler's skull.'

'Oh,' gasped Kitty.

'And,' said Jack, 'you didn't think to notify the police?'

'No,' said John.

'Might I ask you why not?' said Jack.

Maisie noticed that Tindall, sitting behind John, had put down his notebook as if preparing to grasp him from behind. Nairn, sitting between John and the Cannings, also seemed more alert.

'You may well ask,' said John, infuriatingly. 'But you won't like the answer.'

'All the same, Mr Hermanson, will you tell me why, having found Keith Sadler's murder weapon hidden in the boot of Mr Bradshaw's car, you did not notify the proper authorities?'

'Because,' said John, 'to coin a phrase, the show must go on.'

*

For perhaps thirty seconds everyone was talking at once. Maisie watched Jack slowly turning his head, attempting to listen to all the conversations at once, trying to work out if there was anything to be learned from the hubbub. Eventually, he raised a hand and the noise subsided.

'Thank you, Mrs Belt. You may return to your post.' She got up and Barry went to follow her. Jack gestured to stop him. 'Constable Goodbody, I'm sure Mrs Belt can find her own way.'

'Yes,' she tittered. 'I hope I can manage that.'

Maisie watched her exit upstage right, towards the green room, rather than the stage door, and guessed she was going to pour herself a nip of brandy before resuming her duties. She wondered if Jack expected her to do that and had kindly made it possible by preventing Barry from going with her.

No, it's because Barry has yet to give his evidence.

'Mr Hermanson,' said Nairn – and Maisie realised it was the first time the inspector had spoken for some time – 'I am obliged to make you aware that you may be charged with an

329

offence of knowingly withholding information material to a police investigation. Do you understand?'

'Oh, yes, I grasp the burden of your song.'

'Sergeant Wingard,' said Dorothy, 'is there another reason why the cash box might have ended up in the boot of Andrew's car?'

'Would you like to provide us with a possible scenario?' asked Jack, only mildly interested.

'Don't be so bloody ridiculous,' shouted Clive. 'Why are you trying to protect him? Obviously, he did it. He was sleeping in the theatre and the nightwatchman nabbed him and he panicked. That's all there is to it. Then he hid the cash box in the only available place. It's not as though he could secrete it in the building or take it home with him, is it? He had nowhere to go. Then he killed himself in his guilt and shame, like NVE said.'

'I'm missing a chisel,' said Micky, unexpectedly, without unfolding his arms or opening his eyes. 'I reckon he pinched it to break it open, not that any of this has anything to do with me.'

'Or it does,' said Clive, harshly.

Micky roused himself, shuffling his bottom back in his chair and gripping the seat with his two strong hands.

'What did you say?'

'Well, if Andrew didn't kill himself,' said Clive, 'whose fault might it be?'

'What did you say?' repeated Micky, threateningly.

There was an ugly pause and Maisie was struck by the idea that Micky might be devoted enough to NVE to rig the hanging to do away with a troublesome brother.

'Who set the safety?' demanded Clive, with a note of triumph in his voice. 'Tell me that.'

'Don't you dare—' began Micky, launching himself across the circle, bumping into the chair that Mrs Belt had vacated.

330

Jack stepped in front of him and Nairn got up out of his seat to complete the barricade.

'One thing at a time,' said Jack quietly. 'We'll come on to the safety line and how it failed in a little while. I suggest you take your seat once more, Mr Petherick.'

'Do you?' asked Micky rudely.

'We do,' said Fred Nairn, 'if you don't want to be charged with obstruction.'

'Yeah, right,' said Micky. 'You've proper got the whip hand and you're not afraid to use it.'

'Will it help to remind you,' said Nairn, 'all of you, that the innocent have nothing to fear? Sergeant Wingard and I are simply trying to get at the facts. Mr Petherick, if that doesn't reassure you, I would be interested to learn why.'

'All right, all right. I'll sit down. Just tell Clive "lifetime achievement" Canning not to make any more accusations.'

Micky returned to his seat and resumed his pose – crossed ankles, arms folded – but his eyes were now open and alert.

'Constable Goodbody,' said Jack, 'would you be kind enough to tell everyone what you discovered just before this evening's performance?'

'Yes, sir.' Barry cleared his throat and pushed the wad of cotton wool deeper into his ear. 'Before tonight's performance, I noticed poor old Harold Farr. He used to be a farm labourer but he got too old. Now he lives off charity and what other people throw away. I went to speak to him.'

'This is a fascinating story,' said John. 'Aren't we all diverted?'

Barry ignored the interruption.

'He was rootling in the waste bin just outside the theatre café. People often drop their crusts and whatever in there when they're late and running into the show. You've probably all seen him.'

'Does it matter if we've seen him?' said NVE.

331

'I noticed,' persisted Barry, 'that he was wearing gloves – string-backed gloves – and that seemed unlikely. I asked him where he got them and he told me he found them in the bin. I asked him when and his answer was vague, at first, but we narrowed it down to overnight or very early morning on the day the body was discovered, well before the council team came round to empty it.' Barry stopped. 'The bin, I mean.'

'The morning after the night of Keith Sadler's murder,' said Clive, as if reinforcing a key piece of information in a play.

Barry frowned and poked at his ear.

'I'm sorry, sir,' he told Jack. 'It's the vertigo again. Do you think I could be excused?'

'Go ahead, Constable,' said Nairn.

Barry left the circle, weaving a little, putting a hand on Liam Jukes' shoulder as he went past.

'Don't touch me,' he squawked.

'I'm sorry,' said Barry, exiting upstage left.

'Have you hurt yourself, Mr Jukes?' said Jack. 'Mr Canning has damaged his foot or his ankle. I wonder if the two injuries are connected?'

'Can you not keep going?' bleated Liam. 'What about the string-backed gloves?'

'Isn't it obvious?' said NVE. 'They were my brother's. Obviously, he would have string-backed leather gloves, like a moustache-twirling villain in an Ealing Studios comedy. That's it, isn't it?'

'A print from a leather glove,' said Nairn, 'was found on the polished shaft of a standard lamp, stored in the basement room, alongside the curtains where the body of Mr Sadler was concealed.'

'But Kitty and Adélaïde both have leather gloves,' said Liam, his eyes flicking from one to the other.

'Shut your silly mouth,' said Clive. 'That's my daughter you're maligning.'

'*Et moi aussi*,' said Adélaïde quietly.

And me, too.

'I'm not saying you did it, either of you,' insisted Liam. 'That would be ridiculous. I'm just saying that a glove is a glove. And I agree with NVE. Why keep cudgelling our brains when he's already taken the easy way out?'

'You think that's easy?' asked Micky. 'You didn't feel him in your arms, fighting and writhing for breath, and me not able to get any purchase and lift him—'

'Again,' said Jack quickly, 'we will come to the moment of Mr Bradshaw's death shortly.'

'The leather of the glove is a natural skin,' said Nairn. 'The print left on the standard lamp could only have been left by those that Mr Bradshaw used in his crime, then discarded in the most convenient way – the waste bin on the grass near the theatre café.'

'What a stroke of luck you had in Harold Farr,' said John, sarcastically. 'Perhaps you ought to have thought of it yourselves.'

'Detective-Sergeant Tindall searched that bin – and the three others around the car park – immediately after photographing the corpse. Harold Farr had already taken the gloves away early that morning.'

'Yes, well, fair enough,' said John. 'I see you know your business and I should shut my silly mouth.'

'We all agree with that,' said NVE.

'Constable Goodbody retrieved the gloves,' said Nairn, 'giving poor old Harry a few coins in return, and sent it to the station. The leather, with its unique pattern of creases and lines, was compared to Detective-Sergeant Tindall's photograph of the print on the standard lamp and was found to be a match. Confirmation was brought to Constable Goodbody at the stage door during this evening's second act.'

'Yes,' said Dorothy. 'All of this fits together – I almost want to say it all fits like a glove – but why are we still talking about it? We accept your conclusions, Inspector, and yours, too, Sergeant. Andrew committed a terrible crime.' She addressed herself to the director. 'I like to think, NVE, that it happened in a sudden shock, that he would never have planned it. But Keith must have come upon him and, there he was, with the cash box in his hand and...' She stopped then started again addressing Jack. 'Anyway, that's all done with and we accept your conclusions. How could we not? And isn't it clear that Andrew must have been consumed with regret and determined to end it all and did so in a way that, perhaps, his vocation as an actor persuaded him was a good idea.'

'I, too,' said NVE, 'am convinced that this is what occurred.'

'No, I can't believe it,' came the voice of someone who had barely spoken. It was Sam Smithers. He was outside the circle, in one of the chairs left behind by the ensemble players and the stagehands when they were dismissed. He stood up. 'Look, I went to the pub for a quick half, but then I was in the theatre throughout the afternoon, practising my cues in the lighting box and then, when I did the lamp check, there were three bulbs gone and I had to replace them, so I was up and down to the grid.'

'That's very interesting,' said Jack. 'And what did you see?'

'In the grid? Dust and cables,' said Sam, with a smile. 'No, sorry, I shouldn't be facetious. What did I see? An almighty fight broke out.'

FORTY-THREE

Another wave of argument flowed across the stage, from all sides of the circle. Maisie was aware of Adélaïde shifting her position on the low chaise longue, resting her cheek against the velvet and closing her eyes. She heard her speak:

'This does not concern us. We were not there.'

Eventually, the babble of voices subsided.

'Before we get on to the fight,' said Jack, 'I'd like to consider the rope. Mr Petherick?'

'Do you want technical details?' asked Micky.

'Yes, please.'

'Well, it's from Chouinard, a US company that supplies climbers.'

'It's surprisingly thin,' said Jack.

'Quarter inch.'

'But it can support a man's weight?'

'It can catch a man falling from a mountainside with minimal stretch. It's made of Perlon with a slippery sheath on the outside so it runs nicely. I don't know what else to tell you.'

'How would you cut it?'

'With a sharp knife.'

'Not scissors?'

'They'd have to be very good scissors.'

'And would it be possible to cut it almost through, leaving only a few fibres?'

'Obviously. What sort of a question is that?'

'And those fibres would be strong enough to give the impression of a sound safety line when you attached it to

Mr Bradshaw's harness, but would give way under the impact of his fall?'

'Yes. Is that what happened?'

'That is what we believe happened,' said Jack.

'Can I see?'

'No, you'll have to take my word for it,' said Jack. 'In your judgement, however, would that require any particular skill, to organise all that?'

'I guess.'

'A certain amount of dexterity? A familiarity with ropes?'

'If you insist.'

'One would have to take care to cut only just enough and no further,' said Jack. 'You, for example, Mr Petherick, might have accomplished it easily?'

'But I didn't.'

'Thank you. Now, Mr Smithers, would you come into the circle and take Mrs Belt's seat?'

'Of course.'

While this was happening, Maisie was thinking about the company members who had experience with ropes and knots and so on. Sam, for example. As a theatre technician, he must be one of them. And, before getting the understudy to Macheath, Liam Jukes had been in stage management. And Andrew Bradshaw himself had been a Sea Cadet. Someone else had served in the senior service. Who was that?

'You say a fight broke out,' prompted Jack.

'That's right,' said Sam. 'Of course, I didn't catch the beginning. I was re-rigging a lamp and it was awkward to get at.'

'Can anyone help us?' asked Jack.

'It began in the stage door hallway,' said John, 'as I was trying to tell you earlier. I poured oil on the troubled waters and hoped, to mix my metaphors, that the storm had blown itself out. But no.'

336

'I was on the stage and Andy was helping me out,' said Liam. 'He'd taken pity on me and was helping me run his lines – well, my lines, now, I suppose – something the management has failed to do, Miss Dean.'

'Who else was there?' Jack insisted.

'Adélaïde had left the building,' said Liam, 'but Kitty was helping as Polly and Winnie was lovely, as she always is, as Lucy. To give him his due, Andy was a dream to work with – you might be glad to know that, NVE – directing with a light touch, just reminding one of what was good and making sure one kept it in.'

'This all sounds very satisfactory,' said Jack.

'Yes, but then Micky came on and wanted to check the scaffold and Clive chose that moment to blow up.'

'You didn't say Mr Canning was present,' said Jack.

'Well, he wasn't in the scene we were doing but he was lurking somewhere.'

'Why was that, Mr Canning?' asked Jack.

'I like to be on stage before the performance. It grounds me.'

'Because,' contradicted John, 'he had squared up to Andrew in the stage door hallway half an hour before and the combat had left him unsatisfied.'

'I see. And then, Mr Jukes?'

'Well, he went for him – Clive, I mean, went for Andy – and he knocked me over in the process and I've got a God-awful bruise all up my shoulder, and Andy sort of pulled him, like in judo, you know, with his own weight, and he fell on his face and we all laughed because, after all, it was funny – I'm sorry, Clive – such a big man, floundering, and he said all sorts of awful things…'

Liam stopped.

'Things?' asked Jack.

'Must I?' said Liam.

'Let me help you,' said Jack. 'Mr Canning accused Mr Bradshaw of propositioning and humiliating his daughter last night.'

'Well, yes,' said Liam. 'I'm sorry, Kitty.'

'Everyone knows,' said Kitty. 'I don't care.'

'Mr Smithers, is that what you saw?' asked Jack.

'Yes,' said Sam, uncertainly.

'Is there something you would like to add?'

'It's just that it didn't stop there. Clive was back on his feet and running round the scaffold and bellowing and Andrew was laughing at him and keeping out of his way by being quicker – you know, keeping the structure between them – and Clive was more and more furious, and the others were trying to stop them both. The noise brought everyone else on – Miss Dean, NVE. Everyone still in the building, except for Mrs Belt, was on the stage seeing what was happening.'

'And how did it end?'

'NVE and Miss Dean got everyone to come to their senses and go to their dressing rooms.'

'Quickly?'

'Not especially, no.'

'Then what did you do?'

'Well, I carried on re-rigging my lamps.'

Jack turned to Micky.

'So, in all the drama, Mr Petherick, perhaps you didn't have a chance to check the safety line?'

'Hah,' said Micky, rudely, 'but I did. Last thing before I left the stage, I gave it a sharp pull. If it had been cut or weakened, I would have noticed.'

'That's very useful,' said Jack, thoughtfully. 'Thank you.'

There was a pause as everyone considered why that was important.

'Because,' said Sam, giving voice to everyone's thoughts from where he was sitting in the centre of the circle, 'that means the rope was cut between that point and the performance.'

'Yes,' said Jack. 'Or rather, between that point and five to seven, the half.'

'I think,' said Nairn, 'we'll now speak to everyone in turn, in private. Miss Dean, we'll use the green room, if that's convenient.'

*

The questioning became a procession. The circle of tired faces on stage drooped more and more as, one after another, they were summoned, then returned, accompanied by Tindall or Wilson.

Maisie checked her watch. It was almost midnight and she realised she wished she was with Jack and Nairn, asking questions, at the heart of the investigation. She felt – and she knew it was irrational – that she had been unfairly excluded. She had her private investigator day-dream, again, solving baffling crimes, respected by police and criminals alike, her exploits documented in the press…

'They were very kind,' said Adélaïde, quietly, when she returned from giving her evidence.

'You were very quick,' said Maisie.

'We were not here, you and I. From the half, no one could have approached the scaffold without being seen, so the sabotage was accomplished before we returned.'

'Yes,' said Maisie, her mind wandering to another possibility.

Then it was done and Jack and Nairn were back, without having called Maisie at all.

'I say,' said John, 'does Miss Cooper have nothing to add?'

'I interviewed Miss Cooper shortly after the end of the performance,' said Jack. 'I already have her testimony.'

339

'And nothing you have heard has suggested that she needs closer questioning?'

'No.'

'Good,' said John. 'Miss Cooper, Maisie, if I may?' Maisie met his awful, red-rimmed eyes, wondering what was coming. 'You have been a shining light of kindness and good sense. Thank you for helping us, for helping Adélaïde. I am sorry that this unpleasant climax should have tainted your experience with us.'

'Seconded,' said Dorothy.

'Thank you,' said Maisie doubtfully.

'Now, if you please,' said Jack, 'I have one more question and, finally, a routine formality to accomplish.' He paused, then, to everyone's surprise except Fred Nairn's, Maisie thought, he said: 'Detective-Sergeant Tindall, were you able to retrieve any prints from the Chouinard rope so well described by Mr Petherick?'

'It has a nice smooth sheath,' said the tall bony man with small round glasses. 'So, yes.'

'Good. Tomorrow, ladies and gentlemen, we will invite you all to the station to provide prints of your own. You are at liberty to refuse to do this, but your refusal will be noted.'

'Is that the final formality?' asked NVE.

'I'm afraid not. We are obliged to search each of you before we can allow you to leave the stage.'

'Do we take it that you have established a clear timetable?' asked NVE.

'A timetable?'

'Who was where and when,' said Dorothy, 'in the crucial period between the bust-up and the half?'

'Our enquiries are on-going,' Jack prevaricated. 'Gentlemen, shall we begin?'

'Well, yes, if we must,' said NVE, standing and holding out his arms.

Nairn patted him down, getting him to turn out his pockets.
'Would you take off your shoes, please, sir?'

'My shoes?'

'Yes, sir.'

'This is too much,' bellowed Clive.

'Too much?' asked Jack.

'This procedure,' protested Clive. 'There is no need.'

'Why would you say that, sir?'

'I, for one, resent the indignity of a manual search. Do you not all?' he asked, sending his appeal around the circle.

'It's simply routine,' said Dorothy.

'You were in the Navy, sir,' said Jack. 'Is that right?'

'I was. So what?'

'You have experience with ropes?'

'God, so do a lot of people.' Clive stood up and Maisie was struck once again how big he was. 'What the hell is this?'

'Do you refuse to be searched?' asked Jack.

'Refuse? No. Come on, then. Let's get it over with.'

He spread his arms wide as NVE had done.

'Thank you, sir,' said Nairn, patting him down. 'Now, your shoes, if you wouldn't mind?'

'It's an indignity,' repeated Clive, balancing on one leg and removing his left shoe.

'May I?' said Nairn.

Clive held it out.

'What in hell's name are you looking for?' he demanded.

'And the other?' asked Nairn.

Clive dropped his left shoe and pushed his foot back into it, then he stood on one leg again, to remove the right. He held it out with his thumb tucked inside.

'Here, satisfied?'

He went to put it back on, but Nairn stopped him.

'One moment, if you please.'

'You've been limping, Mr Canning,' said Jack. 'But you didn't hurt your foot or your ankle in the fight. What is it that you have concealed inside your shoe that has been making you limp?'

There was an odd little pause. For a second or two, nothing changed. Then, Clive began to bellow.

'It was after he made a fool of me on the stage. I followed him into the green room and he had my award in his hand and he was tossing it up and down, spinning it in the air. I told him what I thought of him, that I would make sure everyone in the business knew what they were dealing with if they ever thought of employing him. Then—' Clive almost sobbed. 'He didn't take me seriously and I had to watch as he deliberately smashed my award against the frame of that wrought-iron chair. The crystal shattered into pieces and he laughed at me,' shouted Clive. 'My life's work shattered into pieces. He laughed and I didn't know what to do, but he ran away from me and, and…'

Maisie watched as Clive's face became slack, all the rage and resentment leaving it. She realised that his outrage at Jack's questioning had been an act. Clive had been trying to defend himself with the skills he knew best – those he had learned as an actor. Knowing, now, that his fingerprints must be on the rope, there was no way to evade his guilt and his performance of righteous innocence collapsed.

Then Clive physically collapsed, too, landing with a thump on his upholstered dining chair.

'My life's work, in fragments on the threadbare carpet,' he whispered.

Nobody else moved and Maisie had a moment of flashback, like in a film – Clive Canning at lunch in the green room, carving a ham joint with a slim pocket knife, and then claiming the honour of having served in the Royal Navy – the senior service.

'What did you do, Clive?' asked Esther in a whisper.
'Dad?' said Kitty.

Clive held out the shoe. Nairn went to take it but, before he could do so, Clive turned it over and something shiny and hard fell with a clatter onto the boards of the stage.

EPILOGUE

The next morning, the Friday, the television room at the Dolphin & Anchor was drenched in sunshine. The south-facing windows were open. Spring had finally fully sprung. Down on the cathedral green, two cherry trees had come into bloom. The bells were ringing as an enthusiastic team practised their peals. The air was warm and there was only the faintest odour of cigarette smoke and stale milk left in the room.

Maisie was waiting for Jack. He had promised to drop in and explain his reasoning – the moments she had not been witness to, above all.

Zoe put her head round the door.

'Not here yet?'

'No, not yet.'

'I've made coffee.' She came in with a tray on which a silver coffee pot, a china jug of cold milk, cups and saucers with doilies and a bowl of brown sugar lumps were balanced. 'I got the brown sugar specially from Sainsbury's because I know you like it better.'

'Thank you.'

Zoe put down the tray.

'I saw Charity downstairs. Is it true she came to give you a date for the Bunting Manor trial?'

'It will begin next week. It shouldn't take very long, I'm told.'

'Then what?' asked Zoe. When Maisie didn't reply, she added: 'I don't want you to go.'

'Then you must come and stay in Paris,' said Maisie, lightly.

'I have a proper job now,' said Zoe. 'I'll have to earn some holiday first.'

'That's a good attitude,' said Maisie.

Zoe removed the pots and crockery from the tray, laying them out on the glass-topped coffee table.

'I was thinking of getting Phyl to help me to learn French,' she said.

'Aren't you living in the annex of the hotel?'

'I changed my mind. I realised I was going to miss the Big House in Bunting. And Phyl, too. There's an early bus each day or I can use the moped if it's fine and in November I'll get my provisional licence and take my driving test.'

'Not in her disastrous old Land Rover?'

'No,' laughed Zoe. 'She's going to buy a new one.'

'Well, that's a good idea, too,' said Maisie.

Zoe put her head on one side.

'Are you all right?'

Maisie sighed. 'I'm fine. Go on with you.'

Jack appeared in the doorway.

'Okay, anything you need, I'll be downstairs,' said Zoe and left.

'Thank you for making time to do this,' said Maisie.

'I only have a few minutes,' said Jack, with a smile. 'Shall we?'

'Yes, go ahead.'

He sat down and poured coffee for them both, drinking thirstily. Maisie didn't touch hers.

'I suppose it was simple, in the end?' she said. 'You just discovered that Clive was the only person who could have sneaked onto the stage in the key time period.'

'Yes, that's right. To start with, Sam was busy in the grid for a while, so that narrowed it down. Then the kerfuffle at the stage door and the understudy rehearsal with Liam Jukes and the others. Then Sam and Micky both signed back out again and went, I think, for another out-of-hours drink at The Bell, though they say they just went for a walk in Priory Park. On the way out, they saw Andrew Bradshaw, Liam Jukes, Winnie Brahms and Kitty Farrell adjourning to the green room. Esther Canning was there, too.'

'But there was nothing to eat,' said Maisie with a frown.

'Too nervous in any case, apparently. Why do you mention it?'

'She loves her food. I rather like her. She's going to have a lot to cope with.'

Jack nodded, with a sympathetic frown.

'Then, they all – except Andrew Bradshaw – went their separate ways, which was when Clive came upon Bradshaw and the crystal award was smashed.'

'Yes,' said Maisie, feeling herself shudder at the memory of Clive's fury. 'Where was Miss Dean?'

'Discussing the future of the show with the director.'

'In Fort Knox?'

'Yes,' said Jack, 'though not quite so impenetrable, as it happened. And the door was open so they would have seen John Hermanson and any of the others, had they gone past.'

'Which they didn't.'

'No.'

'Who else?'

'That's it.'

'So, Clive and Andrew were the only ones who had opportunity,' said Maisie. 'When were you sure?'

'When we came back in from the individual questioning.'

'And you didn't entertain NVE's melodramatic suicide option?'

'It was a possibility, but Clive had a strong motive. Several, in fact. And Andrew Bradshaw seems to me to have been an irredeemably nasty piece of work, not likely to kill himself. No, he was more likely to fight dirty to the last.'

'I suppose so.'

'And Clive was very keen for us to entertain NVE's suicide scenario at the same time as accusing Micky Petherick of incompetence. He was clutching at straws. Plus, his limp, of course. There seemed no convincing reason for that.'

'Just before the knife fell out of his shoe onto the stage, I remembered him using it, the first time I met him, at lunch in the green room. But why did he…?'

'Keep it about his person?' said Jack with a smile. 'We think he was worried we would inspect the dressing rooms and it would give us ideas. Then, I suppose, he anticipated being searched himself, so he concealed it in the ridiculous high-heeled buckled shoe from his costume.'

'I see,' said Maisie, then she frowned. 'I've missed something, haven't I?'

'Unusually, Maisie, you have. You remember he claimed he hurt himself in the big bust-up where Liam Jukes got his shoulder bruise – that does exist, by the way, as we saw in his reaction when Barry touched it by chance – but Clive didn't limp in the show, did he?' said Jack. 'Not even in that magnificent dance-fight sequence.'

'No, of course he didn't,' said Maisie, feeling stupid. 'I should have seen that.'

'And when, towards the end of questioning everyone on stage, we took them off one at a time, Fred and I got confirmation from Tindall of the print on the rope.' Jack drained his cup and sighed with satisfaction. 'That noose looked very sinister the first time it came on.'

'I agree,' said Maisie, feeling wary. She had her own ideas about the noose. 'So that's that?'

There was a knock at the door.

'Come in,' said Jack.

It was Nairn.

'Sorry, Jack, we need to…'

'Yes, of course.' He stood up. 'Maisie, are you free this evening? Could we perhaps have a drink before the show?'

'Yes,' she said. 'I would like that. Come at six. I must be at the theatre for the half. Liam is going to give us his Macbeath.'

'I'll do that.'

Jack and Nairn left, leaving the room very empty. Maisie drifted to and fro, telling herself to let sleeping dogs lie. In the end, though, she couldn't.

She left the TV room and found her way past the chambermaids hoovering in the corridor to Adélaïde's room. She knocked and thought she heard a faint reply, so she went inside.

Adélaïde had pushed back the furniture and was in the centre of the carpet, wearing her white pyjama-like two-piece, doing yoga.

'I'm sorry,' said Maisie. 'I'm interrupting.'

'*Non, non, je viens de terminer.*'

'All right, if you've just finished, I need to ask you something.'

'Yes, but speak English. It is good practice for me.'

Adélaïde got up and perched on the end of the bed. Her face was shiny from exertion and her hair clung damply to her forehead. Still, Maisie thought, she looked stunning.

'It's this. You remember when the bust-up occurred, the first one, just after lunch, and then the afternoon run-through was abandoned?'

'And you and I came back here. Yes, of course.'

'Well, what did you do?'

'What did I do?'

Maisie hesitated. What was she trying to say? Was it even important? It was the question that had come into her mind, just after the onstage tragedy, while Dorothy and Sam were asking what she thought were the wrong ones. She sat down at the desk chair in the window, turning it towards the bed.

'Adélaïde, do you remember when you told me what you would do if someone had murdered your brother?'

'When what?'

'You told me you would kill them and you mimed hanging them with a rope.'

'What is this about?'

'It's about the noose. It's about the fact that the noose wasn't really a noose and someone must have retied it, to turn it into a proper slip-knot.'

'What is that?'

'*Un nœud coulant.* And I just remembered that you were more or less brought up on boats and, when the bust-up happened, you sort of drifted away upstage behind the scenery and it might have been you who retied it because otherwise Andrew might not be dead. He would have had a terrible shock – perhaps even a broken neck – but Micky would have been able to lift him down more easily if the rope hadn't tightened and… Look, I'm not a police officer. I just need to know.'

'That is very interesting,' said Adélaïde, tapping her very white teeth with a fingernail. 'I did not think of that. But you, Maisie, you think of everything.'

'I'm sorry. I want you to know that I've said nothing, but it will come up, the question of the noose—'

'But it must already have come up,' interrupted Adélaïde, 'don't you think?'

Maisie pondered for a moment, looking into her lovely eyes.

'Yes, I suppose it must have.'

'Your clever policeman will have thought of it, won't he?'

'Perhaps.'

'And Clive was a sailor once, you remember, and perhaps can tie a *nœud coulant*?'

'Are you saying that I should ask him?'

'Ask your Jacques? As you say, it isn't our business. Why would you even mention it, if Clive has made his confession?' Adélaïde gave Maisie a dazzling smile. 'Now, that is all settled. I think I would like to do more yoga. I am getting fat òn this terrible English food.'

Maisie left Adélaïde and went downstairs, standing for a moment in the doorway of the hotel.

She thought about the Aristotelian elements of drama that NVE had told her about. Yes, they had all been present: Thought, Song, Plot, Character, Spectacle and – finally – the mystery had been unravelled by Speech.

She wondered if she ought to believe the words of the glamorous French actress who was always so convincing in everything she said – and who she had seen in intense debate with Clive Canning, when she was trying on the tight Balmain-copy dress, while she and Beryl were struggling with the zip.

Did it matter, after all?

Zoe came to tell her Phyl was downstairs, very much looking forward to their lunch.

'You do see life, don't you?' said the young woman, as they descended to the lobby.

'I do,' said Maisie, meaningfully.

'And?'

'I think, in future, I'm going to try and mind my own business.'

The End

Maisie Cooper is no detective, thank you very much. But she might just solve a murder . . .

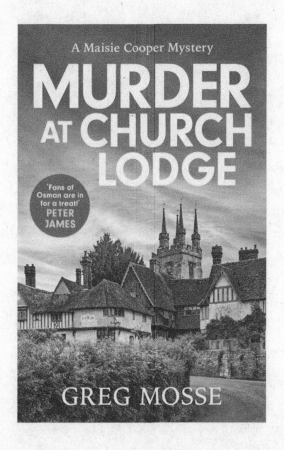

Go back to where it all started with *Murder at Church Lodge*, the first Maisie Cooper mystery novel.

Available now.

Something is afoot in the little village of Bunting . . .
Luckily, amateur sleuth Maisie Cooper is on the case.

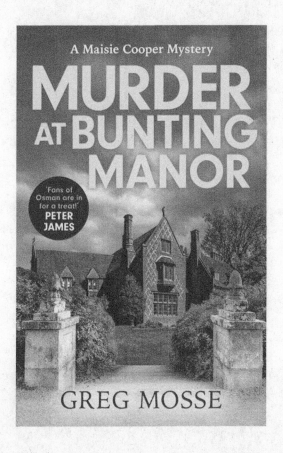

Experience book two in the cosy crime series from
Greg Mosse, where crimes and murder abound . . .

Available now.